more classic CRUMP

Hodder Moa

A catalogue record for this book is available from the National Library of New Zealand.

ISBN: 978-1-86971-108-5

Scrapwaggon: first published in 1965
Bastards I Have Met: first published in 1971
Wild Pork and Watercress: first published in 1986

A Hodder Moa Book
More Classic Crump first published in 2007 by Hachette Livre NZ Ltd
4 Whetu Place, Mairangi Bay
Auckland, New Zealand

Front cover: Barry Crump Collection
Printed by Griffin Press, Australia

SCRAPWAGGON

Dinny and Watcher, city dustmen who also indulge in a spot of rubbish-disposal unknown to their Council, lead profitable and peaceful lives — apart from a few hassles with Dinny's neighbours, who don't appreciate the mountain of 'treasures' he's accumulated in his garden. Then Dinny's daughter turns up to stay. He and Watcher try every trick to move her on, but she's inherited her Dad's obstinate streak, and soon she too is on the scrapwaggon.

Irate neighbours try to ban the whole squalid set-up. The City Council learn of the racket. They also discover that Dinny and Watcher aren't so easily sacked after all. . . .

Scrapwaggon, first published in 1965, is Barry Crump in top form. Dinny and Watcher are two of his most memorable creations. Old friends will find them just as hilarious on second meeting; new readers are promised a load of fun on every page.

Give a man a yard and he'll take the whole blasted street. . . .

Harry Taggit, in the back bar of Alf Cooper's pub.

BARRY CRUMP

SCRAPWAGGON

Illustrated by Roger Hart

Contents

TEN CHAPTERS
NUMBERED FROM ONE TO TEN

with subtitles
which you'll see when you
come to them

Among the events faithfully recorded in this book there is reference to a gentleman called Mr Bung Sumple, and in case there's going to be any fun poked at him about his name, I'd better tell you right now that he wasn't christened Bung Sumple by embittered parents or anything like that. His real name is Eugene Sumple. The Bung was tacked onto him because he couldn't sing quite as well as Bing Crosby when he was a young bloke. He gave up singing years ago but never managed to do the same with the nickname.

B.C.

Give a man a yard . . .

ONE

GIVE A MAN A YARD . . .

Among the sedate respectability of the homes in Essentry Crescent on the borders of the city, there was a Number 17. And nobody who passed along Essentry Crescent failed to stop for a second astonished look at Dinny Virtue's place. It was a truly arresting sight. Some of the remarks inspired by the sight include:

"I suppose you'd get used to it in time."

"Hell!"

"What a beaut!"

"It's an offence against decency."

And, "I wonder if there's a distributor-shaft for my old Kelthorpe in there?"

Dinny Virtue was a Refuse Disposal Officer who was considerably stronger on collection than disposal. He'd never been able to distinguish between the perks and the junk, an inability that affects many of us.

At first the perks had been more or less catalogued in long rows from end to end of Dinny's half-acre yard, but "Furniture" had long since overlapped on one side into "Mechanical", and into the fence on the other. "Trunks and Boxes" had been dragged out and scattered. "Books and Toys" had been spilt out of "Trunks and Boxes" and the whole glorious tangle was festooned with the pages of wet books, kapok, and feathers. "Tents and Canvas" had been unrolled and blown into odd corners of the yard. It was no longer possible to tell where "Domestic" was originally centred, a very popular heap. The whole thing had become one great "General", and when Dinny had been unable to go any further along or out he went up, piling junk on junk. It would be safe to say that science, art, and workmanship have not yet achieved the outrageous effect that Dinny had created by accident. And it was difficult to ignore the crazy feeling that he'd once got hold of some inside information that one day there was going to be a terrible shortage of old bed-wires and soggy portraits of the Royal Family.

Dinny's relationships with his neighbours were generally pretty uncertain, but few of the people around hadn't at one time or another called on him for something they needed, though he'd known them to ransack stores and warehouses from one end of the city to the other before coming to him for some unprocurable bit or piece. The City Council engineers themselves had been known to blushingly call on Dinny and request permission to search for some unobtainable part or piece of machinery they'd thrown out years before. Looking across that magnificent conglomeration you just knew that what you wanted, whatever it was, was in there somewhere. No one had ever been able to prove it wasn't.

Although Dinny's interest in his collection of perks was largely amateur, the junk that had passed through his yard had practically paid for the middle-aged house that stood amongst it. A rumour, probably started by one of his singularly humourless neighbours, claims that the landlord he used to rent the place from had returned from a visit abroad to find himself faced with selling out cheap, or shifting Dinny out. Even if this were the truth, he probably got off pretty lightly, all things considered. An extension of the same rumour claims that the day Dinny paid his deposit on the house, property values in Essentry Crescent dropped by a clean fifteen per cent. But it's a free country.

Dinny Virtue ignored all these side-effects of his activities and went quietly about his own business, which was considerable.

Bung Sumple, a gentleman who'd survived twenty-eight faultless years in the City Corporation Valuer's office, was faced with the formidable task of evaluating the property at 17 Essentry Crescent, during a routine survey. There was promotion due to Mr Sumple in the near future, and despair on his brow as he read through yet another draft of the report he was trying to compose:

> *The property situated at 17 Essentry Crescent, N.E. 1, owned by Mr Dinford Reginald Virtue, is considered a local eyesore. No degree of accurate evaluation is possible, and although the building itself (built August, 1944) appears sound, as far as it is possible to ascertain, the property is unlikely to become a saleable proposition in the foreseeable future. . . .*

Mr Sumple screwed up the report and threw it into his waste-paper basket, along with the earlier drafts. Then he swore, for the first time that year, at the wasted time he was going to have to catch up on, and went home to swear again at his wife.

Dinny woke up very carefully with the feeling that his eyelids were stitched together. He had a hangover. But he knew how to handle hangovers. He had a method of sneaking past while they weren't watching. He lay very still for a few moments getting the hang of it. This one was a beaut, about force-six on his private hangover-scale.

With the very top-front edge of his brain he thought about some plastic bags he'd brought home yesterday, and reached slowly out with one hand to feel along the side of the bed. His fingers closed round the neck of the bottle and he drew it slowly out of the boot it was jammed into. Then he sat up, swung his legs over the side of the bed, heaved one blurred eye half open and raised the bottle in a single smooth movement. Then somebody started knocking on the back door and ruined everything.

For a ghastly moment he was caught unawares. Before he

could get his mind shut the hangover surged up from behind him, speared through his brain, arc-welded his eyeballs and short-circuited his whole nervous system. An alarm sang in his ears and his stomach fell up and down inside him as though it was in a washing machine. He put the bottle on the floor with a thump that ran up his arm and caused the walls of his head to cave in, and rammed a handful of blanket into his face to stop it from exploding. His heart tripped and fell and his own fists began shaking themselves in his face. He thought very hard about the plastic bags and waited for it to pass. Dinny was in a bad way, and somebody was still knocking on the back door. If he hadn't wanted to see who it was he'd have probably hidden in his blanket and waited till they went away. But he hardly ever got visitors.

The hangover eventually sank away and perched restlessly in the back of his neck, as though daring him to make a false move. He got to his feet and glided carefully to the bedroom doorway, with his eyebrows held hard high on his forehead to hold back the headache. Down the hall and out through the kitchen. He throttled the door handle for a few moments to get control of the shakes and then drew the door open. There was a girl standing there.

She was about twenty-two or three, Dinny guessed. Beside her on the path was a fairly big suitcase he could have got her thirty bob for if she wanted to sell it. In her off-side hand she held a shopping bag kind of thing, with a green scarf spread over the top of whatever filled it and tucked in round the sides. The bag was Australian bullock-hide, worth about twelve bob with the scarf thrown in. Her jacket, blouse and skirt weren't new but there was still plenty of wear left in them. Twenty-five and six the lot, to the jumble-sale bloke on Thursday. Brownish kind of hair and fairly new shoes (not worth handling these days), and that was about it. She was about the same height as the handle of the swamp-hook leaning against the wall by the door and looked a bit nervous on it; picking at a big button on the front of her coat and staring at him as though the hangover was visible.

She didn't speak at once and Dinny wasn't in any hurry, so he left it to her. He rarely had a visitor like this, even if she had come to the wrong place, which nobody had ever done before. Maybe one of the Jehovah's Witnesses? — No, they always hunt in packs. Saleswoman? — Not a very good one if she was. He remembered the Welfare Officer who'd called in once to see if he had any kids living there. Could be, but a bit innocent-looking for that caper really. Quite a tidy little carcase on her, by the look of things.

No, he couldn't place this one at all. He was just about ready to give in and ask when she spoke.

"Hello Father," she said.

"Uh — What??"

"Don't you remember me? I'm Leila."

"Er — Oh yeah. Sure. How are you?"

"Aren't you pleased to see me?"

"Yeah, 'course I am. You just took me by surprise for a moment." He looked around and up the junk-lined path towards the gate. "Where's your mother?" he asked suspiciously.

"Mother died two months ago."

"Hell," said Dinny. " — I mean, that's real tough. 'Struth. You'd better come in and sit down for a while."

He had to let her carry her own bags. If he'd bent over to pick them up just then his head would have rolled off his shoulders, slopped onto the ground and seeped away. He led her into the kitchen and managed to pull a couple of chairs out from the table. They sat down.

"I didn't know about it," he said. "Haven't heard from any of you for — let's see — eleven, nearly twelve years. You were only a little bit of a . . ." Dinny's voice trailed off as the hangover thundered back again. She reached over to put her hand on his arm and he pulled it away so sharply the jolt set his eyeballs on fire.

"I understand how you feel, Father," she said gently.

When the pain in his head subsided until it merely felt like someone scrubbing the inside of his cranium with a wire brush, he said: "Where'd it happen?"

"It was cancer," said the girl. "She was in hospital for the last three months. They kept her under sedatives. She wasn't in any pain at the end."

"That's nice," said Dinny absently. "Where's — whatsisname?"

"He went off with a lady friend two days after mother was admitted to hospital," she said primly.

"Pretty good at that, isn't he?" observed Dinny.

"I had to stay on and attend to all the arrangements. I tried to get in touch with you because I knew you'd want to be there for the funeral, but I couldn't find a trace of you."

"Probably just as well," said Dinny. "I don't go for these emotional do's much. They upset me," he added quickly.

"It's taken me two weeks to find you," she said. "The police helped me in the finish, after I told them how urgent it was. It's marvellous how helpful people are when you're in trouble."

"Very decent of you to go to all that trouble to let me know," said Dinny.

"Oh it wasn't too bad really," she said. "I had a little money to tide me over."

"Well, drop in any time you feel like it," said Dinny generously. "I always like a bit of a yarn about old times." He just wanted to crawl away and lie down for a while and keeping up this polite conversation was becoming too much of a strain on his depleted reserves.

"But I've come to live with you, Father," said the girl.

"Like hell you have," said Dinny, taken by surprise again. "I mean, I can't have women living here."

"You're my father," she said, as though that solved everything. "There's nowhere else for me to go. I won't be in your way, and I can make myself quite useful." She glanced around the kitchen, an indoor replica of the yard outside.

"Look," said Dinny, "I'm sorry. You just can't stay here. It's absolutely out of the question."

"But you're my father," she repeated.

"I might be your father," argued Dinny weakly, "but I haven't seen you for twelve years. We're practically strangers. Your mother wouldn't want you staying here either."

"Mother told me to come," she said with an air of finality.

Dinny had had all he could stand. He got unsteadily to his feet and stumbled across the kitchen. "She would," he muttered.

"Do you mind if I do a bit of tidying up?" she asked meekly. "I don't want to barge in, but I'd enjoy having something to do."

"Go for your life," croaked Dinny, turning away to his bedroom.

"Is there a room I can put my things in?"

Dinny waved weakly up the hall towards the two spare rooms and closed his door behind him.

He sat on the edge of the bed. His head felt like an old knot someone had been trying to pick undone with a sack-needle.

His mind always seemed to dissolve when he needed it for something important, and now, just when he needed all his wits about him, he had the added handicap of one of his worst hangovers. He picked up the wine bottle, and then put it down again and went along to the bathroom for a wash. On his way back to the bedroom he saw Leila out in the kitchen tidying up around the sink.

"You know I'm only a garbage-collector?" he called out to her.

"I wondered where all the things came from," she said.

"What'll all your friends say when they find out your old man's a garbage-collector?"

"I haven't got any friends here," she replied. "And I don't have friends who care about things like that anyway."

Dinny went into the bedroom and drank from the wine bottle. Then he went back to the kitchen.

"I'm a very heavy drinker," he said. "I get drunk all the time."

"I can see you need someone here to look after you," she said. "It's too much for anyone, working and running a home too. Lots of people turn to drink when things get too much for them like this."

Dinny closed the bedroom door behind him and sat on the bed for a while. He was losing ground, and he didn't like the look of it.

When he came out again Leila was busy wiping down the table, scraping at the worst places with a knife. It was the first time Dinny had seen the whole surface of that table since he'd brought it home a year ago. It didn't look any better to him for being clean.

"I think it's only fair to tell you I've been in gaol," he announced. "I can't ask a young girl like you to live with a hardened criminal."

"Have you really?" she said interestedly. "We'll have to rehabilitate you."

"Drunk and disorderly," said Dinny hopefully.

"How long were you in gaol?"

"Four hours . . ."

"What's it like?"

Without answering Dinny returned to the bedroom to try and think of something else. He took two three-gulp drinks from the wine bottle, saw that it was nearly empty, and finished it off. Then he had to wait for his stomach to settle before he could go on with his thinking. When he went back to the kitchen for another go, she was busy throwing the plastic bags he'd brought home yesterday into a big cardboard box she'd got from somewhere.

"I'm getting married again!" he almost shouted.

No answer.

"To a widow. With eight kids!"

As soon as he'd said it he knew he'd overdone the kids. But she didn't seem to think so.

"Wonderful! I love children. Isn't it lucky? I'll be able to baby-sit for you."

"But we're going to live in Spain," he announced triumphantly. He waited to see what she was going to say about that one. She said:

"Help me carry this box outside, will you please, Father."

Obediently Dinny went to help his daughter carry the box outside. When he realised he was being practically ordered around in his own house he almost dropped his end of the box, but they were nearly out to one of the rubbish-heaps by then anyway. His favourite and most recent acquisitions usually enjoyed a brief term inside the house before finding their way outside, and here she was, within half an hour of barging in, turfing stuff out with complete disregard for its value. He threw the box angrily on to the heap. Leila retrieved it and began to shake it empty.

"I'll need this again," she said. "There's lots more rubbish to come out."

"Look," said Dinny desperately, "I might as well tell you the truth right now. I just can't afford to keep you here. I haven't got any money. I'm heavily in debt. I — I lost it all at the races. I'm a terrible gambler . . ."

"It's nice of you to take me into your confidence like this,

Father," she said sweetly. "As a matter of fact I might be able to help. I'm quite good at figures. Let's go through your books later, shall we?"

"Don't keep books," he said ungraciously.

"You must have a bank book," she said. "We can start with that. Tomorrow, when you've got over your shock."

"We're not starting with anything," snapped Dinny. "You can just . . ." But he couldn't think exactly what it was she could just, so he stalked back into the refuge of his bedroom. He knew he hadn't said enough, but at the same time he had the uncomfortable feeling that he'd said too much.

There was only one thing left to do. He'd have to go and see his partner, Watcher, about it. He kicked off his slippers and shoved his feet into his shoes as though he was trying to stamp them out. Then he strode out through the kitchen, determined not to say another disastrous word till he'd talked it over with Watcher. Leila was standing on a chair taking things off the mantelpiece and putting them down on the table.

"Going out?" she enquired.

"No," said Dinny cleverly.

"I'll cook those sausages in the cupboard for dinner, with potatoes and onions. When shall I expect you back?"

"I don't know."

He slammed the door behind him but it bounced open again.

He felt strangely foolish as he strode indignantly down his junk-lined path to the gateway, like a man who's come out with odd shoes on.

"Watcher'll have this fixed up in no time," he told himself hopefully.

Leila closed the kitchen door and smiled thoughtfully to herself. She liked her father, she decided. The prospect of living here was quite a pleasant one. Dinny would be all right once he got used to the idea.

TWO

PREAMBLE

To say that Watcher Amble was unusual would be no more inaccurate than any other description of him. People seldom realised how little they knew about Watcher unless it was actually pointed out to them. He'd talk freely and sensibly on any subject you liked, except himself. And when there was anything to cover up he could cover it up so thoroughly that an eye-witness would be tempted to doubt the evidence of his own observations.

For example not more than a handful of people ever knew that his name hadn't always been Watcher Amble. The "Amble" was original, but the combination of his real christian name with it lent itself so irresistibly to a variety of ludicrous nicknames that he never even gave his proper name on official forms and things. And his signature was a tiny scribble that would have given a graphologist cross-eyed nightmares.

He'd left his never-mentioned home environs at the earliest legal age and raced his name from place to place, but it always seemed to catch up with him. Then he got a job in a factory where he had to sit all day watching for foul-ups on a fast-moving production line. His workmates, a pretty rough bunch, misunderstood but respected his reasons for not wanting to divulge his name. At first they referred to him as The Watcher, and then it became just Watcher. And for over twenty-five years he'd stuck to this, the first unembarrassing nickname he'd ever had.

It was hard to imagine that Watcher had ever worked anywhere but on the City Council refuse-collection gangs, or lived anywhere but in his hut made from two obsolete tramcars. He blended so perfectly with his surroundings that it was easy to imagine he'd been picked up with the first load of refuse ever collected and stayed in the game ever since.

This was the man Dinny was coming to consult about the problem of his daughter arriving to live with him. Dinny had worked with Watcher for several months before finding out that he was a pretty decent sort of a bloke, when he let you get to know him. For four years Dinny and Watcher had been partners, workmates, and friends.

"Come in," said Watcher. "How's things, Dinny?"

"Been better," said Dinny grimly.

"Seen you looking better. Still crook from last night eh?"

"Yeah."

"We did knock it around. I was a bit seedy myself this morning. Think I've got a bottle here somewhere."

Watcher opened a cupboard and got out a bottle of dry sherry. He put it on the table.

"Here, rip a bit of that into you."

"Where's your glasses?"

"No sense dirtying glasses for just the two of us," said Watcher.

"I'll wash 'em," said Dinny.

"That's what you always say, then you forget at the last minute and I've got to do them."

"I don't ask you to wash up at my place, do I?"

"Okay," said Watcher. And he got two dirty glasses off a shelf and slid them on to the table, the dirtiest one towards Dinny. Dinny absently reached over for the cleaner glass, wiped his thumb round the rim and poured himself a drink.

"We're in the cart," he announced.

"What's up?"

Dinny told him all about how his daughter had turned up from twelve years ago and was trying to move in and live with him. By the time he'd finished, the wine in the bottle was down to the bottom of the DRY SHERRY on the label. He waited for Watcher to say something.

"Didn't know you'd ever been married," he said. "And a daughter, too!"

"Yeah, I've been married," admitted Dinny. "Couldn't stand the wife any longer in the finish so she left me and ran off with a poultry farmer. The bottom fell out of eggs not long after that, and they went away down south somewhere. I got a letter from her once, asking if I'd take her and the kid back and forgive them. I dropped her a line saying okay but she wrote back that she wasn't really serious, just wanted to know if I would or not. That's the last I heard of them, till now." Dinny drank from his glass and waited for Watcher to solve everything.

"Well what do you reckon?" asked Dinny impatiently.

"Don't see that there's any problem," said Watcher, bunging the cork back into the bottle.

"No problem!" shouted Dinny, grabbing the bottle and pulling the cork out again.

"No," said Watcher. "As you said, she's cleaning up your house for you, and that's something it could use. I've noticed it getting a bit untidy over there the last week or two."

"She's clearing all my gear out of the house," corrected Dinny. "And a lot of that stuff's perishable. And what about our organisation we've built up over the years? What about our conference tonight on the Parnell contract? Do you think we're going to be able to hold business conferences with her listening in on our plans? I tell you she's going to disrupt our whole organisation!"

Watcher shared the last of the sherry out between the two glasses and put the empty bottle on the floor.

"See what you mean," he said. "It could get awkward."

"It's awkward already, I tell you. She thinks she's here to stay."

"Can't throw your own flesh and blood out on the street."

"I'd throw her out quick enough," growled Dinny, "but I don't think she'd go. She never bothers to come near me for twelve years, and then as soon as she's stuck for somewhere to live she comes runnin', expecting me to welcome her with open arms."

"Bit of a problem all right," admitted Watcher sagaciously.

"Well, what are we goin' to do about it?"

"Hard to say without seeing her," said Watcher. "What's she look like?"

"I hardly know her, I tell you. We're strangers. I haven't seen her since she was about six or seven years old."

"How old is she now?"

"'Bout nineteen or twenty."

"Good looker?"

"Nothin' startling."

"Look," said Watcher. "Tell you what, you go on home and I'll drop round later. Just on a chance visit like. After I've had a look at the situation we'll work out what's the best way to handle it."

"No fear," said Dinny. "I'm not goin' back there on me own. You can come with me."

"That's no good. We've got to be subtle about it. Don't want her to think she's got us rattled. You just go home and act as if nothing's happened. And don't say or do anything till we've had a conference about it later."

"Okay, but I don't like it. You haven't got another bottle of grog anywhere around, have you?"

"No more grog," said Watcher authoritatively. "We've got to keep a clear head for this. We'll need all our wits about us."

"Well, don't leave it too long before you come over," said Dinny.

"Be there in an hour," Watcher assured him.

And he was. He found Dinny sitting sullenly at the kitchen table while Leila hurried busily back and forth between the rubbish-heap and the room she'd chosen for herself with boxes of "rubbish". She was pleased to meet Watcher, made them a cup of tea, and left them alone. They sat in the unfamiliar kitchen and talked about the Job. After about half an hour Watcher had seen enough. He whispered to Dinny to come over to his hut after tea. Then he slunk out. Dinny sat on alone in the kitchen wondering what was going to happen. The girl came down the passage with another armful of his gear.

"Oh! Has your friend gone? I didn't say goodbye to him."

"He doesn't like women," said Dinny shortly.

"What a shame. He's such a nice man too," she sighed. "He must have had an unhappy love affair in his past." And she went out with her load, leaving Dinny sitting there with pursed lips and eyes.

He put in a couple of hours sorting through a new box of perks in the wash-house. He usually enjoyed looking over new perks, but this lot seemed to be nothing but junk. He went through the motions all the same, and pretended not to hear when Leila called out that his dinner was on the table. She didn't call out again and after a while he was so curious that he had to go through to the kitchen for a look.

His dinner was on the table. Leila's plate, knife and fork had been washed up and put away. He could hear her sweeping in her room up the passage. He wasn't going to eat any of her fancy grub. It could stay there till it went rotten for all he cared. He went over to the table to see what she'd cooked. Then he took a quick bite off the end of one of the sausages to see if it had been cooked properly. It had, but now there was a big bite mark, so he had to eat the rest of the sausage to destroy the evidence. He carefully arranged some mashed potato and onion over the place on the plate where the sausage had been, so as not to give her the impression he was going to let her cook for him.

It's funny about sausages. They're not like most other meat. Nobody remembers how many slices or hunks of beef or pork or mutton they've put on a plate, but it's different with sausages. If someone cooks six sausages and puts three on each of two plates, they remember. And if one's missing they're likely to notice. Dinny hadn't realised this about sausages before. He thought it over for a few moments and eventually decided to confuse her. He'd take a little from the potatoes and a little from the onions, to make her think she'd put out a smaller meal than she really had. He could lick the fork clean afterwards and leave everything just as it was. She'd never have a clue that he'd even touched her meal.

But it didn't work. For a start he accidentally took too much potato and tried to spread what was left over more of the plate. That made it look too flat so he left the potato for the time being and ate a few more onions to get the proportion right. Then he scraped the potato back into a sort of heap but there was potato left all over the plate where it had been. He carefully licked the plate clean all round the outside and started again to rearrange everything.

He was so engrossed that he failed to hear her coming along the hall. When she walked into the kitchen Dinny was sitting with his chin on the table, trying to build a hollow pile of cold mashed potato on his plate with the handle of his fork.

"Has your dinner got cold?" she enquired concernedly. "What a shame! The very first meal I've cooked for you, too. I was sure you must have heard me call you. If I'd known you were so busy I could have kept it warm for you."

Dinny slowly raised his head from the table but not his eyes.

"Would you like me to heat it up again for you?" she asked. "It wouldn't take a moment."

"Not hungry," he mumbled, getting up from the table.

"The way you were rattling your plate I thought I'd have to cook you some more," she laughed, turning back up the passage. "Just leave your plate on the bench, I'll fix it later."

Dinny grabbed his coat from behind the door, snatched up the two remaining sausages and ate them on the way round to Watcher's hut. He wouldn't have to put up with it much longer, once Watcher got to work.

Watcher had his lamp lit and a bottle ready. In fact the bottle was almost a third over-ready by the time Dinny arrived. Watcher poured him a drink.

"Got any ideas?" demanded Dinny.

"Plenty," said Watcher. "But she's going to be a tough nut to crack, all the same. Might take a bit of time."

"Why don't we just go round and tell her to get the hell out of it?" said Dinny impatiently. "That wouldn't take much time."

"Make you look a proper joe, wouldn't it," observed Watcher. "No, that's not the answer. You can't just kick her out. It's out of the question."

"Can't I!" said Dinny hotly. "If she's still here this time tomorrow I'll . . ."

"Cut it out," interrupted Watcher. "If you were going to be able to throw her out you'd have done it by now."

"It's a free country," insisted Dinny. "I'll have her out of there if I have to get the cops on to her. They'll shift her!"

"She's not twenty-one yet and you're still responsible for her. And the cops'll never interfere in a family row unless someone's getting knocked around. Let's face it, you're not going to be able to throw her out and you know it."

"Why not?" Dinny wanted to know.

"Because you're her father and she's not doing anyone any harm."

"She's only disrupted me whole life, that's all. A man's got a right to his privacy."

"And she's got a right to have somewhere to live," said Watcher.

"She's perfectly capable of getting a job and somewhere of her own to live. I don't care what you say."

"When she gets over losing her mother she'll probably do that."

"It didn't take *me* this long to get over losing her mother," said Dinny ungraciously. "So you reckon there's nothing we can do about it," he challenged, draining his glass. "You're just going to sit back and let her overrun me whole life. Wreck all our plans for making big money. Tie our hands. Rob us of our freedom, and the little bit of fun we get out of life. Take over everything we've built up over the years. A fine mate you turned out to be."

"Now take it easy," said Watcher, pouring a splash into Dinny's glass and a lot into his own. "You're getting carried away again. You'll never break into big business if you're going to throw a Charlie every time a bit of a problem crops up. You have to sit quietly back with a bottle of plonk and nut out all the angles. That's the way fortunes are made."

"But you just said there was nothing we could do about it."

"I didn't say any such thing. I simply pointed out that you can't turf her out, that's all. We've got to be subtle about it. — Now listen. I reckon the best thing that could happen would be for her to leave off her own bat. What we've got to do is make her *want* to go. That way everybody'll be happy. But as long as she doesn't want to go she won't think about doing it."

Dinny thought it over while he topped up his glass.

"I reckon you might just have stumbled on to something there," he said thoughtfully. "All we've got to do is belt her around a bit — starve her out . . ."

"No, no, no! You'd never belt anyone around and you'd starve yourself to death before you'd see a mad dog go without a feed, you know that. That's why you'll never make a fortune without me to keep you from going off half-cocked."

"Well what, then?"

"We'll have to make it so she can't stand the place," said Watcher. "Everyone's got things they don't like. What we've got to do is find out what this daughter of yours doesn't like most, and give her the works."

"Don't think she's too keen on the booze," said Dinny helpfully.

"The trouble with things like booze and gambling is that they're liable to back-fire on you," said Watcher thoughtfully.

"How do you work that out?"

"She might take it the wrong way, and think she has to save us from our weaknesses. We don't want to risk making a soul-saver out of her. Once they get the idea they're really needed Old Nick himself wouldn't shift them. I've seen it happen before. The booze might work but we'd better try one or two other things first."

"What things?"

"First of all we'd better find out as much about her as we can. What happened after I left your place this afternoon?"

"She just went on throwing out all my valuable equipment," said Dinny.

"What did she say after I left?" insisted Watcher. "She must have said something."

"Well she said what a nice bloke you were."

"Hmmm, that makes it tough."

"What do you mean, makes it tough?"

"Never mind. What else did she say?"

"She said you must have had a messed-up love-life,"

remembered Dinny. "You see! She's started on sex already. Before we know what's happening she'll have young blokes hanging around, poking about with all my valuable gear, climbing in and out the windows all hours of the night. And then she'll get herself into trouble and I'll get the blame for not keeping an eye on her."

"Hey, now," laughed Watcher. "You've got your tail in the air again. Keep calm, this is serious business. What made her say that?"

"Say what?"

"About me having a mixed-up love-life."

"I don't know. I think it might have been something I said about you not having much to do with women."

"You're getting pretty chummy on it, aren't you? How come you got to talking about men and women with her in the first place?"

"We weren't," said Dinny. "That's all that was said. I hardly spoke to her all afternoon."

"Anything else happen?"

"No. I spent a fair while going through that new box of gear we picked up on Friday. She just cooked a feed and went on throwing things outside."

"What's her cooking like? They often use that to get a man won over."

"All right I suppose," said Dinny uncomfortably. "Didn't take much notice of it."

"Have to watch out for things like that. You didn't eat any of her cooking did you?"

"What? — No, no," lied Dinny, and he drained his glass.

"Good. We'll have to be careful not to get too friendly with her, especially you. We don't want sentiment entering into it. Try not to let her get into the habit of doing anything she might think makes her indispensable."

"I'm not likely to go getting friendly with her," growled Dinny. "I wouldn't . . ."

"Okay, okay. Keep an eye on her. Watch for anything that might give us an idea what puts her teeth on edge. There's bound to be something. I'll think about it tonight and we'll have another conference at work tomorrow. We've got that bloody Horne Bay run. I'll pick up the scrapwaggon and come over to your place about half past nine."

"Do you think I ought to tell her you're going to move in and we need the spare room? Or something?"

"No. We don't want her to get so much as a whisper that we're up to something. If she gets suspicious the whole thing's had it."

When Dinny got home Leila was hanging up some washed clothes in the kitchen. She put on a cup of tea.

"I didn't know whether to wait up for you or not," she said.

"You don't have to worry about me," he growled.

"Of course I worry about you. I know how you feel just now. It's a terrible strain. What you need is a jolly good sleep."

As he stalked off to his bedroom she called after him: "Your cup of tea's ready, would you like me to bring it in to you?"

"No, I wouldn't," he snarled, jamming his bedroom door shut.

He got into bed feeling as though he'd spent all day going round tying tins on to dogs' tails.

Scrapwaggon

THREE

SCRAPWAGGON

Watcher picked up the scrapwaggon from the Council depot and arrived to collect Dinny just after nine o'clock. Dinny wasn't ready. Watcher blew the horn and sat in the truck to wait.

It didn't really matter what time they started in the mornings as long as they got their work done. They had their runs worked out so neatly that they seldom did more than four hours' work on any day. They'd worked out all the available short-cuts and organised quite a few that weren't available. Then they'd had to arrange some interesting methods of passing the time they'd saved to make it look as though they were working hard.

"It doesn't matter how little you actually do," Watcher often said. "As long as it looks like a lot everyone's happy."

But they had to be careful not to let their boss run away with the idea that they could handle any extra work. It was a knack of being flat-out both ways at once.

Dinny emerged from his jungle of perks looking worried and climbed into the truck.

"Slept in, eh," grinned Watcher. "Have to dock your pay for that."

Dinny didn't answer so he let it drop.

They did a street, one driving and the other collecting the tins of trash in turns. Then they pulled into one of their private sub-depots to go through some interesting stuff a doctor had thrown out. It wasn't as good as it had first looked. Mostly old books and magazines and medicine-bottles.

"Deceptive, this stuff," said Dinny. "It doesn't look much but some of these books might sell for three or four bob."

"Better leave it," said Watcher. "We lose too much on the handling with that kind of stuff."

They got into the truck for a conference and a snort from the "survival kit" they kept behind the seat (a thermos of sweet sherry, for use only in emergencies such as hangovers, wet days, time to pass, opportunities, and conferences).

"How's it going at home?" asked Watcher, passing Dinny the thermos for the first drink.

"No good," said Dinny. "She thinks she's there for keeps all right. I didn't know where I was when I came out of my room this morning."

"Got the place cleaned up, eh?"

"No, cluttered up. She's got her washing hangin' all over the kitchen. Have to keep duckin' under things every time I want to move round."

"Change from stepping over things," observed Watcher, taking the thermos and drinking from it. "We'll have to keep a lookout for a thermos that's not broken. The rust and stuff in this one's turning the plonk sour."

"But they're underclothes and things," insisted Dinny. "It's not right."

"She's your daughter," pointed out Watcher.

"That's what she said when I tackled her about it," said Dinny. "But it doesn't make it any better as far as I'm concerned. We'll have to get her out of it. I couldn't live with anyone like her, even if I wanted to. She's got the place looking like a morgue. There's no atmosphere in it any more."

"Plenty of atmosphere in a morgue," grinned Watcher. "Had a look round in one once."

"Never mind that, what are we going to do about Leila?"

"What was she like when you left this morning?"

"She woke me up with cups of tea three times. Just came

barging into me private room as though she owned the place."

"Sounds like a good worker."

"Too bloody good. That's the trouble," complained Dinny. "A man can't go on being bitchy at someone who never does anything wrong. She tries so hard to please me all the time it's gettin' on me nerves. And she thinks I'm just upset about her mother kickin' off."

"You haven't softened up on her, have you?" asked Watcher suspiciously.

"No I haven't, but it's against human nature to keep on ignoring someone all the time. I tell you we'll have to do something quick, before I pack up altogether."

"Think I've got an idea," said Watcher.

"What is it? I'll try anything."

"All this washing and cleaning up she's doing."

"What about it?"

"We're going to make her ashamed of us," announced Watcher.

"Huh?"

"We'll go round to your place for lunch. The sight of us in our working clobber and the old scrapwaggon here parked outside might just be enough to convince her we're not worth puttin' up with."

"I'll have a go at anything," said Dinny.

"Right. It's near enough to lunch time now. We'll stop on the way and pick up a bit more rubbish to top off the load. Got to make it look right. Keep your eye open for a couple of good ones, there's usually one or two along College Street."

Watcher screwed the top on the thermos and put it behind the seat. Dinny, who was behind the wheel, drove, while Watcher emptied a few extra cans of rubbish artistically along the top of the load.

"That'll do us," he said climbing into the cab beside Dinny.

"Looked like a few perks in the one before last. We'll go through it after lunch."

They pulled up at Dinny's place and got out of the truck. Watcher looked around the yard.

"Say, you're getting quite a collection here," he said admiringly. "Haven't seen some of this before. Where did it come from?"

"Inside," said Dinny shortly, going on up the path.

Watcher whistled softly, shook his head and followed Dinny. Leila came down the passage into the kitchen just as the two men were getting seated at the table. There was no washing hanging in the kitchen but there was a piece of rope strung twice across the room that Watcher hadn't seen before.

"Oh hello," she said pleasantly. "If I'd known you were coming home for lunch I could have got something ready for you. Have you got time for me to cook up something now?"

"We never eat lunch," grunted Dinny.

"Well I'll make you a cup of tea. You'll need something to keep you going."

"Thanks," said Watcher. "I could go a drink. Hope it's not too much trouble."

Dinny turned to stare at him. He was just going to say something when Watcher went on: "Dry work on the old rubbish cart, eh Dinny?"

"Er — yeah," stammered Dinny.

Leila poured their tea, put the milk and sugar on the table for them and then went to the back door. "Just call out if there's anything else you want," she said. "I'll be out by the fence. I'm clearing a place to put a clothesline."

"What the hell are you being nice to her for?" hissed Dinny as soon as she was gone. "You'll have her thinking . . ."

"Don't panic," said Watcher calmly. "I think you might have

been overdoing it a bit. If you talk to her like that all the time she'll end up thinking you're just a big gruff daddy whose bark's worse than his bite, and she won't take anything you say seriously."

Dinny was confused. "That's all very well for you, but you don't have to — shhh, here she comes."

Leila came in the door and caught them in the act of looking guilty.

"Is that your truck out on the road?" she asked.

"Yeah, that's the old scrapwaggon," said Watcher.

"We always park it out there," added Dinny.

"Could I go and have a look?" she asked. "I won't touch anything."

Dinny glanced at Watcher to see what he'd say to that.

"Sure, help yourself," said Watcher.

The girl went out and the two men sat in silence for a few moments. Then Watcher said: "Good legs eh?"

"Uh, what?"

"She's got a decent set of pins on her," said Watcher.

"I wish she'd use 'em to cart herself off somewhere," growled Dinny. "You can see what she's doing to the place, can't you?"

"Yeah. Wonder what she wanted to have a look at the scrapwaggon for?"

"Probably pretending to be interested in our work," said Dinny. "Let's get back and finish the run. At least we can talk out on the job without anyone listening in."

"Ar, you worry too much," said Watcher, following him outside.

"Where'd Leila go?" asked Watcher as they approached the truck.

"Probably took one look and went for her life," said Dinny.
"Not much to look at at the best of times," said Watcher. "Well I'll

go to . . . Have a look at that!"

Leila was standing on the centre of the rear wheel of the scrapwaggon reaching into the back. She saw the men coming and held up a heavy old book for them to see.

"Look," she said. "A *Webster's Dictionary* in perfect condition. It must be worth quite a bit."

"What the hell are you doing up there?" shouted Dinny.

She dropped the book back into the rubbish and jumped down on to the footpath. "You said I could have a look, Father," she said scoldingly.

"We didn't mean you could climb all over the bloody thing," blurted Dinny.

Watcher had reached into the back of the truck for the book Leila had dropped. He passed it to her. "Here y'are," he said cheerfully. "It's all yours. Compliments of the management."

She took the book and ran to the house with it. Dinny looked suspiciously at Watcher. "What are you up to?" he demanded.

"We did tell her to help herself," said Watcher.

"You told her, you mean."

"Hmmm. Anyway that's one trick we can cross off our little list," said Watcher. He climbed into the truck.

"You mean her not being put off by the scrapwaggon?"

"Not only that," replied Watcher, "but that girl's a born scavenger if ever I saw one. A real chip off the old block."

"I don't believe it," said Dinny. "She's just pretending, to try and win us over so we'll let her stay. Anyway we've got her a bit rattled."

"Rattled?"

"The way she got upset when I told her to get off the truck," said Dinny smugly.

"She might be pretending about a lot of things," disagreed Watcher. "Everybody does, if it comes to that. But I don't think she was pretending about being interested in this load of stuff, and I don't think she was rattled either. No one could pretend that well about a thing that puts them off."

"What about all my good gear she threw out of the house?" asked Dinny.

"Did shc throw out any really good stuff?"

"I haven't had a chance to check up on it yet, but . . ."

"Might pay you to look it over," said Watcher. "You are inclined to be a bit over-enthusiastic about perk-collecting, you know."

"Are you trying to tell me she's a better judge of perks than I am?" demanded Dinny hotly.

"No fear," said Watcher patiently. "No amount of talent could ever make up for your experience. You've got nothing to worry about there."

"Well what are we going to do now?"

"I think we'll try something else tonight," said Watcher.

"What?"

"Tell you about it in the pub after we take the truck in," said Watcher. "It'll take careful planning."

They dumped their load and collected, sorted and dumped the rest of the run. Then they took some new perks round to Dinny's place and threw them over the fence. Leila came out to see what they were doing but they told her they were in a hurry and drove off, leaving her peering into the pile of stuff they'd brought.

When she'd finished looking at the new perks Leila turned to go inside and caught a glimpse of somebody's face beside the curtain in a window of the house opposite. She waved and smiled. The curtain fell across the face. It must be the Mr Tweek she'd heard her father and Watcher talking about. Arthur Tweek had enjoyed a full and rewarding career as a traffic officer. His punctual efficiency; his devotion to duty and detail; his level-headed courage in the face of danger or emergency; his scrupulous fairness and courtesy in dealing with the public; the precision of his reports and the honest accuracy of his evidence, had been a source of irritation to everyone he worked on, everyone he worked for, and everyone he worked with, for almost forty years. He retired from the service at sixty with all the above-mentioned qualities in perfect running order.

Officer Tweek had been planning for his retirement at an age when most people are still wondering whether or not to get married. Perhaps it was just as well. A Mrs Tweek who'd survived this long would have been a woeful creature indeed.

Being a bachelor, efficient, willing, and intolerable, Officer Tweek was kept almost permanently on relieving duty. He would relieve officers away on holiday, or ill, or until they could be replaced. He was sent to places and functions where the local traffic men were overloaded with work. Anything to keep him on the move, and wherever he moved he irritated people. But this arrangement suited Officer Tweek nicely. The department not only supplied him with free lodgings wherever he went, but subsidised his search for a place to retire to.

Long before he retired he'd decided on the centre and the suburb that would suit him best. And he knew the distances he wanted to be from the shops, the bus-routes, the hospital, the sea, the courthouse, and other people. He chose the house and had two different valuers go over it twice — and had the courts go over the speculator he bought it from.

Officer Tweek (ret.) settled into his own home to enjoy the years of untroubled leisure he'd so conscientiously provided for. His privacy was shielded from the curiosity of his neighbours on either side by two boundaries of elegant thirty-foot black poplars, which wouldn't have to be trimmed for at least twenty years. And from his deck-chair on the front veranda he could choose between a view of his garden and the houses across the street, or the houses across the street and the top of the hills on the far side of the harbour. Mr Tweek had every reason to feel pleased with the foresight that had promised to make his retirement as unblemished as his working life had been. He settled down to wait for the end of his life with a clear conscience.

But Mr Tweek had not foreseen or provided for that particular brand of injustice that strikes a man down in his moment of triumph. He had scarcely had time to get his new neighbours properly antagonised when Dinny Virtue moved into Number 17, straight across the street from him.

Mr Tweek watched with apprehension, indignation, shock, and finally outrage, as Dinny added daily to the construction of the monstrous eyesore that dominated his only view.

Officer Tweek had risen up against this threat to the dignity of his retirement. He fought it with all the old fire that for almost forty years had rendered the nation's highways unpleasant for the innocent and guilty alike. He complained in triplicate to the proper authorities, and then went over their heads and complained in person. He consulted his solicitor. He presented petitions signed by nearly half the residents of Essentry Crescent. He studied the by-laws and the regulations. He enquired abroad for the owner of Number 17. He enlisted the support of his neighbours and quoted endlessly from the Regulations. He sent telegrams to his local M.P., letters to the editor, and urgent messages to *Truth*, demanding that something be done. He shouted at Dinny from the street. He complained about noise, nuisance, devaluation of properties, health, rats, hazards, victimisation, and the inefficiency of whoever he was complaining to.

He tried to sell his house.

There was nothing anyone could do about it. Dinny kept

himself to his yard, his job, himself, and later on his friend Watcher. He'd decided that the old codger across the road was nuts, and left it at that.

After more than eight years of campaigning the results of Mr Tweek's efforts added up to Dinny holding the honour of being the biggest nuisance in Essentry Crescent, after Mr Tweek. But he never gave up trying to find some way to have that man and his hideous rubbish swept off the face of his retirement. He couldn't even sell his house and go away from it all. After a life spent in the service of justice, Mr Tweek could get none for himself.

And now that man was openly living with a girl young enough to be his daughter.

After they'd put their truck in at the depot Dinny and Watcher adjourned to the pub.

"Well what's this new scheme of yours?" asked Dinny impatiently.

"Swearing," said Watcher. "I've been working it out. If we don't do it now it'll never work, she'd know we were just bunging it on."

"Swearing?" frowned Dinny. "You mean bad language?"

"Yeah. It's one thing not many women can take much of. We'll go round to your place after the pub. Pretend to be a bit shikker, not much, just enough to be merry."

"And start swearing?"

"Yeah."

"Why don't we take some grog and make a proper job of it?" suggested Dinny.

"No fear. We don't want to louse it up with a crook performance. We want to make her think we swear *all* the time, not just when we're drunk. We'll just bowl in and let rip with a few jokes and the odd word or two here and there, natural like.

Have to be careful not to overdo it."

"Okay," said Dinny dubiously. "I sure hope this works. Me nerves are packin' up on me."

"If it doesn't work we'll have to try something else," said Watcher. "The important thing is to work it so that when she does leave she won't be able to blame us."

They not quite rolled up at Dinny's place just on dark that evening. Leila was at the stove with steaming pots.

"Hello," she said. "I'm glad Mr Amble came. I've cooked enough for all of us. We can all eat together — unless you have some business to talk about."

There was a brief silence while Dinny and Watcher gathered their wits and their words. Then Dinny blurted: "D'you feel like any blasted tucker, Watcher?"

"Blowed if I know," replied Watcher.

"What the broodin' hell's this?" Dinny asked, looking at something under the table.

"Stew," said Leila calmly. "I was wondering about food. Would you like me to make out a list of the things we need?"

"Is there any broodin' grog in the broodin' place?" asked Dinny.

"Yeah, I'm as dry as a beggar," added Watcher politely.

"I haven't seen any round," said Leila. "Have you got any in your room, Father?"

"Broodin' hell," whispered Dinny. "No broodin' booze."

"Yeah. No brooding booze," echoed Watcher helpfully.

"Yeah," said Dinny. "We should bug — go back to the pub and get some."

Leila put some plates on the table. "If you're going to bugger off back to the pub for some grog you'll have to hurry. They've been closed for an hour," she said casually. "Will you have your bloody tucker now, or shall I keep it till you get back?"

She served them their food and they ate in a squirming silence. Watcher bolted his food and stood up.

"Well, it's getting late," he said. "Think I'll be getting back to me hut. Big day tomorrow. — Thanks for the feed, miss."

"You're welcome," she said pleasantly. "I hope Father brings you often."

"Yeah, well thanks a lot. See you in the morning, Dinny."

"Wait on," said Dinny desperately. "I think I'll just walk some of the way with you. I always like to get a bit of fresh air before I turn in."

They walked for a while in silence. Then Dinny said: "She was pretending that time all right."

"So were we — only she made a better job of it. Upstaged us good and proper."

"Wonder where she picked up all that language?" said Dinny. "I didn't think she'd know about things like that."

"She's not exactly a baby," Watcher reminded him. "And don't make any mistake about the kids these days. She could probably teach us a thing or two."

"You don't think she's one of them juvenile delinquents, do you?" asked Dinny in alarm.

"Not a show. She's just an ordinary girl who's been around a bit more than most, that's all. I'll tell you something else too, she's about the smartest piece of work I've come across in a long time."

"Well it looks like she's got us whacked, anyway," said Dinny despondently.

"Oh we're not whacked yet, by a long shot. She's just got us temporarily stonkered, that's all. We'll come up with something that'll rock her, don't worry."

"None of these ideas of yours seem to be working out," accused Dinny.

"Not on their own," admitted Watcher, "but all added up

together they'll have the same effect in the long run. We'll have to work on a completely different angle."

"What about the booze?" suggested Dinny. "We haven't tried that yet."

"Might be worth a try. There's no telling what might work. But she's probably livened that we're up to something by now. We'll have to be extra crafty about it."

"It's hard to imagine anyone who looks like that, being like that," said Dinny, kicking in wonder at a stone on the roadside.

"She's no different from anyone else," said Watcher. "One thing, we know she's quite capable of keeping her end up, whatever happens to her. She won't have a nervous breakdown on us, or anything like that."

"Yeah, but think what'd happen if she got some kind of foothold in our set-up."

Watcher laughed. "She has already, and a pretty strong foothold at that. But we'll come up with something, don't let it get you down. I'll just cut through here to my hut. See you in the morning, same time. I'll pick up the waggon. There's only the two-hour run tomorrow."

Two days later Bung Sumple's boss asked Bung for his still unwritten report. Mr Sumple promised to have it on his desk the following day without fail. The following day Mr Sumple spent his lunch hour and a half in the private bar of Alf Cooper's pub, and returned to the office in a condition which the typist described as "tiddly". He scribbled distractedly all over two report forms and his blotter, and then had to go home early with a violent headache.

One for a jack

FOUR

ONE FOR A JACK

It was over a week before they got the booze campaign organised. They'd been neglecting their side-lines and devoting too much of their time to trying to get rid of Dinny's daughter. Several small "contracts" for filling had to be attended to, and the new tyres on one of the Council trucks had to be changed for worn ones they'd collected from a trucking firm's garbage-heap. Forty sheets of old roofing-iron had to be dropped off a few at a time where a bloke they knew was building a boatshed.

"We'll try the booze on her as soon as we've got time to do it properly," said Watcher, passing a full dustbin up to Dinny on the truck.

"But in the meantime we're getting out of drinking form," complained Dinny. "Our boozing's fallen right off. And our organisation's being neglected. They've paid a contractor to do that Everton Street job I just about had lined up. That's five quid we could have picked up if we'd had time to arrange it properly. We hardly ever see each other these days."

"It's no use turning on the grog unless it's the real thing," said Watcher. "And if we wait a while before we try it she won't be so suspicious."

"It's all right for you," said Dinny. "You don't have to live with her."

"Ar, she's not all that bad," said Watcher.

"She had me playing bloody cards last night," said Dinny indignantly.

"Poker?"

"No. Strip-Jack-Naked," snarled Dinny. "A bloody kid's game."

"Not a bad game that," consoled Watcher. "Used to play it meself."

"Well I've got more to do with me time than play games. I've got a business organisation to look after. She's costing me a small fortune."

"You've got to admit she's made a fair bit of difference since she's been with us," said Watcher reasonably.

"Difference! You're telling me she's made a difference! I should have got the police on to her in the first place."

"It was no use then so it's too late to think about it now."

"Well I just hope this grog trick works, that's all. If it doesn't I'm going to sell out, lock, stock, and barrel, and take off somewhere."

"What? Give up all we've worked and strived to build up? One of the biggest perk-organisations in the country, and you want to walk off and leave it just like that?" Watcher was getting excited now.

"It's no use if I can't call me home me own," said Dinny. "A man's freedom comes first. It's no good amassing a fortune if you're not going to be free to enjoy it."

"You're a beaut," said Watcher. "You're enthusiastically unenthusiastic one minute, and the next you're enthusiastically enthusiastic again. You're too enthusiastic."

Dinny stood there on the trash-waggon, frowning over whether Watcher had just praised or abused him. Watcher leaned on the side of the truck and passed him up a cigarette to help him think.

"We haven't even tried the booze one yet, and you're already talking as though it was a complete flop. We haven't tapped our resources yet."

"Well when are we going to do it?" asked Dinny.

"Have to get the grog first. We'll need a fair bit, and our finances aren't too healthy at the moment. I had to pay back that six quid the bloke's wife paid us for those loads of filling. He reckoned there was too much paper in it and it blew all over the place."

"Why didn't you tell him to take a running jump at himself?"

"Couldn't argue with him. Threatened to complain to the Council about it."

"Hell. Best to pay up when they come at that," said Dinny. "We can't risk any complaints or they'll start keeping an eye on everything we do. I've got twenty quid at home anyway; we can use some of that for our grog."

"Twenty quid! Where'd you get it?"

"Well you know how people sometimes think my place is a junk yard?"

"Er — yeah."

"Well, people have been coming round looking for odd things while we've been out, and Leila's sold quite a bit of my best gear. I tore a strip off her when I found out, but she didn't seem to realise how serious it was."

"Hell man," said Watcher. "You should have told her to go ahead and sell as much as she likes. That's good business."

"I did," said Dinny, shuffling his feet in the rubbish on the back of the truck.

The big booze-up was organised in the greatest secrecy.

"If our security on this breaks down," said Watcher solemnly, "the blokes in the pub'll come round like flies for the party, and we don't want Leila to think it's an event. It's supposed to be our normal way of living."

They bought the grog over several days so as not to create any excitement in local drinking circles.

"You blokes are really hitting it along lately," said Alf Cooper the publican to Dinny, who'd called in for his second suitcase of bottles in the same afternoon. "I don't know how you stand up to it."

"We're used to it," said Dinny awkwardly. "We — er — it's a matter of practice."

They stored the grog in Watcher's hut under lock and key, and on the day set aside for its use they loaded it all into the scrapwaggon and covered it with sacks and trash. Then they drove to Dinny's place and parked the waggon outside the gate. It would be quite safe there till it was time to spring their surprise and get the truck back to the depot.

They had an hour or two to kill, so they prowled around in the yard, pretending to be looking for something. Leila made them cups of tea, which they insisted on having out in the fresh air and sunshine. And they were so careful not to make any slips about what was uppermost in both their minds that they hardly spoke to each other at all. Then as the time was drawing near, Leila came out to where they were squatting intently around a cracked motor-block and said: "The stuff you've got in the truck isn't stolen, is it?"

"No," said Dinny indignantly. "We paid hard cash for every drop of it."

"Don't know what you're talking about," said Watcher quickly.

"If it's drink and it's not stolen," she suggested, "why don't you bring it inside? It'll be getting terribly warm out there in the sun."

She helped them to carry it all in. Dinny lined up all the bottles on the bench and the mantelpiece in the kitchen, while Watcher took the scrapwaggon to the depot. He returned in a taxi so as not to miss anything. Dinny and Watcher sat at the table and opened a bottle of beer each.

"What's the party in aid of?" enquired Leila.

"We're returning to our old habits," Dinny said. Far too loudly.

"Oh? What habits are those?"

"We used to have a few drinks here every weekend," said Watcher.

"Drunken hoolies," corrected Dinny.

"Lasting for days," added Watcher.

"Weeks!" gloated Dinny. "*Orgies*!" he almost shouted.

"I wish you'd told me," said Leila. "I could have got some nice food to go with your drinks."

"We never eat when we're drinking," said Dinny.

"Don't touch food for days on end," said Watcher.

"Heavens. I hope you don't make yourselves ill," said Leila. "Perhaps I'd better go down to the store for some aspirins and something to settle stomachs, just in case."

"Never use any of that kind of stuff," said Dinny.

"Never need it," said Watcher.

"Don't want it," said Dinny.

"I don't suppose you'll want me hanging around then," she said. "I'll go off to the pictures if you like. Is there anything you want before I go?"

The men were silent.

"It's all right if I go out, isn't it?" she asked.

"Have to think about that," said Dinny, glancing at Watcher. "I think we'd better have a conference," suggested Watcher. They took their bottles of beer into Dinny's bedroom to hold a conference on what to do about Leila going off to the pictures.

"It's no good staging all this for her if she's not going to be here to see it," said Dinny.

"She's a bit young to be wandering around on her own late at night anyway, isn't she?" said Watcher concernedly. "Anything could happen to her."

"Friday night, too," said Dinny. "If anything happened to her we'd be responsible for letting her go out alone."

"You're her father, you know, Dinny. It's your responsibility."

"Yeah, that's right. But I can't *make* her stay home if she doesn't want to."

"We could carry on without her and be ready for when she gets back," said Watcher.

"I don't know, Watcher," said Dinny, drinking solemnly from his bottle. "I don't think I'd be able to relax and enjoy myself, seeing as how I'm responsible and all that. I'd be too worried. Sitting here boozin' while me only daughter's out goodness knows where on her own. It wouldn't be right."

Watcher drank from his bottle. "In that case there's only one course open to us," he said.

"What's that?"

"We'll have to give her the choice. We can't force her to stay, but if she wants to hang around and find out the truth about us, let it be her decision."

"You're dead right," said Dinny. "Let's go and tell her. *You* tell her," he added. "It's your idea, and I'm a bit hazy on the details. I might muck it up."

They went back to the kitchen, took their places at the table, filled their glasses and drank deeply. Leila was putting something on the stove.

"How was your conference?" she asked. "It looks serious."

Watcher cleared his throat. "We've been discussing this matter, your father and I, and we've decided that seeing as we're more or less your — er — guardians, we feel a bit responsible."

She just stood there looking puzzled. Watcher continued: "How old are you, lass?"

"What's that got to do with it?" she asked.

"We're not sure that a young girl like you ought to be going out on her own," said Dinny. "It mightn't be safe."

"Good heavens," she said. "I've been going out on my own ever since I was twelve years old. I'm eighteen, if you must know.

As a matter of fact I'll be nineteen next Wednesday week."

"We thought you might like to wait till one of us can come with you," lied Watcher.

"Oh that'd be nice," she said. "When?"

"Some time next week, when we've finished our booze-up," said Dinny. "Pour yourself a beer, seein' as it's your birthday next Wednesday week."

"Just one glass, though," added Watcher solicitously.

Leila got herself a glass from the cupboard and poured herself a drink from Dinny's bottle.

"It's awfully warm and frothy," she said, wiping her lips.

Dinny and Watcher glanced at each other. They were still on their first bottles.

"It is a bit," admitted Watcher.

"Doesn't worry us, though," said Dinny. "We're used to it."

"We thrive on it," added Watcher.

The men sipped their beer and talked about times when they'd had *really* crook beer. Leila finished cooking some lamb chops and eggs, offered again to get some for the men, and then sat down between them and ate her meal. By the time she'd finished they were almost visibly drooling. They drank determinedly on for a while, talking about perks, pubs, and deals they were working on. Nothing important in front of the girl, just everyday stuff.

Eventually Watcher said: "This is the worst beer they palmed off on us for years."

"You can say that again," said Dinny.

"Too fresh."

"They don't give it time to brew properly these days," agreed Dinny.

"All chemical beer. Not like the stuff we used to get."

"Spiggott's beer never travels well," said Dinny expertly. "Gets too shook-up. Takes weeks to settle properly."

"Yeah. We should have got something else."

"Of course we're out of condition. You have to take that into consideration ."

"Yeah. Normally we'd clean this lot up in one sitting."

"Is all your beer ruined?" asked Leila politely.

"Not exactly ruined," said Watcher, trying not to burp. "It'll probably come right when it's had a few days to settle and cool off."

"There's some wine there," said Leila. "Shall I get you some of that?"

"No thanks," said Dinny quickly.

"Doesn't mix with the beer," explained Watcher.

"Shall I make you some sandwiches?" she suggested. "Wouldn't hurt," said Dinny with exaggerated carelessness. And they ate sandwiches as fast as she could make them until they'd used all the bread in the house. Then they sat round the table twiddling their conversational thumbs.

"Who'd like a game of cards?" asked Leila.

There was a brief silence.

"Okay," said Dinny resignedly.

"Sure," agreed Watcher.

Leila ran off to her room to get the cards. Watcher and Dinny glanced at each other again and then at all the bottles of grog around the room.

"She bluffed us that time," said Dinny.

"We bluffed ourselves," corrected Watcher.

Leila returned with the cards and handed them to Dinny to shuffle. "Strip-Jack-Naked?" she suggested.

"Okay," said Watcher. "Long time since I played it though. How does it go again?"

"One for a Jack, two for a Queen, three for a King and four for an ace," said Dinny.

They went on playing Strip-Jack-Naked until half past one next morning.

Reorganisation

FIVE

Reorganisation

"We'll have to have an emergency conference," announced Watcher over Dinny's kitchen table.

"What's up?" asked Dinny.

"We're getting too many complaints about our filling. They don't mind tins and bottles and stuff, but there's too much paper in it. Makes too much of a mess."

"People wrap everything in paper these days," said Dinny. "There's nothing we can do about that."

"If we don't do something about it we're going to lose valuable contracts," said Watcher grimly. "They've already cancelled two loads the Potter crowd wanted on the Lawrence Street section, and two of the others have got contractors in to cover up our jobs. If this goes on we'll have to start taking some of our loads out to the Council tip, and you know how that cuts into our time."

"We could back-load a few loads of solid stuff from the tip to keep our quality up," suggested Dinny.

"Too much time and work involved. It'd all have to be hand-loaded. Besides, they'd start getting curious about us if we started taking stuff away from the tip."

"We can't risk that," said Dinny. "I wouldn't be surprised if they don't start looking into our activities as it is. We're getting too big to operate under cover any more."

"Yeah, you're right. Looks like we'll have to drop the filling side of things for the time being and concentrate on perks and — Shhh, here's Leila."

Leila came in with a basket of washing. "The old green washing machine does a faster job than the last one you brought home," she said. "But I still like the wringer on the one outside. Between the three of them . . . Good heavens! What's happened to you two? You look as though the end of the world has arrived."

She put her washing on the end of the table. "Aren't people putting enough perks in their rubbish lately?"

"No, there's always plenty of perks," said Watcher. "It's another branch of the business we're worried about."

"We'll just have to drop it altogether," said Dinny to Watcher.

"Going to be a bit tough after all the time and work we've put in building it up," said Watcher.

"What is it?" asked Leila curiously.

The two men glanced at each other. Watcher shrugged. "It's a lurk we've had going for a fair while," he explained. "Instead of taking our rubbish out to the Council tip we've been selling it for seven-and-six a load to people who want filling on their sections or big holes filled up. Saves us time and brings in a bit of spare cash."

"That's a good idea!" said Leila. "What's gone wrong with it? Aren't there any more holes or sections to fill up?"

"No, it's not that. We could get enough contracts to keep us going for years. But people are complaining about all the papers in our stuff. Odd one or two going crook about smells and dogs scattering bones and things like that, but it's the paper they're really down on. People want the filling but they're not prepared to put up with a bit of mess that goes with it."

"We can't afford to be investigated," said Dinny. "If Council gets on to us our whole organisation'll collapse."

"How do they get on at the Council tip then?" asked Leila. "You don't see paper blowing everywhere like it used to."

"That's different," said Watcher. "They burn everything out there."

"Then why don't you burn yours?"

"No, we couldn't. . . ." Dinny and Watcher looked at each other.

"We could on the Potter job," said Watcher.

"And the one at Eastwood's," said Dinny.

"What about the Haddock Street job?"

"Have to ask them first, but the old girl in Seldon Road won't mind."

In their enthusiasm they'd forgotten about Leila, who contentedly went on folding her washing at the other end of the table.

A few days later Dinny was pulling at a heap of rubbish they'd just tipped off the truck while Watcher waited for him.

"Come on Dinny. That stuff's no good to us. Put a match to it and let's get out of here. I feel exposed."

"Thought I saw a bike-pedal with good rubbers on it in here," said Dinny.

"What the hell do you want pedal-rubbers for?"

"Somebody asked Leila for some the other day and she couldn't find any round the yard. Told me to keep a lookout for some."

Watcher went over to help Dinny free the old bicycle frame he was pulling at. They dragged it out and shook off some wire and paper that was caught on it.

"There y'are," said Dinny. "A whole set of perfectly good rubbers. We'll need a spanner to get 'em off though. Might as well take the whole thing home and let Leila tackle it. She's pretty good with a spanner. The frame might come in handy for something one day."

"Leila's doing quite a bit of business lately," observed Watcher. "She always seems to be picking up orders."

"Yep," said Dinny with a trace of pride. "She's got orders for things from half the women in Essentry Crescent. And some of the people have got the flashest homes in the district. Wonder if their husbands know they're getting stuff from us?"

"We're not branching out into the blackmail business," said Watcher, throwing the bicycle frame onto the back of the truck. "Come on or we'll miss the pub."

On a small dairy farm thirty miles from anywhere significant, on a wild slashing night in April, a tree was struck by lightning, six sheets of iron blew off the cowshed roof, and three heifer calves and Harry Taggitt were born. The calves, which bore broken-coloured testimony to the ingenuity of a neighbour's mongrel bull, appropriately enough called Houdini, were sent to the works, while Harry survived to inherit the dairy farm when he was thirty. He sold it as soon as it was his to sell. Then he invented an infallible betting system for racehorses and had never dared to look back. He rented Number 21 Essentry Crescent and paid off large lumps of back rent every time he had one of his big wins.

Harry would probably have made plenty of friends except for one thing: He thought and spoke of everything in terms of horse-racing, and spoke so badly that it made everybody impatient to get away from him. He seldom saw a racehorse from one year to the other, but anyone who didn't know what won the Auckland Cup from 1929 to 1965 was a bloody immigrant, as far as he was concerned. His only interest in a newspaper was the list of acceptances for the next race meeting.

Harry was the City Council pay clerk and had never embezzled a penny in his life. Everyone he met, whether he knew them or not, was greeted with: "Got a winner for Trentham, mate?" or "What's going to win the cup?", depending on the time of year. Harry loved women, every man-jack of them, regardless of their age or what they looked like, but his obsession with horse-racing rendered him eminently unmarriageable and he was unlikely to ever be nominated for the Matrimonial Stakes.

Dinny's yard, three houses along the street from his place, never worried Harry Taggitt particularly, though if he was pressed he was prepared to admit they "oughter put the 'obbles on 'im". He was "among the starters" in Mr Tweek's anti Dinny's-yard activities, but he was waiting for the odds to shorten and was always "off his oats" whenever it came to actually doing anything. Mr Tweek had had hopes at one time that Harry would be a valuable ally, since he worked for the same people as Dinny, but it never worked out.

The only time Mr Tweek had seriously asked Harry's opinion about what should be done, he suggested that Mr Tweek cover the field with Dinny and hope for a double. He'd drawn too far out to race against him. Mr Tweek never bothered to interpret Harry Taggitt's advice, or ask for it again. And yet it was Harry Taggitt who came nearer than anybody had yet managed to disrupting Dinny and Watcher's organisation.

Watcher arrived at Dinny's place for a conference and there on the kitchen table was what looked like a big rusty cage.

"What do you think of that?" said Dinny, proudly banging the top of the thing with his hand.

"What is it?"

"A meat-safe," said Dinny. "Leila made it up," he added, opening the door of it. "See? There's three safes, one inside the other." He opened the second door. "They've all got holes in them, but if flies do get into the outside one they'll be lucky to find the holes in the next one. And if they get into the second one," he opened the third door, "they'll be dead long before they ever find their way into the inside one!" he finished triumphantly.

"Er — yeah. Sure," blinked Watcher.

"I always knew them safes was worth hangin' on to," said Dinny.

"Yeah, well we'd better have a conference," said Watcher, remembering the purpose of his visit. "An emergency conference. The Council's on to us."

Dinny quickly put the safe on the floor and sat down.

"Hell," he said. "What happened? Someone complain?"

"No. When I was putting the scrapwaggon away just now old Archie gave me a message from Bilter. He wants to see both of us in his office before we start work in the morning. Harry Taggitt saw us parked on the Haddock Street job and Bilter heard him asking Archie what we were doing there. Don't let on we know that, or Archie'll cop it for telling us."

"It was bound to happen sooner or later," said Dinny. "We just got too big for them."

"We're not going to be too big if they give us the bullet," said Watcher. "Our whole organisation's based on the Council job."

"What are we going to do then?"

"Depends how much Bilter knows," said Watcher thoughtfully.

"We could tell him we were tipping the stuff off there to save mileage on the truck," suggested Dinny. "That might help."

"If they find out we've been selling the stuff, nothing'll help," said Watcher. "It could be theft, the way the law works."

"Who owns rubbish anyway? The people who throw it out or the ones who pick it up?"

"Never run into anything on the ownership of rubbish," admitted Watcher. "I've always thought it belonged to whoever picks it up first."

"That's not what they'll go us for anyway," said Dinny. "I can just hear old Bilter: using their truck, in their time, selling their refuse. Betraying the Council's trust in us. He'll most likely tear a few strips off us and let us off with a warning."

"Even if they did let us stay on they'd keep such a close watch on us it wouldn't be safe to keep on with any of our side-lines," said Watcher.

"Yeah. We'll be bloody lucky if they don't prosecute us."

Leila came in looking puffed with a big bag of groceries. She put them on the bench and flopped into a chair.

"Hello," she said, sweeping her hat off and shaking her hair. "Another conference? How's it going?"

"We've decided to leave the Council," said Watcher.

"But I thought you were both quite happy with your job?"

"We're happy enough," grunted Dinny, "but we're not so sure about the Council."

"They've unearthed our filling business," said Watcher.

"Oh. That's bad."

"It'll be worse than bad if they start investigating us," said Dinny. "There's no tellin' what they might dig up."

"Have they told you what they're going to do?"

"We've got to report to the boss in the morning," said Watcher. "We know for certain we'll probably get the sack over it at least."

"Yep, we're finished," said Dinny. "The whole organisation was built up around the Council job. Now it's finished we'll have to start all over again with something else. Eight years of back-breaking labour gone for nothing."

"But the Council job is only a small part of your work," protested Leila. "What about all the other things?"

"Can't work them without the old scrapwaggon," said Watcher. "Everything depended on that truck."

"Couldn't we get a truck of our own?"

"We'd need at least five hundred quid before we started," said Dinny.

"Then we'll get it," said Leila.

"Where would we get all our raw material from?" asked Dinny. "Even if we did get a truck?"

"Right here — the Council tip — demolition jobs," she said.

"There's rubbish all over the city, it's just a matter of looking for it."

"Be all right if we could swing it," said Watcher.

"There's probably two or three trucks out in the yard here," said Dinny. "It's just a matter of finding one and putting it all together."

"That'd take years," said Watcher absently. "What have we got that's worth five hundred quick quid?"

"Nothin'," said Dinny.

"If there's not five hundred pounds' worth of something somewhere in this yard," said Leila, "I'll be very surprised. What can we get a ready sale for? There must be something."

"Copper's worth forty quid a ton just now," said Dinny. "There's plenty of that around."

"White-metal, bronze, brass, lead — they're all fetching good prices," said Watcher. "But who's going to dig it all out?"

"Me," said Leila. "Just show me what it looks like and I'll start gathering it tomorrow. There's no telling what I might find."

"Please yourself," said Dinny. "I'll show you what to look for in the morning. But I still think you're wastin' your time."

"Nothing to lose," said Watcher. "We'll need every few bob's worth of perks we can get, by the looks of it." He stood up. "I think I'll go home. You'd better come round to my place early in the morning, Dinny. We'll go down and see what old Bilter's got up his sleeve. Goodnight, Leila."

"Goodnight, Mr Amble. And don't worry about it. Everything's going to work out all right. I'm sure of it."

"Goodnight."

Watcher was waiting at the corner of the road next morning when Dinny came hurrying along and fell into step beside him.

"Sorry I'm late," he puffed. "Not used to getting up this early.

And Leila held me up to explain about the scrap-metals. She's started fishing out stuff already."

"She's keen enough, I'll say that for her.'

"You never know what she might find," said Dinny. "I couldn't tell you what's in amongst all that stuff myself off hand. And you know how the demand for things keeps changin' all the time. Stuff that wasn't worth anything a few years back is practically priceless today. Worth quids, some of it."

"What sort of things?" asked Watcher absentmindedly.

"Can't think of any on the spur of the moment," said Dinny. "But there's perks in that yard of mine that've been unobtainable for years!"

"That's because it's *all* in your yard," said Watcher. "Here we are. Let's go in and get it over with."

Dinny stopped at the gateway of the Council Depot. "I think I'll let you go in and talk to him, Watcher. I'll just wait out here and you can tell me all about it later."

"Bilter wants to see both of us," Watcher reminded him.

"He might be satisfied with just one," said Dinny. "If he insists I'll be right here. You can give me a whistle."

"Okay, I'm going in to get it over with. Can't stand the suspense."

Dinny watched Watcher go into the office building and settled down to wait, half behind the gatepost. He was still far from settled when Watcher came out again and waved him round to the yard behind the building. Dinny caught him up in the driveway.

"What did he say?" he asked shakily.

"Week's notice," said Watcher. "Let's grab the waggon and go somewhere we can talk. Our Hale Road sub-depot'll do for a quick conference."

Watcher eventually pulled the truck into their Hale Road conference place and got out the survival kit. This was a real emergency.

"What's up?" demanded Dinny, grabbing the thermos. "What's this week's notice business? What did he say?"

"Just said that the pay clerk, Harry Taggitt, saw us parked on that place up in Haddock Street when we should have been over in Aspin Bay. Wanted to know what we had to say for ourselves."

"What did you tell him?"

"Told him we were thinking of buying the place," said Watcher, grabbing a turn at the thermos.

"What'd you say that for?"

"Couldn't think of anything else to say," said Watcher simply.

"Well, go on!"

"He said he'd had complaints about our dumping, too."

"Did he say who potted us?"

"Yeah. The caretaker and the 'dozer-driver out at the tip. Said we'd been disrupting the whole system by not putting the stuff where we were told to."

"But we haven't dumped a load at the tip for weeks!" said Dinny. "It must have been one of the other trucks. We've been framed!"

"Think I was going to tell Bilter that?"

"What did you tell him then?"

"Nothin'. I just stood there and waited for him to say something. Thought it might have been a trap. Then he said he was giving us both a week's notice. Told me to be sure and tell you."

"Thanks," said Dinny, taking the thermos. "So you don't think he knows about our side-lines?"

"No. If he did we wouldn't be here now, you can bet on that. I think he wanted me to start crawling around his office asking for our job back, but it's no good to us now anyway. The first time we made a blue they'd be on to us like a ton of rotten cabbages."

"Suppose you're right," said Dinny. "Let's get this run cleaned up. We should get enough fillin' in a week to finish off one or two of the small jobs."

"We're not giving any of our valuable filling to those blabbermouths out at the tip, after the way they've been talking about us behind our backs," said Watcher. "That's for sure."

They finished the Council run early in the afternoon. Then they did one of their own and decided to knock off. Watcher stopped the truck outside Dinny's place.

"Aren't you coming in?" asked Dinny. "I think Leila's expecting you for a feed."

"Not tonight, thanks," said Watcher. "Think I'll go home and have an early night. It's been a big day."

"Yeah, sure," said Dinny. "See you tomorrow."

Watcher was still trying to wake up next morning when Dinny arrived and burst into the hut.

"Quick. Get up. Come and see what Leila's done. I got the truck outside. You can eat over home. Wait till you see this!"

Watcher sat up in bed rubbing his face with his hands. "What time is it?"

"Wake up man," said Dinny. "Come and see what Leila's done."

"She find a truck yesterday?"

"No. Brass! Copper! Lead! Everything. She's got over half a ton already and she hasn't scratched the surface."

"Half a ton, eh?" said Watcher.

"Throw a pair of pants on and come and see for yourself."

Watcher got out of bed. "Half a ton," he mumbled.

"More," said Dinny. "Don't you see what that means?"

"No," said Watcher, looking under the bed for one of his socks.

"If Leila can get half a ton in a day, the three of us can get a ton and a half, easy. That's over fifty quid a day. I tell you she's hardly scratched the surface."

Watcher, knowing Dinny's enthusiasms as he did, didn't take this one any more seriously than he usually did — until they got to Dinny's yard and he saw for himself. Leila was already at work, digging around in a big heap of everything. She only stopped to say hello and then went on rummaging. At intervals along the path leading to the house, hitherto the only uncluttered area in the whole yard, were several large heaps.

"See this?" said Dinny, walking over to the heaps. "This is all brass — this is the copper — here's the white-metal, zinc, and lead. (A bit of aluminium mixed up with that lot.) And this is the stuff she's not sure about. We'll go through it later. How does it look?" he concluded.

Watcher was for the moment more stunned by the variety than the quantity or value. He was a perk-man himself, and over the years he'd become almost accustomed to Dinny's amazing yard. But this was as though everything he'd ever touched or seen had been gathered up and suddenly spread out in front of him.

There were brass taps and plugs and door-handles, bed-knobs, gongs, bolts, spikes, spokes, bells, brackets, wheels, window catches, hinges, switches, latches, locks, catches and clips.

There were copper fittings, connections, joints, nuts, disconnections, plates, unions, washers, attachments and teapots.

The white-metal, zinc and etceteras were lengths, widths, angles, shapes, sizes, depths, flats, rounds, squares, holes, concaves, convolutions, convexes and doovers.

The pile of miscellaneous was simply made up of pipes, weights, sheets, lumps, knots, blobs, balls, rolls, blocks, knobs, coils, hunks, bits and pieces.

This was just a first impression. Few men could have been confronted with all that at once and still believed in it.

"There's over half a ton there already," said Dinny proudly.

"Is that all?" said Watcher hypnotically.

"What do you think of it?" insisted Dinny. "We haven't scratched the surface yet, I tell you. You can see for yourself. Imagine what must still be in there!"

The idea was too much for Watcher.

"I think we'd better have a conference," he said.

So while Leila cooked them some breakfast Watcher and Dinny conferenced at the table.

"How much worth do you reckon you've got already?" asked Watcher.

"According to the weights and prices Father gave me it's about thirty-seven pounds' worth," said Leila. "I worked it out last night."

"At that rate we're really sitting on a fortune," said Watcher.

"It's pretty good where I'm working at the moment," said Leila. "But I've had a look at a few other places where there's hardly any of the stuff we want. I think we're going to find it mostly in pockets here and there."

"We'll get enough for a truck of our own, though," said Dinny.

"We don't need a truck or a business," said Watcher. "With a couple of days prospecting every week or two we could live off this yard for the rest of our lives and still leave enough to cover our death duties."

"No fear," said Dinny. "I'm making this sacrifice to get us on our feet. I don't like parting with me gear. It's taken me years to collect it all together. As it is I'll probably be left with hardly anything in the metal line but cast-iron."

"That's worth seven quid a ton," said Watcher.

"You're not selling off my good stuff indiscriminately, I tell you. It's got sentimental value."

"Now don't quarrel, you two," said Leila, putting plates of bacon and eggs in front of them. "It isn't going to be as easy as you seem to think. There's a lot of hard work to be done. Just because we had one good day doesn't mean it's all going to be like that. Most of the small stuff is buried under big heavy things and hard to get at. You'll have to help me shift it around."

"That's easy," said Dinny. "We'll hook a rope on to it and drag it clear with the truck. We can get a fair angle from out on the road."

"And are you sure we'll be able to sell it all?" she asked.

"Yep. That bloke in Haining Street'll take the lot. He's always coming round here trying to make me offers. No trouble there."

It was a busy week. Every morning one of the men collected the scrapwaggon as soon as the Council yards were open. By lunch time they'd have fulfilled their obligations to the Council and their clients. Then they used the truck in the afternoons to pull heavy objects clear of new places to prospect. Leila worked steadily away and the piles of scrap-metal grew until new finds had to be carefully placed on the heaps. If they were thrown they'd avalanche down the sides into the rubbish that surrounded them. To get to the house they had to climb and scramble. Groups of people constantly assembled and dispersed in the road outside, speculating hopelessly as to what exactly was going on in the yard of Number 17. Mr Tweek telephoned the Council and wrote letters.

Watcher and Dinny put in all the time they could helping Leila, but Dinny wasn't a very efficient prospector: he kept re-discovering things he hadn't seen for years and getting carried away with what Watcher described as nostalgia. He'd often get so mixed up in the past he'd forget what he was looking for. He was usually nominated to return the scrapwaggon to the depot when they'd finished with it in the afternoons.

On the day before their week's notice expired Dinny drove the truck in to the depot, parked it, turned in the keys, and was ambushed in the driveway by his almost ex-boss, Mr Bilter.

Norman Bilter was one of those people who are hard to imagine unless you're actually looking at them. And then there is no doubt about it. He devoted his working hours to writing reports to The Committee and working out what he was going to say to the next of his "chaps" he'd be obliged to reprimand. At home he had his wife. His favourite broadsides were "Betrayed Trust", "All One Big Happy Family Here", and "I'll Try To Keep This From The Committee But I Can't Guarantee Anything". He'd been a foreman on the City Council since before there was a City Council, and genuinely believed himself to be considered "a bit of a wag". He ambled around the corner of the office block and intercepted Dinny with disgracefully-acted surprise.

"Oh, Mr Virtue," he said. "I'm pleased I ran into you. I've been wanting to see you and Mr — e-r — Ambler.' Would you mind stepping into my office for a moment please?"

"I'm in a bit of a hurry," said Dinny doubtfully.

"I won't keep you a moment. I think you'll be interested in what I have to say to you."

In the office Mr Bilter sat behind his desk while Dinny stood against the wall to one side. Mr Bilter pulled his old trick of pretending to read a report to make his visitors nervous.

"If you're busy I'll drop in tomorrow," said Dinny nervously.

Mr Bilter lowered his report and suddenly noticed him.

"Oh yes," he remembered. "I wanted to see you about your week's notice. You and Mr — er — Ambler, isn't it?"

"It's up tomorrow," said Dinny.

"Yes, yes. I rather thought we might have received an explanatory report from you both. As a matter of fact I've left the matter rather open with The Committee in the hope of hearing from you." His words barked around the room like something trying desperately to escape.

"Yeah, well we'll think it over," said Dinny uncomfortably.

"You realise that in a case such as this, betrayal of the trust we've placed in you, we must be firm. However, Mr Godfrey reports that you have been first to arrive for work every morning this week. In view of this extra effort you are making, and your long service with us, we are prepared to reconsider our decision on the matter. I want to be fair about this, and I don't mind telling you that you and Mr — er — Ambler were thoroughly investigated. I must say I'm very pleased with the results." He smiled as though he'd just laid an egg, and sat back in his chair to remember what came next.

It wasn't the first straight-out lie Mr Bilter had told Dinny, but it had the same disconcerting effect.

"Beg your pardon?" he said.

The smile dropped off Mr Bilter's mouth as though he'd just broken his egg.

"What I'm saying is that if you can give us your assurance that nothing of this nature will happen again, we're prepared to let the matter drop. You and Mr — er — Ambler can continue with your duties, and no reference to this will be included in your employment files. I had to tell The Committee that I'd personally take the responsibility. But I've a great deal of faith in you chaps."

"I don't know if we will be able to stay with you," said Dinny uncomfortably. "We're going into business on our own account. I'd have to have a conference with my partner before we came to any decisions about work."

A similar look would have crossed Mr Bilter's face if someone had just whispered in his ear that the chairman of The Committee was carrying on with Mrs Bilter.

"I see," he grated warmly. "Congratulations. May I ask what kind of business you're going into?"

"We might be able to offer you a contract price for our present collection area," said Dinny.

"Well naturally such a proposal would have to be brought before The Committee," said Mr Bilter doubtfully.

"That's okay. Drop us a line and let's know what they reckon about it. I'll write my address down for you if you like," he offered.

"Well actually we didn't realise that you and Mr — er — Ambler would treat this so seriously," said Mr Bilter. For the first time in years he was lost for words, with the result that he was beginning to talk sense.

"A week's notice is a week's notice," pointed out Dinny.

"We — er — haven't taken any steps to replace you," said the new Mr Bilter.

"That's going to be awkward," said Dinny unsympathetically. "There's going to be a right old mess in the area if you don't get someone schooled up on it pretty soon. You can cut people's power off and increase the cost of living, anything you like. But if you don't collect their rubbish they really perform."

"Yes, yes. Quite. Perhaps you and Mr — er — Ambler might like to stay on and help us out until we can come to some arrangement," said the new Mr Bilter anxiously. "In fact I had this very thing in mind when I assured The Committee that you chaps would never let the Council down in an emergency," added the old one.

"I'll speak to my partner about it," said Dinny. "We'll let you know what we decide as soon as we can. I'd better get goin' before I miss me dinner. See you tomorrow." And he left the old Mr Bilter sitting in his office wondering what he was going to say to The Committee.

That night there was another conference at Dinny's place. He told Watcher and Leila as much as he could remember about his interview with Mr Bilter.

"Load off our mind," said Watcher. "Several loads, when you come to think of it. Bilter'll keep out of our hair, and we can use the scrapwaggon to cart our scrap in."

"How much do you reckon we've got ready to sell?" asked Dinny.

"Tons," said Leila. "We've put the lead into bags, there's about four hundredweight of it. But I'm afraid I've lost track of the other stuff. It's just too difficult to estimate."

"We'll have to cash in on it now anyhow," said Watcher. "No room for any more. It's leaking back into the other stuff as it is."

"Right," said Dinny. "I'll ring that dealer from the depot in the morning."

Non-ferrous

SIX

NON-FERROUS

Like most people who have nothing else to be, Ernest Looper was fiercely proud and prejudiced. His father had died of disappointment when Ernie was still a whimpering boy of nineteen, and his mother never forgave him for his voice dropping.

Ernie had never been able to look ahead, or back, but by looking sideways and trusting nobody he'd managed all right. At forty-five he'd worked his way up from the ground floor to the basement, and although his success owed itself almost entirely to other people's ignorance, his own was unimpaired. He was a self-made scoundrel.

The 'phone in his office rang. He let it ring six times before he snatched up the handpiece.

"Looper Metals. Looper speaking, what can I do for you?"

"Dinny Virtue here. We were wondering if you'd be interested in a load of brass."

"I think we might be able to help you, provided it's good brass. Where can we inspect it?"

"We'll bring a load over to your place this afternoon, if you like," said Dinny.

"I think I'll be in all afternoon," said Ernie. "I'll be happy to have a look at it and give you a quote."

"Right, see you then."

Dinny and Watcher finished their garbage-run by eleven-thirty that morning and they and Leila spent two hours loading most of the brass on to the scrapwaggon. Ernie Looper came out of his office as Dinny and Watcher drove into his yard with what looked like a load of trash.

"You can't come in here with that," he yelled angrily. "I don't want a mess in here."

"I rang up about a load of brass this morning," said Dinny. "We've got it under here."

"Is it stolen?" asked Ernie shrewdly.

"No, it's from my place."

"Hey, I know you. You've got that junk-yard up in Essentry Crescent. So you've decided to sell out, eh?"

"Have a look at this," said Watcher, pushing aside some of the trash that covered the load.

Ernie Looper had a look, and then another. He walked around the truck, pushing aside the trash here and there to look some more.

"What is it?" he asked.

"Can't you tell brass when you see it?" asked Dinny.

"Is this *all* brass?"

"Yeah," said Watcher. "All brass."

"We've got a bit more at home," said Dinny. "Couldn't bring it all in one load."

"I see," said Ernie sightlessly.

"Well do you want it or not?" asked Watcher.

"Oh yes, I'll take it. But I'll have to check it before I can give you a quote on it. . . . Not that I don't trust you," he added quickly. "It's just that we often get people coming in here with all sorts of things in mistake for brass."

"You tryin' to tell us we don't know our brass?" said Dinny indignantly.

Ernie glanced again into the back of the scrapwaggon. "Oh no," he said. "You know your brass all right."

They drove to the gasworks to put the truck over the weigh-bridge, then back to Ernie's yard to tip it off. He showed them where he wanted it tipped off and Dinny backed up the truck and raised the hoist. Ernie was a little stunned at the multi-voluminous vision of all that brass cascading on to the ground from the back of the scrapwaggon. He stumbled to his office and fetched a notebook and a ready reckoner and checked the tare weight painted on the side of the truck against the weighbridge note.

"Three ton, sixteen hundredweight and twenty-five pounds," he quoted.

"Thought the old waggon was groaning a bit coming up the hill there," grinned Watcher.

"We'll go back for the rest of the brass, if you like," offered Dinny.

"Yes, you do that," said Ernie, clutching his hands in front of him as though he was rubbing tobacco. "You could put it over the weighbridge on your way back to save time. In the meantime I'll start checking this lot."

The rest of the brass made up roughly half as much as the first load and took almost as long to throw onto the truck. Leila insisted on helping and was looking exhausted by the time they'd finished.

"You go and have a rest," Dinny told her. "You've been overdoin' it a bit lately."

"I'm all right, really," she said. "I'd like to come for the ride this time, if there's enough room for me."

"Sure," said Dinny. "You just take it easy while we throw these bags of lead on."

The two men loaded the bags of lead and got a cushion for Leila to sit on between them in the cab. After they'd got the weighbridge ticket Dinny drove back towards home.

"Hey," said Watcher, "you've taken the wrong turning back there. This isn't the way to Looper's."

"I think we'll just dump this lead off again before we take the brass in," said Dinny, turning into Essentry Crescent.

"But that'll make the load read four hundredweight more than we've got on," protested Watcher.

"That's right," agreed Dinny.

"That's cheating, and you know it," said Leila indignantly.

"I know Ernie Looper too," said Dinny. "I think we'll come out about even in the long run. You'll see."

Watcher and Leila sat in the truck while Dinny threw the bags of lead off the truck and dragged them back into the yard. Then he drove to Ernie Looper's yard in a disapproving silence.

Ernie was scratching around in a small pile of their last load when they backed up to the heap. Watcher handed him the weighbridge ticket and he checked it in his notebook.

"Twenty-six hundredweight, nineteen pounds," he said. "We'll make it twenty pounds," he added generously. "Let it go right there."

As he reached over to throw the hoist into gear Dinny caught a look from Leila that would have smelted all the brass they'd just cheated Ernie Looper out of.

"How much is all that worth?" he asked, climbing out of the truck.

"Well I can't check every bit of it," said Ernie reasonably, waving towards the pile of brass. "So I've weighed out a test hundredweight — here it is. Now look at this." He picked up several odd-sized lumps from beside the heap. "You can see for yourself; this is a bit of bronze and all the rest is cast-steel."

"It is too," agreed Dinny.

"It weighs just over five pounds," said Ernie. "I'll put it on the scales again and show you if you like."

"Take your word for it," said Watcher impatiently.

"I want to do the right thing by you on this," went on Ernie, "but if I lose five pounds on every hundredweight I'll do money on the deal. I don't have a very big margin on this kind of stuff, you know."

"What are you getting at?" asked Watcher. "Isn't the stuff good enough for you?"

"The bulk of it is," said Ernie quickly. "But I'm afraid I'll have to take five pounds off for every hundredweight. I have to protect myself."

The look Leila gave him would have smelted the whole load.

"We could load it all up again," suggested Watcher wearily.

"No, that's fair enough," said Dinny. "What's the lot worth at that?"

"I won't be able to tell you until I've had time to work it all out," said Ernie. "Do you want to wait?"

"No, she's right," said Dinny. "Just give us a receipt for it and we'll pick up the cash tomorrow."

"Right. I'll have a cheque ready for you by about half past eleven."

"Cash," said Dinny.

"Well, if you'd prefer cash," said Ernie uneasily. "It's a little more trouble, that's all."

"No trouble to us," said Dinny. "Would you be interested in a load of copper?"

"How much have you got?"

"About the same."

"Yes, I think I might be able to handle it for you," said Ernie helpfully. "Bring it in any time you like." And his ready reckoner closed like a hand on money.

As they drove out the gate Leila said: "Those things he showed us didn't come out of our brass, I know they didn't. He just put them in to cheat us out of our money."

"Crafty hunk of work, that one," said Watcher. "We'll have to watch him."

"He's not crafty," said Dinny. "He only thinks he is. If any dealer found five pounds of rubbish in a hundredweight he'd lop off at least ten pounds to make up for it."

"I was furious," said Leila. "I could have hit him on the head with his own piece of cast-steel."

"I can see that lead coming in mighty handy," said Watcher.

"Yeah," laughed Dinny. "While he thinks he's robbin' us he'll be happy enough to take everything we got. He's the only scrap-metal buyer in the city. But we'll come out pretty even on the deal."

Three days later they'd shifted all their scrap-metal to Ernie Looper's except for the lead, which they sold to the gasworks to establish a contact there. By insisting on being paid for each load before they dumped the next one, the only one they never got paid for was the last load of miscellaneous stuff. But they'd allowed for that.

On the day the project was completed Watcher and Dinny left the scrapwaggon at the depot, bought a carton of beer on their way past the pub and retired to Dinny's place for a conference.

"Have you noticed?" asked Watcher. "We haven't touched the grog for nearly two weeks."

"Hell, I'd forgotten all about it," said Dinny.

Leila put a bottle-opener and glasses on the table as soon as they came in.

"We're havin' a conference to work out how much money we've made," said Dinny.

"Four hundred and eighty-six pounds, fifteen," said Leila happily.

"Er — Yes. Well we'd still better have a conference to work out what we're going to do about it," said Watcher.

"The money's non-taxable, too," went on Leila. "It's a sale of assets. I checked up."

"We don't usually bother about taxes," said Dinny, pouring himself a drink. "They get a fair whack out of our Council wages as it is."

"We'll have to pay taxes if we're going into business. I'll do all that kind of thing anyway. You don't have to worry about it."

"Four hundred and eighty-six smackeroos," said Watcher. "And you can't even see where it came from," he added reverently.

"I can," said Dinny. "All that stuff was underneath the big gear. It doesn't show much on the outside, but it's eaten into me holdings. We've got to keep this yard stocked-up, you know. It's the backbone of our whole organisation."

"It's not an organisation," said Watcher, reaching for the bottle. "It's a bloody empire."

Leila suggested that now they were expanding they should get themselves an official name for the organisation. But the men disagreed on the grounds that if they started calling themselves fancy names people might begin to wonder why. So they stayed unofficial for the time being.

"We ought to get a policy and stick to it."

"Specialise in unusual stuff. We don't want to be competing with the army-surplus stores, second-hand dealers, Woolworths, and the Council Tip."

"What about the truck we're going to buy?"

"Don't need one as long as we've got the old scrapwaggon."

"We can use the money to speculate with. Build on it."

"We can be independent of the Council any time anything goes wrong now."

"But with a truck of your own you wouldn't have to be dodging the boss all the time."

"We're used to workin' that way now."

"That's half the fun of it," said Watcher. "But we'd better see Bilter pretty soon and find out what he's done about getting us a contract. He's had a week to talk it over with his committee."

"If you ask me he's goin' to try and stall us off," said Dinny. "Keep us on wages as long as he can. That's the impression I got anyway."

"We'd better bail him up tomorrow and find out exactly where we stand," said Watcher.

"You could drop in on him when you go for the waggon in the mornin'," said Dinny brightly.

"You always leave me to handle Bilter," protested Watcher. "We're both in this together, you know."

"But you're our public-relations expert," said Dinny flatteringly. "And besides, if the two of us get talkin' to him we might contradict each other and blow the whole works."

So Watcher knocked on the door of Mr Bilter's office next morning and waited the usual twenty seconds to be told to come in. Mr Bilter was pretending to be thoughtful over a report by screwing his face up, but it looked more as though he had something in one of his ears. Watcher closed the door behind him and waited patiently to be noticed.

"Ah, Mr — er — Ambler," said Bilter at last. "What can I do for you?"

"Dinny and I have been wondering when you're going to let us know about working on contract. We've been holding off our other arrangements for over a week now."

"Yes, yes. I see," said Mr Bilter uneasily.

Watcher saw at once that he was stalling. "We'd like to know where we stand with the Council," he said respectfully.

"Quite right. As a matter of fact I'm pleased you came in to see me this morning. I fully intended asking you to drop by."

"What's the verdict?"

"Verdict?" echoed Mr Bilter vaguely.

"What did the committee say about us offering to work on contract?" asked Watcher patiently.

"Oh, that."

The truth of the matter was that Mr Bilter had never reported the matter to The Committee in the first place. He'd only intended to reprimand the chaps for loafing on the job and throw a scare into them. He'd had no idea it was going to backfire like this. Watcher's visit shattered his hopes that everything might smooth itself out and the incident be forgotten. The consequences of his little bluff were becoming more serious all the time. Two of his oldest employees sacked for a minor breach of the regulations, no effort made to replace them, the pay clerk not notified, and no report made to The Committee. And there was a memo on Mr Bilter's desk from the chairman, informing him that owing to the present shortage of labour, no labourers were to be dismissed until the circumstances had been referred to The Committee.

It was perhaps inevitable that one day Mr Bilter would outwit himself but for Dinny and Watcher to have him over a dustbin like this was a very timely stroke of luck for them. It was outrageous to Mr Bilter.

"You realise that a proposal such as yours, which involves a change of policy, requires lengthy negotiation, Mr — er — Ambler," he blustered. "Before we can set such a precedent The Committee has to investigate every aspect of the matter very exhaustively."

At the mention of "investigation" Watcher had a bad moment, but Bilter forged ahead reassuringly: "I appreciate your desire to — er — better yourselves, but I can't stand by and let two of my best chaps enter into anything ill-advisedly. Why, I'd feel personally responsible if your venture were to fail because of an oversight on my part. My loyalty to The Committee and my high personal regard for you and Dinny places me in a very difficult position. I have to try and do the best I possibly can for both parties. I had to put forward some very convincing arguments to get this before The Committee in the first place," he confided blinkingly.

Mr Bilter's own verbal momentum was beginning to restore his confidence. He went on: "There was considerable opposition from some of The Committee members at first, but I'm glad to be able to tell you that I'm gradually swinging the balance. I don't mind telling you, Mr — er — Ambler, I'm staking my reputation and judgment against that of The Committee. That's how much faith I have in you and Dinny."

Mr Bilter knew from experience that if he kept it up long enough he'd have Watcher agreeing with him. Everybody had their breaking-point. He paused to assess the effect it was having on Watcher, who saw the opportunity and spoke:

"We're not all that interested in the refuse run," he said. "We'd like to have the contract, but we can get plenty of other work. We just want to know how we stand with the Council."

"But it's my duty," said Mr Bilter desperately.

An hour later Watcher got out of there, feeling as though he'd just spent a month in a Turkish bath. He collected the scrapwaggon and drove round to pick up Dinny.

"How did you get on with Mr Bilter?" asked Leila, greeting the exhausted Watcher at the door.

"You were there long enough," said Dinny.

"Don't know what's eating him," said Watcher, "but he seems to be desperate for us to stay on the job."

"What about the contract? What did he say about that?"

"Lost track of him in the finish. Far as I can make out there's nothing doing. Reckons he's still trying to swing it with his committee."

"He probably hasn't even told them about it," said Dinny.

"Looks to me like he might have been ticked off about giving us the sack in the first place," said Watcher. "We've been with the Council long enough."

"Do you think he knows something about our organisation and wants evidence to dob us in?" asked Dinny.

"No," said Watcher definitely. "If Bilter had anything on us he'd hit us with it. Wouldn't be able to resist it. Anyway he said we needn't take the waggon back to the yard every night. We can keep it here to save time and just shoot it in on Wednesday mornings to be serviced. Felt a bit sorry for him in the finish. Told him we'd stay on in the meantime."

"Keep the waggon out overnight?" said Dinny wonderingly. "That's sure something for old Bilter!"

"It wasn't his idea," said Watcher. "He pinched it from me."

"Well it suits us nicely," said Dinny. "Business as usual and we don't need to buy our own truck yet. I didn't like the idea of partin' with the old scrapwaggon. She's been a great asset to us."

"Never let us down yet," agreed Watcher.

"But you will be careful not to get into trouble, won't you," said Leila anxiously.

"Bet your life," said Watcher, following Dinny outside.

Made men

SEVEN

MADE MEN

Under the new system the organisation did a roaring trade. Dinny swapped two hundred and fifty glass insulators and a gallon of green printers' ink for three good go-kart wheels and one buckled one. Watcher found three-quarters of a beer carton of blue identification-rings for fowls' legs and Dinny sold them to three different poultry farmers for a net profit of twenty-eight bob. Then Leila sold a burnt-out 1½-horsepower electric motor out of the yard for ten bob. A dozen pocket-compasses Dinny bought off a dealer who wasn't keeping up-to-date on his prices for 15/6 each, sold for 17/6 to a rival dealer. Watcher found a drum of D.D.T. powder which he immediately sold for thirty bob. Then half a gross of gate-hinges cost Dinny a fiver on the deal. They made a clean-up by selling a dairy company back fifteen tallow-drums they'd thrown out two weeks before and couldn't get replacements for. They broke even on two prefabricated coffins and lost money on twenty-five axe-heads Dinny swapped for a quarter of a mile of grade-4 sandpaper with a manufacturing fault through it. A set of bar-stools were good, and five new pairs of trousers Watcher got off an old lady for a quid each — were stolen. Leila sold several more things from the yard and didn't tell Dinny. They got two more contracts for filling.

At the end of the month Leila figured out all the profits and losses and expenses in a special organisation book and announced a total profit of £35-15-6, but they could only find £28-10-9 of it, so they had to write the balance off as expenses.

"If this keeps up, we're made men, Watcher," said Dinny, reclining in the cab of the scrapwaggon. "There's no limit to what we can do, now we're on our feet financially. We'll probably have to rent another yard to take the overflow from the one at home before long. We can go round the factories and buy up all their flops — I've always wanted to do that. We could even put up a sign and advertise in the papers if we wanted to."

"We ought to do something for Leila," said Watcher. "That's what we ought to do. To show her how we appreciate all the work she's been putting into the organisation."

Dinny returned to earth from visions of himself in a limitless yard, inspecting the perks as his workers streamed in the gate with them.

"Too right," he said. "You're dead right. That girl's been a great asset to us."

"We'll get her something special," said Watcher. "A present."

"I know," said Dinny. "We'll make her an official presentation of the next real good perk we get."

"Cut it out," said Watcher. "She's surrounded by perks all the time."

"I'm not talking about second-hand perks that've been lying around the yard," snorted Dinny. "I mean a new one, straight off the scrapwaggon. We could even get a whole load of them and let her take her pick."

"Lay off it," said Watcher. "We're going to buy her a proper present out of a shop."

"Better quality in some of these perks than anything you'd buy in a shop these days," said Dinny. "I don't care what you say."

"We're still going to buy her something out of a shop," said Watcher. "Let's get this load dumped. We might have time to go into town and pick something out for her this afternoon if we get finished in time."

The choice of a presentation for Leila involved Watcher and Dinny, four different shops, and five different assistants, in a two-hour disagreement. It started with the choice of which shop to buy the present at. Dinny wanted first to try an auction mart, and then a conglomerated pawnshop. He eventually agreed to settle for a hardware store, and nothing less.

Then he wanted to get her a set of spanners, a range of cold chisels or a pair of gumboots. While Watcher was trying to get him to settle for a pair of tablecloths, the assistant walked away and left them, so they went to a department store instead.

The department store floorwalker and two of his assistants thought they were going to start fighting and escorted them stiffly off the premises. In a third store they finally agreed to settle for a book, and went off in search of a bookshop. Then the argument flared up again because Dinny wanted to buy a *Pictorial Engineering for Beginners*, and Watcher insisted on *Home Decorating for You*. They still hadn't reached agreement by closing-time.

"Why don't you each buy your friend a book?" suggested the taut assistant.

And that's what they did — neither showing the other what they'd bought. Then there was a short discussion on what cards to put in the books. The manager eventually made them take plain ones because he wanted to close the shop. They each then had to borrow his pen to write in secret on the cards. Then they found that the assistant had gone home and the manager had to make an angry job of gift-wrapping their books.

"Good thing we don't have to do this every day," said Watcher as they left the shop. "That bloke'd get on your nerves after a while."

"Bad-tempered lot of sods these shopkeepers," agreed Dinny.

Leila had their dinner ready for them when they slunk into the kitchen with their presents coming unwrapped in their hands.

"You're late tonight," she said. "Did you have a busy day?"

"We picked up a couple of things for you on our way home," said Watcher, shoving his present at her as though it was contagious.

Leila took the parcel and lifted the paper away from it.

"A book. How nice!" she said. "*Countries and Peoples Around the World*," she quoted from the cover.

The card fell out of the book and landed on the floor by Watcher's foot. He slid his foot over it but he was too slow. Leila had seen it.

"A card," she said bending down for it. "Let me see what's on it."

Watcher reluctantly took his foot away. Leila picked up the card and turned it towards the light. Watcher wondered miserably what the hell he'd bought that book for and why he'd written that on the card, and he cursed the manager of the shop for hurrying him.

"'For Leila, with love respects from Watcher'," Leila read from the card. "Oh Watcher, you dear old thing." And she kissed him hard on the face.

"I had the 'love' crossed out," he stammered. "Put it in by mistake."

"Oh go on with you," she laughed. "What's wrong with putting 'love' on a card, may I ask?"

Dinny had been fidgeting in the background all this time, and Watcher turned just in time to stop him sneaking off up the passage.

"Dinny's got something for you too," he said quickly. "Come on, Dinny. Give Leila her present."

It was the only time Watcher ever saw Dinny blush. Leila had to almost drag the book away from him.

"Am I allowed to ask what I've done to deserve all this?" she asked.

"Appreciation for helping the organisation," said Watcher.

"*Countries and Peoples Around the World*," read Leila from the cover of Dinny's book. "Oh you silly old things. You've both bought the same book. What happened?"

"We — er — we had a bit of a rough time working out what to get so we both bought something in the finish," said Watcher uncomfortably.

"How sweet of you," she said. "What's on the card?"

"Hell," was all Watcher could say. Dinny was beyond words. Leila read the card he'd put in the book. Watcher waited interestedly to hear what Dinny had written on his card.

"'Compliments of the Season'," read Leila. "'Yours Faithfully, D'."

She threw her arms round Dinny and kissed his horrified whiskery cheek.

"You funny old things," she said. "Fancy both buying the same book. I love you both."

Almost simultaneously Watcher and Dinny both reached into the cupboard for the wine bottle. Leila skipped around them laying the table, kissing them each on top of the head every time she went past.

"Oh, I've got a surprise for you too," she said. "I almost forgot. We're losing one of our neighbours."

Dinny immediately thought of the neighbour on his right as you face the road, who'd built a six-foot fence three years before and hadn't spoken to him since. But it was the neighbour on his left as you face the road who had triumphantly announced to Essentry Crescent at large that he'd finally sold his house, against the overwhelming odds of his next-door neighbours. It had been up for sale since 1957.

"Old Kirkwood won't be any loss as far as I'm concerned," said Dinny. "But it's not often they sell houses around here."

"Wonder who bought the place," said Watcher.

"We might get some nice neighbours," said Leila. "The ones we've got now hardly ever speak to you."

The man who'd bought the place next door with the idea of letting it had reason to regret the investment. He advertised with flagging optimism and lowering rental for two months before finding a tenant. The kind of people who usually lived in that kind of neighbourhood just weren't equal to the challenge of living next door to Dinny Virtue's yard.

Ashley Nash didn't ask to be born and his parents didn't mean him to be. His father rejoined the ship when Ashley was still on the breast, from which he was taken early. His mother was impatient for him to get his early life over and done with so she could carry on with her own, and in the rush forgot to tell him it wasn't his fault. Ashley obediently grew up into a strapping lad as quickly as he could, and at sixteen he left home with just enough education to bewilder him and a conviction that he owed the world an apology. The last of his self-confidence was dispersed by a crop of pimples when he was seventeen.

On a visit to the country when he was eighteen Ashley went on his first horseback ride. The horse bucked him off and accidently kicked him in the face. The healed result was a rugged, craggy, beat-up set of features that could only conceivably have belonged to a professional light-heavyweight boxer.

If he noticed the change in other people's attitude towards him he certainly had no idea what caused it. He didn't realise that his timorous smile could now be interpreted as nothing but an arrogant grin. The way he stood whenever he was talking to anyone, as though getting ready to run at the sound of a harsh word, was now nothing but the natural, ready-to-spring stance of a born fighting man. The way he always moved around, as though he was being watched or followed, had become a bold swagger. Nobody with a face like that could ever skulk. His reluctance to meet people; his inability to look anyone in the eye; his unwilling handshake; his fear of opening his mouth in case he said something foolish — all these nervous mannerisms were automatically and unanimously misconstrued as part of the strong, silent, laconic, explosive nature of the man he looked. It was simply impossible to imagine anyone with a face like that being any other way. Even his name had a new menacing ring to it.

When he was nineteen Ashley discovered with a shock that other people were the same as him, and with the new confidence this knowledge gave him he began to enjoy life a little.

When he was twenty Ashley Nash had his one experience with love. He was spending his Christmas holidays at Waikaremoana and on the fifth day he was there he decided to explore a narrow, overgrown track that cut sharply up the side of a steep bush-covered ridge. He was toiling along, about halfway to the top, wondering how long it had been since the path was last trodden, when he suddenly saw a girl coming down the track towards him.

It might have been the unexpectedness of it, or the remoteness, or the time of year, or the fern — anyhow, whatever it was, it was love at first sight for Ashley. He'd never seen this girl in his life before, but he fell irretrievably in love with her right there and then. In a daze he watched as she floated gracefully down the path towards him. As she drew level she smiled and said: "Excuse me".

With his manners done up to the very top button, Ashley stepped politely back over the edge of the track and went plunging and rolling and crashing down the almost vertical hillside through the undergrowth. He finally landed with a jarring slosh in a shallow muddy creek two hundred feet below.

It might have been the shock, or the way he crashed down

through the bush, or the sound of the girl's voice, but whatever it was, by the time he'd climbed back up to the track Ashley had fallen out of love again. He never saw her again anyway.

When he was twenty Ashley was boarding with a family who didn't really want him there, working in the Meteorological Office and dreaming all day of inventions. He'd always had a flair for inventing things, but it was only now that he really started exercising it. And once he got started he really churned them out. Only all his discoveries had always been discovered before by someone else. He rediscovered things by the dozen, from indoor aerials and folding tables to slotted needles for mending fishing-nets. He found again for us such things as the polythene glasshouse, the patent gas-lighter, the gin-trap, a machine for painting the white line up the middle of roads, wallboard, snowshoes, putting your head between your knees to stop you feeling sick, the ramset-gun and the granny-knot.

Once he came close to striking something really valuable. Ashley had always been interested in glue and sticking things together. He wouldn't use a nail unless he absolutely had to, or a screw. Apart from having re-invented the dovetail joint he wasn't interested in joinery, or pegging or bolting or binding. But if two things could possibly be stuck together with glue, he'd mix up the right glue and stick 'em so stuck there was no getting them apart again without smashing them. And one day when he was experimenting around with different glues he found a combination that would stick glass on to rubber, or rubber on to rubber, or glass on to glass, instantly — and under water!

But nobody was interested in manufacturing patching-outfits for divers and he eventually gave up looking in the papers for something his glue could be used for.

But Ashley Nash didn't give up inventing, no sir! He went on turning out his rediscoveries at the rate of about half a dozen a week, and it was pretty certain that if he stuck with it he'd sooner or later come up with something that hadn't already been invented. If the wheel hadn't been discovered before then, it would never have got past Ashley. However, a detergent he invented which ate holes in the plumbing system of the house finally gave his landlady the courage to tell him to get out.

We make no excuses for the coincidence that Ashley Nash's new address was Number 15 Essentry Crescent, right next door to Dinny Virtue's place. If it hadn't been him it would have been someone else. The place couldn't stay empty forever, in spite of the neighbours. There's a housing shortage.

And it bears recording that, while the average citizen recoiled in varying degrees of shock at the sight of Dinny Virtue's yard, Ashley Nash was absolutely fascinated by it. It was an inventor's paradise.

"There's a man living in Number 15," said Leila excitedly, when Dinny and Watcher came in for dinner one night.

"On his own?" asked Dinny interestedly.

"He's the only one I've seen."

"How long has he been there?"

"I couldn't say. This morning was the first time I saw him. He came out and went off towards the bus stop this morning and came back just a little while ago. I passed him in the street on my way to the shop."

"Did you speak to 'im?" asked Dinny.

"Yes, I said hello, but he just put his head down and went past. I don't think he was being rude, though. He seemed very nervous."

"What's he look like?" asked Watcher.

"James Michener," said Leila without hesitation.

"If he's anything like the rest of 'em who live round here he won't be too nervous to start complaining about the stuff in me yard," said Dinny. "Blockin' his view, fallin' into his fence, blowin' into his garden. It always takes 'em a few months to find out we're not to be complained at. Old Tweek still thinks he's goin' to get the wood on me one of these days. He's been tryin' to get me out ever since I came here. I'll bet anything you like he gets on to this new bloke and tries to put 'im against us.

With the arrival of a new resident in the house next door to Dinny's yard, Mr Tweek's hopes soared to new heights. No one would voluntarily go and live in a position like that unless they had a very good reason. And no one had seen any furniture go into the house, or the man himself. He'd just appeared. He was probably a detective, getting evidence on Dinny for the new owner of Number 15.

Mr Tweek watched the newcomer very closely for two days, and then decided that his first guess had been right. There was no mistaking the watchful stealthy figure that strolled past two or three times a day, loitering casually past Dinny's yard. Mr Tweek hadn't spent forty years in uniform without being able to pick a plain-clothes man when he saw one. In fact it had always surprised Mr Tweek that they looked so obvious. Then one day as he watched the detective walking past the yard peering furtively over the fence, the woman that man Virtue was living with came out of the house. As soon as he saw her the detective spun round and walked quickly back to Number 15 and vanished inside. He'd been right all along. The man *was* a detective! Mr Tweek waited impatiently to see what he was going to do.

But he didn't do anything for a whole week, and Mr Tweek decided to take action himself. He was going to offer assistance to the detective. After all, nobody alive knew as much about this case as ex-Officer Tweek. At dusk he called on ex-Sergeant-

Major Fulton, who lived just along the street in Number 30.

Sergeant-Major Fulton (ret.) was perhaps the nearest thing to a friend or ally Mr Tweek had. Being an ex-army man, his regimented existence and his bellowing uncamouflaged voice rendered him unapproachable to anyone but collectors for charity, the wine-and-spirit merchant, Mr Tweek, the dachshund bitch two houses along, and anyone he could corner. He was a big man with small red, white, and blue eyes. His flesh had a soggy appearance as though it had been boiled along with his shirts and he peddled his frayed personality up and down Essentry Crescent in search of someone who could stand him.

He professed to share Mr Tweek's strong feelings about Dinny Virtue's yard, but apart from calling Dinny a "scrimshanker" and prescribing a spell in his regiment twenty years ago for him, ex-Sergeant-Major Fulton's only qualification as a supporter of Mr Tweek's cause was that he'd listened to so much of it he'd become committed.

Mr Tweek told the ex-Sergeant-Major of his discovery about the new chap in Number 15 being a detective and his plan to offer help. Ex-Sergeant-Major Fulton agreed to accompany him because he was too cowardly to refuse.

These two retired public servants lugged their sense of duty furtively across to Number 15 and knocked discreetly on the front door with it. After a short wait the door opened and the mendacious features of Ashley Nash peeped out.

"Good evening," said Mr Tweek. "I'm Officer Tweek, and this is Sergeant-Major Fulton. Both retired," he added.

"Yes?" asked Ashley apprehensively.

"We won't ask you your name," said Mr Tweek understandingly. "We understand how it is with you boys. We'd just like to have a word or two with you if you can spare the time."

Ashley slipped out through the door and closed it behind him.

Except for three blankets and a rickety chair he'd lifted over the fence from the yard next door the night before, the house was completely unfurnished. He couldn't possibly invite anyone inside.

"Don't worry about your equipment," said Mr Tweek shrewdly. "We won't give anything away."

"What equipment?" asked Ashley, his mind flashing guiltily to the incriminating chair.

"Your tape-recorders and things," said Mr Tweek, gesturing knowingly towards the closed door. "I used to be a detective of sorts myself, as a matter of fact. You don't have to explain to me."

"I — I don't know what you're talking about," stammered Ashley.

"Perhaps we'd better explain to the feller," rumbled ex-Sergeant-Major Fulton.

"Yes," agreed Mr Tweek. "You see we both live in this street. As a matter of fact I live directly opposite Number 17 here — That mean anything to you? — No? Well, I've been here for nine years, and the Sergeant-Major has been here for three years."

"I've only just arrived here," said, Ashley politely.

"We know exactly why you're here, of course," said Mr Tweek, "and we think we might be able to help you with your investigations."

"I think you've come to the wrong place," said Ashley. "I don't know about any investigations."

Mr Tweek began to look a little disturbed. If he *had* made a mistake, and the Sergeant-Major told anybody . . .

"This blighter next door here," said ex-Sergeant-Major Fulton, waving towards where Dinny's junk loomed in grotesque silhouette above the fence. "How do you feel about this — er — rubbish of his?"

"I haven't thought about it," said Ashley nervously.

"But you're living right here beside it," protested Mr Tweek. "Closer than any of us. You must know how it feels to have it staring you in the face every time you look out."

"I don't notice it much," lied Ashley.

"Come now, old chap," grunted ex-Sergeant-Major Fulton. "We're only here to try and help you, you know."

"Yes," said Mr Tweek earnestly. "Everybody in this street will be right behind you."

"What for?" asked Ashley.

"To help you get this man and his disgraceful rubbish out of this street, once and for all. Make it fit for decent people to live in again. Free from ugliness and disease."

"But I've never met him," said Ashley. "What would I want to get him out of here for?"

"It's the junk in the yard that's the worst," said Mr Tweek shakily. "We all have to work in together if we're going to have any success."

"Oh I don't mind the junk," said Ashley. "In fact I saw some things I wouldn't mind buying, if the man wants to sell them."

Mr Tweek and ex-Sergeant-Major Fulton went home.

"He could still be a detective," said Mr Tweek haughtily, as ex-Sergeant-Major Fulton stopped at his house.

"Didn't say he wasn't," barked the ex-Sergeant-Major. "Didn't say he wasn't." And he closed his garden gate on Mr Tweek's next remark:

"Well I'm going to watch him very closely from now on. There's something very odd about that fellow, and I'm going to find out what it is. But I'm almost certain he's a detective all the same."

Mr Tweek watched Ashley come and go along Essentry Crescent, and the more he watched the more convinced he became that he was a detective, here to get evidence on Dinny

Virtue. He'd worked with the police and C.I.B. often enough to know a detective when he saw one. He was finally so certain that he decided to stand by and be ready to help if he was needed in any way.

Mr Tweek was still standing by the night Ashley walked the whole horrified length of Essentry Crescent with a nanny-goat trotting along beside him on a chain. It was snatching mouthfuls of flowers and hedges as they passed them. While Ashley waited for a car to pass before he crossed the road, the goat made a mess on the footpath right outside Mr Tweek's place. Ashley led the goat across to Number 15 and tied its chain to a tree in the front lawn, in plain view of the whole street.

Mr Tweek snatched up the telephone and dialled a number he knew by heart. This was going to be nipped in the bud, and he knew just the by-law to lodge the complaint under. There was no answer to his ring and he suddenly realised it was after six o'clock. He looked up the home number of the only councillor who hadn't been rude to him about his complaints in the past and dialled it.

The councillor's wife answered and offered to fetch the councillor from his dinner if it was urgent. It was, Mr Tweek informed her.

The councillor was quite curt when Mr Tweek identified himself, and then lost his temper completely when he heard what he'd rung up about. He called Mr Tweek such unpleasant and uncalled-for names that Mr Tweek had to break the connection.

He wasn't going to let *this* go unreported. He'd been abused over the telephone in filthy language by a city councillor for doing his duty as a law-abiding citizen. He dialled the number of the police-station watch-house. This was going to raise some action. It did. The telephone conversation with the constable at the watch-house was even more succinct than that with the councillor.

Ashley patted his goat and went inside to eat his fish and chips before they got cold. He'd always wanted an animal of his own.

"The man next door brought a goat home," said Leila excitedly. "A pretty little brown and white one."

"Wonder where he got it from?" said Watcher.

"Could be a good perk," said Dinny. "He ought to be able to sell it without much trouble. Never thought about dealin' in animals."

"Might want to just keep it for a pet," said Watcher.

"He brought it home on a chain," said Leila. "It's tied up on the front lawn, eating one of those little trees Mr Kirkwood was so proud of."

"That bloke might turn out all right, after all," said Dinny.

"A goat!" exploded ex-Sergeant-Major Fulton. "The audacity of the feller! The blighter can't be allowed to get away with it. This will have to be reported."

"I've already reported it," said Mr Tweek, "but I think perhaps if you yourself lodged a complaint tomorrow it would lend added weight to mine."

"I'll certainly do that," roared ex-Sergeant-Major Fulton, with no intention whatsoever of doing it. "I'm going to demand action on this, by George. What does that scrimshanking Virtue think we have here, a confounded menagerie?"

"Sergeant-Major — I'd appreciate it if you'd keep my little mistake about that chap being a detective just between ourselves," said Mr Tweek awkwardly. "If it were to get round it wouldn't help our complaints get a proper hearing."

"Confound it, man," boomed the ex-Sergeant-Major, "you're not suggesting that I'm one of those — gossip-mongers, are you? I don't go round spreading stories. More to do with my time. Can't answer for the feller himself, though," he added.

"We didn't actually *tell* him we thought he was a detective," said Mr Tweek.

"Well you did all the talking, Tweek. I hardly spoke to the feller."

"We could always say we were just checking up on him," said Mr Tweek uncertainly. "That's if he does say anything about it. We *were* checking up on him anyway, weren't we?"

"Of course, old chap. Naturally," said ex-Sergeant-Major Fulton reassuringly. "Absolutely nothing for you to worry about. I'd put it right out of my mind, if I were you."

Felicitations

EIGHT

FELICITATIONS

Felicity Cambert was born to her parents in the nineteenth year of their marriage, when they were both in their early forties. The delighted couple gave her everything that was available, including discipline. Although she was their only child, they were determined that she shouldn't be spoiled, one way or the other.

They had her immunised against all the immunisable diseases and saw that her diet was balanced — but she wasn't made to eat anything she didn't like. She was encouraged to mix with other children and bring them home to play — as long as she asked first. They answered all her questions — as factually as they could. They had braces put on her teeth and let her wear her hair in whatever the prevailing fashion happened to be at the time for youngsters of her age. Her preferences were always courteously listened to and considered, and her misbehaviour punished firmly and fairly.

They provided her with a pony — which she could ride or not as she chose. They bought all the recommended books for the various stages of her development so that she could read them — if she felt like it. They bought a violin for her to try out, and hired a piano teacher to see if she preferred the piano. She went to dancing-classes of her own accord and also briefly attended a school of elegance for young ladies.

She grew up in the pleasant atmosphere of the big new rambling house on her father's 150-acre stud farm, half an hour's drive from the city. And she was educated at two tastefully chosen schools.

Felicity emerged from adolescence as an immunised, obedient, healthy, handsome, well-read young woman. She could dance, read music, ride, drive, and elocute.

On the other hand she was sloppy, bit her fingernails, and had no sense of rhythm or taste. And she seemed to have been immunised against education by mistake. So Mr and Mrs Cambert were pretty well back where they had started. The sole fruit of their otherwise happy union, and their combined and well-informed efforts to nurse it to maturity, was a twenty-one-year-old extrovert with a mind like a tennis racquet, who still had to be reminded when to take a bath. She was presentable enough, if you were quick, but the odds against her securing a passable husband were overwhelming. She was no more interested in men than she was in everything else. She could do nothing useful enough well enough to enable her to make her own living, and her weary parents gazed wistfully across rooms and tables at her, wondering where they went wrong.

Felicity herself was quite content to carry on as she always had done. She knew that she wasn't particularly useful or ornamental, but she wasn't sensitive enough for it to worry her unduly. She displayed only a perfunctory interest in the subject of young men when more or less told to do so by her mother.

When Felicity was a slightly stupefied but contented young woman of twenty-four, her father, who was now in his late sixties, decided to play the last card in what had started out as a full hand.

In spite of her assuring them that she'd just as soon stay home, they packed her off on her own on an expensive round-the-world tour. Then they sat back with their fingers crossed.

She returned unscathed. Without souvenirs, postcards, foreign words, answering any of their letters, a suntan, duty-free cigarettes, or impressions. She hadn't even been homesick, had trouble with customs and passports, or lost her purse in Cairo. She wasn't pregnant, and she couldn't remember the name of the ship she travelled on. Her six months abroad had made no difference to anyone, not even her fellow travellers. As she had told her parents before she left, she might just as well have stayed home.

She settled back in at home and contentedly looked after her mother, who was now a frail, wispy, sixty-six years old. She fetched and fussed happily about the house, helping anyone who wanted help, from the cook to the nurse who was pretending to cure her mother of old age.

In spite of her mother's poor health, it was her father who died first. The farm manager found him lying out in the paddock one sunny afternoon. Felicity was very sad at the loss of her father. She tried very hard to cry, but couldn't quite make it.

The nurse held off her mother's old age for eighteen months after that.

The first thing Felicity did on finding herself the owner of the estate was to sack the middle-aged farm manager because of something that happened twenty-two years before on a heap of superphosphate bags in the implement shed. Then she got the solicitors to hire another manager and put the place up for sale. She had sufficient brains to realise she wasn't equipped with enough of them to cope with the responsibility of making decisions involving 115 head of pedigreed stock, 150 acres of high-pressure pasture, three employees, two houses, and an annual turnover of around £12,000 a year. It was all she could manage to sign the deeds and transfers and things.

She was robbed handsomely by the buyer of the estate, and then by her own agent. Then the solicitor thought he might as well have a whack. She bought a house in town because at thirty-seven years of age she found herself a wealthy woman who knew nothing but how to live in a house. She was handsomely robbed on that deal too. She moved into Number 34 Essentry Crescent, with an elderly couple, who'd been with the family for ten years, to clean up after her.

Felicity Cambert also saw Ashley Nash lead his nanny-goat along the street and tie it up in what she still thought of as Mr Kirkwood's lawn. She saw most of what went on in the street from her front-room window. From one angle she could even see part of Dinny Virtue's fabulous yard. She'd have given anything for a yard like that. . . .

She turned from the window at the sound of someone knocking at the door, and heard her housemaid go to answer it. And ex-Sergeant-Major Fulton entered the room. He'd been calling in almost every day lately. Felicity thought he must be lonely and was vaguely sorry for him. She'd never been lonely herself, but she could imagine what it must be like.

"I say, have you heard about that blighter who's moved into Kirkwood's old place, m'dear?" began ex-Sergeant-Major Fulton harassedly.

"Into Kirkwood's old place?"

She'd discovered this conversational gimmick years ago, and for ex-Sergeant-Major Fulton it was just perfect. She simply had to repeat three or four key words of his last statement each time it was her turn to speak, and he'd go on for hours, doing all the thinking for both of them. All she had to do was sit back and listen. There were no noisy arguments and he was quite convinced that Felicity Cambert was a brilliant conversationalist.

"Yes m'dear," he said, plunging himself into the chair he always sat in. "It seems he's gone and brought a confounded goat into the street."

"A goat into the street?" she repeated with a trace of astonishment.

"Yes m'dear. Heaven knows where it's all going to finish up, what with that fellow Virtue and his great heap of scraps, and now this johnny bringing this wretched animal here. Tweek wants to report it to the authorities, but I've told him to hold his fire. He's done enough damage already lately, without going off half-cocked on this thing. He's too quick off the mark, old Tweek. Too quick off the mark altogether."

"Yes, too quick off the mark," agreed Felicity.

"Oh, so you've heard about him dragging me over there the other night to confront this chap with some evidence he'd got hold of? He thought the fellow was some kind of detective, spying on someone in the street. Tweek refused to tell me who it was. Confound the man, he's made me damnably curious. In any case he was quite wrong about this chap. Can't blame the fellow for getting a little hot under the collar really. Got to put yourself in his place — woken up in the middle of the night by an absolute stranger and confronted with some unsupported frumpery about being a spy. Reminded me of Austria during the war, with the Gestapo. Fortunately I was on hand to prevent it from developing into anything unpleasant."

"It's fortunate that you were on hand, all right," said Felicity.

"Yes," agreed the ex-Sergeant-Major with himself. "I managed to get things smoothed out between them in the finish. I must say, though, the feller would have been perfectly within his rights to take disciplinary action with Tweek."

"Quite within his rights," echoed Felicity.

"Yes," he went on, "a nasty-looking customer, when he's aroused, too, m'dear. Wouldn't surprise me if he was a prize-fighter with a circus, or something of that kind. I've mixed with that type quite a lot overseas, y'know. Nasty bunch. If this chappy had attempted to assault Tweek I would have been forced to use the old judo on him. Can't take risks with people like that, have to get them on the ground before they hurt someone. Wouldn't have liked to have to do it though; the feller had every right to order us off the property."

"Every right," agreed Felicity, squirming in her chair.

"But it still doesn't give the blighter the right to go bringing this confounded goat into the street. I must say I'm in full agreement with Tw — " The ex-Sergeant-Major's voice was choked off in his throat as Felicity rubbed her nose on the back of her hand, sniffed and swallowed noisily.

Now it may be true that ex-Sergeant-Major Fulton was a chronic gossip-monger. He might even be described as indiscreet. It might even be true that the big brass anti-aircraft shell standing to attention by his front door at Number 30 Essentry Crescent *did* come from Dinny Virtue's yard one night. It might be true, too, that ex-Sergeant-Major Oliver Fulton's discharge papers hinted at something unpleasant surrounding his departure from Her Majesty's Service. But whether these things were true or not, the one thing above all that he was scrupulous about was cleanliness. It was as though all his scruples had been channelled into this one thing. He couldn't abide filth, or even dirt. Untidiness made him uncomfortable, dust made him fidgety, and mud caused him to squirm, but this kind of thing was absolutely unbearable. The last time he'd visited Felicity she had stopped to scratch her back against the doorway of the sitting-room with a cup of tea in each hand, slopping tea into his saucer. The time before that he'd been unable to keep up his end of the conversation because she'd started scratching herself in all sorts of disconcerting places. Another time he'd had to leave early because she took off her slipper and rubbed between her toes with her thumb.

Rather than hurt the lady's feelings ex-Sergeant-Major Fulton had borne all these stomach-churning incidents with hearty stoicism, but the revolting thing he had just witnessed — the sniffing — was more than his delicate constitution could withstand. If he hadn't picked up the faint whiff of big money in the propinquity of Felicity Cambert he'd have got up right there and then and walked out. Things being as they were he gritted his back teeth, smiled with his front ones and forgot what he'd been saying.

"You've forgotten what you were going to say, haven't you," smiled Felicity. "I'm always doing that."

"No, m'dear," he said in his most avuncular manner. "I'm afraid you're wrong this time. As a matter of fact it suddenly occurred to me that every time I visit you the conversation always turns towards things like that fellow Virtue's latest activities, or someone else in the street here. You never mention your past life. It crossed my mind that perhaps you had some unpleasant — er — thing in your past you don't care to — er — talk about."

"No one ever asks me about it," said Felicity.

"Yes yes yes," said the ex-Sergeant-Major. "Of course one doesn't like to pry into the private affairs of one's friends, m'dear. But I have been concerned that a delightful young lady such as yourself should be shut away from the world like this. I had thought that possibly . . ."

He forgot what he was going to say that time because Felicity had just screwed her little finger into her ear and was revolving it around with a long-time-ago look on her face. But she had been listening.

"Don't be silly," she laughed. "I've always lived like this. I like living in houses, I've always done it, ever since I was a little girl."

"Of course, m'dear. Quite right." Ex-Sergeant-Major Fulton rallied his conversational troops. "Are your father and mother still with us, m'dear?"

"With us?" she asked.

"Er, alive," he said quickly.

"Oh no, they're both dead," said Felicity. "That's why I had to sell the farm and come to live here."

"Farming folk, eh!" he said jovially. "By George, isn't that a coincidence now? I was born and bred on the land myself, boy and man, until the old call came and I was needed overseas to help keep old Jerry off French soil . . ." He broke down again as Felicity began to squirm noisily in her chair again.

"I had to sell our farm," she said. "I couldn't look after it all on my own."

"No brothers or sisters, m'dear?"

"No. Just me."

"It must be very difficult for you, m'dear. As a matter of fact I dislike to discuss mercenary matters, especially with my friends, but any time you need help of a financial nature, m'dear, please don't hesitate to consult me about it. As a matter of fact I became so tired of all this money nonsense a few years back that I got all my capital together and hit the stock exchange. Made enough to retire on in comfort for the rest of my life. Made a little too much, as a matter of fact. I used a system an old soldier told me just before he died in my arms."

"Just before he died in your arms?" exclaimed Felicity.

"Yes, m'dear. Rather not go into that, if you don't mind. Yes, I used a selling and buying system that old soldier told me about and now I've got quite a tidy little pile invested here and there. More than I'll ever be able to use, so if you should ever need a few hundred pounds . . ."

"How much did you get?" asked Felicity interestedly.

"Well, I've never been able to get the exact figures," said ex-Sergeant-Major Fulton. "Changing values and rates of exchange and all that y'know. Well over a hundred thousand, I should say."

"I didn't get mine off a soldier," said Felicity. "It's just the money I got for the farm."

"How much did you get for your farm, m'dear? Perhaps if it

were handled sensibly it would be enough to keep you independent for a good many years."

"I don't know how much there is left," said Felicity. "It's all in Mr Stalker's bank."

"The things you women do with your money," laughed the ex-Sergeant-Major. "All your eggs in one basket. Haven't you ever heard of a run on a bank?"

"I think so. What does it mean?" asked Felicity doubtfully.

"They always keep it pretty quiet, m'dear, but sometimes a bank goes bung, just like any other business. It's all very complicated . . .." There was a longish pause. ". . . I — I'm afraid I haven't time to explain it to you just now. I'll have to be going. 'Bye now."

That longish pause and the ex-Sergeant-Major's sudden departure was because Felicity had suddenly poked out her rolled up tongue and coughed wetly, straight into his face.

From behind her curtain Felicity watched him hurry down the footpath to his place and smiled mischievously. She knew she shouldn't really do things like that to the poor ex-Sergeant Major, but it was such fun watching him squirm, and he was such a terrible bore.

Establishing neighbourly relations with Ashley Nash was not a simple thing to accomplish. Once Watcher waved to him and another time Dinny called out "G'day", but he pretended not to see or hear and scuttled for cover. They might have put him down as a crank and forgotten about him, but Leila had actually spoken to him in the store and reported that he was "a very nice man". So they went on being prepared to like him if they got the chance.

The nanny-goat had stripped fifteen years from the departed Mr Kirkwood's shrubbery and started on the hedges by the time

Dinny and Watcher got to meet their new neighbour, and then it was more or less a chance encounter. Dinny, clambering reminiscently through the hills and valleys of his estate one Saturday afternoon, was surprised to observe a backside sticking out of a heap of old beehive frames and bent tubular scaffolding. The backside was that of the elusive Ashley Nash.

"G'day," said Dinny pleasantly. "Can I help you?"

At first Ashley wouldn't come out. And when he did he just stood there in speechless embarrassment.

"You're the bloke from next door here, aren't you?" asked Dinny to start the conversation.

"Yes," mumbled Ashley. He didn't quite add "sir" to it.

"Lookin' for something?" enquired Dinny. "I might be able to help you. Got lots of stuff here," he added waving proudly around.

"I thought there might be something I could make a bench out of," blurted Ashley. "I was going to pay for it," he added anxiously.

"That all?" grinned Dinny. "You won't find much in there for a bench. Over here's the place. I'll show you. Come and have a look."

Ashley followed Dinny clumsily over the heaps to a staggering collection of boxes, boards, broken chairs and tables, sofas, stools, and other furniture.

"There's all sorts of stuff in there," said Dinny modestly. "It depends what you want the bench for, really."

"I think that table there would do," said Ashley, pointing to a small office-desk with two of the legs bent in.

"Okay, she's all yours. I'll get Watcher — that's me partner — and we'll shove it over the fence for you."

"How much is it?" asked Ashley reaching into his empty pocket.

"Forget it," said Dinny. "You can have it for a housewarmin' present."

"I don't mind paying, really."

"Garn, the thing's not worth much anyway. You might be able to do us a little favour some time, you never know."

"Anything you like," said Ashley without hesitation.

"I'm Dinny Virtue, by the way." And he held out his hand.

"Ashley Nash," said Ashley shaking it. "Pleased to meet you."

"Same here. Now we'll get this bench over the fence for you. I'll just see where Watcher is."

"I — I didn't want it today," said Ashley. "I have to find somewhere to put it."

"Okay. We'll bring it over tomorrow if you like."

"Thanks very much. I'm very grateful."

"See you tomorrow then."

"Yes. Thanks. Goodbye." And Ashley clambered quickly out of sight over the jumble of the yard towards his place.

That night Ashley Nash put his bed-wire and four boxes, his chairs, his table, and quite a number of other things back over the fence into Dinny's yard where he'd got them from.

Next morning Dinny and Watcher dragged out the desk Ashley had chosen and fixed up the legs for him. Then they carried it out the gate and round to Number 15. Leila helped them because of it being something of an event. A friendly neighbour in this neighbourhood was a rare thing.

Ashley met them at the door and they juggled the desk right into the house for him, in spite of his frantic assurances that he could manage it on his own, he wasn't ready for it yet, he didn't want it, and he was going to keep it for an outside bench. They put the table down in the kitchen and looked around the empty echoing house. A heap of blankets in one corner and dust in all the others was all that was there.

"You've got no furniture," said Dinny brilliantly.

"I'm having some sent," said Ashley unconvincingly. "It hasn't arrived yet."

"He's been living here all this time without a stick of furniture," said Leila accusingly to Dinny and Watcher, as though they should have known.

"We'll soon fix that," said Dinny. "We'll have this place fixed up with the best of everything before you can see which way it came from. Watcher, come with me."

Under the weakening protests of Ashley, Dinny and Watcher ranged across Dinny's yard, pulling out things as Leila called out what was wanted next and lowering them over the fence to Ashley and Leila. By sundown the house at Number 15 Essentry Crescent was fully furnished with a stunning variety of semi-serviceable furniture. A different lampshade in every room and two to spare. Pictures on the walls. Pots and pans under the sink. Mats on the floor. Blankets on all the beds. And an almost tearfully grateful neighbour.

From that time on their friendship with Ashley Nash grew along with the piles of perks they deposited in his yard for him to invent things with.

"I say, Tweek," said ex-Sergeant-Major Fulton. "Have you seen what they're doing across the road here? That blighter Virtue and his — er . . ."

"Of course I've seen," snapped Mr Tweek. "They've started putting their junk in the yard of Number 15."

"Might be quite harmless, of course," said the ex-Sergeant Major. "It may be just temporary."

"Temporary my foot!" snarled Mr Tweek. "Don't forget I saw how he started on his own yard. It's exactly the same. He puts a bit here and a bit there, and before you know it the whole place is one big mass of junk, getting higher and higher. It never stops."

"We can't have them turning the whole street into a junk yard," bombilated ex-Sergeant-Major Fulton. "Have to put a stop to it."

"How?" grated Mr Tweek.

"Well, there's always the authorities, Tweek. We'll simply have to explore all the avenues until we get satisfaction."

"And what avenues are there left to explore?" demanded Mr Tweek bad-temperedly. "I've even reported it to the owner of Number 15, and he won't do anything about it. If the owner won't complain nobody *can* do anything about it. But just let them break one regulation and I'll have them. And I've got a plan that's going to make them break the law without doing anything or being able to do anything about it."

"That's the spirit, Tweek. Fight fire with fire, by George. It's up to us to keep the street free from this kind of thing. What's this — er — plan of yours?"

"It can't fail," said Mr Tweek looking slyly around. "I might need your help, but we mustn't tell a single soul or it mightn't work. Now listen . . ."

In the Spring

NINE

In The Spring

Leila was seeing a young man off at the gate. Watcher eyed him disdainfully.

"Third time that young Norman's been round here lately," he said. "First he wants a spindle-shaft for a hand-operated wood-drill, then it's a spacer-plate for a motorbike clutch, and now he's after a coupling for an over-sized ball joint. Must be mounting a wood-drill on a motorbike trailer or something."

"He's hangin' round after Leila, that's what he's doin'," said Dinny. "He asked me just now if he could take her out tonight."

"Bloody hell," said Watcher. "What did you tell 'im?"

"I didn't know what to tell 'im. Took me by surprise. Said he'd better ask Leila. I think she took 'im up on it. Don't know what's got into her. He looks like a cross between a cowboy and a Rosicrucian."

"That's the fashion these days."

"Hell!" was all Dinny could think of to say.

"He's got a flash car."

"Yeah. A car like that might just turn a girl's head. Wonder what made him pick on Leila? I didn't know she was all that attractive, did you?"

"Never took much notice, to tell you the truth."

"Well, we can't let it go too far. A bloke like that for a son-in-law wouldn't be much use to the organisation. In fact, he'd be useless."

"Can't stop her going out with him," said Watcher. "Not as if she was going to marry the bloke anyway. All girls her age go out with young blokes."

"Don't like the looks of it," said Dinny pessimistically. "I suppose she's got to go off sooner or later, but I was thinkin' of someone with a truck or something. That car of his would be useless in this game."

"He'll have a game of his own," said Watcher. "He's not the type to come into the organisation, even if he was invited."

"That means he'll probably whip Leila off before she has a chance to fill all her orders, and we'll get a bad name."

"No need to worry about it just yet," said Watcher. "We'll keep an eye on 'im and see if it calls for any action later."

"Do you think we ought to have a yarn with her about it?" asked Dinny.

"Like hell. That's the last thing we're going to do. We'll just follow them tonight and see how keen this young bloke is. If it looks serious we can try and head him off. But we mustn't let Leila get the idea we're buttin' in on her private affairs."

That night, when Norman's little Morris drove bravely out of Essentry Crescent under its load of banners, the scrapwaggon went charging after it. The oddly assorted convoy travelled along the main road into the city, but Dinny was too close. Norman saw the scrapwaggon following behind him, and asked Leila if her father and Watcher had intended going into town that night. Leila, who didn't know of the presence of the waggon right behind them, informed Norman that her father and Watcher never went out at night except on very special jobs. Then at some traffic lights the scrapwaggon got jostled right up behind Norman's little car, towering hungrily above it. The truck had had a blocked idling jet for the last day or two and Dinny had to keep revving the motor to keep it from stalling.

"Do you think they might have spotted us?" he asked uncomfortably.

"Everybody else in the street has," grinned Watcher.

"What'll we do?" asked Dinny with a trace of panic.

"Just pretend we're going the same way as them. We can explain something later."

So they followed the little car. Down the main street, round two blocks and back along the main street again. Norman was so flustered that he overshot the odd one or two parking places that were unoccupied. Then he couldn't stand it any longer and dashed off down a side-street and out around the unlit reserve at the edge of town. The baleful yellow headlights of the scrapwaggon roared after him.

"He's trying to give us the slip!" yelled Dinny, slamming the truck into second gear and juddering it around a corner after the terrified scuttling Morris.

"Don't blame him," said Watcher. "Better turn it in before we run the poor sod into the ditch. I think we've done our dash for this time."

They went back to Dinny's place for a conference and decided to say nothing about their night's work unless they absolutely had to.

"Have to leave things to settle down for a while after this little lot," said Watcher.

"We might have put 'im off already," said Dinny.

"It'd put *me* off," said Watcher.

"Wonder what Leila's going to say?" said Dinny uneasily.

"Have to wait and see."

So they opened a bottle of sherry and waited to see. Leila arrived home at a quarter past one in the morning, to find her two guardians still waiting to see what she was going to say. The sherry had obviously failed to fortify them. They greeted her with all the over-exaggerated surprise afforded someone who's been away for months and suddenly arrived back unexpectedly.

"Father," she began, "and you too, Watcher Amble; if you ever do that again . . ." She threw her green stole impatiently on to a chair-back.

"Do what again?" asked Watcher innocently.

"Yeah, *what?*" put in Dinny trying to look astonished.

"You know jolly well what I'm talking about," she cried. "Following us like that. I've never been so embarrassed. And poor Norman was so nervous we nearly had an accident. Our whole evening was ruined!"

"You've had plenty of time to recuperate," said Dinny pointedly, looking at his bare wrist.

"I've been having cups of tea with Norman's mother and father, if you must know. And I'm going there for dinner on Thursday night, so there."

She turned and flounced off to her room. Dinny and Watcher both reached for the wine bottle.

"Looks bad," said Watcher.

"We'll have to do something," said Dinny.

"We've done plenty already, if you ask me," said Watcher.

"Well I'm not having that young fancy-pants for a son-in-law," said Dinny, crashing his fist lightly on to the table. "And that's final."

"Okay," said Watcher resignedly. "I'll try and work out something tonight and let you know tomorrow."

Norman called for Leila on Thursday and trod up the path as though he might be ambushed at any moment from the tall junk that grew thickly on either side. He knocked on the door as though it could explode, and when Leila led him into the kitchen he might have been crossing a minefield.

"It's all right," Leila said. "You don't have to be nervous. Father and Mr Amble haven't said anything about you since I told them off about last Friday night. They're not here just now anyway, they went off somewhere half an hour ago."

"We've got him shook," said Watcher to Dinny behind their pile of old car-seats and bundles of baling-wire. "Now we'll shake him some more."

They tip-toed about their dirty work and slipped back into the tangle of the yard to watch the results of their handiwork from concealment. They got into position just in time before Leila and Norman came down the path.

Norman had an uneasy premonition that something was wrong as he reached to open the car door for Leila, but there was nothing he could have done about it by then anyway. As he opened the door there was a sudden angry *bzzz* inside the car and he slammed the door again quickly and jumped back. His car was full of blowflies. Hundreds of them. Thousands! Big bad-tempered bluebottles. Crawling all over the rugs and windows, steering-wheel, dashboard, windscreen and air-freshener. Thousands of blowflies.

Norman's courage was completely outnumbered. He ran this way and that for a few yards, shaking his hands as if the blowflies were all over him.

"Your car's full of blowflies," said Leila interestedly.

"It's never been full of blowflies before," Norman appealed to her. "What are they doing in there?"

"Trying to get out by the look of it," she said.

Norman rushed to the car, opened the door and waved his hand frantically into the roaring horde of agitated blowflies, with his averted face screwed up so tight it was going to be hard to get undone.

"That's not helping," said Leila impatiently. "You're shooing them all back in." She went round the car and opened all the doors. "Now for goodness sake, Norman, stand away. They'll go away on their own."

Norman stood blankly back and watched the droning exodus of

blowflies from his beautiful little car. The last few on the windscreen and rear window were going to have to be chased out individually.

"That's not fair," he said to her. "It's just not funny."

"I didn't put blowflies in your car," said Leila shortly. "It won't hurt the frilly thing anyway."

"It's not frilly," said Norman indignantly. "It's the best looked-after car in the whole district, I'll have you know. That's what."

"It's gaudy," said Leila.

"There's plenty of girls who'd be proud to be seen in that car," said Norman haughtily. "I notice you didn't mind riding in it the other night."

"It's ugly," said Leila.

"It happens to be the only car that colour in the whole city," said Norman. "It's distinctive."

"It's disgusting," said Leila.

"If that's the way you feel you won't be invited out in it any more," threatened Norman. "How do you like that?" he finished smugly.

"I do," said Leila. "I'm going home. You can get someone else to decorate your ugly little car."

And she went back to the house, leaving Norman hissing courageously at the last few stubborn blowflies in his car. He drove away with the job still uncompleted.

Dinny and Watcher strolled casually into the kitchen and got surprises to find Leila still there.

"Thought you were going out somewhere?" said Watcher.

"Hasn't your boyfriend come for you yet?" asked Dinny.

"Where did you get all those blowflies?" demanded Leila.

"What blowflies?"

"Yeah, what blowflies?"

"You both know very well what blowflies. Where did you get

them all from? That's what I want to know."

Dinny and Watcher glanced uneasily at each other.

"Put some ripe meat in a two-gallon jar," said Watcher.

"We let 'em breed up in there," said Dinny with a trace of pride.

"We put them in the young bloke's car for him to deliver for us," interrupted Watcher. "The lid must have come off." He trailed off weakly and they both waited for the blast from Leila.

"Well in future I don't want any help with my boyfriends. I can get rid of them myself, thank you."

"You mean you weren't serious about that young feller?" asked Dinny.

"Of course not," she said. "I wouldn't get serious about Norman. He's shorter than I am. He just pestered me until it was easier to go out with him and get it over with than keep on refusing. I'd have had him put off by now, if I'd been left alone to do it myself."

"Thought it might be something like that," lied Watcher, "but we didn't know if you'd be able to handle him on your own."

"Well in future just you remember that I *can*," said Leila firmly. "A woman has her own ways of handling situations like that, and cars full of blowflies isn't one of them."

"We — er — know it's none of our business," said Dinny, "but when we kick off all this'll be yours." He waved around at the tumbled heaps of junk that spread across the yard from corner to corner. "And we wouldn't like to see all we've built up over the years fall under bad management. We want you to marry a good businessman who's not frightened of a bit of hard work."

"Don't be silly, Father. I've got no intention of getting married off to anyone, and even if I had, there's only one man around here I'd dream of marrying, and there's little enough chance of that."

Just then Ashley Nash sidled up the path.

"G'day Ash. How's it going?"

"Fine, thanks. I think I've found a job you might like to have a shot at."

"Yeah? What's the guts of it?"

A friend of Ashley's had put culvert-pipes through the bed of a creek that ran through a block of land he'd bought on the edge of the city. He wanted several hundred yards of filling to level off the ground for a riding school he was starting up. He would pay ten bob a load for as much as they liked to bring. They went out to see the bloke and inspected the job. A verbal contract was taken out on the spot. It was the best job they'd got on to yet.

They were just getting the new filling job nicely organised when something they'd always half feared might happen, happened. Bilter caught them. Caught them red-handed.

They were travelling through the city with two hundred and fifty sheets of corrugated iron and a dismantled 500-gallon water-tank on the scrapwaggon, when they were pulled up by a traffic cop. He led them round to the Traffic Department weighbridge and found that they were almost as grossly overloaded as they looked. Then he informed them that he was also booking them for their load being a hazard to other traffic.

Dinny and Watcher had been prepared for a traffic offence ticket. The one who was driving, Dinny, produced his driver's licence, and Watcher gave his name as that of their boss, care of the City Council. But it didn't come off. The traffic officer rode with them round to the depot and dug up Bilter, who tried not to beam as he surveyed their load of iron.

"Thank you, officer. I'll deal with these chaps. If your department will just advise me what action is being taken." He wanted Dinny and Watcher to himself.

"In Gorman Street eh?" he almost chuckled. "With a load of

nothing but iron. On one of our trucks. I always knew you two were up to something, of course, and here's my proof. You're going to have a time trying to talk your way out of this one, aren't you?"

"No," said Watcher.

"Don't talk to me like that, Ambler, I warn you. This is going before The Committee. I'll tell you that before we go any further."

"Post our wages," said Watcher, turning to get his things out of the cab of the scrapwaggon. "We might as well get off to the pub, Dinny."

"Where do you think you're going?" demanded Bilter. "Come back here this instant! I haven't finished with you two yet by a long chalk!"

"Oh yes you have, Mr Bilter," said Watcher. "We're not staying here to be abused and bitched at by you for half an hour before you give us the sack. We're leaving right now."

"But you can't," insisted Bilter. "I haven't even sacked you yet."

"Well you're too slow. We've already left."

"Yeah, you missed out," put in Dinny, following Watcher towards the gate.

Bilter was still protesting as they passed out of earshot.

"D'you think he's going to kick up a stink?" asked Dinny.

"Don't know," replied Watcher. "He won't be able to resist telling his committee, but he hasn't got a single detail about it. That's why I made us walk out like that before he could ask any awkward questions. They'll probably just write us off their books and leave it at that. There's never been any complaints about our work, that's one thing in our favour."

"Well, what do we do now?"

"Wait. If nothing happens within a couple of weeks we'll know they're not going to do anything about it."

The Council posted the balance of their wages and holiday pay, and that was all. For the first week or ten days Dinny and Watcher were busy reorganising the organisation. Two hundred and eighty second-hand sheets of corrugated iron had to be found to fill the order Bilter had interrupted, so they hired a truck and collected the same lot from the Council tip and delivered it.

Then they went into the city, Dinny, Watcher, Leila and Ashley, to buy a truck of their own. For sentimental reasons they bought one the same year and model as the scrapwaggon they were so used to, and in a week or two it would have been hard to tell the difference.

Leila solved their immediate difficulties by pointing out: "You don't have to collect your filling a rubbish-tin at a time now. You can go straight to the Council tip and take your pick of all the best stuff."

"Can you do that?" asked Ashley doubtfully.

"Course you can," said Watcher. "People have been perking stuff from tips for hundreds of years."

"It's the born right of every citizen," added Dinny.

"I say, m'dear," said ex-Sergeant-Major Fulton, pondering into Felicity Cambert's front room, where she sat, as usual, at the window. "Tweek's sticking his neck out a bit far this time, isn't he?"

"Sticking his neck out?" asked Felicity politely.

"Yes, m'dear. Haven't you heard? I understand he's dug up some regulation saying you can't carry on a business within two hundred feet of a public park, reserve or playground. He's having his place officially declared free for public picnics and things. Says it'll force this Virtue blighter and Co. to pack up and clear out altogether."

"Oh," said Felicity.

"Yes, m'dear. Rather drastic, don't you think? Hope the fellow knows what he's doing. Wants it kept very hush-hush for the time being, but he's already begun negotiations with the authorities and got a very favourable reaction to this public park thing."

"A favourable reaction?"

"Yes, m'dear. I'd say it was the finish of this Virtue chappy around here. Can't say I've much sympathy for him really, after the shocking mess he's been making over at Number 15. Given a little more time they'd have had the whole street one great scrap-heap. It's got to stop somewhere."

"What a shame," said Felicity. "It'd be as dull as anything around here without Mr Virtue's yard. It's the most interesting thing in the whole street. I love to watch them with all their things. I think you and Mr Tweek should be ashamed of yourselves for trying to get them kicked out."

Ex-Sergeant-Major Fulton looked as though he'd suddenly become covered from head to foot with chilblains. As a matter of record he felt like it too.

"Er — yes. — Well well. — Quite — er. — Must be running along now. Mustn't fall behind, eh? — Ha ha! — Yes. — Well, 'bye now." And he blundered backwards out of the room. He always seemed to leave Felicity Cambert's house in confusion or embarrassment. Ex-Sergeant-Major Fulton made up his mind not to call on her quite so often in future.

If that woman was having some kind of joke with him, she'd better watch her step. Ex-Sergeant-Major Fulton wasn't to be fooled around with.

As he reached his gate the ex-Sergeant-Major met Harry Taggitt arriving home from work via the pub and the T.A.B.

"Any winners for Saturday, Fulton?"

"I say, have you heard about Tweek?" asked ex-Sergeant-Major Fulton on the spur of the occasion.

"What's he been up to now?" asked Harry uninterestedly.

"He's turning his place into a public playground," he said, with puzzled indignation. "What with that, and this Virtue blighter's rubbish-dump over the road the neighbourhood soon won't be worth living in. Should be something done to restrain them."

"Old Tweek's been running pretty wide on the turns lately," said Harry carelessly. "He wants swabbin' if y'arsk me." And he went on to his own place, next door to Mr Tweek's proposed public playground.

Watcher and Dinny had been on a tour of the excavation and construction jobs around the city and found several places where they could pull in among the officially-hired owner-driver trucks every now and again for a free load of filling. They tried it out with three sample loads and it worked perfectly. Then they picked up a hundred and fifty mended sacks and swung a deal with two 44-gallon drums of ex-navy insect repellent. A very satisfactory day all round. They went home early to tell Leila about it and found her sitting in the kitchen with Felicity Cambert, the pair of them talking away like auctioneers.

"What's up?" asked Dinny apprehensively.

"This is Miss Cambert, from just along the road," introduced Leila.

"We know," said Dinny. "More complaints about the yard?"

"Oh no," said Felicity. "I just popped over to tell you about Mr Tweek."

"What's he up to now?" asked Watcher.

"He's having his place made into a public park or something, so that nobody can carry on a business within two hundred feet of it. He told that awful Fulton person it would give him an excuse to have you closed down and shifted away."

"Tweek's always trying some caper like that. He's been at

it for years," said Watcher.

"This one sounds serious," said Dinny thoughtfully. He turned to Felicity. "How come you bothered tipping us off? I thought you were on Tweek's side."

"Tipping you off?" asked Felicity blankly.

"Why did you come and tell us about it?" asked Watcher.

"Don't be awful, you two," said Leila. "Miss Cambert has been very kind to warn us. There's no call for you to be rude."

"I was just telling Leila," said Felicity, "what fun it would be if we moved all your things over to my place. There's scads of space, and Mr Tweek wouldn't be able to do a thing about it. I'm not within two hundred feet of his public park."

"Thanks all the same," said Dinny, "but it's too big a job."

"It'd take months," said Watcher.

"Yeah. We'll have to work out some way of gettin' around Tweek without having to shift everything. But don't worry, we'll think of something."

"Well if you do need somewhere to put things you can always use my yard," said Felicity disappointedly.

"That's pretty decent of you, miss, but . . ."

"We have been thinking of starting a separate depot for the brass and copper and other non-ferrous stuff," said Watcher casually.

"Yes," said Leila. "Remember all that trouble we had sorting out the scrap for our new-truck money?"

"Yeah," said Dinny. "We're goin' to have to expand sooner or later. Sure you wouldn't mind, miss? We could pay you a little rent for the space. In the old days we used to back in and tip the whole load, if there was enough good stuff in it, but we've given that up now. We're gettin' selective. You'd only get the best stuff."

"I'd love it," said Felicity. "I've wanted heaps of things like yours ever since I came here."

Watcher and Dinny looked at each other with stretched, astonished faces, and suddenly they were all laughing.

Leila brought them back to earth. "But we still have Mr Tweek to deal with," she reminded them.

"Yeah," said Watcher. "We'd better ask Ash over for a conference tonight. He's the bloke next door," he explained to Felicity.

"Handles all our non-metal stuff," said Dinny.

"He's saving up to buy that house," said Leila. "The owner's going to let him have it cheap."

"Right then," said Dinny. "Conference here tonight after dinner. Perhaps Miss Cambert would like to come along? It might involve her yard."

"Felicity's staying for dinner," said Leila, "so she'll be here anyway."

Felicity giggled happily and within a few moments the two women were picking up conversational revolutions so fast that Dinny and Watcher retreated to Ashley's place for a preconference conference.

"If it comes to the worst we might have to get a lawyer," said Ashley when they'd told him about Tweek's latest threat to their organisation.

"Have to try and keep it from coming to that if we possibly can," said Watcher. "But I don't like the looks of it."

"There's bound to be something in the yard that'll help," said Dinny philosophically. "It's never let us down yet."

Ex-Sergeant-Major Fulton finished off a flask of brandy for morning tea, brushed his hair and his clothes, and called on Mr Tweek sucking a Lifesaver.

"I say, Tweek," he expostulated, "have you noticed anything odd about Miss Cambert recently?"

"No," snarled Mr Tweek ungraciously, "only that she's spent nearly every day this week over at Virtue's junk-yard. And that they've pulled her front fence down and driven their truck over the footpath into her garden with loads of their junk three times, and spread mud all over the public footpath and up the road. And put dirty old sheets of metal over the kerb — that's all I've noticed."

"You don't think she's actually — er — gone over to the other side, do you?" rumbled the ex-Sergeant-Major.

"Was she ever on our side?" demanded Tweek. "What did she do to help protect the neighbourhood from Virtue and his gang? Well, it doesn't worry me one little bit. They're all going to get what's coming to them when I spring my little surprise on them. After next Wednesday there's going to be a lot of changes made around here. And I'll have the law to back me up."

"Er — yes. Quite looking forward to it too," said ex-Sergeant-Major Fulton worriedly. "I must say it's been going on quite long enough. Can't understand Miss Cambert behaving like that, though. Just goes to show one can't be sure who one's friends are. It's just as well you didn't take her into your confidence, Tweek. She could have upset the whole scheme."

"How do you mean, upset the whole scheme?"

"Well — er — if she'd known about your intended — er — action, she might have forewarned this Virtue blighter. Thrown a spanner in the works."

"Well, she doesn't know about it, so she can't. You and I are the only ones who know anything about it. I've got them trapped at last and I'm going to be there to see Virtue's face when the police serve the order on him."

Leila and Felicity had been prospecting a new load of perks that Dinny and Watcher had tipped off the day before in Ashley's yard, and Felicity was crossing to her place with a big bulge of brass and copper in the front of her skirts, when she was intercepted by ex-Sergeant-Major Fulton.

"I say m'dear. You haven't mentioned anything to our friends over the road about Tweek's plan for next Wednesday, have you?"

"We're not interested in what Mr Tweek does," she said without stopping. "And I certainly haven't said anything to anybody about next Wednesday."

Injunction

TEN

INJUNCTION

On Wednesday morning ex-Officer Tweek triumphantly led an unwilling constable with a big envelope up Dinny Virtue's path. It was the first time Mr Tweek had ever set foot in the yard which had been haunting his waking and sleeping hours for nine years. He knocked on the door and stood back so that the first thing Dinny would see when he opened it would be the constable. It was.

"Hullo there, constable — Mr Tweek. Come on in. What can I do for you?"

The constable went into the kitchen and Mr Tweek had no option but to follow him. Watcher, Leila, Ashley Nash, and Felicity Cambert were all sitting around the table.

"Are you the proprietor of this — er — place?" the constable asked Dinny.

"Yeah, me and my partners here," said Dinny. "I'm the legal owner. What's up? You can talk in front of me friends."

"I have an injunction here," said the constable, unfolding his document, "restraining you from conducting a business within two hundred feet of a public park or reserve. I have to warn you that any further activities here will render you liable to arrest for contempt of a court order."

"And I'll be watching you, Virtue," crowed Mr Tweek. "You're finished round here, the whole lot of you. I've got another order being processed to make you clear all your junk out of sight of the street too."

It was obvious that the constable wasn't enjoying his job.

"I'll handle this, thank you, sir," he said to Mr Tweek. "I'm afraid he's right, sir. You will have to give up your activities in this neighbourhood. It comes under Section 14, Clause a of the Public Recreations Act, 1932. 'No person shall carry on, or cause to be carried on, a business within two hundred feet of a place set aside for public recreational purposes.'"

"Where's the public park around here?" asked Dinny.

"My place," said Mr Tweek. "I've donated the grounds to the Council for a public reserve."

"Good," said Dinny. "We must come over there for a picnic. But there must be some mistake," he continued, turning to the constable. "This isn't a place of business, it's an officially recognised charitable fund-raising organisation." Watcher passed him a letter which he handed on to the constable. "Here's the letter from the Government Department that sponsors the drive, accepting our offer to donate all our profits — after our wages and expenses, of course — to an officially recognised charity. And we're authorised to accept and pass on donations too, if you'd care to give a few shillings to the cause and help save some hungry child from malnutrition or something."

"I'm afraid that places a different complexion on the matter," said the constable to Mr Tweek, peering at the letter and then at his court order. "This law doesn't apply to non-profit-making organisations."

"Let me see that letter," snapped Mr Tweek, plucking it from the constable's hand. "It's dated the day before yesterday. You knew about this! You planned it. I'm going to take you to court for this. You're not getting away with it."

"That'll be enough, sir," said the constable firmly, taking the letter from Mr Tweek's trembling grasp and handing it back to Dinny. "I'll have to make a full report to my superiors about this, but I don't think you'll hear from us again, sir."

Mr Tweek made a very impolite and undignified exit. The

constable followed him more decorously.

"Well that's that," grinned Ashley.

"You're a genius, Ashley," smiled Leila happily. "It was all your idea.

And Ashley writhed in blushing embarrassment.

Not only did poor Mr Tweek's plan to have Dinny and Co. banished, bag and garbage, from Essentry Crescent go awry, but the method he used turned cruelly against him. The legalities had required him to publish notice in at least two news papers that his grounds had been declared open and free for public use, and to erect a sign. And it seemed that this was just the kind of informal locality that a number of Ladies' Guilds required for their multifarious social functions. It saved them cleaning up after themselves too.

In the first month no less than eleven meetings and tea-parties took place in the pleasant surroundings of Mr Tweek's front garden, and with such a perfect conversation-piece just across the road they were all a great success. This number was much less than the monthly average later became.

At first Mr Tweek attempted to attract sympathisers to his anti-Dinny and Co. cause, but he never got anywhere. And eventually he shut himself inside the house whenever a herd of cachinnating women trampled and littered his once flourishing gardens. He rudely refused all requests for extra chairs, hot water, or the use of his front veranda for a speakers' rostrum, but still they continued to use his place as what it had been proclaimed — public. There was a wedding reception that left the lawns and paths spottled for weeks afterwards with confetti. And a kindergarten mass-birthday-party that was practically the finish of Mr Tweek's lawn, flower garden and sanity.

During the holiday season there were several complaints about noisy parties carrying on into the early hours of the morning, and once the police were called to deal with something that resembled a brawl, which had broken out among Mr Tweek's shrubbery.

For some reason Mr Tweek could no longer bear the sight of ex-Sergeant-Major Fulton, and for some reason ex-Sergeant-Major Fulton could no longer bear the sight of Mr Tweek. Their relationship corroded to the point where they each pretended that the other never existed.

Perhaps the reason why Mr Tweek and ex-Sergeant-Major Fulton could no longer bear the sight of one another was because ex-Sergeant-Major Fulton had taken to blundering around the fringes of Dinny and Co.'s various departments until he'd blustered himself on to speaking terms with them by sheer brandied persistence. In fact they'd got to the stage where Dinny and Watcher had asked the ex-Sergeant-Major's advice about a load of ex-army motorbike and bren-carrier parts they'd bought up cheap. Ex-Sergeant-Major Fulton had somehow agreed to have the load temporarily deposited in his yard for him to go through and evaluate for them — for a small commission, of course.

Harry Taggitt had always kept his garden fairly tidy because tidy gardens were a bit of a fetish in Essentry Crescent. A kind of reaction against Dinny's yard, as nobody wanted to risk being accused of following his example. But when Ash Nash's yard fell under Dinny and Co.'s untidy influence, Harry began not to bother with his own grounds so much. Now that someone had set a precedent no one was likely to criticise him for neglecting his gardens and hedges a little. Then when Felicity Cambert followed Ash Nash's example so whole-heartedly, Harry Taggitt almost lost the interest he'd never had in gardening altogether. And when Mr Tweek, right next door to him, made his place into a public park and started having messy, noisy groups of people coming and going all the time, Harry didn't bother even mowing his lawns any more.

Then Harry struck a big win, paid off his back rent and nearly all his debts, and bought himself a Ford car of 1935 vintage. The third time he drove out in the car he returned in a taxi and the car followed next day at the back of a tow-truck. They put it on his front lawn for him to work on, and work on it he did. Whenever he wasn't racehorsing, Harry was either banging or tinkering with his car, or over at Dinny's yard, buying, borrowing or looking for something he needed.

Long grass grew up around the car and dismantled parts spread in an ever-widening radius. Harry had announced that he was going to "do the car up to the last nut and bolt", but if appearances were anything to go by the car was deteriorating faster than it was being done up.

The doing-up of Harry Taggitt's car had become more of a hobby than a project, but it assumed the proportions of a crime in Mr Tweek's averted estimation. He regarded Harry as a treacherous menace to everything decent and respectable, just like Dinny Virtue, and he never spoke a civil word to either of them again.

Leila and Felicity ramble contentedly on through their happily-littered lives, and in their spare time they're inexorably manoeuvring Ash Nash into romantic situations with Leila: ultimate, inevitable goal — marriage!

Ashley is using up all his spare time with his inventions, his goat, and paying off the deposit on his house. All his spare courage is needed for unsuccessful attempts to point out to Leila that there is no need to go to all that trouble.

Dinny and Watcher are the same perk-hungry, conference

holding pair they always were, except that they don't know what Leila and Felicity have in mind for Dinny as soon as Leila's safely married off to Ash Nash.

Dinny's neighbour on the right, as you face the road, who never speaks, still never speaks. He's built a two-foot-six extension on to the six-foot boundary fence, and wistfully pretends that Essentry Crescent is still the same as it was in the days before Dinny Virtue came to live there.

BASTARDS I HAVE MET

BARRY CRUMP

Illustrated by
Graham Kirk

An informal encyclopedia of some of the types of Bastard you run into these days, complete with ungarnished reports of the author's personal encounters with them, and the whole thing immeasurably enhanced by Graham Kirk's inspired drawings.

These stories are dedicated to the Bright Bastard, whoever he was, who first coined the title phrase of this priceless volume of disquisitions on Bastardry — and to those of us who know how he felt.

CONTENTS

He wasn't a bad poor bastard,
He'd share his only crust.
And never a better horseman
Dragged his stockwhip through the dust.

BILL

Introduction

NOW BEFORE YOU GO running away with any wild ideas about the title of this book I'd better get one thing clear — it wasn't my idea. It was suggested to me on several hundred different occasions, over the years, by several hundred different people, in several hundred different places, at several hundred different times, in several hundred different ways. A man's got to be pretty thick to ignore such a hint. So I got to thinking about it.

Then I borrowed a dictionary from the schoolmistress and looked up the word *bastard*, to see what it's supposed to mean. Here's what I found.

> **bastard, n. & a. (Child) born out of wedlock or of adultery, illegitimate; (of things) unauthorized, hybrid, counterfeit; —*file* (with serrations of medium coarseness); — *slip*, sucker of tree (also fig., = *bastard* n.); (Bot) nearly resembling another species (— BALM); (Zool.) — *wing*, rudimentary extra digit with quill-feathers. (ME,f.OF f.) *bast.* (BAT-) packsaddle (used as bed by muleteer) + — ARD; cf. BANTLING.**

Nothing much use in that lot. One of those dictionary blokes is going to fall back into a heap of his own verbiage one of these days and smother himself.

I decided to stick to our meaning of the word, and then something occurred to me, something so glaringly obvious, so utterly simple and fundamental that it took me a quite a while to get it sorted out in my mind.

It was nothing less than a damning indictment of the very structure of our whole society. A shocking omission! No wonder the country's in an uproar! No wonder the students are playing merry hell all over the place. How can we blame the workers for striking for more pay? How inevitable that we can't understand what the devil our politicians are raving about! How inescapable that our very newspapers can't report even a simple incident or statement without getting it distorted! How right my landlady is to invade my privacy with her constant threatening demands for money! How futile to hope that they won't be forced to raise even higher the prices of such essential commodities as tobacco and beer! — When there's never been a single book or poem, or TV documentary, or song; or even a speech, devoted to the common or garden Bastard!

Do you realise that the only bastards we ever hear about are only ever there to be a kind of contrast to some scungy hero? And an exhaustive and comprehensive survey carried out by myself in the public bar of the Timberlands Hotel one Saturday afternoon reveals that bastards outnumber heroes by more than fifteen thousand to one. (This figure is very conservative and can be checked quite simply — all you have to do is go into a pub and listen).

Now, now, good reader, there's no need to mark your place and go rushing off to spread the alarm among your loved ones. The matter is under control. You see I, too, was staggered. The situation must be remedied at once!

And so, with the almost overwhelming sense of responsibility to my fellow man and posterity that the work demands of me, I hereby present, without prejudice or regard for the feelings of censors or other would-be inhibitors, this absolutely scrupulously honest, truthful, factual, unvarnished stark and courageous account of — The Bastards I Have Met.

2
Actual Bastard

IT'S ONE OF THE strange truths about Bastardry that the people we are most reluctant to call bastards are those we know to be Actual Bastards (*Bastardus fairdinkumus*). That is, people whose parents either knew themselves or each other too well to risk putting their relationship on to a more formal basis, or who didn't get to know each other well enough. After all, you just don't go round discussing marriage with comparative strangers, do you? It's not always advisable to tell them too much about your past, let alone discuss a future of wedded bliss with them.

Gordon Meltzer, a bloke I worked on the Forestry with, was an Actual Bastard, and, like most Actual Bastards, there was nothing to distinguish him from any other kind of bastard. In fact Gordon was more of an Honest Bastard (*Bastardus truthus*) than anything else. He told us once how he'd given up volunteering the information to people that he was an Actual Bastard. Not because he was ashamed of it or guilty about it, but because of *their* reactions.

The trouble with Gordon was not that his old man didn't make an honest woman out of his mother, but that he didn't stick around long enough to teach Gordon how to be *dis*honest. Gordon couldn't tell a lie to save himself. He was so honest that people often found him very disconcerting, which doesn't say much for the state of the society, or do much for getting Gordon any close mates.

I'll never forget the time our forestry boss came and told us that they'd asked him to see if any of the blokes from the planting gangs would like to apply for training as rangers. If we did we could have a day off to go in to the head office for an interview. Gordon and another bloke and I decided to have a go at it, and in we went to see Mr Blund himself, The Controller of Forests.

The office girl showed the three of us into Mr Blund's office

Bastardus fairdinkumus

and he sat us down and took our names. Then he asked the other bloke why he wanted to be a Forestry Ranger, and he told him, openly and frankly, how he'd always liked the open-air life; how he believed that forestry was one of the nation's most important assets and it was vital to the economy and progress of the country that it be properly administered and protected, and how he'd decided that to be a part of this great and developing industry was the most worthwhile thing he could make a career of etc. etc. etc.

You could see by the way the Controller looked at him that he was overdoing it a bit, but he waited until he'd finished. Then he said to Gordon, "And why do *you* wish to train as a ranger, Mr Meltzer?"

"I don't know, actually," said Gordon with his customary lack of deception.

"But surely you must have *some* reason for applying for it," prompted the Controller.

"Well, my mates wanted to come in and see about it," said Gordon.

"You mean you just came along to keep them company," said the Controller.

"It's a day off on full pay and a free trip into town," Gordon reminded him. It was almost as though Gordon was inviting the Controller of Forests to be in on a good thing. The C. of Fs. was looking from one to the other of us very suspiciously by this time, but there was nothing we could do to shut Gordon up. "We don't have to go back to camp until tonight," he added.

"I see," said the Controller. "So you just came in to apply for a position as a trainee ranger in order to get the day off — all of you," he added, looking at the other bloke and me. "It seems to me that you chaps have simply taken advantage of our invitation for applications to get yourselves a paid day off. Is this correct?" he said to Gordon.

"Yes," said Gordon.

That rocked the controller of Forests. He didn't get where he was by dealing in the kind of commodity Gordon was dispensing. It took him a few moments to work out how to reply to Gordon's one-word occupational suicide — or rather, suicides. There were three of us on the skids.

3
Bad Bastard

AND NOW, LEARNED READER — fellow student of bastardry, patient peruser of these propaedeutic ponderations, Decent Bastard (*Bastardus goodblokeus*) — I cannot risk my reputation for straight-shooting, down-to-earth, commonsense and unbribable honesty. I must now deal with the category of bastard that brings to all of us the most horripulating recollections of all the worst kind of bastard we've run into.

(I'll have to return this dictionary to the schoolmistress. It's causing an element of anafractuosity to creep into this, the first and only maieutic, tendentious prolegomina yet produced on the vitally important subject of bastitudinariousness.)

But onward — you will already have gathered that the type of bastard I'm going to deal with now is the Bad Bastard (Bastardus skulduggerus).

Read this out loud: "He's a bad bastard, that one."

Louder — so you can hear it — See what I mean?

The bad bastard is a combination of every other kind of unpleasant bastard known to you and me, and between us both you've got to admit we've met a few of 'em. He even has a go at pretending to be a Decent Bastard, when he thinks it'll take genuine D.Bs. like you and me in.

Of all the abuse and condemnation, criticism and contempt, rejection and indifference that we can bring to our aid in times of exasperation and outrage, there's nothing to beat calling someone ". . . a bad bastard."

It implies that there's no hope for him. He's simply incorrigibly bad. He warrants no sympathy or attempt at rehabilitation. He's always been a bad bastard and he always will be. If he ever gets caught, and they do sometimes, or hurt, or cheated (rare), or if he simply runs into a bit of ordinary bad luck, the Bad Bastard has only got what's coming to him. He's been asking for it for

Bastardus skulduggerus

a long time. Nobody will stand by him, mainly because he doesn't bloody well deserve it.

I feel that this is an appropriate occasion to introduce you to a whole new aspect of bastardry. In these times of exaggeration, when the use of superlatives in speech is almost as common as it used to be in motion-picture advertising, we're often stumped for words when it comes to describing something that is genuinely extraordinary. Not so with bastardry. The description of any type of bastard is simply and effectively doubled by putting in front of it the word "real". A *Real* Dirty Bastard, a *Real* ugly Bastard etc. etc.

I've brought this to your notice at this point because the bloke it is my inescapable duty to tell you about now was a *Real* Bad Bastard. He was such a thorough-going bastard that if you'd seen his mother and father's marriage certificate, duly signed and dated, with his own birth certificate attached, you'd still swear it was a forgery.

I don't want you to get the idea I'm prejudiced or anything, it's just that I didn't like the look of the bastard from the moment I slapped eyes on him. It wasn't so much the way he looked, it was the way he *was*. There was something not quite right about him. He was short and stocky and grubby-looking. About thirty-five or -six, I'd say, with his hair swished straight back. When he spoke he talked without expression, as though he was reading out loud.

And there was something clammy about him. He had clammy eyes. And besides all that he whistled under his breath and rapped on the bar with the edge of a coin, half-catching your attention all the time.

He told us his name was Howard Blake, but one of the blokes told my mate Clive Piper that he'd run into him driving buses up north and he was calling himself Henry Cook there. But whatever his name was there was no doubting his B-rating. He walked into the pub one night and took three dollars off the blokes at the dart board. Then he came over and cleaned up all our best "guns" on the pool-table. And he never shouted once. Not once! He'd just get a beer and sit on it for half an hour at a time.

He turned up again the next night and got stuck into us again, so some of us got our heads together and decided to have a go at getting him boozed, because it didn't look as though he could takc much grog. But he drank double-whiskies and jugs of beer, on us, all night, and the only difference it made was that he started whistling as he sauntered round the pool-table sinking balls one after the other. Yes, the bastard actually *whistled*!

He got to coming in every night after that — he'd landed a job with the Ministry of Works. It wasn't long before he couldn't get us to play darts or pool with him, but there were plenty of people passing through and we used to have to watch while this cunning bastard talked them into playing pool for a jug of beer, for even as much as a dollar a game sometimes. And then he'd proceed to thrash the strides off them. Sometimes they wouldn't even get a shot, he'd sink the lot off the break, which, often as not, he'd talked them into giving him.

And on Saturdays, when he had a few under his belt, he'd start getting sarcastic. And then he'd go round acting as though he was an old mate of yours, bludging drinks and interrupting yarns and conversations.

Ted Butler told this bloke to get lost one day and he blind-hit Ted in the side of the face with a glass and cut his cheek. So Ted took the bastard outside to pin his ears back for him, once and for all, but he dropped Ted with a dirty punch in the throat while they were going out the door. And then he dropped two of the blokes who butted in to stop him putting the boot into Ted while he was on the ground. Bang! Bang! Just like that. The bloody little bastard could fight like a thrashing machine.

Then the cops arrived and we were all expecting him to get run in for assaulting Ted with the glass, but the cunning bastard talked his way out of it! That was when Stevie the barman said: "He's a Bad Bastard, that one. A Real Bad Bastard."

That was what he was all right, and he really lived up to it. He stole and bludged and cheated and got the blame and got away with it all over the district for months. He'd thieve the harness off a nightmare. We knew it was him who broke into the bottlestore of the pub one night, so did the cops, but he turned up in the pub the next night as bold as brass, trying to talk someone into a game of pool for fifty cents. And no one could do anything about it.

The Ministry of Works knew it was him who was selling M.O.W. diesel to the private contractors over on the hydro scheme, but when they gave him notice to quit he kicked up such a stink with the union that they had to drop the matter and keep him on. And somehow he *still* went on flogging their diesel. They never found out how he was doing it as far as I know.

And then, in the manner of all Bad Bastards, he did a moonlight. Disappeared, just like that. One night we noticed that he hadn't been into the pub for a few nights, and one of the M.O.W. blokes said that he didn't think he'd been at work either. He was gone all right, and a couple of weeks later they found out that young Judy Grimwood was four months pregnant. It was never actually proved who the father was, but we had our ideas all the same. So did old Harry Grimwood.

Goodness knows where that bloke is now, but if you ever run into a short, stocky, grubby-looking bloke, about thirty-five or -six, hair swished back and whistles under his breath and raps on the bar with the edge of a coin, half-catching your attention all the time — you want to keep out of his way, it might just be him, and he's a Real *Bad* Bastard.

4
Clever Bastard

I WAS WAITING IN the Department of Labour and Employment one day when I heard a conversation start up at a slide a bit further along from the one I was waiting at. Or I should say I heard *half* of a conversation start up, because the Labour and Employment bloke was inside the room and I couldn't hear him. But the other character's voice was as loud as his personality was. I couldn't *not* hear him.

This is how it went.

"G'day. I . . . er . . . was lookin' around for a job and they reckon you blokes are the caper so I just dropped in to see if you could put me onto something."

"— — — — — — — —?" (Something from the L. and E. bloke.)

"Charlie. Charlie Roberts, but me mates usually call me Wrecker because of something that happened once."

"— — — — — — — —?"

"Eighteen next month, but I can pass for twenty-two or -three easy enough."

"— — — — — — — —?"

"Well I'll have a crack at just about anything. What y'got?"

"— — — — — — — —?"

"Ah . . . well I haven't *been* working just lately, as a matter of fact. Been on holiday, sort of."

"— — — — — — — —?"

"Let's see now . . . Must be about six weeks since I threw the last job in."

"— — — — — — — —?"

"Bridge job. Over in the King Country. I was only there a couple of months. Didn't hit it off too well with the foreman."

"— — — — — — — —?"

"No, nothin' like that. As a matter of fact him and me didn't see eye to eye about me trottin' his daughter round."

"— — — — — — — —?"

Bastardus smartfartus

"Aw . . . he reckoned she was too young or something. she looked big enough to me, though. Turned out she was only fourteen or fifteen or something like that."

"— — — — — — — —?"

"Cut it out! A joker can't go round asking people their age when he hardly knows 'em properly, can he?"

"— — — — — — — —?"

"No, I didn't get around to asking about a reference. Never go in for 'em myself, as a matter of fact. Anyone can write himself out a reference if he wants one. I mean, if a bloke's going to give a man a reference he either gives 'im a good one or you don't bother askin' for it. No one's going to flash a crook reference around if he's after a job, now is he?"

"— — — — — — — —?"

"No, they gave me a week's pay instead of notice. I was thinkin' of going to you blokes about it but I decided it wasn't worth it in the finish."

"— — — — — — — —?"

"Well it wasn't only the foreman's daughter, actually. There was a bit of a stink about a truck."

"— — — — — — — —?"

"Had a bit of a prang. Ran it into the ditch."

"— — — — — — — —?"

"No, well as a matter of fact I wasn't actually supposed to be driving it at the time."

"— — — — — — — —?"

"Funny you should mention that. I was just thinkin' of goin' in to get a licence the day after it happened. That wasn't what they really went crook about anyway."

"— — — — — — — —?"

"Oh, we'd just been in to pick up a couple of bottles of booze for me mate's birthday."

"— — — — — — — —?"

"No, we were dead stone cold sober."

"A couple of crates. A fair bit of it got busted and some nosey parkers came along before we could get it cleaned up properly. And you know how beer stinks when it's busted all over the place."

"— — — — — — — — —?"

"Well it does."

"— — — — — — — — —?"

"Well it might have been all right anyway, only one of the blokes got knocked around a bit. Probably wasn't hangin' on properly, if you ask me."

"— — — — — — — — —?"

"Don't know exactly. Something to do with his back. They whipped him off to hospital anyway. I was a bit worried about it for a while there, as a matter of fact. I mean, I didn't know but he might have kicked the bucket of something. Them ambulance blokes won't let on what's wrong with a bloke when they take him away."

"— — — — — — — — —?"

"Oh he's as good as gold now. Got a cushy job in the office after that, I believe. They reckon he's in for a good slice of compo. out of it. Partial disablement, they reckon. Some jokers get all the luck."

"— — — — — — — — —?"

"Well I'm not too fussy, mate. Anything'll do me."

"— —?"

"Dairy farm? Yeah, I worked on a dairy farm for four months one time."

"— — — — — — — — —?"

"Up north. Morrinsville."

"Funny you should mention that. The boss was a bit of a bastard, but it was his missus who wore the pants. It was her who gave me the push, as a matter of fact."

"— — — — — — — — —?"

"Well she reckoned it was because they couldn't afford to keep me on, but I'd spotted her watchin' me teach the daughter how to ride a bike the day before she gave me the push. The old bat just didn't trust a bloke, if you ask me. It's no good workin' on a place where they don't trust a man. He's better off out of it all together . . . Where is this place, by the way?"

"— — — — — — — — —?"

"Woodville, eh. How many cows?"

"— — — — — — — — —?"

"Sounds okay. Wouldn't mind havin' a look at it. A man can always throw it in if it's no good, can't he."

"— — — — — — — — —?"

"Well thanks, mate. That's mighty decent of you. What's this bloke's name?"

"— — — — — — — — —?"

"Boggs eh! That's a beaut."

"— — — — — — — — —?"

"Good. Thanks. I'll go up there tomorrow . . . They tell me you blokes'll pay a man's fare if he's stuck for cash to get to a job. That right?"

"— — — — — — — — —?"

"Yeah, I am as a matter of fact. Been having a crook run of luck lately."

"— — — — — — — — —?"

"Good, that'll do me. Thanks a lot . . . You don't happen to know if this bloke Boggs has got any daughters, do you?"

"— — — — — — — — —?"

"Ah well, you never know your luck."

"— — — — — — — — —?"

"Okay then, I'll be seein' you. Ta."

And with that, our friend slouched out of the Department of Labour and Employment, slamming the door behind him.

How's *that* for a Clever Bastard (*Bastardus smartfartus*)!

5
Dozey Bastard

YES, STAN FUDD WAS a true-blue, dyed-in-the-wool, honest-to-goodness, fair-dinkum, jumped-up-never-to-come-down, gold-plated, Dozey Bastard (*Bastardus drippus*). Not a bad truck-driver, mind you, but a Really Dozey Bastard, all the same.

I was driving trucks at the time. Big artics., long hauls. Auckland — Napier — Gisborne — Palmerston North — Wellington, runs like that, and usually two or three of us would set off together and stay more or less together as long as we could.

One day, when my mate Mike Foote and I were getting ready for a routine run down to Palmerston North and back, the boss came and introduced this new bloke, Stan Fudd, and asked us to show him the ropes and keep an eye on him. He was to drive a third rig and bring back a load of refrigerated fish.

So off we went, Mike up front, the new bloke in the middle, and I brought up the rear. It's a fairly long run down to Palmerston North but we were all empty and got there in eleven hours — one o'clock in the morning — and had a kip in our usual pub.

The new bloke could handle a truck all right, there's no doubt about that, but by the time we'd loaded up and had a feed he was looking a bit weary on it. Not used to the long runs. And by the time we'd made it back up to Taupo he was looking really beat, so we stopped for an hour to give him a spell.

Back at the depot we were told to get some sleep because there was a rush job on and we had to leave for Napier early next morning.

Stan turned up yawning and hollow-eyed and when we stopped for lunch at Taupo he almost went to sleep at the cafe table we were sitting at. So Mike went to his truck and came back with a jar of tablets he kept in his cab.

"Here, take one of these," he said to Stan. "It'll keep you awake."

Bastardus drippus

"What are they?" said Stan.

"Methedrines," said Mike. "They'll stop you going to sleep on the road. There's a rough stretch between here and Napier and we don't want you going over the bank."

"Okay, thanks," said Stan, taking one of the pills and washing it down with coffee.

"You'd better take a few of these," said Mike, pouring about fifty of them onto a table napkin for him. "Just take one when you feel yourself getting sleepy."

"Thanks," said Stan. "I need something like that."

"You have to be careful not to take too many of them," warned Mike.

But I don't think Stan can have heard him — or perhaps it was just that he was a Dozey Bastard — because he took to those methedrine pills like nobody's business. He drove non-stop to Napier and didn't even wait until morning to head back.

I was trying to sleep in the same hotel room as him and he flounced and creaked around in his bed for a couple of hours and then he got dressed and went out for a walk around. He woke me up in the early hours of the next morning to tell me he was going to head on back to Auckland.

His truck was in the yard, unloaded, serviced and ready to take off again, by the time Mike and I arrived back late that night. And when we met at the depot two days later, Stan, hollow-eyed and wildly excited, whispered hoarsely to us (although there was nobody else within earshot) that he hadn't been to sleep since he'd got back from Napier but he felt terrific.

"I've been having long discussions with the wife," he confided to us. "Our whole lives have been changed!"

"You want to take it a bit easy on those methedrines," Mike told him. "You'll go right off if you keep taking too many of them."

"I've hardly touched them!" protested Stan quickly, looking guiltily around the yard.

"Just take it easy, all the same," said Mike. "Give them a rest for a few days."

Stan got held up at the depot that morning so Mike and I left ahead of him, but he passed us later in the day, grim-jawed and black-eyed, heading south as though he was in an army tank or a jumbo-jet.

He got out of step with us, we couldnt keep up with him. He was making half as much again as us, and we were on big money.

Then the jar of methedrines disappeared out of Mike's truck and we started getting worried. We asked Stan about it and he accused us of picking on him — just like his wife had been lately.

"He won't be able to keep it up," Mike said to me. "It won't be long before it catches up on him."

And it wasn't. We'd caught up with Stan at an eating place well down the line and were having one of our rare meals together. But Stan wasn't hungry and picked at the edges of his food as though he'd already eaten too much, but he drank five cups of coffee and then drank all the milk out of the jug on our table. We tried to talk to him but he was almost incoherent by this time. Raving wildly for a few minutes and then lapsing suddenly into a sullen brooding silence. And before Mike and I had finished eating he abruptly left us, saying as he went that he had to get going.

We decided that if he got any worse we'd have to get the boss to lay him off for a few days. It didn't look to us as though Stan had been eating or sleeping anywhere near enough over the past couple of weeks (ever since the methedrines) and we estimated that he'd lost between a stone and a half and two stone in weight.

It was about half past one the following morning when we came up to Stan's truck, stopped in the middle of the road on a long straight, with the motor running and the lights on full-beam and the cab door hanging open. There were fifty-yard-long black streaks of rubber on the road where he'd slammed on his brakes at high speed. It's a wonder he hadn't jack-knifed her.

We pulled over and stopped our trucks and got out to look for Stan. We'd gone past him. He was back up the road looking around in some fern down the bank, lighting matches and calling out, "Hoi, Hoi there! Where are you?"

It was just as well it was us who'd found him. We led him back to the trucks and made him drink some coffee from the thermos I carried in my cab.

And this, as near as we could gather, was what had happened

to him. He was just driving along making good time when the little naked man who'd been scampering along in his headlights with his umbrella up for about forty or fifty miles suddenly disappeared with a scream under the front of the truck. Stan stamped on his brakes and jammed the 22-ton rig to a hell of a stop but there was no hope for the little man. By the time we'd arrived Stan had searched through the tyres and wheels of his outfit and right back up the road, but there was no sign of him.

We found twenty-six of the two hundred-odd methedrines he'd nicked from Mike's truck in his shirt pocket and had no conscience about confiscating them. Then we shifted Stan's truck to a safe place off the road and locked it up and took him about 40 miles to our nearest stopping hotel and put him to bed.

He slept for a day and a night and was looking a little better when we picked him up on our way back and drove him to pick up his truck. He was a day and a half late getting back to the depot but we'd organised a breakdown yarn for him and he didn't get into trouble over it.

"Not that he didn't deserve to," said Mike. "Us long-distance drivers have been using methedrines for ten years that I know of, and they're a damn good thing if you use them sensibly. But it only takes someone like Stan to get everyone calling them dangerous drugs. Anything'd be dangerous in the hands of a Dozey Bastard like that."

And you have to admit that Mike was right. A Dozey Bastard.

6
Enigmatic Bastard

I DON'T THINK IT'D be too presumptuous of me to describe Suggy Benson as an Enigmatic Bastard (*Bastardus perplexus*). The only Real Enigmatic Bastard I've ever run into, as a matter of fact. There's been so much talk flying around about him that it's got right out of hand altogether, so I've decided to set the facts down while there's still time, and then people will be able to form their own opinions about him.

Though I personally knew Suggy as well as just about anybody (he's dead just now) I still can't make up my mind about him. There's those who say he was nothing but a lazy, shiftless, selfish criminal, with no regard for anybody else — or their property. And then there's those who swear that Suggy was a thoughtful, considerate friend to anyone in trouble; a Good Bastard. Only rob people who could afford it. A 'Robin Hood' kind of bloke.

I don't know — both sides of the story are true enough, I suppose. All I know is that if you were with Suggy Benson you were all right. You'd never go short of a feed or somewhere to sleep, or even a job, if you wanted one. He had bunks all over the country, did Suggy. There was the university gymnasium and the hothouse and one or two other places in Auckland. The Te Rapa racetrack buildings in Hamilton. Hot pools at Rotorua and Taupo. A church and a school in Wellington. Railway carriages and one or two other little spots in Christchurch. And a lean-to that backed right up against a baker's ovens in Dunedin. Just to mention a few of the more obvious ones.

And wherever he went he had his own special lurk for getting a feed. Never knew him to go hungry, old Suggy, and he went through a few rough spots, believe me. For absolute emergencies, for example, there were the Albert Park goldfish in Auckland. Trout in Rotorua and Taupo. Pigeons in Wellington and Dunedin. And ducks in Rotorua and Christchurch — to mention a careful few. Yes, Suggy could swipe a duck or pigeon or goldfish —

Bastardus perplexus

anything you liked — from right under your nose and you'd never know it was happening.

You see, Suggy Benson was the most terrific thief you ever saw in all your born days. If he wanted something it'd never occur to him to go and buy it, or ask for it, or anything like that. He'd just swipe it. And he'd swipe it so naturally that quite often eyewitnesses wouldn't realise what he was doing.

The thing about Suggy's pinching was that he didn't seem to mind whether he got caught or not. They reckon no one will ever know exactly how much stuff Suggy knocked-off in his time. He seemed to have a genius for lifting the kind of stuff you don't miss for a while, and then you wonder just when it went off, and whether someone might have borrowed it — or what the hell had happened to it.

It wasn't always like that though. For instance there was the time Suggy pinched a whole truckload of Maoris. They were on their way from Ruatahuna to Ngaruawahia for a *tangi*, with one of their cousins in a coffin under some sacks on the back of the truck. They pulled up at the Murupara pub and the driver and his mate went in to leave a message with one of their other cousins and they got held up in there. Suggy wandered out of the pub a bit later and noticed the truck parked there with all the flax baskets and blankets and old ladies and kids on board. So he hopped in and drove the whole caboodle back to Ruatahuna. Everyone on the truck thought they were going back to pick up some people, or something that had been left behind.

When they got there Suggy pulled up outside the store and wandered off without saying anything to anyone, and it was hours before they livened that something might be up. And when it was all sorted out nobody knew what to do about it. They reported it to the local cop when they got back from the *tangi* about a week later, but he didn't believe them so they let it slide. No one thought to mention it to Suggy. It wouldn't have seemed to be worth making an issue of, I suppose, especially once they got talking to him.

And while they were away at the *tangi* Suggy had moved in with one of the families and was almost a relative by the time they got back. But don't run away with the idea that those Maoris were suckers, or dumb, or anything like that. The Passenger Transport Company found themselves in exactly the same kind of position the time Suggy drove one of their buses out of the city terminal and spent the whole afternoon picking up people around the suburbs and running them into town, or wherever else they wanted to go. Then he put the bus back where he'd got it from and it was a week before they found out it had been taken.

The first the company heard about it was when they got a letter from Suburban Buses Ltd. asking them to explain what an Otahuhu Bus had been doing on their North Shore run a couple of days before. They hadn't even missed the bus and eventually decided that the best thing they could do was tighten up on their security a bit and hush the matter up as best they could, to try and save themselves the embarrassment of an enquiry into how someone could have used one of their buses for a whole afternoon and then put it back without being spotted.

One of the things about Suggy was that he looked so *innocent*, even when he was actually in the act of whipping something. There was the time he scored three bolts of high-class suit material from a department store: Suggy had been in there getting a new pair of socks for himself and he was just leaving when a bloke staggered in the door with a big parcel. Suggy thought it might be blankets and it was getting on for winter, so he pulled the bloke up. "I'll take that," he said to him. "Okay," said the bloke. "Sign here." So Suggy signed something and took the bolts of cloth. When he found out what it was he gave someone one of the bolts in return for making the other two bolts up into blankets for him.

They put Suggy on probation once, but he never bothered reporting. The probation officer picked him up from the billiard room one afternoon and drove him round to the probation office and spent about half an hour tearing strips off him. Suggy promised to be a good boy in future, walked out of there, hopped into the probation officer's car on Friday night and put it back on Sunday afternoon, when he got back to town. And he never heard another word about it.

It seems that when the probation officer came out and found the car gone he didn't do anything about it because two of the other probation officers had the use of the same car. When the three of them got together later in the week to try and work out which one of them had clocked up six hundred and forty-one miles over the weekend, of course they all denied *having* the car on the weekend. And each of them was convinced that one of the others was lying, the real truth never occurred to them. The nature of their work had evidently made them distrustful of everyone, including each other.

And so it went. Suggy spent his whole life being casually disinterested in anything to do with the due order and course of anything he happened to come into contact with. He was quite indifferent to the precedents and standards of the system; absolutely unaffected by prescriptions, or formulas, examples, customs, methods, routines, norms, tenets, commandments, conventions, codes, recipes, regimes, precepts or discretions.

Of course a man who ignores everything consistent with order and routine isn't going to have an easy time of it. Suggy certainly didn't. I happen to know that the one year the Income Tax people collared him they discovered to their horror that he could only remember twenty-six of the jobs he'd had during the preceding financial year.

"But that's an average of less than two weeks on each job!" the Income Tax Bloke said to him.

"I've got an idea I put in a few days driving for a firewood bloke in the King Country," recalled Suggy helpfully. "Can't remember what his name was, though. In fact I'm not quite sure whether it was last year or the year before. . . ."

Suggy fought in the Second World War, you know. Too right!

And I heard that from the time he was called up until his outfit arrived in the Middle East every bit of Suggy's leave was cancelled because of his continuous casual attitude towards army regulations. Every bit of his *official* leave, that is. Some of his mates used to swear that he was A.W.O.L. for more of the time than he was there for his C.O. to confine to barracks. They only just got him onto the boat in time to ship him overseas (they'd finally found him shoeing a horse before he left for a mate of his who had a crook back).

Once they'd actually got Suggy over there and out into the desert where all the action was, his record changed dramatically, and yet his behaviour remained exactly the same as it always was. He was wounded twice and returned himself to front-line duty twice. He was captured once, and immediately escaped, and returned himself to the front lines again.

He was mentioned in despatches a number of times mainly for his level-headedness and calm courage under heavy enemy attack. One officer reported that, against direct orders, Private Benson deliberately left his post and advanced across eighty yards of open terrain under heavy enemy fire, disabled an enemy tank by climbing up and dropping a hand-grenade through the hatch, and then returned, unhurt, to his post. This action undoubtedly enabled them to hold their position, but the officer requested advice on how to deal with Private Benson for disobeying a direct order from his superior officer.

One of Suggy's mates said to me, years later, "He was a brave bastard all right. A Real Brave Bastard (*Bastardus heroicus*), there's no doubt about that. It's a wonder he didn't get himself killed half a dozen times over."

In fact Suggy was recommended for the V.C. three times, but each time they tried to present him with the thing they found out that he was due to come up for court martial for something or other, and by the end of the war the two things had eventually cancelled themselves out. His discharge was honourable, as it bloody well should have been.

A lot of people might have said that Suggy shouldn't have done a lot of those things; that he was breaking the law and ought to have been punished for it; that he was a bit of a Bad Bastard. But before you make up your mind one way or the other, I think you should know a bit about Suggy's background. You see, I went to school with Suggy for a while, and I don't know anything about psychology but I think what I have to tell you might throw some light on why he was like he was and did the things he did.

As far as we could find out, Suggy had been left behind at his Uncle Charlie's place at the end of the Christmas holidays, and he was staying on there because they had trouble keeping a farmhand on the place. We were both ten or eleven years old at the time, in the same class at school, Suggy was waiting at the end of Boundary Road with the Wallace kids on the day school started for the year and he came in on the school bus and told Mr Fusk his parents wanted him to get to our school for that year because of family arrangements. That's all you had to do to get into a school in those days. Getting out of them was a different matter.

They were only about thirty-five kids at the school and everyone, from standard one up to standard six, was taught in the same room by the headmaster, Mr Fusk, and nobody liked him. In fact he was a Real Rotten Bastard (*Bastardus putrefactus*). He quickly nosed out the kids who could be persecuted without the risk of them getting too much sympathy at home, and he had Suggy sorted out within a couple of days of him starting at the school. On the third day he called him out in front of the whole school and went through his hair with two pencils held like a knife and fork. Then he dropped the pencils into the waste paper basket with an exaggerated air of disgust and told him to go and sit down again.

And he soon found out that Suggy was liable to get into trouble if he was late home from school, so he always kept him in to punish him for real or imagined breaches of his regulations. The school bus was too small to take all the kids from out our way in one load and had to make two trips of it. If Suggy was held back till the second trip he could usually just make it home in time for the milking by running like hell through Wallace's place. I don't think Fusk ever found out about that. By this time we were all on Suggy's side. He didn't say much when Fusk started in on him and most of us older blokes reckoned that Fusk was going to have the new bloke broken before he was finished.

Now I'm going to have to tell you about one of the girls in standard two — you'll see why later on. This girl was so nervous of Fusk that she would usually wet herself if he kept at her long enough. When this happened he'd make her stand up on her desk while he strutted back and forth apologising to the rest of us for having to ask us to study in the company of "this — this disgusting thing."

Yes, Fusk was a Rotten Bastard all right, and that's what started Suggy talking to him. It was just after lunchtime one Friday and Fusk had had that girl I've been telling you about standing on her desk for about twenty minutes and he was going to get stuck into her any minute. We all knew it. And then Suggy put up his hand and kept it up until Fusk said: "Well, Benson. What is it?"

"Please sir, some of the boys aren't paying attention sir."

"Er . . . yes, Benson. Any boys who can't answer questions at the end of the period will be kept in. Now sit down, thank you Benson."

But Suggy evidently wasn't ready to sit down yet.

"It's hard to concentrate when some of the boys aren't paying attention sir," he said.

"Yes, I'm sure it is, Benson. Now sit down and we'll get on with it."

I just wanted you to know, sir, that I like Social Studies very much, sir. And when some of the boys aren't . . ."

"Yes, Benson. Now sit *down* please!"

"I hope I haven't made you angry or anything, sir. I was just trying to help, sir."

"Yes, Benson. Now that's enough, I don't want to hear another word about it. Sit down!"

"I didn't mean to make you wild, sir. I was only . . ."

"Benson! Sit down this instant!"

"Yes, sir," said Suggy still standing, "I'm very sorry, sir. I didn't mean to make you angry with me, sir. Because I think you're the best teacher I've ever had, sir, and when some of the boys . . ."

"Leave the room, Benson! Get out of it! Go on, leave this room at once! Get out!" He was fair livid by this time.

"Yes sir," said Suggy. "Shall I take my book, sir?"

"What book?"

"My social studies exercise book, sir. This one."

"Yes, yes! Take the thing and get out!"

"Yes sir," said Suggy. And at the door of the room he stopped and said, "Sir?"

"What!" shouted Fusk.

"Where shall I go, sir?"

"Anywhere! Just get out of my sight! Go on! Out!"

"I just thought there might be something you'd like me to do outside for you, sir."

"Just get out! Get out! Get out!" shouted Fusk, slapping at his table with a book. "Get out and stay out!"

Suggy went out and then popped his head back round the door and said, "When shall I come back, sir?"

The "boys who weren't paying attention" thoroughly enjoyed Suggy's interruption, or perhaps I should say *dis*ruption, of Fusk's dreary social studies class. And Fusk had more on his mind than dealing with us, even if he could find out who we were or if we really hadn't been paying attention. And the girl he was getting ready to embarrass everyone with was spared from him that time. In fact she got to be spared quite a lot by Suggy's interventions, as time went on. Fusk would start on the girl, and Suggy would immediately say something like, "Sir?"

"Now, Benson. I'm warning you, boy. I'm in no mood for any of your impertinence . . ."

"No sir," interrupted Suggy. "It's just that I've found your notebook."

"Where?"

"Up there, sir," said Suggy, pointing to the corner of Fusk's missing notebook, just visible under a pile of maps on top of the cupboards.

"How did it get there, Benson?"

"I don't know, sir. I just noticed it. Just now, sir."

And Fusk would say, "By heaven, Benson, if I thought for a moment . . ."

And once again Fusk's attention would have been diverted from little Janice Weedborne. And Fusk hated Suggy more than ever. We all knew that if Fusk ever got one over on Suggy it'd be too bad for Suggy, but he went on baiting Fusk, even when he didn't need to. I remember once when we were out in the playground and Fusk came stalking around to put a stop to any fun that might be going on. He came near the game we were playing and Suggy went up to him and said, "Sir?"

"What is it this time, Benson?" said Fusk with the nervous twitch of his right wrist he'd developed since he'd met Suggy.

"Are you very well-to-do sir?"

"Don't be impertinent, boy. I've warned you about that sort of thing."

"My Aunt Meredith told me that well-to-do people always know things, sir, and I thought you must be very well-to-do because of you knowing such a lot of things, sir."

"I'm not interested in what your Aunt Meredith says, Benson. And I'll thank you not to speak to me about personal matters in the future. Now go and pick up that piece of paper and put it in the rubbish basket."

"I think it might be Brian Laing's, sir" said Suggy.

"I didn't ask you whose it was, Benson. Just put it in the rubbish basket! And don't bother me again!"

"Don't you like talking to me, sir?"

"I'll talk to you if you don't do as you're told at once, Benson. Now jump to it!'"

"I'm very sorry, sir," said Suggy. "I was only . . ."

"You think you're clever, don't you Benson. I warn you, boy, if I ever have any more of this impertinence from you I'm going to report you to the school inspectors — and your Aunt."

And Fusk turned and walked stiffly away towards the school building. At the steps he turned unexpectedly and caught us all grinning. It wasn't going to be a very pleasant afternoon for any of us, but it was well worth it. Suggy was our school hero by this time and whatever he did was okay as far as we were concerned.

Within fifteen minutes of us sitting down for the afternoon lessons Fusk had Janice Weedborne standing on her desk for being too slow getting her books out. He left her there for a while and then walked over and looked her up and down as though she was bouncing. There was a hush and then he suddenly barked, "What are you standing up there for, you idiot?"

Janic Weedborne began to climb down from the desk. Then Fusk said, "Don't you answer your teacher when he asks you a question?"

"Yes sir," she said.

"Well answer me then," he shouted. "What are you standing up there for?"

"Because you told me to, sir,"

"And did I tell you to get down again?"

"No, sir," she whispered.

"Well you'd better get down before you make another of your disgusting messes. I can't ask respectable people to sit among that kind of filth, now can I?" he demanded

Then Suggy spoke up from the back of the room.

"Please, sir. I think your dog's been sick under Troughton's desk, sir."

Fusk turned slowly. "Has he now, Benson. Well you can have the pleasure of cleaning it up."

"Yes, sir," said Suggy. "Isn't your dog very well, sir?"

"What are you talking about?" said Fusk sarcastically.

"Well it's got stuff coming out one of its ears, sir. And . . ."

"You will stay in after school this afternoon, Benson, and write on the blackboard two hundred times 'I will not speak in class unless I am spoken to,' you understand?"

And so it went, until the incident of the school bus. Somebody threw an apple-core at somebody else and it just missed the bus driver and caused him to swerve across the road. Somebody yelled out that Suggy Benson threw it and he was put off the bus to walk home. Next morning at school Fusk was a strutting figure of pompous concern. He assembled the whole school, all thirty-eight of us, in the main room and then stalked thoughtfully back and forth across the front of the room looking grim.

"It has been reported to me," he boomed, "that one of our pupils here has, by an act of complete irresponsibility, seriously endangered the lives of a number of you. Not to mention our bus driver, whose presence of mind we have to thank for the fact that some of us," (he lowered his voice) "are here today."

A long pause, then, "Benson, stand out here."

Suggy went up the front and Fusk said to him, "Benson, since you have so grossly abused the facilities provided for you, I have no option but to deny them to you. You will no longer use the school transport."

"But sir, I never threw that apple," said Suggy.

"Don't you think you've done enough already, Benson, without calling your teacher and your schoolmates liars!" said Fusk quietly.

"But sir. . . !"

"That will do, Benson,"

Fusk turned sadly back to the rest of us standing in the hall. "And if there is any further trouble of this kind from Benson I will be forced to expel him from this school. I would ask you all to report to me at once if anything of this nature occurs again. Your lives are too important for me to ignore the risk involved in permitting this — this wretched fellow to remain in our midst unless he changes his dangerous ways. That will be all, thank you, Benson."

At the back of the hall Colin Martin started crying in his hands. And the next day Colin Martin's father came to the school and talked to Fusk out in the corridor. Then Fusk brought him into the classroom looking flustered. We knew what it was all about; quite a few of the kids knew it was Colin Martin who had thrown that apple core in the bus, and we'd had a "talk" to him about it the day before.

"It seems," began Fusk, "that young Colin has admitted to Mr Martin here that he was responsible for throwing the apple core that — er — narrowly missed the bus driver on Tuesday afternoon. It was — er — very — er — courageous of the lad to come forward like this. And it was very kind of Mr Martin to spare his valuable time to come along and — er — help us clear the matter up. In the meantime I will have to decide what is to be done about it. Apparently the lad was trying to throw the apple core out the window and it — er — it bounced . . ."

I was there that afternoon when Suggy came up to Fusk in the playground.

"What do you want, Benson?" said Fusk.

"I just wondered if it was all right for me to use the school bus again, sir."

"You will use the school bus when I say you can," snarled Fusk. "And don't think I've forgotten this. Now get out of it!"

So Suggy went on walking three and a half miles to and from school every day. By cutting across the paddocks he wasn't far behind the school bus and I don't think his aunt and uncle ever found out he'd been kicked off the bus, but somehow all the sting seemed to have gone out of him. Some of us were a bit worried in case Fusk had broken his spirit. He even seemed to have given up Fusk-baiting. Then one morning the school inspector arrived on a routine visit. I still remember him — a bony, bustling little man with a sharp nose, voice and Adam's-apple. He put his suitcase on Fusk's desk and said.

"Morning, children. Everything all right? You can sit down."

We all sat down, except Suggy. He just stayed standing up and we knew that this was going to be *it* as far as Suggy and Fusk went.

"No, sir. Everything's not all right, sir," said Suggy in a clear voice.

The inspector stopped looking through the roll and looked at Suggy for a few moments.

"I beg your pardon?" he said to him.

"I have a complaint, sir."

The inspector turned to Fusk. "Who is this boy, Mister Fusk?'"

"Benson, sir," said Fusk frowning. "One of our most difficult boys, I'm afraid. He unfortunately . . ."

"Yes, yes," said the inspector. "You say you have a complaint, Benson."

"Yes, sir."

"Well, what is this complaint?"

"There's a dog in the classroom, sir. It smells something awful and I think it's unhealthy."

"A dog, you say?" And we could see right away that this particular inspector didn't like them.

"Yes, sir."

"Where is the animal?"

"It's over here, sir," said a boy in the far corner.

And Fusk's dog was shoved out from under the desk and shooed up the aisle. An old, old, spaniel, with patches of bare hide where the hair had fallen out of him, and weeping blind eyes and cankery deaf ears. The inspector was openly horrified.

"Who let this in here? Who does it belong to, Mister Fusk?"

"He's mine," said Fusk uncomfortably.

"Take it at once from this room," ordered the inspcctor. "And don't let it within the school grounds again. I advise you to have the — it put away."

The inspector turned away from the sight of Fusk picking up

his stinking dog and carrying it awkwardly out the door. Suggy was still standing at his desk.

"Thank you, Benson. You were quite right in reporting that to me. I'll see that you aren't criticised for it. You may sit down."

"There's another matter, sir," said Suggy.

There has never been a quieter schoolroom than ours was for the few moments after Suggy said that. Then the inspector began to get a bit annoyed with him.

"Well, what is it this time?" he said impatiently.

"I've been unjustly treated at this school," said Suggy.

The inspector tapped on the desk thoughtfully for a while. I see," he said, looking around. "Do any of you others consider that you've been unjustly treated?"

No one spoke up. The inspector looked back at Suggy.

"I hope you realise that you are liable to be severely punished for falsely claiming that your schoolteacher has mistreated you, Benson. It's a very serious charge to make."

"Yes, sir. I know," said Suggy.

He was magnificent, none of us had ever heard anyone speak to a *school inspector* like this. And none of us ever heard it again, either.

Then Fusk walked back into the room and saw Suggy still standing and the inspector looking cold and grim.

"Mister Fusk. This boy claims he has been unjustly treated here. I think we should dismiss the rest of the pupils while I hear what he has to say."

So Fusk sent everyone except Suggy into the playground with instructions to play quietly. Then he waited in the corridor while Suggy told the inspector all about it. Suggy must have been making a good fist of it too, because it took a long time. Then they sent out for Colin Martin. He came back and sent Janice Weedborne in. Then two or three others, mostly prefects and things. Then Suggy himself came out and told a livid Fusk that the inspector wanted to see him, sir.

We played around till after lunchtime and then Fusk came out and told us the whole school was dismissed for the day. We could go home. Suggy rode in the school bus and nobody would have anything to do with him, just in case.

And next morning Fusk was gone. There was a relieving lady teacher called Miss Gurney, who turned to be as soft as Fusk had been hard. We gave her hell, looking back on it. Reaction for Fusk, I suppose.

But the funny thing about it all was that Suggy could have been a hero and he wouldn't be, no matter how hard we pressed him. He could have been the leader of any gang he wanted. He could have been best-friends with anyone around, but he wouldn't. He wasn't even particularly interested in Janice Weedborne, who we knew was the cause of Suggy starting on Fusk in the first place.

The reason I've told you all this is because it strikes me as worth pointing out that the same can be said of most of us. You see, whether he could have changed his attitude towards things or not, Suggy never did. He responded to the army exactly as he responded to Fusk when he was a young bloke at school, and the same as everything else he ever did. He was a hero on some occasions, and, for doing exactly the same things, a villain on others. And sometimes he was a villain at the time and a hero later, and vice versa.

I suppose you could say that he was everything, good *and* bad, that everyone who knew him claims he was. At different times, of course, just like the rest of us.

If you ask me that's a pretty good reason why we ought to try and give up judging each other on one performance, usually the kind of performance that it suits us to believe of the person under judgement. It doesn't make sense when you think about it. And yet we all do it, every one of us, all the time — even such hand-picked and faultless bastards as you and I.

In fact the only person I ever knew who didn't pass judgements on people was a bloke called Suggy Benson.

7
Filthy Bastard

Most of us know the difference between the Dirty Bastard and your actual Filthy Bastard only too well. But for the benefit and enlightenment of those who don't know I'll touch briefly on the subject.

Your Dirty Bastard (*Bastardus begrimus*) is simply unfastidious. He's often malodorous, fusty, mucky, scummy or dreggy. He may even be a little mangy, but your actual Filthy Bastard (*Bastardus filthus*) leaves him for dead. A Filthy B. is downright unwholesome. He's offensive and insanitary, feculent, scorbutic, pestilential, verminous, impetiginous, leprous, louse-bound, fly-blown and gangrenous. He's often inclined to be a little sickly as well.

And such a man was old Yorky Spudding. A Filthy B. of the first order. His existence was justified if only because he could be used as an example of how filthy a man can get if he devotes himself wholeheartedly to it for long enough.

Yorky was a pig-farmer and it's a fairly safe bet that few other occupations could have enhanced his aura as well as this one did. And apart from telling you that the cleanest things around there were the pigs, I won't describe Yorky's piggery or the way he maintained it. Such things don't only defy accurate description, but there's no point in upsetting everyone.

Yorky himself had the usual attributes of the fully-qualified Filthy Bastard. He was as filthy as he looked, or looked as filthy as he was, whichever way you cared to look at him. Creased, wrinkled, ragged, caked, clogged, cluttered, smeared, splashed and maggot-gagging. You could tell from a hundred and fifty yards away that he was a genuine gold-plated Filthy Bastard, and if you were down-wind you'd be cheating. If he hadn't been so obviously authentic you'd have sworn they'd spared no effort or expense to have him made-up for a horror movie.

And this brings me to the odour of him. Though odour is not

Bastardus filthus

the word for it. In fact an exhaustive search of the schoolmistress's dictionary brings to light no adequate language to describe the way old Yorky stank. Words like nauseous or fetid fall far short of doing justice to the almost audible fermentation of the way Yorky and his environment ponged.

There was a rumour, probably true, that Yorky's ten acres had once been in the Borough and they'd fought for years until they got the boundary shifted so he'd be in the Country.

One of the things about Filthy Bastards is that they themselves never seem to think there's anything wrong with the way they are. And Yorky was no exception to this. Take the way he never gave up advertising for a housekeeper, for example. He put literally hundreds of ads in the newspapers for a "Housekeeper to care for middle-aged farmer and light farm duties. Live in, etc. . . . Very few of the housekeepers who came to be interviewed for the position ever got out of the taxi at Yorky's gate, and none of them ever spent the night there.

I know I haven't mentioned anything about what Yorky actually *did* to get himself into such an outrageous condition and keep himself in it, but common decency prevents me from describing the Filthy Bastard in greater detail than I have done already. You wouldn't thank me, gentle reader — Hygienic Bastard (*Bastardus sterilizus*) — for going into greater detail about old Yorky. I did note down details of a number of his more well-known escapades and activities, but it was no good. No matter how I tried to temper the acrid material I had to work with, I eventually had to discard it altogether, for fear I'd be accused of exaggerating his filthiness in order to shock my readers.

I make no apologies for moving hastily on to more wholesome subjects.

8
Good Bastard

YOU HAVE TO BE very careful calling someone a Good Bastard. (*Bastardus virtuus*). We can all be Good Bastards when we feel like it and a convenient occasion presents itclf, but to be a Good Bastard all the time, whatever the circumstances, isn't so easy. In fact Real Good Bastards are pretty rare.

The only bastard I ever met who I could honestly say was a *good* one was Mr Jeffries. He lived in the district I was brought up in, and that's about as close as he and I ever got.

He was always polite and considerate and as far as I know he was never known to utter a derogatory remark about anyone in his whole bloody life. He went to church religiously, worked hard, kept a nice garden and always had a gift and a cheery word for anyone who was sick or hard-up or down on their luck. He mowed lawns for old ladies — and kept it up for years. He passed the hat round whenever there was a reason or a chance to. He could be relied upon absolutely and was very active in charity drives and appeals.

He was a great driving-force behind the local Civil Defence Organisation, but there's no doubt that if there *had* been an emergency involving the Civil Defence (and there never was) Mr J. would have been kept well out of it. He was far too good to have been any use in a real emergency.

He was a member of every committee, guild, fraternity, movement, circle, fellowship, brigade, group and panel that couldn't find an excuse to exclude him. And he got more mail than any other private individual I ever knew. He must have written thousands of letters to people all over the world, all of them good ones, of course. In fact Mr J. was so downright bloody good that no one could stand him. Even such spare-time Good Bastards as professional ecclesiastics and dedicated social workers would unashamedly groan aloud their exasperation, in the hearing of anyone who happened to be within earshot, whenever they saw

Bastardus virtuus

that an encounter with the good Mr Jeffries could not be avoided.

Children found him dull and boring and were often quite rude to him, but, being a Real Good Bastard, Mr J. never complained or retaliated or gave up being nice to them. His few and lukewarm friends treated him abominably, but he made excuses for them. His boss promoted men from under and around him, and Mr Jeffries always congratulated them warmly.

In the finish his wife couldn't stand it any longer and she up and left him without even bothering to tell him why, and, like a true Good Bastard, Mr J. took the blame.

Even the Jehovah's Witnesses found that there was nothing they could teach him about human goodness. The only kind of person I could think of who would be able to take the good Mr J.'s goodness would have to be someone as good as himself, and although I've kept a wary eye out for them all my life I've never come across another one. But then it's not likely that I'm moving in the right circles for that kind of thing these days.

It'd be nice to be able to tell you that Mr Jeffries eventually reaped the rewards of his long lifetime of service to his fellow man, but, alas, I have to report that he was carried off during an epidemic by a squadron of Asian-flu germs, against whom he'd never so much as uncorked a bottle of vapour-rub or fired a salvo of aerosol in his whole virtuous life.

I wonder where he is now. I somehow can't see him or heaven gaining anything by his residence there, but then the other place doesn't seem right for him either. Perhaps there's a special kind of halfway-house where Good Bastards go when they pass on, where they can spend their days being as good to each other as they like without anyone getting embarrassed about it. I hope so.

9
Hard-case Bastard

WHICH BRINGS US TO the Hard-case Bastard (*Bastardus waggus*). Everyone knows him. He's widely distributed throughout the various strata of society, though he usually prefers the working-class environment. He's often found in the drinking-schools, parties, working gangs, and generally wherever people gather together. In fact it's a measly group indeed that hasn't got its Hard-case to liven things up a bit.

His size ranges from small and weedy to big, fat and benign, and he's often referred to as "the life and soul of the party".

One of the characteristics of the H-c. B. is his inability to endure inactivity or silence, and from the time he wakes up in the morning until he finally crashes at night (often from sheer exhaustion) he's continually on the go. Playing tricks, taking the micky out of the boss, teasing people, and generally organising unusual and often hilarious departures from the normal course of things.

One of the most remarkable attributes of the Hard-case Bastard is his memory for jokes, and when he's not actually actively engaged in some other kind of hard-casery he keeps up an almost continuous running patter of jokes from his seemingly inexhaustible fund of them.

In fact one soon learns not to try telling a joke when there's a H-c. Bastard around because he won't even wait for the laughter from your joke to die down properly before he launches into one of his own. Usually the same type of joke as yours (e.g. Dad and Dave; Englishman, Irishman and Scotsman; Bill Smith and the Pope etc. etc.) whatever it is, but it's always a so much *better* joke than yours. So much better-told and up-to-date, and so much funnier than your pathetic effort, that you feel ashamed of yourself for having had the appalling bad form to try and put one across in the first place.

Fortunately it doesn't usually matter as much as it might do, because once started on a joke-telling session, the Hard-case

Bastardus waggus

Bastard can only be stopped by one of two things: (a) the breaking-up of the group, or (b) the intrusion of something on the group's attention with at least the impact of a power-cut (e.g. the beer running out). As for a genuine Hard-case Bastard running out of jokes — it doesn't happen.

One of the Hard-case Bastards I knocked around with for a while was undoubtedly the very best joke-teller I ever knew — Willy Driver. If we were in a restaurant Willy'd come up with one about a restaurant. If we saw a dog he'd come up with the one about why a dog cocks his leg — or one of the dozens he seemed to have at his very tongue-tip.

He had jokes for every occasion and I never saw him stumped for one, or even hesitate. Doctor jokes, lawyer jokes, travelling salesman jokes, tramp jokes, gangster jokes, mad-house jokes, man-falling-from-a-skyscraper jokes, Indian chief jokes, hospital jokes, chemist-shop jokes, Young Johnny jokes, Eskimo jokes, eunuch jokes, psychologist jokes, prostitute jokes, corny jokes, sick jokes, clean and hairy-dog jokes. And I must say I don't remember him ever telling the same joke twice.

Typical of Hard-case Bastards, Willy was rarely in *serious* trouble with the authorities, but on the other hand he was rarely far off it. He seemed to be always on his last chance with someone or other, or being warned that if it happened again he'd be in for it.

I remember once it was the local magistrate. He pointed out that Willy had been up before him eleven times in two years for minor traffic and other offences, and eleven times he'd had to be warned about contempt of court.

"But I'm accident-prone," interrupted Willy. "I can't help it."

"Silence!" said his Honour, banging on the bar with his little wooden knocker. "Any more of these outbursts and I'll hold you in contempt of court."

"But damn it all, Mick, you know yourself that it wasn't me who lifted them chooks. I was over at Bob's place on the Saturday and I'd have mentioned it to him if it'd been me!"

"You will address me as Your Honour," said the magistrate, banging on his bar.

"Sorry Mick," said Willy. "It was just that I was upset about being falsely accused . . ."

"I'm dismissing this charge because of insufficient evidence," said the Magistrate. "But I'm seriously considering replacing it with one of contempt. I'm not at all satisfied with your attitude towards this court."

"Thanks, Mick," said Willy. "Will you be over the club tonight?"

How Willy got away with it nobody knew. There were rumours that he was related to the magistrate through marriage but I think that was probably just an attempt to explain the unexplainable — how the hell he did it.

Another time it was Willy's boss. He'd warned Willy dozens of times that dozens of things had to stop. But Willy had dozens more little capers up his sleeve. This time it was a two-day rodeo that suddenly turned up and started being held in the boss's front paddock. It didn't take long to establish that it was the Master of Ceremonies, Willy Driver himself, who was behind it all.

There wasn't much the boss could do about it because the rodeo was to raise funds for a swimming pool for the local school and the boss had a great tribe of kids.

"I didn't actually tell them they could hold the rodeo here," explained Willy when his livid boss bailed him up about it. "I told them you'd be only too happy to help out."

Anyone else would have got the bullet right off, but, like most Hard-case Bastards, Willy was a hard man to replace on the job. Their ingenuity comes in real handy when there's any kind of emergency on. And Willy's boss knew this only too well, and what's more Willy knew his boss knew it only too well. And what's more than that, Willy's boss knew his Hard-case Bastards well enough not to have more than one of them on the payroll at any one time. Put a couple of Hard-case Bastards together and they're so busy trying to out-hard-case each other that not much work gets done, though some of the things they come up with get talked about in the district for years.

In fact many of the traditions of an area are established by the activities of Hard-case Bastards. Like the time Willy and another bloke of similar inclinations commandeered the boss's D-9 bulldozer and shoved a huge rock that marked the historic resting-place of a great Maori chief to another location 300 yards farther along the road and replaced it with an old kitchen sofa.

The main critics of Hard-case Bastards are their so-called victims, or people without much sense of humour. Like the time Willy and I had a terrific opening morning of the duck-shooting season. Limit bags, and no-one else did any good. The rumour got put around that we'd been poaching in the sanctuary, but we knew it was only because some of them were a bit sour about us having a bit of good luck and being terrifically good shots.

In fact it's worth noting that the rumour gained a great deal of momentum after the postmaster's letterbox, the glovebox of Jeff Willett's new Rambler, and Willy's boss's overcoat pockets were all found to be stuffed tight with duck feathers. (All these people, I might point out, were notoriously humourless and therefore fair game to a Hard-case Bastard.)

No, there's no doubt about the Hard-case Bastard, life would be pretty dull without him, wouldn't it?

He's the natural entertainer of this world in a way. He really enjoys entertaining other people and doesn't expect any other reward for his efforts than the delight of his audience.

Have you ever noticed that there are very few Real Hard-case Bastards in the entertainment business? Their performance seems to depend on their almost uncanny sense of what they can get away with, and it has a kind of spontaneity that you could never get through a radio or television set. They can get away with things that'd get you or I chucked out on our ears. They've got a hard-case way of telling slightly-off jokes in polite company, or putting the hard word on the host's wife and getting away with it.

I reckon we could do with more of the brand of good humour that inspires the Hard-case Bastard. He ignores the rules whenever he sees the opportunity to do so amusingly, but never deliberately hurt anybody. His ribbing seldom hurts anyone's feelings. He raves almost continuously, but you don't hear him slandering or gossiping about other people, and when somebody's in trouble the Hard-case Bastard is usually the first to come to light with a bit of practical assistance.

There's no doubt that he can become a bit tiresome or irritating at times, but when you think about it life wouldn't be the same without the imaginative carryings-on of the Hard-case Bastard.

Bless him. As a matter of fact, good reader, I can tell by the way you've been reading this that underneath it all you're a bit of a Hard-case Bastard yourself.

10
Intellectual Bastard

I MET A BRILLIANT man once. You couldn't tell he was brilliant just by looking at him, but he was. Everybody said so. He was a brilliant lecturer or architect or something.

He wasn't what you'd call a handsome man, or a well-dressed one. Nor was he particularly charming, or witty, or interesting. As a matter of fact he was bloody rude. He couldn't talk about anything or any one except himself. He interrupted conversations, ate with his mouth open and generally made everyone squirm by his sheer lack of consideration and common decency.

It didn't take me long to see that I'd run into a fully-fledged Intellectual Bastard (*Bastardus profoundus*). He was typical of them; he claimed to be an intellectual but he was really just a bastard. Half a dozen of the hundreds of obscure poems he'd written had been published in obscure literary magazines subsidised by the arts grants, so he called himself a poet.

He was phoney and ignorant, and, like all Intellectual Bastards, he protected his ignorance by assuming an air of shaky superciliousness. His intellectualness was based on such things as throwing references to obscure subjects into the conversation and leaving you stumped for words. There's not a great deal you *can* say to such things, "Of course Domingo Faustino Sarmiento in *Defence of Freedom* claims that the press is a *virtue*, rather than a collection of type-face." You either have to brave his scorn and confess that you've never head of Domingo Faustino Sarmiento, or, agree with him. Either way there's an uneasy silence because he's interrupted the flow of the conversation and the atmosphere of the gathering and it always takes a while to get going again after a thing like that happens. It's not worth trying to pin him down or prove him wrong because nearly everything he says is quoted from some musty book or other and the best you can hope for is to prove the book wrong, while he goes scot-free.

Few people speak so much and say so little as the Intellectual

Bastardus profoundus

Bastard, and they're usually talking such ephemeral, arrant nonsense that nobody could articulate about it, and the "um" and "ah" and croak and groan in between their words like somebody with a speech-impediment.

Most types of bastards are versatile enough to switch from one kind of bastardry to another, depending on the requirements of the situation, but the Intellectual Bastard is so busy maintaining his precarious perch above the rest of us that he can't let go for fear of falling in amongst us. Unthinkable! Everything he has an impulse to say must be carefully processed and worked out before he says it because the Intellectual Bastard must be absolutely correct in all he says at all times.

The result of this is that he's rarely ever right, but since he can't see it he doesn't know about it, and because he doesn't know about it it doesn't matter, because he knows everything that *does* matter.

His humour is a kind of acerbic wit that, boiled down, amounts to petty, catty, criticisms of other people. He can't fight and he can't work and he's a pacifist because he's frightened of losing his temper, and his view of that is as outrageously exaggerated as his self-importance — roughly proportionate to his *actual* importance.

As far as I'm concerned the Intellectual Bastard is a man with a great quantity of information and a great lack of knowledge. The poor bastard's the victim of the Great Academic Confidence Trick, usually worded something like, "You'll get nowhere these days without a degree behind you." And our student, hundreds of thousands of times too often, interprets this as, "I feel like I do because I haven't got a university degree. Once I get *that* everything is going to be all right. I won't feel anxious or inadequate any more. People will be nicer to me. I'll be offered jobs in high places at high salaries. Women will compete for my company. I'll be rich and famous and never have to worry about myself ever again."

And so he embarks on his chosen career of Intellectual Bastardry. After many years of study he finally graduates with the only experiences he's had during these prime years having been ones to do with studying for a university degree, and that's all the *knowledge* he can logically claim to have.

Unfortunately the only people qualified to either confirm or deny this state of affairs are those with university degrees, but by the time they've made it they're so thoroughly indoctrinated and personally committed that to explode the Academic Myth calls on them to acknowledge that their years of study and effort have been almost completely wasted. So they blindly go on supporting something that they know underneath isn't working for them, never did work for them, and probably never will work for them. This causes them to become defensive and aggressive and anxious to prove how much more than us they know — how inferior we are to them.

Perhaps the most effective way of silencing an Intellectual Bastard would be to present him with a ledger, with all he's ever *done* in one column, and the time it's taken him to do it in the other. Which goes to demonstrate that if there was any tangible way to assess the qualities of the Intellectual Bastard he wouldn't exist.

I haven't got a university degree and never had the opportunity to decide whether I wanted one or not, but I'm taking this opportunity, patient reader — Understanding Bastard (*Bastardus allknowingus*) — to tell you how pleased I am that you and I never turned out to be Intellectual Bastards.

11
Jovial Bastard

JOVIAL BASTARDS (*Bastardus jocundus*) are okay. At least they're cheerful.

Toby Mercer was about the *most* Jovial Bastard I ever met. He was so by-jovial about everything it was hard to get him to be serious. He was too big and round and bland to be anything but jovial, no matter what the circumstances were. We used to call him Ho-ho, because of him going ho-ho all the time.

"You couldn't lend me sixteen bucks, Toby," I said to him one day. "They're coming to repossess my car. I'll pay you back on payday."

"Ho-ho," said Toby. "I've only got four dollars left over from backing that double you said was going to pay a fortune last Saturday," And he slapped me on the back and told me I could borrow his pushbike to go to work on after they'd taken my car away.

Of course being a compulsory Jovialist isn't plain sailing. There were places you couldn't take Toby — funerals, for instance. I'll never forget the time I took him to my cousin's wedding. He didn't go over very well at all. Everyone got the impression that Toby was enjoying some huge joke of his own about the marriage. He and I both knew it was *their* guilty conscience. We couldn't help it if it was hard not to see that my cousin and his bride had left things a bit late in the day to get married.

The magistrate fined Toby an extra five bucks for contempt of court once. But he was really only being jovial about being fined thirty dollars for drinking after hours in the pub.

Come to think about it there were quite a few times when things would have gone much better for him if Toby had taken a more serious view of them. I remember once we were on our way back from the races at Ellerslie, broke as seven thousand bastards, and I had a go at getting a bloke in a milkbar to cash a cheque for me. I had him talked into it and was actually writing out the

Bastardus jocundus

cheque, when the milkbar bloke started getting uneasy about Toby grinning.

What's the joke?" he asked me, leaving my cheque on the counter.

"No joke," I said.

"Your mate seems to think so."

"Oh him," I said. "He always does that. He thinks everything's a joke. Don't you, Toby?"

"Ho-ho," said Toby, to show the milkbar bloke how jokey he thought everything was.

And as I watched him I saw the milkbar bloke go right off the idea of cashing that cheque for me.

"Sorry mate," he said, pushing the cheque back to my side of the counter as though it was infectious. "Try the bloke at the service station along here. He sometimes cashes cheques."

But of course the bloke at the service station didn't interpret Toby's ho-hoing any more accurately than the milkbar bloke had.

That night it was freezing cold and we were trying to kip down in a bus shelter when blow me down if a couple of cops in a prowl car didn't spring us. And while I was giving them our hardluck story Toby started ho-hoing again, and in the finish they got suspicious of us and took us in to the station. I could tell they were suspicious because they kept asking Toby questions about drugs. One of them seemed to have the idea that Toby was taking the micky out of him but it turned out all right in the finish. They gave us a cell to bunk down in.

If it hadn't been for Toby's ho-hoing we'd have been stuck in that bus shelter all night — but then if it hadn't been for his ho-hoing we'd have been home in bed and none of it would have happened in the first place.

It was the same the time Toby got involved in a car accident. The other bloke was indisputably in the wrong: he'd failed to stop at a compulsory stop sign and driven blindly out into the traffic, failing to give way on his right, and driven fair into the side of Toby's car. But it was Toby they took in for a blood alcohol test.

He told me later he was overjoyed that no-one had been injured and his car was covered by insurance and not even badly damaged, but the traffic officer described it as, "unnatural levity in the circumstances". It was obvious that the traffic cop didn't know about Jovial Bastards like Toby. It takes more than a minor traffic accident, or a bad day at the races, or a fine for after-hours drinking — or even a broken leg — to quell their joviality; their cheerful sense of optimism. Even so, Toby's brand of it had its drawbacks. His joviality got us the sack in the finish. We were driving trucks for a real Neurotic Bastard (*Bastardus tormentus*) of a bloke. My truck had broken a fan-belt and Toby was giving me a hand to put a new one on it, in the yard, when the boss arrived.

"What are you men doing there?" said the boss.

"Ho-ho," said Toby. "We've got a broken fan-belt. Just putting a new one on. Ho-ho."

"Who told you to do that?" demanded the boss. "Where's the mechanic?"

"Ho-ho," said Toby again. "No need to trouble him with it. We'll have it done in a couple of shakes, ho-ho."

"What's so funny about it," said the boss.

I could see that he was getting a bit strung-up about Toby saying ho-ho to him all the time. *I* mustn't laugh or he'd get really het-up — might even sack us on the spot, which we'd seen him do once or twice before — so I started grinning my head off. Couldn't help myself. Toby didn't help much, either.

"Ho-ho," he said. "It's not as serious as all that. We'll have this old tub back on the road again in no time, ho-ho."

By this time I couldn't hide my stupid grinning and the boss couldn't take it.

"Well *I* think it's very funny," he said sarcastically. "It's so bloody funny you can just ho-ho down to the office and pick up your time. Both of you!"

"Ho-ho," said Toby, as the boss got into his car and roared off.

And that was that.

It's hard for Sour Bastards (*Bastardus bitterus*) like that to believe everyone doesn't feel like they do. And, looking back on it, most of Toby's trouble was simply a matter of people not taking him at face value. They were actually suspicious of his good humour.

I often wonder where old Ho-ho is these days. It's years since I last saw him, but wherever he is and whatever he's doing, he's cheerful about it, no matter how misunderstood his joviality is.

12
Kinky Bastard

HE'S FAIRLY RARE, THE Kinky Bastard (*Bastardus loopus*). Given to playing tricks of a certain kind, often involving such things as books about sex that give you an electric shock when you open them, cushions that make unpleasant noises when you sit on them, flowers that squirt water in your face, itching powder in your sleeping bag, plastic spiders, vomits and other such delightful paraphernalia.

Kinky Bastards must be fairly widely spread because you see from the advertisements that there are people who actually manufacture and distribute this kind of gear — and, presumably, people who buy the stuff.

One Kinky Bastard on his own can usually be kept fairly harmless, but get two of them together and you've got to watch it. Three or more of them in a pack can be downright dangerous. At this point they become what is known as a Pack of Bastards. They're plain irresponsible, rather than deliberately harmful, but you have to be careful when they're about.

I knew one such Kinky Bastard who took great delight in giving people frights. He and a couple of his mates once filled a balloon with oxygen and acetylene mixture and taped it around a spark-plug of the car one of our mates was going on his honeymoon in. The couple came out of the reception with everyone waving goodbye, congratulating them, and wishing them good luck, but as soon as the groom touched the starter of the car the balloon exploded with a deafening bang and a sheet of flame. Blew the bonnet right off the car.

It was two weeks before our mate's new missus had sufficiently recovered from the shock for them to get on with their honeymoon. We knew well enough who was most likely to have done it but naturally they all denied having anything to do with it and there was nothing anyone could prove.

One of the things about Kinky Bastards is that they never learn.

Bastardus loopus

That bunch's next little trick was to pinch the toilet roll from a house we were having a party at and on their way home they ran a strip of it up the road, so that the white line curving around a bend ran on into the bank. The driver of the car that ran off the road there later that night had the usual chances of being injured or killed. As it happened the damage was slight, which was fortunate for everyone concerned.

That was when we discovered a good line of treatment for Kinky Bastards; their own medicine is an anathema to them. Some Kinky Bastard went and put a handful of sugar in the petrol-tank of their car, and another kept squirting dishwashing detergent into their jugs of beer while other Kinky Bastards diverted their attention.

And the hurt feelings of a Kinky Bastard who's had one put across him are touching to hear him complain about. The indignation, the outrage, the persecution and the sheer unfairness of it all is too heart-rending to contemplate. The suffering of a Kinky Bastard is seldom less than the very limit of human endurance.

It's hard to know what's easier to put up with — the Kinky Bastard's pranks, or his grizzling when he's on the receiving end of one of them. Even his apologies are hard to stomach.

It's not much wonder that the Kinky is one of the most studiously avoided of all Bastards. The thing that strikes me most about them is *that* they're Kinky Bastards. They're either too bored or too self-important for ordinary things to have "the desired effect" on them any more. It's got to be "way out", or "weird" or some other such thing, to appeal to their either jaded or undeveloped tastes.

They're welcome to it.

13
Lazy Bastard

ARNEY SLOAN WAS A Lazy Bastard (*Bastardus loafus*) of the first order. He was in his thirties when I met him, and in spite of the fact that he was known locally as "The Late Mr Sloan" I immediately got the unshakable impression that he was going to live for hundreds of years.

It was hard at first to believe it wasn't some kind of act he was putting on but no, it was the dinkum oil all right. He was born, bone lazy. He was so lazy he didn't even move fast enough to keep himself awake half the time, and he'd been found asleep in all sorts of unusual places.

I invited him in for a cup of tea one morning and went into the house ahead of him to get it ready. By the time I'd poured the tea Arney still hadn't come into the kitchen from the back porch, where I'd left him taking his boots off. So I had a look and found him fast asleep, sitting on the top step, leaning against the doorway, with one boot half-unlaced.

It's often true of Lazy Bastards that there's *something* they're not lazy in. Some sport, or hobby or other activity they can be encouraged to put a little bit of energy and effort into, but not so with Arney. He was a *Real* Lazy Bastard. A professional to his untrimmed fingertips. There was *nothing* he wasn't lazy about. I understand it took him four years to get through the primers at school, and by the time he left school at seventeen he'd only made it as far as form one. He wasn't dull-witted, or stupid, or unintelligent, or even careless — just lazy.

In fact it's a pretty safe bet that if Arney had been more widely-known his name would have come into the language as the perfect cliché to describe Lazy Bastards in general. (E.g. "A real *Arney Sloane* of a joker!").

He was literally too lazy to come in out of the rain. Always getting wet because he was too slow getting his coat on or getting under shelter. They'd tried to teach him to swim but had

Bastardus loafus

to give it up for fear he'd drown himself crossing the school swimming baths, for Arney a matter of endurance. And riding a bike or driving a car was absolutely out of the question for him. Neither would travel slowly enough.

Of course they'd investigated the possibility that there might be something physically wrong with Arney, but the doctors and specialists his folks consulted were unanimous. They all reported, in their discreet jargon, that he was simply a Lazy Bastard of average intelligence, ability and stature.

Arney's folks knew better than to even try sending him out to work. He just stayed on to help out round their small farm, and it says a lot of their ingenuity that they'd managed to find ways for him to be useful. For example he was an excellent gardener. He could grow anything you liked, and grow it well. It was well known that his vegetables and flowers were the best around, although many things grew a little impetuously for him at times, and he was in a constant hectic rush to keep ahead of the weeds that he was convinced sprang up behind him as soon as he turned his back. And looking at it from his pace and point of view this would be quite true of course.

His mother told me once that as a child Arney had given them no trouble whatever, too lazy to misbehave, or even get sick, I suppose. It's certainly true that he was never likely to get himself into trouble with the authorities. He was too lazy to do anything illegal, except perhaps loiter.

You may get the impression from all this that Arney was a goof, or a dope, but he wasn't. He was actually quite an interesting bloke to talk to, if you had plenty of time. He had a kind of *pace* about him that was very restful. A way of talking and moving that made you wonder what all the rush and bustle was about anyway. But I must say that after about half an hour of it you'd start getting the feeling that you hadn't had enough sleep the night before. And before you could get away from him you'd be yawning your head off. It always took me an hour or so to get myself moving properly after I'd been having a natter with Arney.

I don't know about you, dear reader — Energetic Bastard (*Bastardus whirlwindus*) — but I used to feel sorry for Lazy Bastards like Arney. Now I'm not so sure. They don't have such a hard time of it when you consider that they never get sent to fetch anything, or do anything there's any hurry to get done. And that includes just about everything in these hectic times. No one expects them to be "on time", or efficient, or stick to schedules, or even pull their weight. They just get left alone to do their own things in their own time. And yet you couldn't really call them Useless Bastards (*Bastardus nonentus*). That's a different category altogether.

Maybe they've been sent among us to remind us that we're taking things too seriously and too fast for our own good. In a world full of criticism of each other, where anything we do is liable to be wrong in *somebody's* opinion, there's few less harmful and objectionable types than the good old Lazy Bastard.

14
Miserable Bastard

YOU'VE BEEN LUCKY INDEED if you haven't run into any Miserable Bastards (*Bastardus woebegoneus*) in your time. Goodness knows, there's plenty of them around, and they never seem to go to any trouble to conceal their miserableness. Mean-ness is one of their main things, and it's a well-known fact that many well-to-do people fall into this category.

If "a man of means" means a mean man, then I think I know what it means. I mean — look at it this way, have you ever met a man of means who wasn't a mean man? Ever tried collecting money for charity? Or hitching a lift on a wet night? Not that they mean to be mean, I don't suppose, but when a man becomes a man of means he usually seems to automatically become a mean man. Or perhaps a man has to be a mean man in order to *qualify* as a man of means. Ah — to hell with it. It's no good trying to make excuses for them; it all boils down to the simple fact that they're bastards — and Miserable Bastards at that.

The Miserable Bastards I'm going to tell you about were not actually men of means, but their Miserableness was unarguable. I'd been hanging around waiting for a job at the shipyards to come up and my money was running out, so I decided to take a temporary job to tide me over. And I finally landed one in an office where they handled accounts for a big distributing outfit. Right in amongst four of the most Miserable Bastards I've ever come across.

It looked to me as though Mr Walker had been promoted to boss because nobody else would take it on. He was always busy and harrassed but you could never tell what he was actually *doing*. He was so preoccupied with things "not getting done" that he had no idea who was shirking and who was working. And when things got too far behind he'd come round complaining that he had to take the brunt. He was one of those blokes who didn't seem to have ever heard about optimism. Nothing ever went right

Bastardus woebegoneus

as far as he was concerned, and he was never more disconcerted than when he was hard-up for something or someone's inefficiency to complain about. Even the men who worked for him complained about his pessimistic view of life, and that's really saying something.

Roger, at the desk opposite mine, was iron-grey and hearty, in a miserable kind of way. He avoided as many of the monthly charge-accounts as he could and bluffed his way somehow through the rest. He was always protesting that his balance-sheets were absolutely correct, or that he hadn't been chosen to play rep. rugby for the college he went to years before.

He seemed to be married but went out of his way to be a bachelor in front of the girls in the outer office. One of them was always on the very verge of cracking him one every time he lechered around her, but Roger didn't seem to be aware of the effect he had on her, or anyone else, for that matter.

Alex, in the far corner of the office, was leathery, lined and leaning, with an aggressive misleading handshake and as miserable a disposition as it's ever been my misfortune to be confined in the same office with. He wore tight collars, chain-smoked, and had been forced to give up his own business because of bad health. He kept bottles of pills in his pockets and desk drawers and was full of endless misinformation about the political situation.

I was a bit chary of Alex, and it seemed to be mutual. Whenever I approached his desk he hastily covered whatever he was doing with papers and books, as though the Overdue Accounts he dealt with were highly classified information. It was rumoured that Alex took his wife's false teeth to work with him in case she ate too much while he was away. He was such a Miserable Bastard he'd pretend not to have noticed you arrive, rather than spend a "Good morning" on you.

Harold fretted nervously over "Discounts and Refunds" at the desk opposite Alex. He was petulant and never to blame, and he'd probably caught his severe miserableness from the environment he worked in as though it was a rampant virus. He was always shifting his weightless support back and forth between Roger's and Alex's phoney lack of antagonism towards one another. He distrusted me because I wouldn't take sides in his one-sided, unspoken quarrels with the rest of them.

Most of the work in the place was finally put together and concluded by Walker's secretary, Mrs Smith, the only one I liked in the whole outfit. But she didn't like me and we hardly ever spoke to one another.

Mrs Smith had been there for uncountable years and during the changes of staff she'd survived she'd had to learn and teach every different job in the office and she was the only one who actually understood how it all worked. I don't think she had any idea that she was the key figure in the whole business. None of them were likely to tell her, either, the miserable bastards.

I stuck it out for two weeks, an eternity, and as soon as old Walker had been round with my first pay-envelope I suddenly decided to leave before the atmosphere of misery and complaint infected me beyond recovery. But I just couldn't walk out without saying goodbye to Roger, Alex and Harold.

So I put everything that was mine into my pockets and went over to where Harold was shuffling through papers as though he'd just lost one of them.

"Here, Harold," I said, slipping him a folded dollar note I'd got ready. "You'd better put this towards it. I'm sorry I can't make it a bit more, but I've had to pay him not to report *me*."

Harold was so taken by surprise that he took the money, and I could see that there was no need for me to say anything else because he'd gone as white as a dismissal-notice. So I nodded understandingly, patted him on the shoulder, and went across to Alex, who shuffled the letter he was writing under some papers on his desk and gave me a hostile look.

"What do you want?" he said. "You'll get us all into trouble if Walker comes in — hanging around the desks like this."

I bent down so close to his ear that he nearly fell off his chair trying to get further away from me.

"You'd better get onto him before he takes this thing any further," I whispered urgently.

"Who! Who! What are you talking about?" he whispered back. And he started shooting quick, nervous glances around the office as though he'd just heard someone was sneaking up on him.

"I'll try and back you up, of course," I whispered, "but it'll cost you hundreds if it ever gets as far as the courts."

And before he could say anything else I left him and went across to Roger, who'd seen that something was going on and had his hearty guilt ready to receive me.

"What's wrong with Alex," he said. "Looks as though he's been caught cooking the books," he joked nervously.

And on the spur of the moment I took him up on it. "I'd be very careful about spreading these rumours, if I were you, Mr Samson," I warned him severely. "Nothing is going to be decided until my report has been considered by the board."

That set him back on his miserable heels better than anything I could have thought up without his help.

"You mean you're from . . ." he stammered. "You've been . . ."

"I'm not in a position to say any more, at this juncture," I interrupted him. "And I strongly advise you to keep the whole matter entirely to yourself."

"Well you won't find anything wrong with *my* books," he blustered guiltily.

"That remains to be seen," I said.

And I left the office, ignoring Alex's nervous jerking and hissing for me to come over to his desk and tell him "who" and "what".

"That should give them something to be miserable about," I said to Mrs Smith on my way past her desk and out into the street.

And I wasn't even tempted to go back and see what happened to The Miserable Bastards.

15
Nasty Bastard

WE ALL KNOW HIM. He infests every stratum of our overloaded society, and he spreads treachery and deception wherever he goes amongst us.

I speak of course, of the Nasty Bastard (*Bastardus notquiteniceus*). The kind of bastard who doesn't know how to be honourable or honest. He doesn't lie and cheat by accident, or to protect anyone else's feelings, or to get himself out of trouble, he does it automatically, without regard for the consequences to himself or anyone else.

One of the unfortunate characteristics of the Nasty Bastard is that he's always on the move, spreading his maliciousness far and wide. This is mainly because his activities start catching up on him after a while and rather than permit himself to be confronted by the truth or face the consequences of his deceptions he takes to his miserable scrapers and sets himself up in his troublous practices somewhere else.

Bertie (the germ) Bell was a Nasty Bastard, and, as with most of his kind, he had the knack of taking people in at first. On acquaintance, even if somebody warned you about him, you were impressed by his worldliness and his adroit knack of flattery; his unconcerned attitude towards money (although he never seemed to actually *have* any). But it wouldn't be long before his true colours emerged. At the first opportunity he'd bounce one of his rubber cheques on you, or — even worse — he'd get you to bounce one on someone else for him, and in such a way there wouldn't be much you could do about it.

Bertie used to hang around the periphery of our group, not being either welcome or qualified to join us. He was the sort of bastard you had to be downright rude to before you could get rid of him. And nobody liked to do that because they knew it'd spoil the atmosphere of the party or drinking-school they were in. He'd make strong men furious with themselves for having

Bastardus notquiteniceus

to cross streets or make excuses of previous engagements in order to avoid his unpleasant company.

Occasionally some misguided soul would take pity on little Bertie and try to be friends with him. This always had the effect of causing Bertie to despise them and they inevitably suffered for their pains. He'd either steal from them, try to get them to steal *for* him, or cause trouble between them and the rest of their friends. So the aim was to avoid Bertie and, temporarily, anyone who was with him. He was too much a Nasty Bastard.

He cheated at games. He stole small change. He passed detrimental information, often *false* information, back and forth between friends and groups. He stole whenever there was an opportunity combined with a good chance of his getting away with it or blaming someone else. He'd start fights and if he couldn't avoid getting involved in them it'd be Bertie who'd use a bottle or a broken glass on someone who was already down. Then he would swear it was somebody else.

Like most Nasty Bastards, Bertie wasn't unknown to the police by any means. It was well known that he had an unenviable list of convictions for crimes involving double-dealing, fiddling, petty-theft, shoplifting, consorting, drug-possession, cashing dud cheques, and other such shabby and wretched offences. And it was less well-known that he was suspected in some circles of being a police-informer, and rumour had it that he was only at large because of the useful information he passed on to the authorities about the criminal scene. So that law-abiding citizens and criminals (and those in-between) all avoided Bertie as though he was a rampant plague all of his own.

Bertie was a journalist and specialised in ferreting out stories of sordid interest for Sunday newspapers. The kind of story that is damaging to the names and reputations of those involved, without making any difference to the world at large. Things like divorce and adultery, sex crimes, and details of perverse and other unsavoury offences — these were the tools of Bertie's unwholesome trade.

And if that's not a Nasty Bastard I don't know what is.

The last I heard of Bertie he was in trouble with a private detective agency. Apparently they'd recruited him to play the part of "the other man" in a jacked-up divorce case. They paid him half the money and told him when and where to report for duty. But while he and the woman were waiting in the motel unit to be caught in compromising circumstances by the people from the private detective agency Bertie decided to take advantage of the situation — no one could be expected to believe he was being something so un-nasty as conscientious — and the result of it was that when the rest of them got there all hell was in the process of breaking loose. The woman was tearing around half-dressed in the motel car-park, yelling out that she was being raped, while Bertie was in the office trying to get them to ring a taxi for him.

They managed to keep the police out of it, but the divorce thing was a complete wash-out. And Bertie only escaped a charge of indecent assault because of his unhesitating willingness to expose the whole bunch of them. They even had to pay him the other half of his fee to try and keep him quiet about it, but this wasn't at all successful. Bertie couldn't wait to tell everybody he met. In fact if the story hadn't been verified by a mate of ours whose brother-in-law runs the motel where it happened none of us would have believed a word of it.

And all that was only a couple of months ago so it looks as though if Bertie is ever going to change for the better it won't be for a while yet.

16
Officious Bastard

YOU FIND HIM IN GOVERNMENT Departments and in the lower gears of business-corporation coggery. He usually asks you if he can help you in a way that leaves you in no doubt that you've got yourself embroiled in the starchy, ritualistic caution of the Officious Bastard (*Bastardus correctus*). And the very presence of one of the Officious Bastards is enough to reduce the average Unruffable Bastard (*Bastardus coolus*) to jibbering obsequiousness.

I went one day to get the electricity turned on in a flat I'd just rented and ran into it head-on. I'd been waiting around in the big glass electricity building just long enough for the atmosphere to un-nerve me when I saw one of them moving towards me. Slow and preoccupied, like a man who's just been told he hasn't long to live and can't work out how to put in the rest of his time. He came right up to me and just as I thought he was going right past he suddenly acknowledged that he'd seen me. He said.

"Can I help you, sir?"

And like a fool, not knowing whether he could help me or not, I said, "Yes." And then I added, "I'd like to get the power put on."

"I see," he said. But he said it very slowly and cautiously, as though I'd told him I wanted to test a nuclear device in the basement of the Power Board Building and he'd never had to deal with such a request before. And then, after a thoughtful pause, he said, "What address?"

I told him the address.

"Are you the consumer?" he asked me.

"Have you filled in your application form?" he asked me.

"No," I said. "I haven't."

"Well you'll have to fill one of those in," he said. "They're on the desk over there."

So I went and got one of their application forms and filled it

Bastardus correctus,

in. Name, address, how long I'd been there, previous address, how long I'd been *there* — etc. etc., and then I had to wait to get to see the same Officious Bastard again. He went through the application form and then told me to wait and went off somewhere.

There's an uneasy guilty feeling when an Officious Bastard takes a form you've just filled with information about yourself and goes off to check it, but this one didn't keep me long. He was back in about five minutes and I could see by the way he approached that something had been decided or resolved.

"Would you come through please," he said to me. "The Credit Manager would like a word with you."

So I followed him into the glassy-eyed office of his Credit Manager, who sat behind a desk that was bare except for my application form.

"Sit down, Mr — er — Mumble," he said. "You're the new tenant of this — er — flat," he accused me, checking everything he said against the incriminating information on the application form.

"Yes," I confessed.

"I see," he said. "We've had a lot of trouble with the previous tenants of this particular property, Mr — er — Clamp. There's still an outstanding account owing for electricity from last May and June."

"I don't know anything about that," I told him. "I just want the power turned on."

"I see," he said. "Well we'll have to get a deposit of six dollars from you. A guarantee, you understand."

"That's okay," I said, getting my wallet out. "When can you turn the power on?"

"There'll be a re-connection fee of two dollars, fifty," he went on. "We had to disconnect the supply for non-payment of the account."

"Here you are then," I said, and offered him ten dollars to show him I had moncy.

"You'll have to pay the cashier in the outer office," he said.

"Oh," I said. "All right then, I'll do that. Is there anything else you want from me?"

"I think that'll be all, thank you," he said. "I'll hand your application on to the Service Department."

"When will my power be turned on?" I asked him.

"Oh — it should be on by tomorrow," he said.

"But what am I going to do tonight!" I said.

"Well, you *have* left it a little late in the day," he said doubtfully, looking at his watch. "All the vehicles will be out on the road by this time. We're very busy just now," he added.

"But I've just moved in," I said. "I haven't even unpacked, and I've only got today off work. There's no hot water or anything."

"We can't help that, Mr — er — Clump. You should have come in earlier."

"But I *couldn't* get in any earlier," I said desperately. "Isn't there anything you can do to hurry it up?"

And suddenly I saw that this particular Officious Bastard had got what he wanted. I was grovelling. He was now prepared to exert his authority on my behalf.

"Well in that case," he said magniloquently, "I'll see what I can do for you. I won't promise anything, mind, but I may be able to have a word with the head of our Service Department."

I was overwhelmed. This bureaucratic dignitary was actually going to pull strings for me; use his far-reaching influence and sway to get the power on for me; bring into play his power-behind-the-throne of the Electricity Department, just so I could have electric light and hot water; plug in my humble electric jug and have a cup of tea — even cook myself sausages and eggs on the electric stove.

Because of this Officious Bastard's great prestige and influence in Power Board circles I needn't after all go to work without my breakfast in the morning. I was benumbed and the humble gratitude I expressed to him embarrasses me still whenever I think about it.

And imagine my feelings on arriving back at my new flat and seeing the power-board truck parked outside.

"That's pretty quick work," I said admiringly to the three electricity men who were even then putting the plug back in, or whatever they have to do to justify the reconnection fee.

"What do you mean, quick work?" said one of the men defensively (I think he thought I was being sarcastic).

"I've only just come from the Power Board Office," I told him. "I thought I'd be lucky to get the power connected at all today."

"Oh, there's nothing much on today," he said. "They just called us up on the R.T. . . . There y'are," he added, closing the junction-box or whatever it was, "You're connected!"

And, sure enough, when I went inside and switched on the nearest electric light — it worked! I had the power on.

But I couldn't shake the feeling that in spite of their efficiency the Officious Bastards at the Power Board Office had put one over on me, which happens every time I encounter them. I wonder if there's something psychologically wrong with me?

17
Poor Bastard

A POSSUM-MAN IS LIKE a possum dog. They're a special kind of people. When the price of the skins drops away to barely worthwhile and doesn't look like it'll ever pick up again, and all the money-hunters quit the game, and there's rumours of synthetic fibres taking over from the possum skin, the genuine possum-man will keep on going; running out his lines and accumulating racks and bundles of beautifully-done skins to send away to the dwindling market. And strangely enough it's never dwindled away completely. They've always managed to keep going.

Except for their loyalty to the profession, there's nothing to distinguish one possum-man from another. I've seen them short and thin, short and stocky, long and beefy, long and thin — but most of them are old-timers. A possum-man who can't remember when you used to have to have a licence to trap them, and a government tag on each skin you sold, is a newcomer to the game. They usually work alone because no two of them will ever agree on the same best areas and methods to get the best possum skins. You still run across the odd possum-man in out-of-the-way pubs, or pass him on the road when you're taking a short cut through some back way or other. You can tell him by his dog, if his vehicle or his appearance don't give him away.

But this yarn isn't about possum-men, I only mentioned them to remind you about them. In fact this yarn is about the only exception to the above rule I ever knew. His name was Cecil Groson and he should have been one of the best possum-men in the game. He'd had plenty of opportunity to be, goodness knows. His old man was one of the oldest of the oldtimers, and still going strong when I knew Cecil. But the trouble was that Ces was an incurable Poor Bastard (*Bastardus upagainstitus*).

I met his old man once or twice. He was trapping on a Maori block in the Urewera and he was camped in a hut I used to use

Bastardus upagainstitus

sometimes, half an hour in from the Wairoa Road. He was a bloody good trapper, old Claude Groson, there was no doubt about that. And he'd talk to you about possums and the bush and the seasons and the spread of the opossum across the country since they were first released here in 1866 — but he wouldn't talk about Cecil. At the very mention of Cecil's name the old man's mouth would shut like a sprung trap and nothing would get him going again until next time you saw him.

You couldn't blame the old man in a way. Cecil must have been a great disappointment to him — he was everything the old man wasn't, and nothing that he was. The only thing in Cecil's favour was that he never gave up trying — and a lot of people would have told you that wasn't *in* his favour, if you'd asked them.

There were two impressive things about Cecil Groson. The first was his appearance. He was tall and lean, and straight and bent forward slightly from the hips like a man who's been used to carrying heavy loads all his life. He had a long hooked nose and his long straight mouth curled downward at the corners. His eyes were round and dark, and his eyebrows curved across his receding forehead like the wings of a descending hawk. No humour there, you'd swear to look at him. Not a man to tamper with you'd say to yourself or your closest mate. But then he'd open his mouth, and that was the other impressive thing about him.

It wasn't that all the top teeth were missing from one side of his mouth and most of the bottom ones from the other side. It wasn't that you could suddenly see that the turned-down mouth was really an upside-down grin (and a pretty stupid-looking grin at that). No, it wasn't the deception of his appearance, or the unexpectedly high-pitched giggle and whine of his voice, or even the slightly ridiculous way he said the slightly ridiculous things he did. It was a kind of *atmosphere* the man had. Hard to put your finger on, but it was impressive all right, you can take my word for that. The nearest anyone ever got to summing it up was probably when my old mate Clive Piper remarked just after Ces had left the pub in quest of another disaster one day — "A bit of a *Poor* Bastard, old Ces."

The only reason a few of us used to let Ces pretend to be a

mate of ours was because we felt kind of sorry for him. Whenever you ran into him he'd have just done something bad. I remember once it was forgetting to hang up the phone properly after he'd rung long-distance, and whacked up a colossal toll account for the bloke whose telephone he was using. Another time he'd got caught in the rain with a thousand first-grade possum skins on a packhorse and nothing to cover them with. Three months' work down the drain. And then there was the time we ran into him in the pub and he'd just poisoned nineteen sheep the night before.

Not that we were particularly surprised to hear about that because Ces had a reputation with cyanide. He'd poisoned things nobody knew you *could* poison with it. Things like goats, and birds, a horse — and once, he swears, an eel, two hundred yards from the nearest creek. He poisoned stoats, polecats, hedgehogs, rabbits, earthworms, pigs, a stag, rats, his dog, and quite a few possums as well.

At first we used to think he was being dogged with his usual run of bad luck, but it was a bit too much even for that. And then we found out why. A bunch of the boys were out pig-hunting and they came across a cyanide line Cecil had laid the day before. And what a line! It was an almost continuous trail of potassium cyanide and flour, right across the watershed. He'd plastered the stuff everywhere. Must have used pounds and pounds of it. The boys doubled back and went round to Cecil's camp to see what he was up to, and there he was. Grinding up big hunks of cyanide out of a tin — with an ordinary meat-mincer — on the table inside his hut. How he hadn't poisoned himself with it no-one could understand.

Nobody would let Ces lay cyanide on their property after that, so he went back to running equally ruinous trap-lines though they weren't so potentially dangerous as the cyanide.

I don't know about the other blokes, but Ces used to make me feel so sorry for him that I couldn't stand the sight of him for more than a few minutes at a time. Not that he used to complain, mind you. He'd cheerfully tell you about his most recent disaster and then he'd go on, just as cheerfully, to tell you about the next catastrophe he was planning. You just *knew* he was going to make a dismal balls-up of it, whatever it was.

By conscientiously going from one cheerful calamity to the next, Ces eventually worked his way out of the district, and you'd only run into him occasionally when you were on your way to or from somewhere else. But it was enough to keep you advised that he hadn't changed much.

I never saw him for about four years at one stage. And the next time I did see him it was to be the last, though of course I didn't know that till much later on. I'd heard the odd report that he was working in the Waioeka Gorge area — on possums, but that was all, until I was passing through there one day and pulled over to the edge of the road to let an old jalopy get past. There'd been a slip. The road was pretty narrow and windy and steep around there and the other vehicle didn't look as though it was particularly strong on brakes. And who do you think was driving it. . . ?

Yes, it was Ces. Same as ever. We sat there yarning through the windows of our vehicles until a Public Works truck came along and we had to shift to let it get past.

"Turn around and follow me!" shouted Ces as he moved off. "I'm camped just down here a bit."And he drove away, waving out the window of his bomb to the blokes in the P.W. truck.

Well I had a perfect opportunity to avoid Ces that time. All I had to do was just keep going. But somehow I didn't like to. He was so pleased to see me, and, besides, I'd had a fair spell without him. I felt I could stand a little more. So I found a place to turn round and drove back. Ces was waiting for me where a track turned off the road and followed a small creek up into the bush. The track got rougher and rougher and just before it became impossible to go any further, we came to Ces's camp. It was a broken-down old hut with possum-boards leaning all around the outside walls. He had his dried skins hanging in bundles in a lean-to at the back of the hut and she stank a fair bit, but apart from that it wasn't a bad camp. For Ces.

He stoked up the fire, chattering all the time like someone who's had nobody to talk to for a long time, and we had a brew of tea in filthy mugs. He'd been there for six weeks, in this particular area, and it was the best place he'd ever struck. Never been trapped before. Of course he'd had one or two minor set-backs

— like having sixty traps pinched off the back of his waggon, and nearly having to go back to using cyanide. But, fortunately, he'd got another fifty traps on credit so he was able to keep going without using poison. And, as I say, it was just as bloody well.

I won't explain how it came about, but I ended up agreeing to stay the night. Ces knew this place out on a farm at the edge of the bush that was absolutely crawling with possums. We were going out there for a bit of sport that night. He had a big hand-spotlight with a practically brand-new battery he'd been saving for an occasion like this. He was to spotlight the possums and I was to shoot them out of the trees, in their hundreds, with his old .22 rifle. And just to make sure of any wounded ones, we took Ces's new possum-dog with us. A fair-dinkum cracker-jack possum-dog he reckoned. Best one he'd ever had. Looking at the dog, and knowing Ces, I had my doubts about it, but as long as he was happy it didn't make any difference whether the dog was no better than any of the one's he'd had when he was down our way.

Now it wasn't that I should have known better than to get myself involved in one of Ces's capers — I *did* know better. And I didn't like the idea of it any the more for that. But, as I said, he was so pleased to see one of the "old mates", and it was me who was handling the rifle. I couldn't see what could go wrong, but that didn't make much difference either. No one had ever been able to foresee any of Ces's disasters. So I wasn't all that terribly optimistic when we pulled up in his truck, about an hour after dark, at this place where Ces reckoned all the possums were.

And I'll tell you what — there were possums there all right! We lit up fifteen or twenty of them with Ces's big torch before we even got into the paddock. They were perched all over the trees and scattered everywhere across the grass out from the bush edge. I didn't get much of a chance for a decent look around because Ces took one sweep with the light and then he and his dog were through the fence and off down the hill, with Ces hissing, "There they are! Come on!", with his spotlight waving around like a crashing car, leaving me to try and finish loading the rifle in the dark.

I caught up with him about halfway down the slope. He had

three possums lit up in a dead popular and he was just about climbing up the beam of his spotlight to get at them.

"Here they are! Here they are!" he hissed at me. "Shoot the little bastards! Hurry up! Shoot! Shoot!"

So I shot. Got two of them, and hit the branch beside the third, and it ran down the tree and jumped out onto the grass at the other side of the trunk. Ces immediately gave chase, yelling to his dog to "Skitchem!", but his dog was busy shaking the fur out of one of the dead possums and didn't seem to hear him. So Ces took off across the paddock trying to keep his light on the possum that was scampering across the ground in front of him.

And suddenly there was this almight crashy and Ces's torch flew through the air like a Catherine-wheel and landed a bit further down the hill and went out on the third bounce.

By the time I got there my eyes were adjusting to the darkness and I could see what had happened. The possum had shot straight under a seven-wire fence and Ces hadn't even seen it coming. He'd cannoned into it at full tilt and bounced about twelve feet back into the paddock. After a while I got him sitting up and explained what had happened to him. And as soon as he could move he crawled off along the fence looking for his light. He found it just through the fence about ten yards down the hill and as soon as he picked it up it flickered on. And it flickered on and off all the time after that.

I wanted to call it a night and get back to the camp, but Ces wouldn't hear of it. We'd come out to shoot possums, and shoot possums we would. So I gave in and we set off again, along the bush edge, with Ces limping badly and bumping his torch on and off and trying not to grunt from the pain of his injuries. At least he wasn't going to go dashing off after any more possums. Not that night, anyway.

We got another four of five possums but with the light going on and off all the time it was a bit awkward and I'd just got Ces talked into working our way back towards where we'd left the truck when he spotted a big buck possum perched in the top of a small punga. He kept the spotlight on-and-off it while I moved in for a shot, and just as I was getting into position, several things happened . . .

First, the possum jumped out of the punga. Secondly, Ces's torch went out. Thirdly, Ces's dog headed the possum off. Fourthly, the possum saw Ces standing there and thought he was a stump and ran up him to get away from the dog, and perched there on Ces's head, with its claws dug into his face and scalp. Fifthly, Ces dropped the torch, and it came on and illuminated . . . Sixthly, Ces's dog jumped up and, Oh God, was dragging the possum off Ces's head.

As soon as I picked up the torch it went out again, and when I joggled it on and saw Ces's face I tried to quickly joggle it out again, but it stayed on. What a mess! For a start he was covered in blood. One of his ear lobes was split nearly right through, and his face was ripped in several deep ragged lines from his forehead to his chin.

Ces's dog yelped in pain somewhere out across the paddock and a few minutes later he came back. That possum must have been a bit too much for him.

Ces was vaguely trying to smear the blood off his face with the sleeve of his woollen jersey and I waited to hear from him so I could tell exactly how badly hurt he was. It looked like a hospital job to me.

Then Ces spoke, "William Tell would have shot that possum right off my head," he said, grinning through the blood.

He was a hospital job all right, but not the kind of hospital I'd first had in mind. Poor Bastard.

I got him back to the truck. I got him back to camp. I got him cleaned up and sticking-plastered and bandaged. I got him into his bunk and gave him a brew of tea. And I got the hell out of there at first light the next morning.

The next I heard of Ces was when one of the blokes found him in the obituary column and brought the cutting into the pub:

GROSON, CECIL EDWARD. Accidentally, at Waioeka Gorge. Son of Claude and Emily. Brother of Jane. Sadly missed.

And it gave the date, just three weeks after I'd last seen him, after the night of the possums.

I got to wondering about it. After all the disasters and catastrophes and calamities and things Ces had survived it was hard to imagine what kind of mere accident could have carried him off. I remembered him waving to the blokes in the Public Works truck the day I met him in the gorge, and when I was up that way a couple of weeks later I ran into a bunch of them clearing a slip off the road. So I stopped and asked them if they knew Ces Groson.

They knew him all right. They knew he was dead, too. They even knew one of the blokes who found him. And, yes, they knew how it happened.

It seems that the Public Works blokes used to drop Ces off a couple of loaves of bread two or three times a week, and when they found that he wasn't collecting it two of them went up to his camp to see if he was okay. His dog was there but there was no sign of Ces. And it didn't look as though the camp had been used for a few days. So they reported him missing and the police and a few of the locals got up a search party.

They split up into two groups and went looking for him. One lot found his trap line. No possums and every trap sprung. Only Ces would have done that. Then the other party found Ces. He wasn't hard to locate. You see, they came across this dirty great cyanide-line, running right through the bush. Cyanide everywhere. They followed it along and found dead wekas, and possums, dead rats . . . and where the line ended they found Ces. Dead. from cyanide. He'd finally rounded off his tally. The variety of kills he made with the potassium cyanide must surely and posthumously, be a record for Ces Groson. Poor old Ces. Sadly missed. You get blokes like that. Poor bastards.

18
Queer Bastard

THE OLD MEANING OF this description of a bastard is long since outdated. In other words, there's nothing queer about queers these days.

No, the Queer Bastard (*Bastardus quaintus*) as we know him today is one who is not quite the full quid, but more peculiar than mad. Whimsical, perhaps, even a little faddy or weird. Possibly even dotty, potty, batty, dippy, dizzy, giddy, screwy, wacky; scatty or daft. But definitely not nuts or crackers. That is, if my old mate Clive Piper is anything to go by. And if *he* wasn't a Queer Bastard nobody was.

Clive was so strange he was often taken for a lunatic at first sight or acquaintance, but once you got to know him you realised that there was a kind of logic to what he did and said. Like the time I was fifty yards from the post office when I noticed that the letter he'd asked me to post for him was addressed to Ho Chi Minh in North Vietnam. I didn't want him getting himself into trouble so I took the letter back to Clive's place to see if he'd like to change his mind about it, and found him taking all the windows out of his house.

"What are you doing there, Clive?" I asked him.

"I'm taking all my windows out," he said.

"What are you doing that for?" I asked him.

"To turn them round — end for end," he said.

"Why?" I said.

"Because they've been up this way for forty years," he said.

"What's the difference?" I said.

"Don't you know about glass?" he asked me.

"What about it?"

"It's liquid," he explained.

"Liquid?"

"Yes," he said. "The glass at the bottom of all these windows is thicker than the glass at the top because they've been up this

Bastardus quaintus

way all the time. I'm turning them round so they'll last longer. Otherwise they'll get too thin at the top and break when I go to clean them."

"What about this letter?" I said to change the subject.

"What about it?"

"It's addressed to Ho Chi Minh," I said. "In North Vietnam."

"So it should be," he said. "That's who it's written to."

"You mean you've actually written a letter to Ho Chi Minh?" I said.

"You've got it in your hand," he pointed out. "I thought you were going to post it for me."

"I will," I said. "I was just wondering why you'd want to write to Ho Chi Minh, that's all."

"It's personal," he said.

So I gave up. Posted his letter and tried to forget about it, but I couldn't forget about him turning all his windows upside-down. I was worried that my old friend might be finally slipping off the wrong side of the wall he'd been balancing on for so long. So I checked up, and you know what I found?

I found that glass *is* a liquid and is never anything else. And that the glass at the bottom of Clive's windows was, after forty years, undoubtedly thicker than the glass at the top. There was some doubt about the efficacy of turning windows upside-down to make them less likely to break, but I wasn't going to argue about that. Clive was okay after all. His old abnormal self.

I went round to his place, almost a month since I'd last seen him, to agree with him about the windows, and found him up on the roof, sweeping it with a straw broom.

"What are you up to, Clive?" I called up to him.

"Sweeping the roof," he called back.

"What are you sweeping the roof for?"

"Because it's dirty," he called down to me. "It gets all the stuff from the factories around here on it. I sweep it every three months or so."

"What's the difference?" I called up.

"The paint lasts three times as long if you sweep it occasionally," he said. "There's a lot of chemicals in that stuff."

"What about the rain," I tried. "Doesn't that wash it off?"

"The paint lasts three times as long if you sweep it down every three months or so," he repeated.

So I waited for him to finish sweeping his roof and when he came down we had a cup of tea.

"Did you get a reply from Ho Chi Minh?" I asked him casually.

"Yes," he said. "It came just yesterday, as a matter of fact."

"What did it say?" I asked sceptically.

"That's personal," he said.

"Did you save the postage stamps on the envelope?" I asked him cunningly.

"The envelope's still on the dresser there. You can have the stamps if you want them."

And, sure enough, he produced the letter he'd got from Ho Chi Minh and let me tear the North Vietnamese stamps off the North Vietnamese envelope. All he would tell me was that some people demonstrate, some people raise funds, others write letters to the newspapers, and he writes to Ho Chi Minh. I'd have given anything to find out what was in that letter, but I never did.

"What sort of a bloke is he to write to?" I asked as a last resort.

"Better than the other joker," said Clive. "*He* didn't even reply to my letter himself. He got someone else to do it for him."

"What other joker's that?" I asked him.

"President Nixon," said Clive. "The stamps off his letters are still around somewhere if you want them."

"No thanks," I stammered. "It doesn't matter any more."

And Clive looked at me kind of thoughtful for a moment or two, and then, "Y'know," he said. "you're a bit of a *Queer* Bastard at times."

"Me? Queer!" I said to him.

"Yes," he said.

"How do you work that out?" I said, settling down to hear him get himself into the usual entertaining tangle.

"You waste time all the time," he said.

"I don't get you," I said.

"Every time you ask me something I tell you — then you ask me again, and I tell you again — then you check up on it later to see if I was putting you crook or not. And I've never put you crook yet, so that means you've wasted all the time you've spent checking up on me so far, and you're *still* doing it. You still haven't found out that it's easier to believe what someone tells you and maybe come a gutser every once in a while, than to make sure everything's dead right before you can accept it.

"And if *that*," concluded Clive. "isn't a Queer Bastard, I don't know what is."

Me neither. If that's the kind of queerness Clive's been writing to people like Ho Chi Minh and President Nixon about I can only hope it had the effect on them that it did on me.

19
Rude Bastard

DON'T LET'S RUN AWAY with the erroneous notion that Rude Bastards (*Bastardus badmannerus*) are ignorant. They not only know about manners and how to use them, they believe in them — providing they don't have to use them themselves. In fact there's nobody more likely to be indignant about the lack of manners than a Rude Bastard.

You'd expect Rude Bastards to be almost exclusively confined to us lower classes, the proletarians, the workers. But I want to bring your attention to the lawyer who makes an appointment with you and then abruptly breaks off discussing your affairs to talk on his telephone for endless minutes, consulting files and making notes, while you sit there like some intruder, wondering what it's going to cost you. These men have secretaries and receptionists to take their telephone calls and tell the callers to ring later, but they're not instructed to do this because Mr Lawyer has his spatulate fingers in so many trust-account pies that he can't afford to attend to one thing at a time any longer. There's a *Real* Rude Bastard for you.

And then there's the doctor who, before you've finished telling him your symptoms, drags his prescription-pad across, scribbles something like the tracks of a drunken fowl on it, hands it to you and tells you to see the nurse on your way out to make an appointment for another dose of the same ignorance.

I don't give a damn how overworked they are. They're well-paid for every patient they're off-hand with. If you or I started skimping our work in that manner simply because we had a lot of it to do we'd be out of our jobs pretty smartly. And a physician who refused to discuss your health with you when you consult him about it is nothing but a Rude Bastard, in anybody's language.

And what about the Magistrate who takes advantage of his position in the intimidating environs of one of *our* courtrooms

Bastardus badmannerus

to make his ill-mannered, corny and sarcastic personal remarks about the character of his victims? As Rude a Bastard as you can get.

The psychologist we're invited to go to for help, only to be told something ludicrous like, "You have a deep-seated personality defect." He's a bloody jargoneer — another Rude Bastard.

The television interviewer who invites an expert to tell the viewers about something he has a specialised knowledge of, and then proceeds to question the veracity of the expert's information in order to gain for himself a reputation for hard-hitting interviewing. A Rude Bastard.

Officialdom, too, has a goodly share of Rude Bastards in its ranks. And personally I've had a gutful of it. The next so-called professional man, official, honorary ranger, policeman, traffic officer, receptionist, or anyone else who has me in a position where I need something from him, and takes advantage of it to exercise his native rudeness, is going to find out that I can be a pretty Rude Bastard myself. And, unlike him, I will have the advantage of being able to help it.

I cordially invite you, mannerly reader, to join the Society For The Giving Of Just Deserts To Rude Bastards, which you can become a life member of by simply informing the next Rude Bastard you run into that you object to his, or her, lack of manners. They'll know what you mean. Good luck!

20
Situational Bastard

BASTARDRY IS NOT RESTRICTED to cataloguing types of people. A man can get himself into a bastard of a situation, for instance, if he doesn't watch it. And I can't think of a better example of this than the time I got collared to look after my sister's kids for a couple of hours while she was getting her teeth fixed up.

There were two of them, both girls, and I didn't know them very well in those days. The oldest was about belt-high and the other one wasn't different enough so I could tell which was Lucy and which was May.

I was a bit out of my depth at the kid-minding caper, but I reckoned the best thing to do was take them into town and buy them something. They seemed to think it was a fair enough idea and they got into the car without any persuading. And off we went, with the two kids jumping all over the seats, nattering like sparrows and asking me all kinds of crazy questions. Apart from that everything was going off okay, but before we got to town they suddenly decided they wanted to go to the toilet. First one of the them, and then the other.

And by the time we'd got to town it was getting urgent — for all of us. They were jumping from foot to foot, hanging onto themselves, crossing their legs, and generally carrying on something terrible.

I was a bit stonkered. I thought of asking some woman to help us out but none of the ones I saw along the streets looked as though they'd have been very approachable on the subject. And then I thought about the student building at the university. I remembered it from the time I was trotting a woman who took lectures there. And the toilets were just inside the main door.

I pulled up outside the place, just in time, by the way the kids were performing, and took them in. There was no one around just then but it didn't make any difference. I opened the door

Bastardus setuppus

of the women's outfit for them and saw that there was another door for them to get through, but they managed to shove it open. It sprung shut behind them and I stood around waiting.

They took a hell of a long time in there and I was thinking of asking the next woman who came past if she'd mind checking up on them for me. Then I heard the youngest one half-crying inside the toilet and woke up to what was happening. That inside door was too tough for them to pull open and they were stuck in there.

And I'd just opened the outside door to go in and let them out when someone came down some stairs behind me and a woman's voice said, "Hey there! What do you think you're doing!"

So I let the door shut again and said to her, "It's okay, lady. I'm just going in here to get a couple of young girls."

"You're doing no such thing," she said. "Get away from there at once!"

And before I could explain, there were people coming from all directions until I was surrounded by them. And that woman was telling everyone in a loud voice how she'd caught me in the very act of breaking into the women's toilet to get at some girls.

"It'll be that perv who's been attacking women in the Domain!" said somebody.

"We'd better call the police!" said someone else.

"Let's grab him before he gets away," said one of the blokes. "There's enough of us here to hold him till the cops get here."

"They're my nieces!" I shouted at them. "Can't you hear them in there?"

"Filthy swine!" said the first woman, who obviously didn't want me to turn out to be anything but a depraved sex-maniac.

Now that was a bastard of a situation if ever there was one. A *real* bastard of a situation. And it didn't improve, either.

"Don't be so bloody stupid," I yelled at them. "They're only little girls."

And I held my hand up to show everyone how big they were.

"Oooo — listen to him!" said one of the women.

"Go and have a look," I said. "They're probably stuck in there. I don't think they can get the door open."

"Well they're not going to come out while *you're* here, are they mate?" said one of the blokes.

"Go and see for yourself," I said impatiently.

"No, thank you," he replied sarcastically. "It's not my cup of tea, that sort of thing."

"Not you, you bloody idiot," I said to him. And I turned to one of the women who hadn't been saying much and said to her, "Will *you* go in and get them. They'll be getting scared by this time."

"I'm not surprised," she said, backing away from me through the crowd as though I'd just indecently exposed myself. "You can hardly blame them, can you."

And in the bit of a lull that happened while they were waiting for me to think up an answer to that one, someone said, " There *is* somebody in there. Listen!"

And sure enough you could hear the kids, both of them, crying and yelling to be let out. But the mob made me get away from the door, in fact *all* the men did (and some of them got ready to grab me in case I made a run for it), while half a dozen women crowded into the women's toilet to investigate.

They brought the girls out and, no matter how hard they tried to get them to admit I'd been molesting them, they insisted that I was their uncle and we'd come to use the toilet. But although they had to let us go I was pretty sure most of them were disappointed that they hadn't apprehended a sexual pervert after all.

"Poor little things," I heard one of them say as we got back into the car.

Which goes to demonstrate that being the victim of an hysterical mob of outraged people is a bastard of a situation to be in.

21
Temperamental Bastard

I'VE PERSONALLY RUN INTO quite a few Temperamental Bastards (*Bastardus highstrungus*) in my time, but the man who stands out as the obvious one to use as an example is a bloke called Basil Wainwright, who I lived with for a few months once.

Basil wouldn't like to know I'd referred to him as a Temperamental Bastard. He used to claim he was a Sensitive Bastard (*Bastardus thinskinnus*), but I'm sticking to Temperamental B. because I refuse to let personal preferences sway me from my determination to be strictly factual in these matters of Bastardry.

Temperamental Bastards are not like us. We only see them as people who have to be very carefully approached until we've established what particular mood they're in this time. But the fact is that Unfeeling Bastards (*Bastardus icebergus*) like you and I just don't know what makes the Temperamental Bastard tick. He's away over our heads when it comes to appreciating the finer things in life.

He *feels* things we don't feel. He thinks things we just don't know about. He's usually engrossed either in exploring the psychological origins of his own suffering, or examining the deeper meanings of his relationships with other people. And he's so persistent in his claims of being absolutely honest that I'm downright bloody suspicious.

I must say that Basil was very patient and understanding with my inability to be patient an. understanding with him. In spite of his earnest lectures I'd still go gallivanting off with my current girlfriend to parties, dances, sailing, fishing, surfing and skiing — frivolous things like that. While Basil and his girl would sit around the flat having serious discussions about the deeper facets of their relationship.

This didn't seem to do much *for* their relationship, though, because they were always either just celebrating a reunion (with

Bastardus highstrungus

another serious discussion!), or parted — this time for ever — because of some unforgivable insensitivity on her part. Never his.

It was never quite clear to me exactly what these serious discussions were about. Sometimes they'd invite me to join in, and they'd get to talking about their mothers and fathers and uncles and aunts and cousins and brothers and sisters and friends and acquaintances, with such intense, analytical attention to detail that I'd eventually have to go to bed before I fell asleep where I was sitting. And sometimes I'd be woken up in the early hours of the morning by a fair-dinkum barney, as shrill and uninhibited as their serious discussion had been subdued and unemotional. Something had gone haywire somewhere along the way.

Although I used to go through a fair few girlfriends, Basil wasn't above changing his from time to time.

"Jenny and I have decided not to see each other for a while," he'd say. And you'd never see her again. Or, "Nola doesn't satisfy the *intellectual* side of my life," he'd say. And that would be the last we'd see of Nola. Or sometimes it'd be, "Penny doesn't understand my sensitivity," and Penny'd be a goner too.

For a Sensitive Bastard Basil could be pretty tough on his girlfriends when he'd had enough of them. That's why I prefer to describe him as a Temperamental Bastard.

As with most of the Temperamental Bastards you find huddled anxiously together in the cities, Basil was very careful not to get himself involved in anything to do with hard work. It was as though he was using up so much of his energy hanging onto his feelings that if he used any of it on anything else his sensitivity would start leaking out all over the place. He wasn't what you'd call a fit bloke, by any standards. He got very little sleep or exercise, he ate the most dreadful artificial tucker, and assaulted himself almost continuously with pills and capsules and all kinds of other medicinal drugs. He'd been doing all this to himself for years, and yet he was basically still quite healthy! It's truly astonishing the amount of punishment the human body can take.

I once dragged Basil off on a tramping holiday and nursed him along for five days, listening to his complaints about the primitive conditions, the food, the weather, his blisters and the general discomfort of it all. Then when we got back to town he spent another week or so telling everyone how much good it had done him; how great he was feeling.

But then I suggested that he join a tramping club and make himself feel good every weekend and Basil dropped the whole subject. It was impossible, he said. Perhaps it was, but the reason he gave was that his creative work had to take precedence over everything else. I'd offended his sensitivity again by suggesting that a bit of exercise was more important than the pictures he painted whenever he was inspired. His paintings, incidentally, were as unfathomable as his way of living.

I don't know about you, tolerant reader — humanitarian Bastard (*Bastardus bigheartedus*) — but by the time I shifted out of that flat with Basil I'd just about enough of Temperamental Bastards. For too long we've been making excuses for them on the grounds of their sensitivity, as though to be sensitive was some kind of virtue.

Look at it this way, if you or I had a sensitive — say — elbow, we wouldn't be likely to regard it as anything but a disability, a source of discomfort. We certainly wouldn't claim it was a gift or a talent or an excuse to suffer, as the Temperamental Bastard so often does. We'd know that the best thing would be a rapid cure; a de-sentization of the elbow!

It's obvious enough that the T.B. is up against it in some way, even if we can't understand what his trouble is, but don't you think it's about time we gave up letting him prescribe his own treatment? I mean, if it was ever going to work it would have surely started to by this time! But it's not, it's getting worse. We've been listening to their jaundiced interpretation of their condition for so long now that we've forgotten what words like sensitive and temperamental really mean. The same kind of fact-dodgers have been slinging the word Creative around until we've lost track of the fact that it's meaningless. Man might be able to do a bit of re-arranging on a not-very-useful scale, but he can't create a single bloody thing — unless you can count situations, and most of the ones we've come up with so far are nothing to skite about.

22
Unlucky Bastard

STEVE CLAUSE WAS SUCH an Unlucky Bastard (*Bastardus rawdealus*) that it was hardly safe for him to get out of bed in the morning. I've never seen anything like it, fair go. It was uncanny. He had everything unlucky going for him that you could imagine, and yet he was such a Decent Bastard you couldn't help liking him.

I was working at the railway workshops when Steve got a job there, and from the very start he was in trouble. When I first started hanging around with him I didn't believe such bad luck could possibly last much longer, but I was wrong. If anything fell it'd be Steve it would land on. He could do things everyone else had been getting away with for years, and Steve'd get caught. Not that he was careless, just unlucky.

He'd been sacked from literally hundreds of jobs through sheer bad luck. I've never seen anything like it. As sure as he'd sneak away for a smoke the boss'd catch him at it.

He even lost his fiancee through bad luck. He was on his way to visit her one evening and stopped to grab a handful of flowers for her from the council gardens on his way through the park; and when he looked up there was a cop standing right there. Poor old Steve got the blame for every flower that had ever been pinched from the park. They decided to make an example of him. They fined him $15.00 and costs, and his fiancee's folks wouldn't let her have anything more to do with him because he had a criminal record.

And then he got the sack. Through bad luck. The blokes had been getting away with a staggering amount of perks from the job, but the night Steve decided to help himself to a handful of two-inch nails was the night they'd decided to spot-check the men at the gates. Steve was the only one they caught, and he was down the road again.

Just as I was getting on the bus with Steve that night outside

Bastardus rawdealus

work, one of the blokes called out that we'd better let the driver know he had Steve on board. I thought he was joking, but at the very first intersection we came to the bus collided with a truck, and Steve was the only passenger who got injured. He broke one of his front teeth on the handrail behind the seat in front of us and we couldn't find a dentist to put a cap on the exposed nerve in his broken tooth until the next day.

Steve had decided to take the ferry to the South Island to look for work down there so I took the day off and went to see him off. We shook hands on the wharf and he was walking innocently up the gangplank with everything he owned in a suitcase, when a scuffle started among some celebrating blokes who had come to see some of their mates off. One of them thought Steve was in on it and gave him a shove. And the shove, combined with Steve's bad luck, sent him somehow sailing down into the water between the boat and wharf, suitcase and all.

We finally twigged that Steve couldn't swim and an heroic onlooker dived in and held him up till they fished them out of the water, but they didn't bother with his suitcase.

They'd collared the bloke who'd pushed him and invited Steve to bring charges against him. But Steve refused. He maintained that he would probably have fallen into the harbour anyway and the wharf police had to let the bloke go in the finish. It was obvious that the police thought he was some kind of nut, but I didn't. I'd known Steve for a couple of months by this time and wasn't a bit surprised that him trying on something like getting onto a big ferryboat had ended in disaster.

He'd lost his ferry ticket along with everything else and they wouldn't believe he'd ever had a ticket in the first place, so he couldn't go on the ferry. He was still wringing wet from his dip in the harbour and it was as cold as hell, so I decided to take him back to my flat and get him into some dry clothes.

I should have known better. The landlady sprung me sneaking this wet bedraggled Steve into my flat and she kept us bailed up on the stairs to remind me of her rules about drinking and parties and visitors and other such immoral carryings-on in the flat. We were just getting away from her when she spotted Steve's puddle of water on her carpet and did her block good and proper.

She didn't look like stopping for a while so I dragged Steve inside and shut the door, which she knocked on a little later to give me a week's notice to get out of the place.

We dried Steve's clothes in front of the heater and that night he slept on my couch. In the morning I gave him some of my clothes and stuff and we packed it into an old kit I had. I had just over sixty dollars and lent Steve thirty dollars of it to tide him over. I decided to take the day off work and personally deliver him to the ferry, but before we'd got to the wharf some blokes with a movie camera set up on the footpath stopped us. I wanted us to cut and run for it before any bad luck happened, but before I could get Steve to take off they'd collared him to tell television-land what he thought about the Common Market developments.

He mumbled something non-committal into their microphone and I was dragging him away before something happened when it did. Someone in the small crowd that had gathered suddenly shouted, "Hey, There's Steve Clause!" And I could tell by the way they said it that here was more bad luck. I was right. A great big bloke and his even bigger mate skinned us for forty dollars Steve had borrowed off him once and forgotten to pay back.

And when we looked around for Steve's kit of gear it was gone. Somebody had pinched it and nobody had seen them do it. So he had no gear or money again.

By the time I'd bought Steve's ticket on the ferry and given him a ten-dollar stake to help him get a job down south I had exactly 75 cents left out of my sixty dollars. My resources were exhausted. There was nothing more I could do for him.

My feelings as the boat pulled away from the wharf were not mixed. I shouted to Steve to stand farther back from the rail and hoped nothing would happen to stop that ferry. I'd done all that could be humanly expected of me. It was somebody else's turn now.

I just managed to hang onto my job for taking two days off without telling them, and I got a much better flat to live in. It was three months before I heard from Steve. Only a letter, but even that made me slightly apprehensive. He sent three dollars and a little note saying he'd hoped to send more but he'd been a bit unlucky. I had no option but to believe him.

23
Vain Bastard

HE CARRIES A COMB and always has a clean handkerchief in his pocket. And that, good reader, is as much as I know about the Vain Bastard (*Bastardus primpus*). I hadn't realised until I undertook to write about him that I'd never had much to do with them. I can't think of a single really Vain Bastard I've known personally.

This must be put right at once, a little research is called for. Wait here — I'm going down town to find a Vain Bastard and get to know him. I'll let you know how I get on when I get back.

LATER — You may not realise this, patient reader, but sixteen hours have passed since you finished reading the above paragraph. I've been down town and looked through some of the pubs for a Vain Bastard. It didn't take as long as I'd expected. I found a beaut in the lounge bar of the Brit. Immaculate, he was, standing there at the bar. Fussy, finnicky and fastidious. Creases in all the right places. In short — resplendent.

It was only when I approached him to introduce myself that I realised I'd been so engrossed in the hunt for a Vain Bastard I hadn't given any thought to what I was going to do when I'd caught one. I decided to play it by ear.

As I reached my quarry I saw why it was that I'd never got close to any Vain Bastards before. There's something about me that makes them distinctly uneasy. This one shrank away from me as though I might at any moment spatter all over his beautiful clothes. But he relaxed a little as he realised that unless I actually touched him none of my scruffiness was going to rub off on his resplendency.

"G'day," I said, "How's it going?"

"Quite well, thank you," he said cautiously.

"Nice day for it," I observed, signalling for the barman to fill my new friend's glass and bring me one of the same.

Bastardus primpus

"Yes it is," he replied fastidiously.

"I'm Barry Crump," I said, holding out my hand for him to shake.

He looked at my hand as though it was dripping with waste-oil, and then when it didn't go away again he shook it.

"Philip —," he said. "Have we met before?"

"Don't think so," I said. "What are you doing for a crust these days?"

"I'm not working at the moment," he said, as though I should have known.

"Waiting for someone?" I asked him.

"Yes, I am, as a matter of fact," he replied. "— Mother," he added, as though it might frighten me off. "We're going to lunch as soon as she gets here."

"Good idea," I nodded. "You've got to eat. I might even join you. Where do you eat usually?"

Well his mother didn't turn up and I eventually dragged my captive Vain Bastard off for a feed at a flash restaurant. Shouted us two bottles of imported plonk to see if there was any vitality under all his plumage, but nothing happened so I carted him off to another pub for a few more snorts. But when I picked up a couple of girls for us to have a night out on the town with, Philip vanished in the direction of the toilet and we didn't see him again. So I had to manage the girls on my own. The whole thing turned out a bit expensive, but I had the information I needed for this discourse on Vain Bastards.

And this, going on what I gleaned from my day with the timid Philip, is what I learned about them.

The Vain Bastard is a hard man to get to know because he's so heavily disguised. It's hard to tell what he's like by the look of him because he's camouflaged by his fancy-dress costume and his hair is so strictly regimented into the shape and style he thinks he looks best in.

And because he's such a Vain Bastard you can't tell what he's like from what he says because he's only interested in subjects pertaining to himself, providing they're flattering subjects. They don't like talking about anything that's not clean and sweet-smelling, and it's no good trying to talk to them at all while you're walking along a city street with them because they're too preoccupied with catching their reflection in shop windows to keep a conversation going.

You can't tell what he's like by his movements because they're influenced so much by the care he thinks he needs to take not to crease or soil his clothes. He walks stiff-legged so as not to put knees in his trousers, and when he sits he perches on his chair as though expecting it to splinter under his weight and deposit him on the dusty carpet any moment.

He eats as though each forkful of food might explode all over his shirt-front before he can get it safely into his mouth, and he's as fussy about his health as he is about his appearance. He's got a thing about germs and believes that to get wet means to get pneumonia.

He uses the toilet, combs his hair, and then washes his hands. He's a fan for jewellery and a sucker for the con-men who manufacture cosmetics. He smells like a whore's handbag of some kind of scent they've put a masculine-sounding label on and conned him into buying by suggesting on television that no woman worth her salt would have anything to do with him unless he reeks of the stuff.

He's dishonest and unreliable because his immediate requirements are much more important than any arrangement he may have previously condescended to make with a member of the common herd. And there's nothing he couldn't do better than the experts if only he bothered to put a little time and practice into it. Poor Vain Bastard.

24
Weak Bastard

NONE OF US DISPUTED that Cedric Fleet was a Weak Bastard (*Bastardus dishwaterus*) from the time he first turned up asking for a job on the Rabbit Board. But none of us realised just how weak he really was. You could see he was weak just by looking at him. There was nothing of him, for a start. Scrawny, wizened, middle-aged and wretched-looking. I put his weight at around six-and-a-half to seven stone. He was almost five foot high when he stood up straight, which wasn't often. He went round hunched over a like a sick man.

"Do you think you could stand up to the work?" the boss asked, looking him up and down.

"I don't know," he said. "I've been a bit crook on it lately."

"Well we need men, I'll give you a trial," said the boss. "You can share the end hut with Crumpy here. He'll show you where to put your gear."

So Cedric moved in with me. The boss told me on the quiet to keep an eye on him, but there was hardly enough of him to keep a decent eye on. I gave him a hand to lift his three big suitcases of gear up the steps into the hut and as soon as we'd got his bunk made up he hoisted his miserable frame into it and flaked out. That didn't matter because new blokes always got a day on full pay to settle in. He didn't even want to eat when I woke up for a feed that night, so I ate it myself and left him asleep.

The next day was Saturday and some of us were going into town to the pub, so I woke Cedric up to see if he wanted to come. But he only drank a cup of tea or two and told me he'd better stay home because the last time he'd gone on the bash he'd ended up with a dose of double-pneumonia.

I stayed in town that night and when I got back to camp next day Cedric was sitting on the edge of his bunk looking anxiously into his shaving mirror.

Bastardus dishwaterus

"I think I'm coming down with something," he said to me. "My tongue's a funny colour."

"So's mine," I told him. "Let's get this hut cleaned up and put a feed on."

That's when I discovered that Cedric couldn't stay in the hut while the floor was being swept because it might bring on his hay-fever. And a bit later I discovered that he had to be very careful what he ate. Most things, it seemed, disagreed with him.

"I've got to watch my health, you know," he said.

"What health?" I couldn't help asking.

I thought I was going to carry him out to the truck when they came to pick us up the next morning, but he made it all right. Then he told the boss he had a rare disease called haemophilia and had to ride in the front of the truck in case he cut himself and bled to death. We didn't know whether to believe him or not but we weren't game to take the risk, so Cedric always rode in the front, just in case.

We were laying poison at the time and every day we'd give Cedric a half-full jam-gun and let him do the easy spots around the truck until he got a bit of his health back. But he never did. He got weaker, if anything, and almost every day he informed us of some new and frightful disability he suffered from.

He'd had one lung removed, and one kidney. He'd had operations on his appendix, his gall-bladder, his back and his ulcers. He was allergic to seventy-eight of the ninety things you *could* be allergic to. He had a steel pin in his ankle and a plate in his hip. (His bones were powdery and brittle because of some deficiency or other). He sure knew a lot of long medical words, and when you looked at him, no matter what outrageous-sounding disease he claimed to be suffering from this time, you simply had to give him the benefit of the doubt.

Weak Bastards usually have a ton of guts to make up for their lack of strength, but not our Cedric. He was weak in all departments. He had neither strength *nor* guts. He complained so long and so convincingly about his ebbing vitality that he was never sent down into gullies for fear he wouldn't make it back up to the top again. We'd hurry to lift things for him or help him over fences or logs. He never had to get out of the truck and open gates, or chop firewood, or do any cooking. He was just too weak.

Although none of us actually said so at the time, we all had a sneaking concern that we might have to carry him back to camp feet-first one of these days, in spite of all we could do to conserve his feeble reserves of energy.

The boss had our sympathy. Even if Cedric had pulled his own weight it wouldn't have been noticeable, and he couldn't even do *that* half the time, let alone a day's work. But you couldn't sack a man out of his job when he was in the condition Cedric was in. So we went on nursing him along and reassuring ourselves that he might start coming right any day now, though none of us really believed it was possible.

And then one morning, just as we were climbing into the truck, one of the blokes yelled out, "Hey . . . what's all that smoke! It looks as though your hut's on fire!"

And it surely did. There was smoke pouring out of the doorway.

"Get some water!" shouted the boss. And we ran to get buckets and things to fight the fire with. But none of us was as quick as Cedric.

"My things are in there!" he shouted. And he ran like a hare to the hut and dived straight into the smoke. And the next thing we knew there was a veritable shower of things flying out through the door. First all his personal gear — clothes and books and things — then all my stuff. Then the pots and billies and all the food out of the cupboards. Chairs, bedding, tools, lamps, cases, boxes, sacks, benches and bags. There was a lot of gear in that hut, some of it weighing more than Cedric, and every bit of it came flying out through that door as though there were two strong men behind it.

Cedric was so engrossed in clearing out the hut that he hadn't noticed the smoke clearing. There were only a few whiffs of it still drifting around by the time he ran out dragging the big sheepskin mat off the floor. When he saw us all standing there he stopped and looked back into the conflagration, but there was none.

To say that he looked as sheepish as the mat he was holding, as he stood there amongst all the stuff he'd thrown out of the hut, would be an understatement.

"I thought I'd make sure nothing got burnt," he said.

We had a look and found that a pair of Cedric's trousers had fallen off the drying-rail into thc embers of the fire. They'd smouldered away to a charred black mess. Apart from that the only damage was the stuff that got broken when Cedric slung it out of the hut with such astonishing strength and energy.

The little bastard was as tough as machine-belting. He'd been using his scrawny appearance to take us for a ride. And we had to admit he'd done it handsomely. He'd been having a holiday at our expense. Needless to say he didn't get any change out of us after that, but we didn't get any work out of him either. As soon as he saw that his jig was up he packed it in.

"I'll have to go back up north before the winter sets in," he told the boss. "I have to watch me rheumatics, y'know."

And the boss paid him off without comment.

25
Xenial Bastard

THE ONLY THING I know about this kind of Bastard — Xenial Bastard (*Bastardus obscurus*) — is that somebody called me one once. And I've returned the schoolmistress's dictionary so I don't know whether I was being praised, criticised, or taken the micky out of.

I'd like to believe she said *Genial* Bastard, but I know she didn't. Anyway, I've never met a Bastard yet who had an accurate idea of his own B-rating, and I don't suppose I'm any different from any other Bastard.

The surest way of finding out would be to ask someone who knows me, and he'll tell you, instantly and accurately, precisely what sort of Bastard I am; but ask him what sort of Bastard he himself is and he'll become evasive, inarticulate and often either falsely modest or boastful or totally dishonest. Whatever he says, the chances of him being able to give himself an accurate B-rating are millions to one — that is, according to a survey I've been carrying out since 1935.

Which just goes to show that if we knew as much about ourselves as we claim to know about other people there'd be more Splendid Bastards like you and me around.

Bastardus obscurus

26
Young Bastard

YOUNG BASTARDS (*BASTARDUS WHIPPER-SNAPPERUS*) are known to everybody all over the world. The main thing about Youngbastardry is that it's seldom permanent and most of the types of Bastard described in this priceless collection were themselves Young Bastards in their time.

The Young Bastard swipes your fruit, rides his bike into your hedge or flower garden, throws stones onto your lawn, breaks the odd window with his slug-gun or shanghai, asks endless questions and generally exasperates us cantankerous Old Bastards (*Bastardus senilus*). He might shout a bit of cheek when you drive past if he's with a couple of other Young Bastards. He may even whip the money out of your milk bottles if you don't watch it.

If you know a Young Bastard well, you can often pick what kind of Bastard he's going to grow up into, but apart from guiding him as well as you can away from the more odious types of Bastardry there's nothing much you can do about it, because by this time his Bastard-type is well and truly settled.

The Young Bastard has an aversion to Old Bastards like you and me trying out our various psychological theories on how to "handle" Young Bastards like him. He finds it very difficult to take anyone seriously who doesn't remember what it was like to be a Young Bastard.

So the next time a Young Bastard gets on your goat, ask yourself how many goats you got on when you were a Young Bastard yourself. Then give him a grin, tell him he's a Young Bastard, and he's your friend for life. You're talking his language.

You may have noticed just back there where I said that Youngbastardry is *seldom* permanent. That was to allow for the alarming numbers of us (not you or I, of course) who never grow up. People who retain intact all the tantrums, the complaining-to-their-mothers, the demands and the freedom from responsibility

Bastardus whipper-snapperus

of their childhood, and yet they still insist on having all the privileges that go with adulthood.

They want the best of everything they've ever had, *when* they want it. And they also want to *not* have it when it's inconvenient. This type of Youngbastardry is mostly found in so-called men, but not exclusively (E.g. the fat woman with the voice and the uncontrolled appetites of an infant.) And the places you find these specimens! The headmaster complaining to his assembled pupilage that he can't go on putting up with some piece of adolescent behaviour or other. ("It's not fair!")

The politician — whining to the nation on television about the dreadfulness of the opposition or the trade unions. ("You kids are going to get us all into trouble!")

The magistrate who tells the peeping-Tom how he has to have beasts like him locked up for the protection of decent people. ("You're not allowed over to our place to play any more, so ha!")

And the unheroic credit manager of a department store who's done a quick check-up on you through his shabby system and tells you he's afraid he is unable to offer you a credit account at the moment. ("Your granny's got something bad wrong with her, so ha!")

The more you think of it the more of them there are. It's a sobering thing to contemplate. If you ask me the less these types have to do with bringing up, or even influencing, our genuine Young Bastards the better.

I was even starting to suspect myself for a moment there.

27
Zealous Bastard

IT DISTRESSES ME TO have to end this section with the description of the Zealous Bastard (*Bastardus fanaticus*), but this is no time to depart from the strict observance of outspoken, unperjured veracity that sets this volume apart from its imitators. So here goes.

The Zealous Bastard, mercifully, seldom appears amongst us, but when he does there' s not much doubt about it. The only snag about recognising him is that it's sometimes difficult not to mistake him for the Humanitarian Bastard (*Bastardus philanthropus*), and *that* would be a mistake.

Of all the Bastards from the Onward and Upward Department the Zealous Bastard takes the cake as far as enthusiasm goes, and Ira Bowmast was a fair-dinkum beaut. You could tell that by the look of him. He looked like a cartoon of a religious racing car. He was a high-octane glass of milk, or a Pomeranian pig-dog. He was clear-eyed and hairy, skinny and overpowering, meek and intimidating. He used to get around in a balaclava, three big jumpers (summer and winter), and enormous overcoat, and Roman sandals with dirty toenails.

He'd appear amongst us and really take up the cudgels on behalf of somebody (never himself) or something, usually some cause or other. But it was always something that wasn't topical, something out of date and unpopular. Something everyone else had lost or never had any interest in. The last time it was getting the Yanks out of Vietnam and most of them were already gone, but Ira accumulated more support for that cause than it had ever had when it was at the height of its fashion.

He'd pursue his chosen objective with a truly inspiring vigour. He'd work so energetically, so purposefully, and with such fervent and consuming, single-minded tenacity that we could only stand back and admire him and leave him to it.

By his very self-denial he usually engendered a fair number of

Bastardus fanaticus

setbacks, but these only seemed to spur him on to even greater efforts, until, one by one, his obstacles were overwhelmed by his sheer unfaltering drive and dedication. And at last his goal would be in sight. The result was a foregone conclusion. The bureaucrats were willing to negotiate with him. Employers were prepared to discuss changes in the working conditions of their downtrodden employees or the government was announcing a preliminary investigation into the possible setting-up of another Royal Commission. . . .

And then, to everyone's astonishment, with the victory he'd worked so long and ardently for within his very grasp, the bastard would go and lose interest in it. As often as not he'd just disappear, leaving all his supporters wondering what the hell to do now.

Every time this happened we'd swear never to take any notice of him ever again, but he'd turn up after two, or six, or twelve months and before we'd know what was happening he'd have us handing out leaflets, or drumming up support for his new cause in some other way. It was hard not to believe that this time it was the real thing. Ira would be so bloody convincing; striving and battling valiantly onward, against all odds and opposition.

Then, just when it looked as though we were really getting somewhere, he'd announce that he was needed up north to help with the Treaty of Waitangi cause, or some such. We'd been had again.

And there's not much you can do about it when you've been caught up in the whirl of enthusiasm that surrounds a Zealous Bastard. He's not humanitarian — as you thought, nor is he ambitious, nor is he particularly interested in what he's been fighting *for*. It's the long, gruelling, up-hill struggle he's interested in — the might-and-main of it all. The challenge of the thing. And there's no challenge in being victorious. Winning a battle simply means to the Zealous Bastard that he has to turn round and find something else to get stuck into. It's the end of the game for him, he's been bowled out . . .

I hadn't thought of it that way before. Wait till I see that Zealous Bastard Ira Bowmast again!

HERE ARE A FEW OTHER BASTARDS I MET AFTER COMPLETING MY A-Z OF BASTARDRY

Introduction

Well it has been a year or three since I produced my alphabetical list of bastards, and since then I have spent the best part of twelve months down on the Coast — at a place called Tangaroa which I disliked from the start but had quite a job escaping from. It was one of those small, damp and scattered places — in some respects thirty years out of date, and fifty years in others, but it boasted as concentrated a collection of bastards you could ever hope to meet in this fair land.

My triumphal entry into Tangaroa was heralded only by a shower of rain and an old brown dog that was lying in the middle of the road outside the store. The town was: a deceptively innocent-looking old pub; a hall that was never used; about a dozen huts and houses; a store/post office with two petrol bowsers; and, just down the road, a long bridge over the Tangaroa River.

I stopped at the petrol pumps and went in to the store. The place was open but there was no-one around. I waited for a while and then rapped on the counter with a fifty-cent coin. But no-one came.

"Shop!" I called out.

Nothing.

"Anyone there?" I yelled.

No-one.

So I went outside. The back door of the house beside the store was open so I went over and knocked.

No response.

I drove along to the pub and went in. There was no-one there. I rapped on the bar with a coin and after a while I heard footsteps so I stopped rapping. But the footsteps hadn't heard me at all. They faded away to a different part of the building.

"Whew!" I said to myself to the mirror behind the bar. I wasn't in any particular hurry but this was bloody ridiculous. Just then someone pulled up outside the pub in one of those Volkswagen buggies towing a trailer loaded with gear, with a little plywood dinghy tied on the top. It looked like some kind of camping outfit but it was impossible to tell what the bloke did by looking at him or his gear. He seemed to have a hell of a lot of sacks and netting and there was a big bundle of flax tied on to the load. He had come a long way by the look of it. The whole outfit, including himself, was splattered with mud.

He got out of his waggon and came into the bar. A big rough-looking bloke with two fingers missing off his left hand and a face like a fritter. He had red hair starting to go grey and was wearing anything you like. He also needed a shave but if you were going to clean him up it would be a fair while before you got around to that.

"G'day," he said.

"G'day," I nodded back.

"What do you do to get a drink around here?" asked the bloke.

"You wait," I said.

So we waited. The big bloke was Nobby Corcoran, who had come over from Canterbury to have a crack at eeling in some of the lakes on the Coast. He had already jacked up to sell his eels to the bloke who ran a venison freezer, four miles down the road, for eight cents a pound, which he reckoned wasn't a bad price.

It wasn't long before the publican turned up. He was Rex Logan — dark, fattish, born and bred on the Coast, proud of it and in no hurry. He had a big wife who looked and talked and dressed and walked just like Rex, except that she did most of the work around the pub and Rex did most of the talking.

Rex had to muck around with his beer system for a while before we got a drink but when we finally did the first few beers were on the house. The more beer we knocked back, the better Nobby and I hit it off. Nobby could use an off-sider and I had nothing to do and nowhere that I had to get to, so we decided to have a go at eeling Lake Douglas together and see how it worked out.

Nobby was a Simple Bastard (*Bastardus straightforwardus*) — not just an honest bastard (*Bastardus truthus*) like you or I, but in spite of being a bit rough at the edges, generous and kind.

Nobby and I spent all next day getting gas and supplies from the store and in the afternoon we moved in to a disused Forest Service hut down thc road from Tangaroa and nine miles from Lake Douglas. It seemed that I was going to stay in the locality for a while, although I'm not at all sure I would have done what I did if I had realised just what an assortment of bastards I'd meet in Tangaroa. They were too good to miss, so here goes.

29
Simple Bastard

IN SPITE OF HIM being a bit on the rough side, I could tell that Nobby was going to be a good bloke to camp and work with. It'd probably take plenty to get him worried or rattled, and probably a hell of a lot more to quieten him down again once he got his rag out. When he had something to say, he said it. And when he said something it was exactly what he meant, neither more or less. And when he didn't have anything to say, he didn't say anything.

He didn't even know how to be sarcastic.

It rained for four days and we spent most of the time in the pub. Our money was just about cut by the time we arrived at the lake with Nobby's boat and his seven chicken-netting eel-traps on the back of my ute.

Lake Douglas was dark and deep and still and clear, with trees and moss right down to the water, except for three or four small beaches of sand and reeds. The vegetation was so thick the lake reminded me of the tropics, but that was as far as any similarity went. This one was so cold it hurt.

We baited the traps with dead hares we'd picked up on the road and it took us several hours to get them spaced out across the lake because the boat would only take two of us and two of the traps at once. Nobby rowed his boat like he did everything else — bloody clumsily. One oar was longer than the other; rowlocks kept slipping out of their holes; there was only three inches of freeboard, and I had to balance the boat and bail out water. She leaked.

"Do you reckon it's safe to wear those gumboots of yours in the boat, Nobby?" I asked.

"Why not?" said Nobby, splashing me with a freezing oarful of water.

"Well, if we were to capsize you wouldn't be able to swim too good with them on."

Bastardus straightforwardus

"I can't swim at all with them on or off," grinned Nobby, "so it doesn't make any difference. This'll do, we'll drop one about here."

I eased one of the baited traps over the stern. It was six or seven feet long and I had to be careful not to tip the boat over too far. I let the trap down on its rope, but before it was completely out of sight, came to the half-gallon plastic detergent container Nobby used for a float.

"The rope's too short," I said. "The hinaki's nowhere near the bottom yet."

"Blast," said Nobby. "Never thought of that. the place I've been working in is only shallow. Hang on to it, I'll tow us into shallow water."

Which took nearly half an hour. We extended the ropes on our traps with whatever we could find in the way of rope, and wire, and flax, and it was well into the afternoon by the time we'd finished laying them. Then we drove into Tangaroa and spent an hour and a half looking for and waiting for the bloke at the store so we could buy some rope and bread off him. We couldn't afford to wait in the pub any more. We had less than a dollar left by the time we paid for the stuff we bought.

"Doesn't matter," said Nobby. "We'll be selling eels tomorrow."

"I just hope we catch some," I said.

Nobby grinned at me. "If we don't, I'll give you my share of the catch," he said.

But it'd take more than that to reassure a bloke who'd never given eels a second thought in his life.

It rained all night and it was still raining next morning when we got up early. We got the fire going, had tea and toast, coats on, and away to the lake to see what we'd got. The rain stopped as we arrived. We tipped the rainwater out of the dinghy and Nobby rowed us out to the farthest trap-float. On the way there I idly wondered how on earth Nobby could have had so much experience at rowing a boat and still be so downright bad at it.

It was at the first trap we lifted that I found out why Nobby had use for a mate. I thought the trap must have been snagged on something at first, but it was full of eels — packed with them.

About seventy or eighty pounds weight and some bloody whoppers amongst them! They were even spilling out through the neck of the trap as I managed to roll it over the stern into the boat. Nobby had to sit right up in the front to keep the stern from going under. Then Nobby leaned forward and held a sack open while I released the gate at the end of the trap and the whole load slid neatly into the sack. Nobby tied the neck of the nearly-full sack with flax while I baited the trap again and lowered it back over the stern.

"How thc hell do you pull 'em up on your own without capsizing the boat?" I asked, shoving a stray slithering eel into a fresh sack with my foot.

"Rocks," said Nobby.

"Rocks?"

"Yeah. You load the back of the boat up with as many rocks as she'll take and row out to your hinaki. Then you shift the rocks into the front of the boat so you can get into the back of it and pull the hinaki in. When you've got enough eels you just chuck the rocks over the side and use the sacks of eels to balance the boat. It's a hell of a lot easier with two blokes, though, isn't it?" he added.

"I can believe that," I said with feeling. "But why not get a bigger boat?"

"It'd be too tough to cart around and handle," said Nobby. "Some of the places I get into are pretty swampy and shallow. This boat'll do us. You should see some of the tidal estuaries over the other side. This is nothing."

"It's something all right," I said. "But I think I can imagine what you mean."

The other six traps were all as full as the first one and it was about three hours before we had our seven nearly-full sacks of all sized yellow-bellies on the back of the ute. I could tell we had a fair load by the way the ute handled.

"Would you call this good going?" I asked Nobby.

"Not particularly," said Nobby. "You always do pretty good at first. We could clean 'em out of that lake in a week or so. We'll just have to wait and see how it goes."

The bloke at the venison freezer, a Dutchman, weighed our

sacks of eels and then emptied them into one of four 500-gallon concrete water tanks he had, fresh water running through from a spring up in the bush behind his place.

"What happens to them now?" I wanted to know.

"I keep 'em alive in the tanks for two or three weeks," explained the eel bloke. "Then I kill 'em and smoke 'em. He waved his arm towards a longish building where all this killing and smoking evidently took place.

"What do you do with them then?"

"Export," said the bloke. "Most of my stuff goes to Holland."

Then he weighed the wet sacks and deducted that from the total he'd written on the back of his docket book.

"I make it 496 pounds," he said. "That okay?"

"Yep," said Nobby.

And at eight cents a pound the bloke wrote them out a cheque for $39.68.

Driving back to the hut I said, "That's not bad money, Nobby. I make it roughly 280 bucks a week. That's 140 each. These eels are really something!"

"Yeah," said Nobby, with a non-commital grin of someone who knows it never really works out that way.

If someone had told me I was going to get a kick out of catching eels in a freezing Westland lake and actually make money at it — I'd have simply felt sorry for them. But I did. The traps kept catching day after day and even Nobby seemed mildly surprised. The locals were beginning to thaw out a bit and some of them even waved or nodded when we drove past or walked into the pub.

In the mornings when the mist was lifting off the surface of the lake and the sun was flooding across the Alps, but not yet high enough to reach into the valleys, the water reflected the snowy craggy cloud-streaked peaks of the mountains and the bushed ridges leading up to them like a giant mirror. And the air was as clear and chill as the water in the lake itself. I couldn't remember seeing anything better-looking.

For a man who'd been making his living for five years by taking eels out of lakes and rivers and estuaries by the ton, Nobby knew astonishingly little about them. He knew they ate meat and were partial to the odd trout or two, but nothing else about their diet. He knew they were supposed to migrate and breed out in the sea somewhere, but he'd never seen it. He knew there was a difference between a silver-belly and a yellow-belly, but apart from the colour of them they were all the same to him. Eels — eight cents a pound. Nobby was a simple bastard.

And when the eels in their traps began to dwindle down to 150 to 200 pounds a day, I shot the odd deer or two up in the big Tangaroa River flats by getting out before daylight in the morning and stalking quietly along the misty bush-edges in the first light. We both laughed at the idea of Nobby sneaking quietly enough to get within rifle shot of a deer and shared the money we got for the meat.

Nobby was a tower of strength when it came to packing out the deer, which weighed up to 175 pounds a carcass. The locals seemed to think I was a pretty good sort of a hunter because they hardly ever shot any deer, and the two professional hunters with their jet-boat had hardly got any either. But then they seldom got out before daylight and went hunting for them. They didn't need to, it was their locality and the way they saw it every deer shot was shot by everyone.

I didn't bother telling anyone that the first deer I shot I had to carry back to the hut, head, guts and all, because I'd forgotten to take a knife with me.

It had to happen that our catch of eels fell off until it was uneconomic, but Lake Douglas kept us going for three weeks before Nobby made up his mind to lift his traps and head further south to try some of the lakes down there. But I had got to like the meat-hunting and the money that was in it so I decided to stick around Tangaroa for a while.

We loaded Nobby's waggon and trailer and then got so drunk having a send-off noggin or two in the pub that he couldn't leave till the next day. He set off in the middle of a mind-blowing hangover, waving his three fingered hand out the window of his VW — and got his two off-side wheels off the track into a patch of swamp and reeds and I had to tow him out with the ute.

Let's face it, Simple Bastards like Nobby are not too bad to have around, and I rather missed my big clumsy mate, even if I was too busy to think about it much. I hunted morning and evening and had to go so far up the river to have a shot that my new-found mates at the Tangaroa pub could have been excused it they'd started calling me an Enthusiastic Bastard (*Bastardus keenus*). It was as though most of the deer had followed Nobby south, so I decided to stick around and have a go at this white-baiting I'd been hearing so much about. I started making a few casual enquiries and discovered that although every Tangaroan knew everything there was to know about it . . .

30
Rough Bastard

SCRATCHER FARRELL WAS THE bloke to see about whitebaiting. He was one of the most successful whitebaiters on the Coast, they reckoned. Been at it more than twenty years and always got more than anyone else.

He liked working with a mate, but for some reason that wasn't quite clear no one ever stayed with him for more than a week or two. Everyone agreed that Scratcher had something wrong with him, but no one seemed to be able to say exactly what it was, except that he "lived a bit hard". I found out *where* he lived a bit hard, about five miles away down a dead-end side road and went to see him.

I got to know Scratcher pretty well over the next few weeks. He was a little wiry bloke about fifty or sixty years old. Sometimes you couldn't get a word out of him and sometimes you could, depending on how you struck him. He told me a bit about whitebaiting in one of his talkative moods and made out a list of the things I was going to need. It was written with a sharpened .22 bullet on a flap torn off a cardboard box.

Scratcher lived a bit hard all right — he was a Real Rough Bastard (*Bastardus hardcasus*). He lived in a draughty old shed with a dirt floor. He cooked his tucker in buckets over a smoky fire in the doorway. The stuff in plastic buckets only got as cooked as it could by having boiling water from one of his galvanised buckets poured into it. You had to literally duck through the flames and smoke to get inside when he had a feed on. When the wind was blowing the smoke into the shed he did his cooking and eating from the outside, and when it wasn't he could operate from inside, more or less out of the rain.

Everything in the shed was hanging from nails around the dry areas of the walls. The dirt floor soaked up the water from outside when it rained and it was often quite muddy. His bunk was the corrugated-iron door off the shed, built up from the floor

Bastardus hardcasus

with blocks of firewood and padded with sacks and coats and his good going-to-town clothes.

For light in the daytime we hung the sack over the one window opening on a nail to one side.

At night he used a candle shielded from the draught by a milk-powder tin cut down the middle. He didn't trust pressure lamps and he didn't like the smell of kerosene. He usually went to bed early anyway, he told me.

Most of his food hung from the roof in sacks with slits cut in them so he could put stuff in and get it out again without having to take his cupboards down. Anything perishable had to be kept in the cab of his old Land Rover because that was the only possum-and-waterproof place he had access to. Every three months or so he got them to send him down a sack of calf milk-powder, a fifty-pound bag of flour, and twenty large tins of golden syrup. The rest of his stuff he got from the store or picked up around the place. He wasn't fussy about what he ate and he used to shoot quite a few birds and hares and things to put in his buckets of stew. He was always on the scrounge for meat and they reckoned he'd pinch the maggotty rib-cage of a goat off one of Ted Packer's dogs, but they were probably exaggerating.

The one good thing about Scratcher and his food was that he didn't like giving any away. I dropped in to see him one morning and Scratcher was eating a skinned, but not gutted, shag he'd shot. He'd fried it in his shovel and was tearing into it with the blackened stumps of his few remaining teeth as though he'd seen me coming and didn't want to have to offer me any. We yarned while he finished his meal and wiped his face on his hands and then his hands on his pants. We then went on chatting about nothing in particular while Scratcher messed about in his open-air kitchen. I then suddenly noticed that he was squeezing something out of a tube into a bucketful of something he had been boiling over the fire.

"Hey, that's not *glue* you're putting in there, is it Scratcher?"

Scratcher had a look at the tube. "Yeah, looks like it," he said.

"You can't eat that stuff!"

"Why not?" said Scratcher, squeezing a bit more in and wiping the nozzle of the tube on the rim of the bucket.

"You'll make yourself crook."

"No, it's okay," said Scratcher. "I put some in the stew by accident the other night and it thickened her up just nicely. It was a bit dark at the time and I thought it was condensed milk," he explained.

"Is there *anything* you wouldn't eat?" I asked.

Scratcher thought this over for a few moments.

"Don't go much on dogs," he said "Or . . ."

"Do you ever go up to town, Scratcher?"

"Yeah, I was up there a few months back."

"Stay long?"

"No, I only wanted to see me sister's kids and buy a few things."

"Well, did you see them?"

"See who?"

"Your sister's kids."

"Oh, them. Yeah, I saw them there. They were playing around in the yard. Everything looked all right so I came away again."

"You mean to say you didn't even go in and have a yarn with them?"

"No, I didn't want to talk to 'em. I only wanted to see if they were okay."

"Well, did you get your shopping done?"

"No, everything was shut, so I came home. Must have been a Sunday or something."

"You mean you drove 250 miles and back just to look at your sister's kids?"

"Yeah, I don't like the towns much."

There was the day I went out to have a look at Scratcher's job with him. It was his official duty to maintain the telephone line between Tangaroa and Boulder Creek, a tiny settlement in the next valley. It was a single wire running through insulators hammered into the trees, roughly nine miles of it, most of it through heavy bush. Whenever a tree or branch fell across the wire they'd let Scratcher know the phone was out and he'd go and walk along the line until he found the break and fix it.

As soon as I saw the line I discovered why it was so notoriously weak. Scratcher had been tying the breaks in the wire with all sorts of stuff. It was incredible that the line worked at all. Quite a few of the gaps were bridged with *barbed* wire, and in one place, where he hadn't been quite able to get the broken ends of wire to meet he'd punched holes in each end of a sardine tin and hooked the wires into them. He'd used a length of dog-chain in one place, and a hook made out of a rusty four-inch nail in another. In another spot he'd used an iron fencing-standard and in another a billy-handle; in another a slasher-head — a stirrup iron . . .

"Hey Scratcher, you can't do this!" I said, kicking at a push-bike wheel that hung nearly to the ground in an old break in the wire.

"Why not?" said Scratcher. "That's been there for months. I brought up a spring-leaf to replace it once, but I had to use it in another place. This works okay though."

"Don't they give you proper wire to patch up the breaks with?" I asked increduously.

"Yeah, I got a whole roll of it off 'em once."

"Well, what did you do with it?"

"Used some of it," said Scratcher, "And I sold some of it to me mates, I'm saving the rest. It's damn good wire, that. Copper, Comes in handy for binding up split axe-handles and oars and things."

"But where on earth do you get all this stuff?"

"Lying around," said Scratcher. "You'd be surprised what you can make do with."

"I *am* surprised," I said truthfully. "I've never seen anything like this in my bloody life."

"Mind you," warned Scratcher, "you can't go using just *any* old thing in a telephone line."

"No?"

"No fear," said Scratcher. "It's got to be *metal*."

"Has anyone else seen this?" I asked.

"No, I'm the only one who ever comes up here. As long as I keep their phone working okay nobody's got anything to worry about."

"I was beginning to see how old Scratcher worked. Although he was a dreadful scrounger he never had much of the fruits of his scavenging around his place because whatever he couldn't eat he was hanging in the Tangaroa-Boulder Creek telephone line. If the people of Boulder Creek knew by what means their only link with the outside world was being maintained . . .

I later discovered another thing Scratcher used his roll of copper wire for. Sewing. Most of his buttons were tied on with it. And the sun glinting on the seams of his trousers or coat revealed that they, too were stitched up with telephone wire. He was the Roughest Bastard I've come across, old Scratcher, and I've come across some Rough Bastards in my time.

31
Literate Bastard

QUENTIN PARSONAGE WAS A tall, old, stooped bloke who used a shaving brush, and wore spectacles and sandals and an old grey suit when he went along to the Tangaroa pub or store. He lived with a green and yellow budgie called Mr Bo Jangles in a very tidy little place just inside the bush half a mile past the Tangaroa bridge. His place had been a shack when he moved into it, but he'd made it so neat and tidy that it was now a cottage. He was as fastidious as Scratcher Farrell wasn't, with everything scrubbed clean and put away in its proper place.

Quentin was a Real Literate Bastard (*Bastardus bookwormus*), who was always on the lookout for something to read. He had the biggest collection of old newspapers and magazines neatly stacked in his kitchen that anyone has ever seen, and Rex Logan, the local publican, reckoned that when Quentin first came to Tangaroa it only took him three weeks to read every printed word in the whole district. And to watch him actually read was rather interesting . . .

Bastardus bookwormus

it

looked

as

though

he

was

skimming

through

the

pages

as

quickly

as

this,

but

in fact he was reading every word as carefully as you're reading these ones. It's just that he was a terrifically fast reader. Sometimes he wouldn't even borrow a book, he'd read it right where it was, even if it took him two or three visits.

He inspected everything he handled to see what was written on it, and people didn't always understand why he examined their money so closely for something he'd bought. When he first came into a place he'd go round reading everything, like a dog sniffing. He read instructions, brand names and labels. He read the proof-marks on shotguns, and the *Made in Japan* stamped into the frames of fishing reels. He'd read your calendar, your cardboard boxes, the radio dial and the name on the fridge door. It only took him two trips between his place and the pub to polish off the whole dashboard, the warrant of fitness, the registration sticker, the lining of a hat, and the service manual I kept in the glovebox of the ute, but a war comic someone had left in my hut staggered him a bit. He fluttered through the pages and then dropped it into the fire as though to save anyone else from being exposed to it, which goes to show he was a man of taste. He liked to read everything but he didn't necessarily like everything he read.

He lived mainly on his pension, his garden and quite a few trout taken by various means from the river. And he drank mainly on anyone who would pay for his booze.

Sometimes when Quentin had a few rums under his belt he would entertain everyone with magician's tricks that mostly never quite came off. The first one I saw him make a botch of was the one where Quentin slipped a match up the hem of his handkerchief on the quiet and then showed everyone how he folded a match up in the handkerchief and broke it up inside it and then tipped it out again in one piece. You're supposed to break the match you've got up the hem of the handkerchief, but Quentin got the wrong one, three times in a row, and when he finally got it right no one was watching any more.

Then he tried the one about which cup the five cent piece was under, but he got confused and as often as not somebody else guessed it right. He dropped twenty cent pieces that were supposed to have disappeared, and forgot how to do tricks with matches arranged on the bar. He wasn't very good with tricks using bits of string either and he was useless at riddles and jokes because after an impressive and long-winded build-up he always forgot exactly how the punch-line went.

In short, Quentin was not only a Literate Bastard, but something of a Clumsy Bastard (*Bastardus ballsupus*) as well, as so many Literate or Intellectual Bastards — remember *Bastardus profoundus*? — are.

Quentin was worst of all with card tricks. Whenever a series of his tricks had let him down again, he'd call for the pack of cards Rex kept under the bar and get everyone ready to be shown a *real* trick. He'd finish off his rum and shuffle and snap the curled old pack and then lay out twenty-one cards on the bar like a Mississippi gambler in a movie and invite you to pick out any card you liked but not let on what it was. When you'd done that, he'd whisk them off the bar again, have another quick rum, shuffle the cards, and then slap them out again and ask you which row it was in now. He'd keep this up until you were beginning to lose interest, and then he'd suddenly flip a card out in front of you and say, "How's that?"

"No," you'd have to say.

Quentin would flip out another card as though the first one was just to get you guessing. "That it?" he'd say shrewdly.

"Nope."

"This one then . . ."

"Nope."

"Darn. I must have done something wrong. Hold on, I'll run through it again."

But he never got it right. The more he tried, the worse he got at it. It wasn't that he didn't *know* the tricks properly, it was because he had to have a fair few rums on board before he got up the courage to do them, and by that time he was starting to get a bit muddled.

He was good for business at the pub, though. Poeple who dropped in for a quick drink would sometimes stay for hours if Quentin was doing his tricks, fascinated by the gamble of whether he was going to get one of them right.

Everyone liked old Quentin and most of his carpentry and plumbing and fencing was done by blokes who'd dropped in to see him and seen what a dreadful botch he was making of it. He was a hell of a good gardener though, grow anything. And he always had a cabbage or a couple of outsized lettuces to wrap up for you as you were leaving.

Quentin was the only one drinking in the pub when I turned up there one morning and Quentin had got straight on to the rum and was away to a great start. He'd brought a couple of enormous cabbages along for Rex Logan and had only just remembered to give them to him when I arrived.

"By strike," said Rex gratefully, pouring a double rum into Quentin's glass. "There's no doubt about you. You must put in more time in that garden of yours than a married man spends at home with the wife!"

"Naturally," said Quentin. "There's a lot more for a man in a garden than in a marriage."

"Get away with you," scoffed Rex. "You're a confirmed old batchelor, you are!"

"Oh, I've been married," said Quentin, replacing his empty glass on the bar.

"Fair go?" said Rex. "I never knew you'd been married."

"Oh yes," said Quentin.

"It's not worth mentioning," said Quentin, "I'd rather talk about gardening. It's more productive."

"Did you have any kids?" I asked, putting the money on the bar for another beer and motioning Rex to fill Quentin's glass as well.

"No, unfortunately," said Quentin.

"What happened?" asked Rex, giving them their drinks and leaning attentively on the bar.

"Oh, it was the usual exhausting treadmill," said Quentin. "Impossible to maintain. My wife was a very beautiful woman actually. A music teacher — well-educated."

Quentin paused for another drink.

"Before we were married," he went on, "she used to say I set her on fire. But after I married her all I found was a scattered heap of soggy embers that wouldn't ignite, no matter what I tried. But I'm not complaining. I was no better myself in a number of other ways."

"How do you mean?"

"Well, in my splendid self-sacrificing superiority, I'd gone and made an honest woman out of her. How grateful she would have to be! I'd married her, hadn't I? All I had to do now was sit back and spend the rest of my days receiving her spontaneous gratitude. But she let me down. Betrayed me. It wasn't like I'd expected it to be, whatever that was. Be so good as to give me another rum, please Rex." He interrupted himself. "A double, thanks."

"Yes, go on," prompted Rex, putting the drink on the bar and sliding the cloves bottle beside it without taking any money.

"Well," said Quentin, and he paused to polish off the rum, "I wasn't going to be treated like that. This woman I'd married not only didn't understand what I needed, but she wasn't giving it to me without my having to ask for it. I was forced to seek these unnameable things at the bosoms of the wife of a fellow lecturer at the university."

"Were you a lecturer at a university?" asked Rex incredulously.

"Senior lecturer in English at Canterbury," said Quentin.

"Well I'll be blowed," said Rex, "How long were you there?"

"Nine years," said Quentin, moving his empty glass on the bar so it'd be noticed. "After my divorce I left the university and took on private tutoring."

"What happened?" I asked. "Did you get caught with the lecturer's wife?"

"No, it wasn't like that," said Quentin. "It wasn't a matter of my wife finding out about it. She knew. All over the country there are men in all walks of life being unfaithful to their wives all the time. And all the women know it. But they can't do much about it because they don't feel what they're traditionally supposed to feel when their husbands take lovers. It's caused them to become better at concealing their husband's infidelities from themselves than the husbands are. There's not a woman alive who could stop loving a man she genuinely loves because of him having an affair with another woman, and yet for years she's been expected to divorce him for it. Of course I didn't realise all this when it was happening to me. I was doing what I was to make her sorry for what she was driving me to do so she'd change her ways. And the more I did it, the more impossible it became for her to give me what I thought I needed so badly."

"What was that?" I asked.

"I'm not sure now, so I can't have had much idea at the time," said Quentin. "And it's as true of a marriage as of anything else that a thing that starts off on an illogical basis can never reach a logical conclusion. We tried to disregard this self-evident truth for three years and then we parted, complete strangers to one another. She went to live in Dunedin and from then on we only ever communicated through lawyers. The last time I saw her was in a courtroom getting her divorce and we were as close then as we'd ever been. — Excuse me, gentlemen. Nature calls." And he polished off his eleventh double rum for the day and left the bar.

"Good old Quentin," said Rex. "You know, he's been around here for over four years now and we never knew he'd ever been married, or a lecturer at a university.

"*Senior* lecturer," I said. "In English!"

"We knew he was well-educated," said Rex, "but this is the first time I've ever heard him talk about himself. What a bloke!"

Just then Quentin returned, a little unsteady on his feet, and said "Feel like a game of darts? I'll play you Aussie rules — lowest score pays for the drinks."

"Okay," I said. "You're on!"

But Quentin turned out to be such a rotten darts-player that I couldn't even contrive to lose a game to him. I was no great shakes at the game myself, but it was all Quentin could do to get one on the board. It didn't prevent us from having a very enjoyable session, though, and we arrived at Quentin's shack, both drunk and broke, in the middle of the afternoon for lunch.

Yes, he was a Real Literate Bastard was Quentin. I've always remembered what he had to say about women and marriage, and I really enjoyed the vegetables he cooked up for lunch.

32
Slow Bastard

EVERYONE RECKONED THAT WEAVER at the store had taken a shine to me, but the only indication I had of this was that Weaver was appearing a little sooner than usual when I went along there for supplies or petrol. Weaver was medium height and build, about middle-aged, with medium colouring and looks. He wore medium kind of clothes.

Somebody told me that Weaver used to be a dairy farmer, but he lost half his herd of cows in a poker-game with a couple of his neighbours, and couldn't afford to go on milking the rest. So he sold out and came to manage the Tangaroa store for six weeks while the owner found a permanent manager. After he'd been there a couple of years, he bought the place.

That was nineteen years ago. He hated Tangaroa and was always complaining about the "Godforsaken hole", but it was obvious that it was going to take him a while yet to move, for Weaver was a Real Slow Bastard (*Bastardus fullstopus*). I don't mean that he was retarded or anything like that; he just took his time to get moving. He owned half the property in Tangaroa by this time, and it didn't pay anyone to try and get him moving any faster than he felt like, which was never very fast. He had the only petrol for sixty miles, and people had been known to find themselves pleading with him to let them have a few gallons at any price because they'd been incautious enough to get uppity or impatient with him.

I had heard all about this, but I found it out for myself the day Weaver ordered me to come over to the house and have a bottle of beer with him. We were on our seventh or eighth bottle, sitting at Weaver's kitchen table, when a big American car pulled up at Weaver's petrol pump and a bloke in a grey suit and moustache got out and went into the store. After a while he came out again and spoke to his blue wife sitting in the car.

"Looks like he wants gas," I said.

Bastardus fullstopus

Weaver grunted and opened another bottle, filled his glass and slid the bottle across the table to me. Then Weaver's customer did a very tactless thing.

He blew the horn of his car.

Three times.

Weaver was drinking at the time and he paused with his glass held at his bottom lip while the horn was blowing and then he went on with his drink. We idly watched as the bloke looked at his watch and paced around in front of the store for a while and then came over the house and knocked on the door as though he had a search warrant. Weaver got up and went and opened the door.

"Do you sell petrol here?" demanded the bloke in a voice that was obviously used to running the show.

"Yeah," said Weaver, totally unimpressed or intimidated.

"Well I'll have four gallons, thank you," said the bloke.

Weaver grunted and shoved his feet into his boots on the porch and his customer led the way across to the petrol pump as though it was a race to get there first. But before he'd gone half-way Weaver was slapping his pockets. Then he stopped altogether.

"Hang on," he said, "I'll have to get me keys."

He took his boots off and came back into the house, finished his beer, put his boots on again and went back out to the pump. I went too.

Weaver unlocked the bowser and shoved the nozzle into the bloke's tank. But there wasn't enough juice in his batteries to run the electric motor in the petrol pump, so he hung the nozzle up again.

"I'll have to start the generator," he said patiently.

"Look here," said the bloke who wanted gas. "How long is this going to take? I'm in a hurry!"

"Dunno," said Weaver. "We'll have to see what kind of a mood the diesel's in." And we left his client mumbling something about ". . . old fool . . ." to his tight-lipped wife, and went round the back to start the generating plant.

Now it wasn't very often that Weaver had to start his generator in the daytime, so after we'd topped up the fuel tank and got her running, he did one or two minor adjustments he'd been meaning to get on to, and by the time we got back round the front, his customer was standing by his car with his petrol cap in one hand and his wallet in the other.

Weaver's pump was one of the old ones, slow as hell. It clicked and dinged steadily over, tenth by tenth, until the four gallons were finally in the tank. By the time he'd hung up the nozzle the bloke was waving a five-dollar note in his face, but Weaver didn't see it until he'd got back from shutting off his generator.

"Two dollars, four cents," he said, reaching for the bloke's money.

"Just a minute," said the bloke, pulling his money away from Weaver's grasp. "That's fifty-one cents a gallon!"

"Yeah," said Weaver.

"But it's only forty-nine cents a gallon in Christchurch."

Weaver didn't bother explaining to him that the petrol had to be freighted to Tangaroa in forty-four gallon drums and siphoned into the reservoir under the pump at a cost in cartage and labour that more than covered the extra two cents a gallon he charged for it. He disappeared around the back and returned with a four-gallon tin and a piece of hose. He shoved the hose into the bloke's tank and started siphoning his gas out again.

"Hey," said the bloke when he saw what Weaver was doing. "What are you doing?"

"Not goin' t' force the stuff on y'," said Weaver. "If y' don't want it, I'll have it back again."

The bloke turned to me. "Is there anywhere else around here where I can buy petrol?" he asked.

"Nope," I said, shaking my head.

"But I haven't got enough to get me back to town," said the bloke.

"Weaver here sells it," I pointed out.

The bloke was beaten and he knew it.

"Look here," he said to Weaver in a very different tone of voice from the one he'd been using. "I didn't mean to imply that you were overcharging for your petrol. I realise that you have your expenses in a place like this . . ."

"You want it or don't you?" asked Weaver indifferently.

"I want it. I want it," said the bloke holding out his five dollars.

Weaver pulled his hose out of the bloke's tank, ran a dribble of petrol from it into his tin and took the money into the store. His far-from-satisfied customer took his change without counting it and drove back in the direction of town. I picked up Weaver's tin. Judging by its weight, it was half full.

"Did you charge him for the full four gallons, Weaver?"

"Yeah."

"But he only ended up with about two gallons."

Weaver grunted something or other and led the way back to his kitchen to fetch a bottle of beer. That sort of thing was nothing unusual to him.

"Everyone gets their money's worth around here," he said.

Weaver was a Slow Bastard, all right. I felt we could get on very well together.

33
Useless Bastard

ANOTHER OF THE NOTEWORTHY citizens of Tangaroa was Ted Packer, a quaint old guy who leased the Muddy River flats for ninety-nine years. Ted was not so much one of the your Dozey Bastards (*Bastardus drippus*) or even a Lazy Bastard (*Bastardus loaferus*) like you or me. No, he was a Useless Bastard (*Bastardus nohopeus*), who ran about 200 tatty sheep and sixty-odd head of beef cattle, mostly on the road. His stock was always getting hit by cars or shot by spotlighters and his dogs were always hungry.

It was generally accepted that Ted was more concerned about his dogs than anything else he had, including his industrious little grey wife, who managed their property while Ted's seven or eight dogs only just managed to keep themselves from starving.

Ted always wore oilskins. Oilskin coat, oilskin sou'wester hat and oilskin leggings. And to see this lean weatherbeaten figure riding up the road on his tired, muddy, brown horse, attended by a retinue of hip-bony, ribby cattle-dogs, it was hard to imagine he wasn't arriving back from mustering all the chamois off the Southern Alps single-handed.

But he was probably just out for a ride and his wife had probably had to catch his horse for him and give him a leg up into the saddle because of his sciatica.

Actually Ted only ever rode along the road because his dogs were pretty good at getting themselves a feed of possum. And it was true that for three or four miles either side of his place there were usually frequent scatters of possum fur, where his dogs had dragged them out of the fern at the side of the road and cleaned up everything except some of the fur. You'd often come across him riding along with a few of his dogs coughing on fur and others still chewing on difficult parts of possum.

Every few days Ted would ride out and chase all his stock from one direction back towards home, but they always ran straight

Bastardus nohopeus

past his gate and in spite of all his dogs he didn't bother heading them off. He just chased them back the other way next time.

A Ministry of Works engineer complained in the pub one day that most of Ted Packer's stock had never set foot on his own property since they were calves or lambs. Once a year Ted trucked some of his stock away to a sale somewhere or other. At shearing time, dipping time, crutching time and lambing time — he didn't seem to bother.

Rex Logan swore that Ted hadn't been up his own river flats for so long that he didn't know his wife was breeding a big mob of mongrel horses up there. The horses and the deer were eating every blade of grass up Muddy River as fast as it would grow, so his stock only had the road to get a feed on anyway.

Rex reckoned that Ted was so much like one of his own dogs he couldn't even lie down without turning around a couple of times.

Ted didn't create a very good impression on passing traffic, either. They usually had to slow down to get past his dogs, who treated the road as their own personal domain, and people would often stop to ask this very colourful drover directions or questions about the district.

But Ted always told them about his sciatica instead, and then followed it up with how he was going to shoot the Governor-General when he got the chance because of something the Governor-General had said on the radio at Christmas time, 1956. And when they politely pointed out that we had a different Governor-General now, he'd say, "Arrgh, they're all the bloody same, them Governor-Generals. Just you let the bastard put one foot on my place, that's all! I'll drop him in his bloody tracks. I'll put one fair through his bloody guts for him! I'll . . ."

At about this point the travellers, who usually included a woman or two would politely thank him for his trouble and drive off wondering what the hell they'd struck.

No one knew what it was that the Governor-General had said on the radio at Christmas time in 1956 that had upset Ted so much, but since Ted's run-down property was so remote from anything that might be included in His Excellency's itinerary, he was unlikely to ever be in any danger from his arch-enemy, Ted Packer.

34
Indispensable Bastard

IF THE NEAREST THING in Tangaroa to a service station was Weaver's store, the nearest thing to a mechanic they had was Joe Bimler.

They've been saying no one's indispensable for so long now that we don't think about it any more, but I had occasion to reconsider that old saying the day I first saw Joe Bimler's workshop. If it was anything to do with cars or trucks, it was probably somewhere among the staggering conglomeration of spare parts that were hung, flung, or slung in Joe's big shed. But if you wanted to know *where* it was, then Joe Bimler was an absolutely Indispensable Bastard (*Bastardus necessarius*).

It was so difficult to accept that anyone could know exactly where everything was in that overwhelming mechanical morass, that you had to rediscover the fact that Joe could instantly tell you whether he had what you wanted or not, and then go and put his hand on it without even having to think where it was. In some incredibly complicated way the place, to him, was actually quite orderly. He'd shake a Commer fan-belt out of the tangle under the far end of the bench, or drag a Vauxhall gearbox out of the long grass behind the shed, as though he'd just put them there the day before yesterday. Joe himself was as deceptively untidy-looking as his workshop. A dark, loose-jointed, baggy, oily bloke, completely uncorrupted by any kind of formal training or education, he'd been married for a few years, but his wife had turned it in and gone back to live with her parents in Motueka.

He had a fleet of four old trucks — starting from number forty-five and only one of them was actually on the road at any one time, but he could only drive one of them at a time anyway, and he was probably the only man alive who could have driven them safely over those roads. With five yards of wet shingle on the back he could pull one of his trucks up from thirty to a dead stop using nothing but the gearbox and the soft going at the side

Bastardus necessarius

of the road. His brakes were notoriously in need of adjustment or repair. They reckoned he'd wear out three clutch pedals before his brake pedal was even shiny.

He hired out his trucks to the Ministry of Works on road work between Greymouth and Tangaroa, though his schedule was a bit unreliable because of his frequent stops for roadside repairs and him having to do most of his travelling at night. Something to do with Certificates of Fitness and Registration and other such formalites.

Joe had once been caught by the M.O.W. engineer who'd hired him, giving his truck a valve-grind on the job. They fired him, but then had to re-hire him because the nearest other truck would have had to travel more than eighty miles to get to and from the job.

Joe was an obliging bloke and he'd cheerfully fix your car for you, if it could be fixed, though unless it was a V8 he was inclined to diagnose the trouble, whatever it was, as being directly traceable to a chronic lack of power. Straight-sixes weren't quite so bad, but he treated anything with four cylinders with utter contempt. Scratcher came into the pub one day with his leathery old feelings hurt because Joe had just told him his Land Rover couldn't pull a hen off its roost.

But there wasn't a mechanic or engineer in the country who could touch Joe Bimler on V8 motors. Give him a V8 and he'd do things with it that would defy every specification the manufacturers darted to claim for it. If the makers' recommended maximum revs-per-minute were 3,500, Joe would get her doing 5,000 just to test her before he slapped her into one of his old trucks.

Or he'd take one that someone had worn out and thrown away, do her up a bit, and get another 50,000 miles out of it.

When Joe was winding up one of his V8s to check her out, the whole village stopped in its tracks. He'd stand there and open her up like a siren, until he produced a high-pitched shriek of a sound that was almost beyond the range of the human ear. And he'd hold it there until you'd swear something had to blow up any second.

Anyone standing round watching moved further back out of

the way. Business at the pub and the store, half a mile away, came to an uneasy standstill. Dogs set up a howling that travelled as far as Boulder Creek. Deer, 3,000 feet up in the Alps, stopped feeding, looked about them with a startled air, and then hurried off into thick cover on the far side of the ridge. The bird-life was stunned into silence for the rest of the day, completely upstaged. Small animals in their burrows and tree-holes and nests got such a fright that there wasn't a possum to be seen on the road for the next three nights. The sandflies stopped biting. The trout in the Tangaroa River moved into deeper water. If it was raining it stopped and if it wasn't raining it started. The trees in the forest produced wavery growth-rings, and dislodged rocks bounded in panic down the sides of the mountains.

Joe, the maestro of the whole ear-splitting performance, stood calmly beside his madly vibrating and leaping machine with the throttle in one hand and a screwdriver in the other, making one or two final adjustments to the mixture or the timing.

The silence when he finally let the whole district off the hook was uncanny. An hour or so after it stopped Joe would drive up the road in one of his trucks and stop outside the pub, give her one or two unnerving bursts of acceleration and come into the bar looking as pleased with himself as though he'd just inherited a whole Ford factory.

"Just slapped a new motor in old forty-seven," he'd announced superfluously. "She should be okay for a while now."

"I certainly hope so," said the publican. "The last time you put a motor in one of your trucks me chooks went off the lay for a fortnight."

It was Joe who gave me the most hair-raising ride in a motor vehicle I've ever had in my life. I was half a mile up the riverbed getting a load of firewood in my ute and on my way back I tore the sump off on an ordinary bunch of reeds that turned out to be growing around a petrified knot of red beech as hard as iron.

Luckily I stopped to see what the bang was and found all my sump-bolts stripped out of the block and the badly-dented sump lying just in front of a rear wheel. I walked all the way out to the road and along to the pub. After a quick beer I went along to Joe's place and found him working on an old hydraulic hoist he'd picked up somewhere. I explained to Joe what had happened.

"Yair," said Joe. "I've done one or two of 'em before. We'll just have to straighten out your sump and tap out bigger holes in the block and slap her on with bigger bolts. They're usually quarter-inch, so five-sixteenth ought to do it. I've got some here."

"Do you think you could tow me off the riverbed?" I asked. "She's out on the shingle below flood level."

"Sure, we'll go and drag her in and do the job right here."

Joe threw a huge snigging-chain on to the back of his currently-functioning V8 truck and off we roared to get my ute. Bouncing out across the riverbed I had to hang onto the glovebox hole in the dashboard to keep myself from being flung into the door or the windscreen or Joe. We backed up to the ute and shackled Joe's big snigging-chain around my front axle and on to a rear spring-hanger of Joe's truck.

"I'll have to keep us moving once we get going across this shingle," said Joe. "If we break through the surface of this stuff we'll both be stuck here."

"Well, okay," I said, "but take it easy on my waggon, will you?"

"Okay," said Joe, opening his truck door. "You right?"

"Yep."

When people say they're going to take off in a motor vehicle they usually only mean that they're going to *move* off along the road, on the surface of the earth. Joe used the term literally.

He took off across the riverbed without even taking up the slack in the chain first. I was plucked from a standstill to full revs of Joe's truck in second gear so suddenly it almost broke my neck. And I never regained proper control of the ute during the whole of that terrible ride.

We careered over the riverbed at a speed that made it impossible for me to think. I slewed from side to side, frantically spinning the wheel one way and then the other to save myself from hitting into the logs and bigger rocks Joe was casually dodging around. We bounced on to the track and out to the main road up a foot-high bank that tore the steering-wheel out of my grasp, and one of the spokes hit my thumb with the force of a backfiring crank-handle.

As soon as we were on the track Joe slammed his truck into third gear with a jerk that must have almost ripped the whole front suspension out of the ute. A little later I found myself seriously wishing it had done.

I just couldn't get control of my vehicle for more than a few seconds at a time. Whenever Joe steered around a pothole or corner, my wagon would start swerving violently from one side to the other. At one point, my off-side wheels rode up on an overgrown log beside the track and the ute rose up to the very point of rolling over, but Joe's big chain dragged me back on to my wheels with a spine-jolting bang that shot me into the scrub on the other side of the track.

Now, I'd travelled that track many times, and I thought I knew it well, but I was getting a vastly different view of it that day. My only indication that we'd reached the main road was when Joe started crashing his truck down through its gearbox. I felt some relief — surely the main road would be easier going!

But we bounced out on to the road, regardless of anything that might be coming and took off towards Tangaroa with the chain flailing around in front of my bonnet. Second — third — top gear, and Joe was flat to the boards. At one point I was sideways-on to Joe's truck and almost parallel with his tailboard. I could see Joe's face in the rear-vision mirror, but Joe wasn't looking back, and then I was snatched round out of a skid and started on another one in the other direction.

Whenever I could spare a hand I kept it on the horn or banged on the side of the ute with it, but Joe couldn't have heard anything over the unmuffled roar of his hurtling truck. It was too dangerous to even jump out. The only thing I had in favour of my survival was that I had brakes and Joe didn't but I was too frightened to touch them.

As far as I knew things couldn't have been much worse, but during a particularly violent swerve out on to the wrong side of the road, I was horrified to see Scratcher's old Land Rover approaching.

So this was to be the way I went out. I didn't even bother

getting ready to meet my Maker. There was nothing he could do anyway.

Ever since that day I've often wondered at the trivial kind of thing that can settle a man's fate. What, for instance, if Scratcher had set off from wherever he did a few seconds earlier or later?

But as it happened, I was just swinging out from behind Joe's truck when Scratcher went past. I caught a fractional glimpse of him meandering along with one hand still raised in a wave to Joe and the other absently picking his nose, as I was hurled past the outside corner of the Land Rover, missing it by a margin as minute as the fact that Scratcher's bomb needed a coat of paint.

The only other near-casualties of the journey were a couple of pub verandah-posts. I was too physically and emotionally exhausted to register a serious complaint when we finally pulled up at Joe's place. The ute was covered with mud and scratches. There was fern and scrub hanging off the bumpers and door-handles and windscreen wipers. Both parking lights and one headlight were broken. Its mudguard and grille had been flogged by Joe's chain until their original shapes were only distinguishable by comparison with another vehicle of the same make and model. My outside rear-vision mirror had been torn off, but apart from that, the ute had hung together remarkably well.

In such ways as this, the greatest film sequences of our times are lost to us.

I was in about the same condition as my ute. My thumb was sprained and swelling; one of my elbows was still hurting from a crack on the window-winder; some skin had been bruised off one of my knees on the bottom edge of the dashboard; I had a bruise on my forehead, and I'd bitten my tongue.

"Didn't you hear me blowing the horn?" I asked Joe.

"No," said Joe, "but it wouldn't have made any difference. You couldn't have got past me anyway."

"No," I agreed.

Joe had the sump straightened out and back on the ute and topped up with oil out of his own drum within an hour. He even managed to get the worst dents knocked out of the mudguard and grille, and Joe found a headlight unit to replace the one that had got broken. He refused to accept any payment for his time and trouble, so I thanked him as warmly as I could and drove slowly to the pub for a very quiet drink.

My driving was anxiously over-cautious for as long as my wheel-marks stayed all over the sides of the road to remind me. It was months before they were all washed away by the rains and I could begin to forget about it a little, and there were times when I concluded that Joe was definitely a Dispensable Bastard, (*Bastardus giveawayus*).

35
Stupid Bastard

EGGY NEWBIGAN WAS NOT so much a Stupid Bastard (*Bastardus clottus*) as a Dangerous Bastard (*Bastard suicidus*), but I suppose that we'd better give him the benefit of the doubt. Eggy was a good name for him for he looked a bit of an egg — let's face it, he *was* an egg, and a proper bloody egg at that. He'd been around Tangaroa for two or three years, doing odd work that nobody else wanted to do. They'd given him a job maintaining a stretch of road but he'd filled all the pot-holes with dirt out of the water-tables and they knew better than to let him near any machinery, so he'd had to be sacked.

Weaver gave him a trial week looking after the store, but within three days Eggy had got the cash register and the shelves in such a confusion that it took Weaver a month to get them right again. He figures that Eggy must have eaten eighteen dollars worth of chocolate and sweets and had to write them off, along with Eggy.

Rex Logan at the pub, against everyone's advice, let Eggy have a go at looking after the bar, but nobody wanted to drink with him there and he had to be put on general work around the place. He rearranged all Rex's stocks of bottles and stuff and Rex couldn't find anything when he wanted it. It took poor Rex three weeks to get exasperated enough to sack Eggy, and by that time he'd burnt holes and grooves in shelves, benches, floors, tables, mats, bedclothes, and books, by leaving his lighted cigarette-butts everywhere. He'd broken glass all over the place, including a big window; he'd set fire to the pub twice, trying to light the fire in the bar with newspaper; he'd tied the pub goat within reach of Mrs Logan's washing; he'd dropped the telephone and broken that; he'd driven Rex's car into the bench at the end of the car-shed and even Joe Bimler couldn't fix it without sending up to town for parts; he'd left the beer tap dribbling one night on a nearly-full eighteen-gallon keg and flooded half the building with beer. And he'd made the pub leak in several places by walking

Bastardus clottus

all over the corrugated-iron looking for one of Rex's slippers he'd accidentally thrown on to the roof . . . All in all he'd been more trouble that he was worth, as usual.

He'd nearly shot Ted Packer with a rifle, so he wasn't very popular in that quarter. And he'd spilt one of Joe Bimler's drums of diesel into the river last whitebait season, which didn't raise his shares with anyone else.

Quentin Parsonage was the last Tangarorian to have lost faith in Eggy Newbigan. He stuck up for him when everyone else was well and truly convinced that Eggy was absolutely hopeless. He responded to Eggy's critics by saying that, after all, there's a little bit of good and a little bit of bad in all of us. And then Eggy rode a horse through Quentin's vegetable garden and Quentin came into the pub with his sandals flapping angrily and his spectacles fairly blazing with indignation. Eggy was leaning patiently on the bar waiting for Rex Logan to change his mind and give him a beer on credit.

"Egbert," said Quentin. "Did you ride your horse through my garden yesterday?"

"Yeah," said Eggy. "I did have a bit of a look around. You weren't there."

"Is that any reason to ride a horse all over my plants?"

"I don't know," said Eggy. "I didn't take much notice."

"Well don't come to my place ever again," said Quentin. "I don't want you there. You are a *wretched* fellow!" he repeated.

And Eggy had lost his only ally in Tangaroa, or probably anywhere else for that matter. And yet he still thought he was popular with everyone.

I should have known better, but when Eggy offered to let me go fifty-fifty on a scrap metal contract he'd got with a North Island company, I agreed to have a look at it. Eggy was lifting four miles of narrow-gauge tramline that ran back into the bush from the old mill, which was two miles north of Tangaroa and half a mile down a side road. Eggy had already sent the first load of tramlines away and had a cheque for seventy dollars to prove it.

It should have been a good lurk. The old jigger-wheels were still there and all it needed was to make up a jigger to wheel the tramlines on as they were lifted. The only snag was that Eggy had taken his first load from the rails nearest the road, instead of bringing them from the far end. The closest rails left were a quarter of a mile back in the swampy bush. He'd loused that job up as well.

Everyone seemed to think that I should thank my lucky stars that Eggy had mucked up the job before I had put any money or work into it, but I couldn't help pointing out to Eggy what he'd done wrong and that the only way to put it right was to bring rails forward and rebuild the stretch he'd lifted, so he could get them all in to the mill. And a week later Eggy walked all the way down to my place to tell me he'd done as I'd suggested; he'd re-laid the quarter-mile of tramlines he'd taken out first.

The only thing wrong was that he'd re-laid them from the *second* quarter-mile of the line.

It's never easy to be tolerant of such idiocy, but I managed to explain to Eggy that he should have taken the rails from the *last*, the farthest away, end of the line first. I eventually seemed to have got the message across and left Eggy preparing to make himself a jigger and take it right to the end of the line and bring in the rails to bridge the second gap he'd made.

Ten days or so later I heard that Eggy had at last got his tramline-salvage job organised workably, but by this time the truck had been back three times to pick up the second load. They were so sick of the waste of their time and money that they'd dropped the project altogether.

But Eggy went on bringing in the tramlines until he had tons of them lying in great tangled heap on the old mill-skids. All he ever sold them was one rail, to Scratcher for two dollars. (It's probably now part of the Tangaroa-Boulder Creek telephone line.)

Scratcher and I were going spotlighting and as we were getting ready to leave the pub Eggy started hanging about wanting to come, so I eventually said he could come and hold the light for us.

"No!" said Weaver, who'd been listening to our preparations.

But Eggy was finally allowed to come providing he didn't touch any rifles and did what he was told. Weaver still wasn't happy about it. Half an hour after we'd got going Scratcher banged on the roof and I stopped and got out. Scratcher had a set of deer's eyes holding well in the powerful light, high up on a slip in the bush above the road. I leaned on the ute, hissed at Eggy to keep quiet and still, and pulled off a fine shot. The deer dropped in its tracks.

Scratcher and I took the torch and left Eggy to keep the spotlight on the spot where the deer had gone down. But Eggy started waving the light around all over the place so we just carried on with our torch. We found the deer, a young stag, lying in a muddy waterhole at the bottom of the slip. We pulled it out and gutted it and rolled and dragged it down to the road. There was no spotlight at all by this time. Eggy had shorted it somehow and blown the bulb.

There was nothing to do but go back to the pub, so we told Eggy to stay on the back and off we went. But we'd only just got going when there was an explosion and a shout, so I jammed on the brakes and jumped out. Eggy had been getting the rifle ready, in case we saw a deer on the road, and he'd put a .303 bullet through the bonnet of the ute and out through the radiator. We took the rifle off him and sat him in the front where we could keep an eye on him, and made it back to the pub without overheating the ute too much.

Joe Bimler was at home and apparently only too pleased to have something to fix, so we left him hunched over my radiator with a soldering-iron and Scratcher drove Eggy and me home in his Land Rover.

Next morning I arrived at Joe's place to pick up the ute and found that Eggy had been there for about an hour already, to lend a hand. He'd been hosing down the muddy deer on the back of the ute, and he'd left the hose running. Everything was drenched and the deer was unsellable. It had gone soggy.

And Eggy had left the hose running when Joe had had to leave for work and taken him home rather than leave him there. But Eggy had walked back and was there to lend a hand when I tried to back my ute out. It slid sideways in the mud and ended up hard against Joe's gatepost. And while I was away getting Scratcher and his Land Rover, Eggy jacked up some wire-strainers and fencing wire he found in Joe's shed and pulled the door handle off the ute trying to drag it away from the post for me.

Scratcher and I arrived back just in time. Eggy had his wire tied on to the steering wheel and already had it sprung to its limits through the window.

We chased the Stupid Bastard away up the road with a stick, throwing rocks and abuse after him, and got the ute out without any further damage.

After that I followed everyone else's example and wouldn't let Eggy hang around anywhere near me, and only had the average number of calamities to cope with.

WILD PORK AND WATERCRESS

BARRY CRUMP

Illustrated by
Malcolm Evans

CONTENTS

One

THE WIFE'S SISTER'S BOY

MY PROPER NAME'S Richard Morehu Baker but they always call me Ricky. My mother was quarter-Maori and I was born in 1974, years later and a lot darker-skinned than my brother and sister, and don't let anyone tell you *that* doesn't make a difference. I always had trouble fitting in. People were always getting a surprise to find out I actually belonged in our family. I was also a bit overweight and not much good at sports and stuff like that.

By the time I'd been at school for a few years I could read miles better than most of the other kids but I wasn't much good at anything else, and they decided I was a slow learner. They shifted me around from class to class, trying to work out where fat Maori boys who can't play rugby or learn simple stuff fitted in. I knew they had me all wrong, but there wasn't much I could do about it.

I've always been able to remember just about anything I want to and it's easy for me to learn things. Too easy. I was worried about all the stuff that was going into my head, and they were shoving more in all the time. The wrong sort of stuff, too. I couldn't forget a lot of it. I used to be scared my head was going to fill up till it couldn't take any more and I'd suddenly go mad, or burst or something. So I took time off school, which I usually had to pay for with more trouble. But heads are only so big.

Anyway, while all this was going on my parents got divorced and my mother took custody of me, mainly because nobody seemed to know exactly where my father was living. He was never allowed in the house when he'd been drinking, and he just did more and more drinking till he didn't come home at all. Things got worse at home and school until in the end my mother couldn't handle me. Looking back, I seem to have spent a lot of time standing in various offices while adults sat around deciding what was going to happen to me next. I soon found out that thin white difficult boys are easier to "do something with" than overweight brown ones.

When I was nine they stuck me in a kind of health camp, but I couldn't stand it and got out of there as soon as I saw a chance. They caught up with me sneaking onto a bus to Wellington to stow away on a boat or plane to Australia, and I was carted off to a social welfare home for delinquent boys which was worse than the health camp and trickier to get out of. I had to spend three nights there before I could get away, but I made it home and decided to hang on there as long as possible. The social welfare people found out I was there and came round a few times, but they left me there.

By this time my mother was getting ready to get married again. My stepfather-to-be liked it better when I wasn't around, but he did his best not to let on about it. My mother used to say that everything was going to be all right and we pretended along like that, but less than a year later I was back in a social welfare home for shoplifting a bag of potato chips. They locked us up in that place and I had a lot of trouble getting away. They found out I was back at home but they left me alone. I think my new stepfather might have stuck up for me that time. He was still trying to like me, and I was getting better at keeping my head down.

The next time they picked me up I was riding a ten-speed bike I didn't even know was supposed to be stolen. I ended up in the same place as before but they were watching me this time and it was nearly a month before I got a chance to get away. I was on the loose for seven weeks — joined up with a bunch of kids who were living in a burnt-out bus near Taupo. They didn't really want me around, either. I was too inexperienced, they reckoned, and I might bring attention to them. We were living off what we could steal out of houses and cars and shops, so I don't suppose I could blame them really.

It didn't last long, anyway. They busted in on us in the middle of the night and carted us all off to the police station, then after a long car ride in the early hours to a prison place, where they locked us up in cells. There was no way of getting out of there. Things were getting worse. This was actual prison.

It turned out that I was too young to stay there, and after four days they got me in this office and told me I was being given one last chance to straighten myself up. I didn't deserve it, the social welfare man reckoned, but if I agreed to co-operate my Uncle Hector and Aunt Bella Faulkner had offered to take me into fostership on a trial basis and wasn't that wonderful of them.

The bloke was lying. Uncle Hec would never have offered to take anyone like me in. He didn't even like kids. It was another shove-around without me being consulted about it. But being in jail's no joke either, so I said all right, and the next day I was delivered to Uncle Hec and Aunty Bella's farm at the end of a windy stony road, eighty-seven kilometres from Gisborne. At this stage I was twelve years and three weeks old.

The Faulkners' farm was up a valley beside a river called the Apopo, and everything about the place was old and falling to bits. You could tell where their place started by all the thistles and scrub everywhere. Their road fence was all overgrown with briar bushes and long grass and they had a rusty old drum on a post with their name on it near the front gate. Two muddy wheel tracks went curving up the hill to their rusty old blue car parked outside the house, which was surrounded by falling rails and a skimpy hedge, with weeds and long grass growing right up to the window-sills round one side and the back. On the other side was Aunty Bella's vegetable garden. There was a path trodden in the grass between the gate and the back porch.

The Apopo river was about a hundred metres from the house, and the old woolshed with its rusty corrugated iron and red-streaked mossy boards was out on the flat between. It was a skin shed, a toolshed, a workshop — it was the only other building on the place apart from the house and everything happened down there. Uncle Hec used to spend a lot of time sitting on a staple-box with a folded sack nailed onto it for padding, tipped back against the wall of the shed, looking up the valley.

The river was quite a big one, stony and shingly and about

twenty metres across at the crossings, with deep pools in between. Upstream Uncle Hec's 140 acres went steeply up from the river flats, which were covered with clumps of blackberry and other scrub. Patches of grass were still quite numerous around the bottoms of the ridges, but higher up there was just manuka and gorse with streaks of new bush in the gullies. Beyond that dark ridges of native bush went right up to a broken blue range shaped like a train crash. It was real steep. From the shed you could see where little streams came falling down between the ridges to make Rough Creek, which ran into the Apopo up at the end of the "Property".

It was an interesting place all right. I'd been there a few times before this, visiting. Uncle Hec was usually taking it easy and Aunty Bella was usually very busy. Aunty Bella was my mother's eldest sister and it was she who'd set up the taking me into fostership thing. I could tell by the way she called me a poor lamb and was inclined to do a bit too much hair-ruffling and cuddling and stuff. She was going to supervise me on correspondence school.

Aunty Bella's was the best place to be hungry I ever knew. I'll tell you more about that later. She always wore slacks and cardigans and had her grey-black hair in a big clip at the back to keep it out of her way. When Aunty Bella was angry she'd call you a scallywag, whatever that was. It wasn't as serious as Uncle Hec getting angry, that's for sure.

Uncle Hec was very old. Over fifty. He called himself a bushman but it was hard to tell exactly what that meant. Most of the family used to say he was a no-hoper, when they talked about him at all. I'd picked up that he'd been in prison for "something disgraceful" when he was young. Another time I'd heard that it was for fighting. He was a grouchy old codger and most of the kids were a bit scared of him. He was supposed to be real stubborn when it came to an argument. He'd had a difference of opinion with the electricity people a few years before and they'd cut the power off, so Uncle Hec told them to come and take their poles and wire off his place. There was a story about him getting a big fine for cutting down their poles with a chainsaw. He was tall and thin with bony knuckles and hairy blue eyes and only bottom teeth.

That was really all I knew about Uncle Hec and Aunty Bella at the time I was dumped there, except that Uncle Hec had the most terrific way of shutting up my mother I ever saw. She never did approve of Uncle Hec, and just when she was getting wound up telling him what a lazy pig he was and how her sister deserved better, Uncle Hec would spit. Right past her. She never finished what she was saying. Not once. You wouldn't have been surprised either, if you'd seen Uncle Hec spit.

They had a daughter, cousin Judy. I'd only seen her a few times. She was a nurse, married to a doctor and living in Africa. She used to send letters describing the atrocious conditions where they lived. I was given Judy's old room next to the kitchen.

Uncle Hec wasn't exactly overwhelmed with joy about me being there at first, so I wasn't exactly overwhelmed with joy about him either. As far as he was concerned I was just the wife's sister's boy from the city and had to be put up with for the time being, till I ran away again or something. But at least Aunty Bella wanted me around.

One of the best things about the Faulkners' place was all the animals. They had eleven chooks and a rooster called Dreyfus, who ran around free-range and perched in the big macrocarpa at night. We were always looking around for where the chooks were laying this time. There were four muskovy ducks half-wild in the swamp across the river among the wild ducks and wekas and pukekos. There were rabbits up the river flats, and hares too. Sometimes bunches of wild goats would come down out of the bush to feed in the fern above the house. There were wild pigs up the back, and deer — Uncle Hec had shot a spiker with his shotgun when he was pheasant-shooting a few weeks before. Its skin with a big hole in it was hanging on a rafter in the shed.

There were supposed to be 250 sheep on the place, but there weren't that many left. I think Uncle Hec used to add one every time we ate one. Two horses called Mack and Rosie lived up the flats and wouldn't let anyone catch them. There were also about thirty big calves living in the scrub up the valley, getting fattened up for "the sale".

I decided to have a good try at fitting in with them. I was worried about the way things were going between me and the social welfare people, so I started off doing everything I was told. And that was plenty — they expected me to pull my weight. Uncle Hec would tell me what I had to do and show me how to do it. Once. After that I was supposed to know all about it. But in spite of that it didn't take me long to work out how to live there and keep out of most of the trouble.

Uncle Hec would get up just after the rooster crowed in the morning and give me a yell. "Okay Ricky!"

I could never figure out why we had to get up so early in the morning and then loaf around all day hardly doing anything, but that's the way they wanted it, so I went along with them.

Uncle Hec would have a wash at the tubs and I'd get dressed and take the bucket from upside-down on the bench and go out to find the house cow, Sally, who was always somewhere down at the far end of the paddock. I'd chase her up to the shed and into the bail at the side, wash her udder and milk her with big musical squirts into the frothy bucket. It's handy to know how to milk a cow. Nothing to it really, and the cream you get is like no other cream. And, while I'm doing this smoke would come pouring out of the chimney over at the house. Sometimes it would hang in a blue streak right along the valley.

When I came in and put the milk on the bench Uncle Hec would be getting around in his long-johns making a pot of tea. I'd have a wash at the tubs on the porch and dry my hands and face on the big towel hanging there. By the time we were on our second cups of tea Aunty Bella would come out and start rattling things around, and all we had to do then was keep out of her way. Uncle Hec would be ordered to go and dress himself decently and I was always asked if I'd had my wash yet.

"Yep," I'd say.

"There's a lamb," she'd say.

I'd sit at the table with a book and Uncle Hec would come in tucking his shirt into his pants and start fiddling with the old battery radio to get *Morning News*, and grumble between the reports that "they're going bloody mad out there". And then the smells of rolled oats floating in cream and brown with sugar, and wild-pork bacon and bright orange free-range eggs and toast would take our minds off everything else. Good breakfasts, those ones.

Around eight o'clock Uncle Hec and I and the chook-bucket would get chased out of the house. We might decide to stack lengths of manuka into the rack and cut a pile of wood for the stove with Uncle Hec's old chainsaw. Sometimes we'd take the Winchester rifle up the flats and shoot some young rabbits for dinner. One each. Or we might have a possum in one of the traps in the old orchard and hang its skin on a board with the others in the shed. Or we might just go down the shed and sit around. Depended mainly what mood Uncle Hec was in. For instance, not long after I came there (four weeks and two days, actually), we were down at the shed and I said, "How come you never have to do much work, Uncle Hec?"

"Because I'm the most successful farmer around, that's why."

"How come your farm's in such a mess, then?"

"Mess?" he said looking around. "Where?"

"Well, all those prickles and bushes along the road fence," I said.

"That's rose-hip," he said, as though he'd grown it there on purpose. "Great stock-food, the old rose-hip. Loaded with vitamin C, lasts right through the winter. Valuable stuff to have around, that."

I watched him carefully. I was suspicious of Uncle Hec. When I was six he'd told me he had a sheep's lung in him because one of his had been ripped out by a flying crowbar in an explosion. He even had a big scar across his ribs to prove it, and I'd believed him for more than a year before I'd made a fool of myself telling them at school about it. I looked around. The only tidy thing on the whole place, outside the house, was the vegetable garden — Aunty Bella's garden.

"What about all the clumps of weeds and stuff all over the paddocks?" I said, pointing up the river flats.

"They're not weeds, that's blackberry. Good tucker, the old blackberry. The rabbits like it, too. If I cleared off all the blackberry I'd have to go all the way up to Goat Gully to get meself a feed. Anyway it's not worth doing too much to this place. The Forestry's supposed to be going to buy up all the land around here and plant it in pines."

"Sounds like a good excuse for being lazy," I said.

"Not too lazy to leap up and flatten any young buggers who get too cheeky with me," he said.

"You'd better not hit me," I told him.

"Then you'd better not get cheeky with me," he said, getting up off his box.

We were standing there like that, looking at each other, when the gong started ringing for me to go up to the house for correspondence. Must have been ten o'clock.

The gong was a big round piece of metal off some old farm machine, hanging on a wire in the macrocarpa tree by the side gate. Aunty Bella used to bang it with a piece of pipe when it was time to eat or when Uncle Hec was wanted up at the house. Sometimes you could hear it down at the Hickeys' place, nearly a mile away. Just as well it rang when it did that day. I didn't know what Uncle Hec meant by "flatten" at that stage.

At ten o'clock every weekday I had to go up to the house and do schoolwork. If Aunty Bella hadn't taken it so seriously I'd have been dangerously bored by those lessons, but she was so good about it I had to try and not disappoint her. The worst hassle was writing it all down neat enough for them. I actually started waking up to some of the things they'd been trying to tell me at school. Correspondence is the best kind of school for people who have trouble fitting in. You get left alone more.

While I finished the schoolwork Aunty Bella would put lunch on. Then I'd go and gong real loud for Uncle Hec and we'd have lunch. It might be cold roast mutton with Aunty Bella's special chutney, and salad from the garden and big slices of oven bread and butter. And cups of tea. Stuff like that. As much as you wanted. Pretty good.

After lunch we usually had a lie on our beds for an hour or two. I read books mostly, especially science fiction if I could get my hands on any. They had hardly any books at the Faulkners', and nothing any good. Aunty Bella joined the library in town for me and I read everything I could borrow around the neighbours.

Around two-thirty or three o'clock Aunty Bella would get active and noisy again, and after a cup of tea or two Uncle Hec and I would drift outside and maybe bring in a load of firewood, or put a post in a gap in a fence, or some other half-necessary job. After an hour or two of this Uncle Hec would move off towards his seat down at the shed. I sometimes felt like going for a walk and exploring around the place. I especially liked climbing up the hills to a high place. It sometimes gave me a kind of free feeling I'd never noticed anywhere else. By this time of day Uncle Hec and I had often seen enough of one another — I could usually tell.

Dinner at night meant another wash and the kitchen full of smells and activity, with pot lids rattling and steaming on the stove, and something smoking and spitting whenever Aunty Bella opened the oven door and stabbed in with her big fork, all the time giving orders like the captain on the bridge of a star-ship. Uncle Hec would probably be grumbling about the quality of the mantles they make these days as he lit the kerosene pressure-lamp.

Then the hot plates of stuffed braised rabbit, a whole one each and one extra, with thick brown oniony gravy and roasted kumara from the garden and fluffy mashed potato — as much as you could eat. Then a third of a big blackberry pie hidden under cream skimmed off this morning's milk in lumps as big as your spoon.

"Please may I leave the table," I'd say.

"Yeah, you'd better get out of here before you bust," Uncle Hec said one night.

"Hector!" said Aunty Bella. "You mustn't say things like that. Ricky's a growing boy."

"He's growing all right," said Uncle Hec. "Outwards. Look at the size of him."

"At least I'm not a skinny old bag of bones like you," I shouted at him.

He put both hands on the table to leap up and flatten me, but Aunty Bella said, "Now that's quite enough from both of you. Ricky, off you go and run the bath. And put those clothes in the wash, they're filthy. You're not wearing them another day."

I'd lie in the bath listening to Uncle Hec trying to get the radio adjusted right and finally leaving it half off the station. Aunty Bella would clatter through the washing up while I'd dry myself on a towel hot from the rack over the stove and get into my pyjamas before drying the dishes and putting them away properly. Then I'd sip a mug of Milo made with hot milk, cop a cuddle from Aunty Bella, and brush my teeth.

"Goodnight," I'd say.

"Goodnight, lamb. Now don't you go reading all hours of the night. You'll ruin your eyes."

"Okay, goodnight."

Uncle Hec would grunt. He doesn't like saying things like hello or goodbye or good morning or good night.

I'd light my candle and get into bed discovering that Aunty Bella had put a hot water bottle in my bed while I was having my bath. I'd discovered that a scallywag is someone who peels the potatoes too thick. I'd read for an hour or so. Around nine-thirty Uncle Hec would grumble his way off to bed saying there's never anything decent on the bloody wireless these days. The last sounds in the house would be Aunty Bella clattering around getting everything ready for the morning. A clank of the milk bucket upside-down on the bench and the day would be over.

I'd pinch out my candle and lie there in the dark, listening to the Apopo river talking away to itself in mangled voices beyond the window, and working out the best way of running away from there — just in case I needed to later on.

Two

A DOG LIKE ZAG

THERE'S QUITE a lot I haven't mentioned about the Faulkners and their funny old overgrown farm. For example Uncle Hec had this dog, a black and white Border Collie cross called Zag. It used to follow Uncle Hec everywhere when it was off the chain but it didn't like anyone else even patting it. A one-man dog, Uncle Hec said it was. I didn't like Zag much at first because he wouldn't let me be friends with him, but that was before I found out he was a champion dog. It was an important day for me, that.

After breakfast Uncle Hec said, "You'd better stick those new boots of yours on today, young feller. We'll see if we can walk some of that surplus condition off you."

"What are we going to do?" I asked him.

"I want to go up to the end of the property and see how many of the cattle I can find. If there's any fat enough we'll bring 'em down and stick 'em in the front paddock for the sale. They must be getting pretty big by now."

We took Zag, who seemed to know there was something on. He dashed around everywhere and jumped up on Uncle Hec till he got growled at. It looked to me as though Zag must have been flattened a few times, the way he instantly obeyed Uncle Hec, but I found out later that those dogs are like that.

We had to cross the river six times and you had to watch where you were putting your feet on the wet stones. I was having to hurry to keep up and thinking we must be near the end of the property by this time, when Uncle Hec suddenly stopped and I nearly ran into him.

"That's fresh pig-rooting up there," he said quietly, pointing up a ferny ridge to a scattered patch of dug-up dirt amongst the fern. "They mightn't be too far away."

And he stood squinting up the ridge.

"Shall we go back and get the rifle," I suggested.

"We might be able to stop one with the dog if we get lucky," he said. "I haven't got a knife on me, have you got that one of yours?"

"Yep," I said, pulling it out of my pocket and opening it up. "It's sharp, too."

"Put it away," he said, "and stay close behind me. We'll climb up to that rooting and see if the dog can pick up a fresh scent."

We climbed up from the river and pushed our way up a faint track through the high fern, and before we reached where the rooting was Zag started getting excited, trying to push past Uncle Hec in the fern.

"Okay, go on," he said, and Zag shot away up the ridge.

"They must be pretty close," Uncle Hec whispered. "We'd better get off this track in case he brings 'em this way."

I got quickly into the fern behind him, and just then there was a terrific crashing and snarling and whoofing just up ahead of us. We could hear pigs crashing off around both sides of the ridge. I saw the fern shake in a big ripple as one of them charged away, and I saw it for a moment as it ran round into the next gully. A big black one with long hair sticking up along its back. I don't mind admitting it made me a bit nervous to realise animals like *that* were running around the place — and there we were with only a dog and a pocket knife.

But that was nothing. Suddenly Zag was fighting and snarling and crashing and driving another one down through the fern and manuka in the gully on the other side.

"He's onto one," said Uncle Hec. "He might stop it in the river. We'd better get down there."

We ran after the dog and pig, crashing and rolling down through the fern, and when we slid down the bank onto the river stones here was this big black pig, going round and round in the water at the edge of the river with Zag hanging onto one of its ears.

"Quick," said Uncle Hec. "Give me the knife."

I pulled it out and he snatched it off me while I was still trying to get it open for him. He ran over and tried to get behind the pig, but just as he ducked in to grab it by the back leg the pig threw the dog off and turned on him.

I always regret I didn't see exactly what happened after that because I was too busy getting up the bank, but when I looked again Uncle Hec was standing in the river up to his knees and Zag had the pig by the ear again out on the stones. Round and round they went, the pig grunting and scoffing and squealing, with the dog snarling and shaking at it. I didn't know Zag could get so savage. I had respect for him over that.

Uncle Hec dived in again and this time he got the pig by the back leg and struggled and turned it over and stuck it in the neck with my knife. The pig's blood poured out on the stones, and even after it stopped kicking Zag had to be booted away from it. He kept wanting to get stuck in again.

"Good pig that," said Uncle Hec, breathing heavily and kicking Zag away again. "What say we singe it, eh?"

"Too right," I agreed, whatever singeing was.

Singeing was throwing a heap of dead manuka down onto the riverbed from a clump up the hill and lighting a big fire. When it was going properly we carried the pig across to the river and dunked it in until it was good and wet when we swung it onto the fire. The hairs sprang short in the flames with a steaming and sizzling and smell of burning. When the bottom side was well heated up we turned it over and scraped the burnt-off bristles with splinters of driftwood, and the whole outside layer of skin peeled away, leaving white skin underneath. When we'd scraped the whole pig we burnt a brown skin on it in the embers and lifted the hot tight carcase out onto the stones. And were we sweating! It's hot work, singeing wild pigs.

Uncle Hec gutted the pig with my knife, which was getting very blunt, and examined the liver. "Perfect," he said, and threw it into the hollow carcase.

We threw the rest of the guts into the fern at the foot of the bank and set off to pack the meat home. It weighed about twenty-five kilos, that pig, but I managed to carry it most of the way. We hung it in the big meat-safe under the lean-to behind the shed. Aunty Bella came down to have a look and pretended to be shocked at the mess we were in. "I think I'll make some brawn," she said.

"All right, eh," said Uncle Hec when we were sharing the soap under the tap.

"All right," I agreed.

I wanted a dog like Zag for my own. I'd decided to be a hunter, but I wasn't quite ready to discuss it with Uncle Hec yet.

Next morning, after a breakfast of liver, onions, eggs, tomatoes and toast, we cut our pig down the middle with the old hand-saw and cut it up on the kitchen bench into roasts and chops and stewing-meat. Then I got sent to two different neighbours with parcels of meat because we were the only ones in the valley without a fridge.

That was the best pork I'd ever tasted, and I've especially liked wild pork ever since — roast wild pork, with crackling and roast kumaras and pumpkin and gravy and watercress. I wanted a dog of my own all right. A pig-dog.

I liked doing things for Aunty Bella, she was a real good sort, and made the most beautiful brawn you've ever eaten. And she could turn a bucket of ordinary old mushrooms into the most delicious bacony creamy toast-soaking stuff you could imagine. She had a bit of magic, Aunty Bella. She was my best friend as well.

Not long after we got the pig (just under a week — okay, four days), we were sitting around down the shed waiting for the gong to go for dinner, and I said to Uncle Hec, "The Hickey's bitch has got a litter of pups by Old Dave's black labrador. Six of them."

"Yeah, I know," he said. "Those pups ought to be just about weaned by now."

"Yes," I said. "As a matter of fact Joe said I could have my pick out of three of them — that's if it's okay with you for me to have a dog."

I was watching him. He shook his head. "No way, mate. You're not bringing any Alsation-Labrador dogs around here."

"Why not?" I asked. This was a bit embarrassing because I'd already told Joe Hickey Uncle Hec wouldn't mind.

"Because they're no bloody good, that's why," he said.

"You just don't want me to have a dog at all."

"You can have a dog, if you want one that bad, but you're not bringing any scoffing bloody wool-classers around here. If you can get the right kind of dog you can keep it, providing you look after it yourself. They have to be kept fed, you know."

"You'll only keep saying they're no good," I said.

"Only if they are no good," he said, and the gong went for us to go and have a wash for dinner — roast pork with all the trimmings.

I left it for a whole day and when we were down the shed again I said to him, "How do you go about getting the right sort of dog, Uncle Hec?"

"You can never tell what a dog's going to turn out like," he said, "but you can eliminate some of the risks."

"How do you do that?"

"Well for a start you have to decide just what you want a dog for."

"Catching pigs, like Zag," I said.

"Well Zag's a cattle-dog, and I reckon they're as good in the bush as anything you'll get. Working dogs are light on their feet, that's important. They'll live on nothing, and life's always a lot easier if you don't have to worry about what your dog's up to. Something with a bit of working-dog in it'd probably do you."

"How do you find dogs like that?" I said.

"You keep your eyes and ears open, and check with me before you bring any home."

That was the best I was going to do for the time being, so I left it at that.

Not long afterwards (two days) I had another run-in with Uncle Hec. I'd dug the point of my knife into my hand and it wouldn't stop bleeding. I went round the shed and showed Uncle Hec. He twirled some cobweb out of the corner of the shed with a stick and put it on my cut hand. The bleeding stopped instantly. Magic.

"How did you do it?" he said.

"I must have put my knife in my pocket half-closed," I said.

"Not very smart, eh," he said, and sat down on his staple-box again.

"I'm smarter than most people," I told him.

"You're a bit smart," he admitted, and I watched him because he didn't usually admit things like that.

"I'm smarter than you, anyway," I said. "You can't even count 161 sheep."

He started getting up off his box and suddenly I was sitting on the ground with my hearing only just coming back in time to hear him say ". . . . asking for that," as he walked off towards the house. I'd been flattened! I jumped up and grabbed a pair of fencing pliers that were sitting on a post and almost let him have it — just stopped myself in time. I'd never been hit like that before. I had extra respect for Uncle Hec over that. He could flatten you all right.

Another thing happened one night when we were coming back down the flats with some rabbits we'd just shot and I was carrying the rifle.

"How old do you think someone would have to be before they could shoot with a .22?" I asked him casually.

"Nothin' to do with age," he said.

"What, then?"

"It's how much brains y'got."

"I've got brains," I said.

"Then you've got to be able to skin or pluck and gut everything you shoot," he said.

It was I who skinned and gutted the rabbits that night. It wasn't as easy as Uncle Hec made it look, but I managed. I cut the heads and feet off them and took them up and gave them to Aunty Bella.

"Heavens," she said, "you've put them through the mincer."

But Uncle Hec had said I was "getting the message", which sounded okay to me.

After dinner that night I got the .22 out of the cupboard and got him to show me how it worked and how to hold it right. We pulled the whole thing to bits on the kitchen table in the finish, and I put it together again. Nothing much to it, really. I usually had to pretend to be dumber than usual when grown-ups were showing me how to do something.

Next day we had a shooting session down by the bend of the river. We fired off two and a half packets of fifty, and by the finish I was putting three bullets in a five-inch group at seventy metres, which Uncle Hec said wasn't bad with open sights. He was good, though. In fact Uncle Hec was the best shot with a rifle I ever saw, which turned out to be very lucky for us a few times.

That night I heard Uncle Hec say to Aunty Bella, "The young coot's not a bad shot," and I couldn't get out of the bath for grinning.

I lived for shooting rabbits for a while. There were dozens of them around and the older ones were getting cunning and hard to sneak up on. I missed a few, but I got a few as well. I thought I'd blown the whole thing one day when Uncle Hec met me at the gate and we were looking at a big hare I'd shot in the neck. I thought the rifle was on safety and pulled the trigger to test it, and it went off and blew a hole in the dirt between our feet.

We stood looking at each other like someone was going to flatten someone, and then he said, "If you ever do anything like that again you can put the rifle in the cupboard and leave it there."

"Yes, sir," I said. And meant it. It was hard to believe, getting away with that one. I wondered if Uncle Hec did something stupid like that with a rifle when he was a young bloke. You don't ask Uncle Hecs about things like that, they'd think it was personal.

It was the best fun so far, going out hunting on my own with the rifle. Uncle Hec had a .303 that just about knocked you over, and a shotgun with hammers you had to pull back to fire it. He didn't like me using the shotgun and I was happy with the .22.

"You can shoot anything you want with a .22, if you know what you're doin'," he said.

One day he sent me up to Goat Gully to get a goat for dog tucker. I got one just up the creek at the bottom of a slip — dropped it right where it was standing. I gutted it, carried it back and hung it in the dog-tucker tree near Zag's kennel and didn't even say anything to any uncles about it.

A young billy-goat. As far as I was concerned that made me a hunter, but I didn't advise Uncle Hec about that just yet.

Around this time, just after I'd turned twelve and a half, I nearly came unstuck with my schoolwork. They wrote a letter saying they were so pleased with the standard of my work that they were considering putting me forward a whole year by stages. I was lucky having Aunty Bella on my side, she advised them against it because I was just settling down and any changes might set me back, and stuff like that. They left me alone for a while after that, but they always had me worried. Fat Maori boys can get into terrible trouble with those sorts of people. I was careful to get a few simple things wrong here and there after that.

A pair of hunters, the Shortage brothers, Bill and Norm, had access rights to hunt up the back of Uncle Hec's place. They came out most weekends during the winter and brought various mates and dogs with them. They usually always got a pig or two and sometimes a deer as well. They were well-known for having a good pack of hunting dogs.

But they got Uncle Hec's back up in a big way one day. Their dogs came out of the bush ahead of them and cleaned up four of his sheep before they could stop them. Boy, he could sure get himself worked up, Uncle Hec. They offered to pay him for the sheep, but he didn't even hear them. They offered to shoot the two guilty dogs right there in front of him, but that made no difference either. He told them never to come back on the place with their scoffing bloody mongrels or he'd shoot the whole bloody lot of them.

We had a few arguments after that because he used to say the Shortages never even offered to pay him for the sheep their dogs killed, and I used to say they did offer but he hadn't heard them. He'd grunt and say, "Well I never heard 'em," but next time he'd be telling someone about it he'd still say the Shortages never even offered to pay for the sheep. You just have to give up on grown-ups on some things.

Anyway, just before all this happened Norm Shortage offered me one of his dogs. He had two of them out of the same litter — they were big fox-terrier crossed with a cattle-dog/red-setter bitch. They were ten and a half months old and just starting to hunt. Norm only wanted to keep one of them, so how would I like to have the other one?

Would I? I looked at the dog he was offering me and I liked it straightaway — red with white patches, nearly-prick-ears, bouncy, cheeky, real fast and intelligent-looking. His name was Willy.

"Here, Willy. Here boy," I said, but it didn't take any notice of me.

"It'll take him a while to get used to you," said Norm, "but once he does you won't be able to kick him out of your road."

"I'll have to ask Uncle Hec first," I said. "He's a bit fussy about what kind of dogs we have around here. Is it okay if I let you know next weekend?"

"Sure," said Norm, ruffling my hair with his hand. "I'll bring him out again next Sunday, okay?"

I was so pleased I hardly even wanted to kick him one for ruffling my hair like that. I don't like people ruffling my hair. Someone was going to get a punch one of these days. Flattened.

During the week I softened Uncle Hec up till he had to tell me to shut up about the bloody dog.

"I'll let you know when I've had a look at it," he said.

On the Sunday Uncle Hec looked Willy over when he jumped out of the Shortages' trailer with their other four dogs. I was watching him, and after the longest time I'd ever waited he gave the smallest nod of his head I'd ever seen. Norm caught my dog for me and I took him on a piece of rope and tied him beside Zag along the hedge. That was the Sunday Uncle Hec's sheep got worried by the Shortages' dogs, so it was a close shave.

"What makes dogs kill sheep, Uncle Hec?" I asked him when he'd cooled down, two days later.

"They live in town and come out here to hunt. The dogs don't know the difference between a pig and a sheep, half of 'em. It's the bloody owners who need shootin', most of the time."

"How do you keep your dog from worrying sheep?"

"Get him used to them. Work them with him. Let him know you don't want him to bite 'em and he never will."

"Do you think Willy would worry sheep?"

"If he does it'll be *your* fault, and *he'll* get shot."

After that I took my dog everywhere I went. In fact most of the places I went were only so I could take him there, which meant a lot of rambling around the hills. Willy was a real obedient dog, and never even looked like chasing the sheep unless I put him round them. He took to hunting with Zag and we started catching good pigs with them from the beginning. It was the best fun ever. I got Uncle Hec to come hunting whenever I could wangle it, which was difficult to organise sometimes because he'd only hunt when we needed meat. I managed to give quite a lot of pork to the Hickeys and two other families further down the valley who all had freezers, and we usually went out on a proper pig hunt once every two weeks or so.

We'd go up-river and climb up a ridge we reckoned was likely to hold something, and we usually got a bit of action before we'd gone far. Willy developed into a neat little finder, and Zag would wait for Willy to bark on something and then nick round to head it off. They pulled off some good ones, working together like that, and we hardly ever came back without "something for the pot", as Uncle Hec used to say.

One morning when I was looking around for Sally the house cow I thought I saw a half-grown black pig trot through a little clearing in the manuka above the house. It was only just getting daylight and it was about as far as you could see, but I let the dogs off and ran up the flat to get ahead of where the pig looked to be heading.

We'd just come round into the first gully past the house when Willy got a scent on the wind and shot up into the scrub. There were two barks when he found it, only about sixty yards up the side, and then a squeal when he turned it round and brought it crashing down and out into the open. When the pig saw Zag it swerved away towards the shed with both dogs catching up on it. They spun it round and stopped it by the woodblock. Willy got on one ear and Zag got on the other and that pig just had to stand there squealing.

Uncle Hec in his long-johns got there just before I did. He pulled the axe out of the woodblock and donged the pig on the head with the back of it and kicked the dogs away. My knife was in my other pants and we had to yell out to Aunty Bella to bring one down from the house. She arrived in her dressing-gown and slippers and I grabbed the knife off her and stuck the pig, which was starting to come round. It was a young boar, about sixty pounds, Uncle Hec reckoned, and we singed it right there beside the woodblock.

"That dog of yours might just turn out all right," said Uncle Hec as we scraped the burning hair.

"He's all right, all right," I said.

"He could turn out all right," he said again.

At that stage neither of us could have guessed how important it was going to be to us that Willy turned out all right.

Three

OTHER PEOPLE

BY THE TIME I was thirteen I could do most of the things Uncle Hec could around the farm, though he would never have admitted it. According to him I always sharpened the chainsaw wrong, or gave the dogs the wrong whistle, or used too much oil on his good sharpening-stone, or deliberately made the horses hard to catch. It was always my fault when we missed out on a pig or deer because if I was on the ridge I should have been in the creek, and if I was in the creek I should have been on the ridge. And all this was supposed to be because I was so fat.

He was hard to live with all right, but in spite of that, Uncle Hec and I were getting along a bit easier than at first. We still had to be careful not to get into a confrontation — we didn't want to have to find out who'd give in first, I suppose. He used to get on my nerves by always referring to how fat I was, especially in front of other people, and I used to get on his nerves by running around the side of the house and jumping on the loose board on the porch. It could shake the whole house when I hit it right, but even if Aunty Bella shouted with fright, Uncle Hec never let on he'd noticed it. I could tell it got him rattled, though.

Aunty Bella was just the opposite. According to her I never did anything wrong.

"He'd bust a bloody anvil," Uncle Hec would say.

"He's a growing boy," she'd say. "It's just a stage he's going through, isn't it lamb," and she'd ruffle my hair and give me a squeeze.

The main thing about Uncle Hec and Aunty Bella, though, was that they liked each other. They were friends, better than any other old people I'd ever known before. It was worth putting up with a lot of other grown-up stuff for that. What kept me from running away from there when things got bad was the way Uncle Hec never cared about my Maori skin. Fat white boys are always less embarrassing to have around than fat brown boys, I knew that, but it never seemed to bother Uncle Hec one way or the other. It was a long time before I gave up expecting him to say something about my Maoriness in an argument, because people like him always do, but he never did. It was a bit of a mystery to me, that.

Aunty Bella didn't count because she was quarter-Maori herself, and she wouldn't have been prejudiced about anything like that anyway. Being accepted by both of them in that kind of way was so good it got scary at times — almost like fitting in.

But the hunting was always the best fun. I usually forgot about everything else when we were out with the dogs, walking through the bush and waiting for that first bark when they made a find. One day they chased a big hind right past me in a narrow creek, and I got such a surprise I didn't think of shooting until it was disappearing around the corner. I've been waiting for the next one to do that ever since.

So, taking it all round, things were pretty good living at the Faulkners'. It was hard to believe the news that was coming over the radio and in the newspapers — hundreds of farmers walking off their farms and going on the dole, gangs and violence and police teams everywhere in the towns, the army running some of the country and the police running the rest, and the people ripping off everything they could get away with. Not much wonder we hardly ever went past the store and post office out on the main road these days.

"They're going bloody mad out there," Uncle Hec would say, and switch of the wireless to save the battery for the next lot of bad news.

It seemed as though everyone was having troubles except us, and then all ours landed on us at once. I was down at the Hickeys' place that day, helping them press some bales of wool, and Mrs Hickey came down to the woolshed and said that Aunty Bella had been taken ill and Uncle Hec had gone with her into the Gisborne hospital. I knew right then that something real bad was happening.

Uncle Hec was going to ring up later and let us know how Aunty Bella was. I was supposed to stay at the Hickeys' that night but I didn't want to. I went home and lit the lamp and had something to eat but I don't remember what it was. I couldn't even read that night — I just kind of knew that things were going to be different from now on.

Uncle Hec arrived home the next afternoon with Mrs Hickey. They were looking for me up at the house, but I was down the shed, sitting on Uncle Hec's staple-box, looking up the valley. Aunty Bella had died at five-thirty that morning. She'd had a stroke. And that was that.

Nothing could have been the same after that. I don't know about Uncle Hec, but I couldn't see across the gap Aunty Bella left in our lives. It should have happened to someone else, not us.

We made it to the funeral in the rusty blue car in spite of Uncle Hec's dangerous driving, and stood around feeling out of place among the relatives and other strangers — hard to tell which was which, and it was nothing to do with Aunty Bella being gone. My mother was living in Australia somewhere and they hadn't been able to contact her. One lady, some sort of cousin, ruffled my hair and said, "Poor thing, I wonder what's going to happen to *you* now."

After the funeral I had to wait for about an hour in the car while Uncle Hec had a private talk with some of his relatives. Neither of us talked all the way home — Uncle Hec's driving takes your mind off most other things anyway.

Uncle Hec took it all well, considering, but it was a bad time for both of us. It was worse because we hadn't realised how much stuff Aunty Bella had been doing around the place until we had to do it ourselves — things like winding up the clock, cleaning out the stove, or filling the water-tank.

After about six weeks, just when we were getting used to our own cooking, other people interfered in my life again. A letter came from the Social Welfare, addressed to Uncle Hec, which smelt like trouble to me. I read it out to him. '*...deeply sorry to learn of your recent sad bereavement, however in the light of the altered circumstances the situation with regard to the fostership of Richard Morehu Baker will* *naturally have to be reviewed. A Mr Draper will be calling on you in the near future to advise you what arrangements have been made...'*

"What does it mean?" I said.

Uncle Hec tapped the letter on the kitchen table with his finger. "It means that you have to go back into one of those welfare homes until they can find another foster home for you, by the look of it," he said.

"Like hell I do," I said, jumping up. "I'm not going into any welfare home."

"You've got no choice," he said.

"Why can't I just stay here?"

"They wouldn't let you, not without a woman in the place."

"You just don't want me here, do you?"

"No mate," he said. "Sit down. There's something I haven't told you about yet."

"What?" I didn't like the sound of all this.

"I can't stay here either."

"What do you mean?"

"You remember at the funeral, I got pulled aside by Wilf and Humphrey and them?"

"Yes."

"Well what they were telling me was that they've decided to sell the farm."

"*This* farm?"

"Yeah, this one."

"But it's *your* farm."

"It's a family property. Our folks left it equally between me and my two brothers and our sister — that's your Aunt Daphne. I was the only one interested in running the place so Bella and I took it over. Now the others want to sell up and split the money."

"But can they do that without you wanting to?"

"Sure, I wouldn't stop them. They reckon my share of the money'll buy me one of those nice little single units in town, where they can keep an eye on me."

"What are you going to do about it?"

"I think I'll take to the scrub for a spell. Trap a few skins, sell a bit of meat."

Aunty Bella had said how Uncle Hec used to disappear into the bush for weeks on end.

"I'm coming with you," I decided. "If we can stay in the bush till I'm fifteen they'll have to leave me alone."

"You can't come with me. You're still under the Social Welfare."

"No I'm not," I said. "I'm under you, and if you're going into the bush I'm coming too."

"Like hell you are. Forget it. It's out of the question."

That night we were still yelling back and forth in the dark between our rooms.

"Like hell you are," was the last thing Uncle Hec said about it, just before he started snoring.

It was very important to me not to get into the hands of the Social Welfare people again.

"Like hell you are," said Uncle Hec at breakfast next morning.

"You're not putting me in any institution."

"It's not *me* who's putting you anywhere."

"You are, by not taking me with you."

"I'd be breaking the law."

"Not if we leave before they officially change things. There's nothing to stop us having a spell in the bush if we want to."

"Forget it, you're wasting your breath."

That afternoon two men in a car came and stuck a FOR SALE sign on the front fence, and that sort of put the lid on it all. It was actually happening, Uncle Hec was right. The only thing for us to do was take to the bush.

"Like hell you are," said Uncle Hec that night. "I'm leaving for the Mangatoatoa Hut as soon as they come and get you, so you might as well get used to the idea."

"You won't get into any trouble. I'll tell them I came of my own accord. I know how to run away — I've done it before, you know."

"You haven't done anything like this before."

"I can handle it, Uncle Hec. True."

"You don't know what you're talking about. Forget it."

Well, it was the hardest argument I ever won, and I had to risk a flattening before he finally gave in and said he'd have to think about it. I had to agree to a lot of stuff that would have to be rearranged later on, but he finally said it.

"We'll get away first thing tomorrer mornin'."

Left me exhausted, that.

We nailed up a box of stuff Uncle Hec wanted kept for him, mostly tools, and wrote "Faulkner" on it with a piece of raddle. Everything else got left just as it was, except that we opened all the gates on our way up the flats so the stock wouldn't starve. It was only an hour or so after daylight when we climbed up onto the spur beyond Goat Gully, heading for the top of the Rakawhaia Ridge. It was a long climb, that. Every now and then we'd stop for a breather and look back down through the mist at the little farm. No talking — I suppose we'd done enough of that in the past few days.

Plodding up through the bush behind Uncle Hec, with loaded packs and the rifle, and the two dogs in behind, I was doing a bit of thinking. It had been such a hassle getting Uncle Hec to let me come with him that I hadn't taken much notice of what we'd brought with us. It sure didn't seem to be much preparation for holding out in the bush for two or three years. My main worry was what we were going to eat.

It hadn't taken us long to pack what we did bring. I had an old pack-frame with a synthetic-fibre sack tied onto it with nylon cord — sleeping-bag, spare pants, singlet and socks. My knife was in my pocket and I had a few books. Most of the spare space I'd filled with food to keep us going. Mug, fork and spoon, a couple of extra books shoved down the side and my green Swandri jacket tied on the top, and that was my load. About twenty kilos, Uncle Hec reckoned.

Uncle Hec had his old pack, sleeping bag, some clothes, a bit of rope, the tea-billy — too little in my opinion. We were carrying the .22 because it was the most versatile rifle. We had 279 bullets for it.

I was wearing my Casio digital watch that my mother had given me. It told the month, the day, the date, the hour, the minute and the second. Uncle Hec was inclined to sling off about it at first. Didn't need 'em, he reckoned, but later on that watch became so important to us that we carried it knotted in a plastic bag and carried it in the zip-pocket of Uncle Hec's pack to avoid it getting wet or damaged or lost.

We'd left a note under a bottle of tomato sauce on the kitchen table saying, GONE HUNTING. H. FAULKNER. R. BAKER.

We stopped on the top of the ridge and rested with our backs against a big beech tree and ate some bread and cheese. The dogs moved around sniffing the wind. The last bits of mist and cloud were blowing through the trees and as far as we could see ahead of us were ridges of bush, nothing but bush, going blue in the distance. It was hard to imagine how anyone could find their way around in it without getting lost. Uncle Hec had been hunting and trapping in the Urewera since he was a boy and reckoned he knew it like the back of his hand, but I didn't trust his memory all that much. I'd seen Uncle Hec forget things almost as soon as they happened — but he was still my best bet.

"Are we in the Urewera yet?" I asked him.

"Yes," he said, waving a piece of bread and cheese towards it all. "What we've got here is about a million acres of unbroken native bush, with about fifty Forestry Department huts scattered through it. I think I can find most of 'em, and they have to keep some supplies in them in case of trampers getting lost and that. The hunting's pretty good in most places. It mightn't always be easy to stick a feed under our belts but we shouldn't starve."

"How far is it to this hut we're going to?" I asked him.

"I've done it in five hours from home," he said. "But we're not in any great hurry. We'll be there before dark."

About half an hour's walk along the Rakawhaia Ridge and we came across an old track, which no one had used for a long time. We followed this track for about three hours, getting deeper into strange bush all the time. This was the real thing all right — there was deer-sign everywhere, droppings and hoofprints, and we kept the dogs close in behind us. We needed them to catch pork for us and didn't want them burning themselves out chasing deer.

We trudged up the longest ridge I'd ever seen and down off the track into the head of a creek I found out later was the Mangatoatoa. The dogs dived over into a hook-grassy clearing in the trees and grabbed a skinny boar. I sat with my load against a tree and let Uncle Hec go down and deal with it. It was too skinny for eating so we left it there and carried on down the creek. The dogs were a bit easier to control now that they'd had a bit of exercise.

On we went, walking through a world of trunks and branches and stones and roots and vines. I could hardly lift my feet or tell up from down by the time we came to the first big forks of the creek, where the country got wider and flatter. My pack was hurting my shoulders and I was just about falling over when we dropped our loads and sat down on the grass against a log. I must admit that it was only thoughts of the Social Welfare department that was keeping me going. "How much further?" I said, almost in a coma from being so tired.

"About an hour down the creek. How are you going?"

"I'm all right," I told him.

"Let's have a brew-up," he said. "I could use something to eat."

Thoughts of food livened me up and we lit a driftwood fire and had mugs of sweet tea, with bread and cold mutton and some watercress we found in a backwater. I felt better after that, but I had to use thoughts of the Social Welfare to get my legs moving properly when we got going again.

We crossed the creek back and forth from flat to flat, cutting across bush terraces with groves of big trees and waist-deep ferns until we came to the Mangatoatoa hut, where a big side creek came in on the right. It was the same as most of the Forestry huts in the Urewera, Uncle Hec said. Painted orange, tin roof and sides, one room with wooden bunks around the walls and a fireplace in one side. Table and shelves, a big locked food-cupboard broken open, one long wooden stool, aluminium camp-oven and billies under the table. Twisted wire hooks hanging over the soggy ashes of the last fire. The smell of old smoke and ashes.

No one had been here for a long time and there wasn't much food around. A milk-powder tin a third full of mouldy brown rice, some suspicious looking curry-powder in a coffee jar, two packets of instant soup with the corners chewed by rats, some broken pieces of candle and a thin piece of soap. It didn't look very promising to me, but Uncle Hec seemed to think it was okay. There wasn't even anything to read there.

We tied up the dogs in case they took off after something they were scenting downstream and got a big fire going, which immediately made everything look much better. We ate the rest of the mutton, the last of the second-to-last loaf of bread, half the rice and some mugs of tea. It was still getting dark when I flopped onto a bunk and went to sleep. I thought I heard Uncle Hec get up in the night to deal with a possum in a trap he'd found and set beneath the tree behind the hut, and next thing I knew it was morning and the fire was blazing and the tea billy was starting to sizzle round the edges.

"Sleep all right?" asked Uncle Hec, poking more wood into the fire.

"Did I ever," I said, sitting up and yawning. "I'm sore all over."

"Not surprised," he said. "You walked right across the Huiarau Range yesterday."

"Is that a long way?"

"It's a bit further than you usually have to walk to get to a hut in here."

"I sure hope so," I said. "I can hardly move."

"Well we don't have to do much today," he said, handing me my mug of tea. "We should be able to get a bit of pork around here, and after a day or two we can take a wander over to the next hut."

"How far's that?"

"About two and a half hours. You can hang round here today and take it easy if you like. I'll just nick out and see if I can knock up an eating-pig for us."

"No you don't," I said. "I'm coming with you."

So after we'd had a feed of bread and rice and sat round for a while, we went up a side creek for a hunt. We'd only been going for a few minutes when we came across a little bush flat freshly turned over by pigs. The dogs shot up into the bush and dragged a little fat boar squealing down into the creek and held it there by an ear each. It was too easy. We carried it out onto the main creek bed and singed it over a driftwood and green manuka fire. That night we cut it up and roasted it in its own fat in the Forestry camp-oven. We ate half of it with a big bundle of watercress. Unfortunately we used up nearly all the rest of the bread.

I was glad we didn't have to walk far that day. I had some blisters on my feet I wasn't mentioning to Uncle Hec and it hurt like anything to walk. I put some paper in my socks when we walked over to the Te Pua hut next day and it wasn't as bad as I thought it was going to be. We climbed up a long ridge, then back down to a big creek on the other side which we followed down to the hut, where there was nothing worth mentioning. The hut itself was much the same as the last one, except that there was no food at all.

We stayed the night at Te Pua, sharpened our knives on a piece of oilstone we found under the steps, and moved on next day across another big ridge to the Tauwharana hut. There was half a five-kilo bag of flour hanging from the rafter and some old yeast in a jar on a shelf, and Uncle Hec showed me how to make a loaf of bread in the camp-oven. You have to keep that yeasty water at just the right temperature and have the fire at the same heat for an hour and a half to get one to turn out right. It was good to know we could actually make our own bread.

Things were looking better in the food department, but by this time I knew I could never find my way out of there on my own. Keeping Uncle Hec in sight through the bush became even more important than finding food. He wasn't my best bet any more, he was my only chance of staying alive.

Four

A TIN OF PEACHES

AFTER THAT we walked hundreds of hours through the bush from hut to hut — Otanetea, Tukurua hut, Ngahirimai hut — all the same and all very scrappy as far as supplies went. We weren't eating for the taste of it any more, we were eating for energy to get to the next hut. And what we ate was usually a mixture of what we had left over from the last camp, what we could shoot or catch on the way, and what we found in the next hut when we got there.

Flour, rice and sugar were the main things we liked to find. We had a rice-bag with a mixture of rice from just about every hut, but it still wasn't much. Tea and matches were no trouble — they were left in almost every hut — but condensed milk, sugar and tins of meat or fish were the rarest and best finds. Once I got the hang of it I got to make better loaves of bread than Uncle Hec, so after a few loaves he got to keeping the wood coming while I baked the loaf. It was his way of saying that my loaf was better than his, though he'd never say it right out.

The dogs mostly did okay on the possums they dragged out of banks and clumps, but we had to be aware all the time of what we needed to make up the next couple of feeds. There were a few other drastic changes as well — there was more to it than I'd imagined, living in the bush. At first I was so busy just walking and trying to keep up that I didn't get much chance to look around. In fact it took me a couple of weeks to realise just where we were and what we were doing.

All this bush — there was so much of it. You could stand on a high ridge and as far as you could see in every direction rose other high ridges of bush, disappearing into the distance, split by slips and creeks and bluffs, but always with the bush growing in and on and around everything. There were times when I really didn't think I'd ever see open land again. Sometimes the country we travelled through was so steep and broken up you noticed every flat area, even if it was only big enough to put your foot on. In other places the ridges were long and easy and open under the trees, and the rivers wide and flat, but I soon found out that you never travel far in the Urewera without coming across rough going.

Uncle Hec was good at getting through the bush. The supplejack vines parted in front of him and closed again in front of me in a series of tough tangles. Pigfern up to your chest seemed to lean aside in front of him and stitch itself together behind him so cunningly that I sometimes had to break the stalks to get through, by which time Uncle Hec would be way ahead again. When crossing rivers Uncle Hec would walk straight through at the head of the rapids, propping one leg downstream against the drag of the current. He made it look so easy I was always getting into trouble. Even when I put my foot exactly where his had been I usually stood on a slippery rock. Overbalancing in rivers can make you very bad-tempered.

The result of all this was that I was always hurrying to catch up with Uncle Hec, and whenever I did catch him it was usually only for a few yards before all of a sudden he'd be away ahead again. Then he'd have a spell till I came puffing up, when he'd move off again, making me keep going to stay caught up.

But after a while it became less of a hassle. I wasn't getting blisters and cramps in my leg muscles any more, and I was learning how to weave my way through the ferns and vines and branches.

"If you try to break off every twig and fern that gets in your way," said Uncle Hec one day without looking round, "you'll be worn away long before you've made any impression on the Urewera."

He was right. The bush had us so absolutely outnumbered in every direction you had to have respect for it. No one could live in there without sticking to the rules. No tawa tree was ever going to reach out and steady me when I tripped on one of its roots. No ridge was going to level off any sooner just because I was too tired to climb any higher. No flooded river was going to ease off to let me across. If it wanted to rain, or blow a gale, or freeze or flood or get dark when we were still two hours away from the nearest hut, it certainly didn't take my preferences into account. The bush just stood there, growing and minding its own business.

I know all this is pretty obvious, but some things take a while to sink in when everything's strange and new to you. And there were things in that bush I'm glad I didn't know about at first. Like the time we were walking through a little valley off the Kahikatea Range and the dogs got excited about something up in the bush above us. We hadn't seen much fresh deer-sign around in that area so in case it was a pig we could eat we let them go, and they dived away up into the bush. We waited for a minute or two and then Zag let out his bark when he finds. Next thing they were both bailing hard. Whatever it was hadn't moved, which was a bit unusual.

"I don't know what that'll be," said Uncle Hec, dropping his pack and checking the rifle. "I'd better go up and have a look. You wait here in case it comes this way." And he took off half-running up the side.

I knew he didn't want me to go up there in case it was dangerous, and I don't know what I was supposed to do if anything did come my way, but I let it pass. The dogs were going mad up on the ridge by this time so I jogged out onto the open riverbed where I could see both ways and hear better. Suddenly Willy let out a yelp. He was hurt. Then there was silence.

I was just going to yell out to Uncle Hec when something came crashing down like a falling boulder through a ferny vine-filled gully and out through a stony place to the riverbed where it suddenly stopped, right under the bank I'd just slid down. It was a huge grey boar, like a big piece of an elephant, with pricked-up hairy ears and dark sunken tufts for eyes. Its mouth was frothing and chomping on its big white tusks and its tail was slapping from side to side while it stood there.

If you'd never heard or seen a pig before you'd know this one was definitely dangerous. And there I was standing right out in the open, thirty feet away from it, and I couldn't tell if it had seen me or not. We stood like that forever, then suddenly this great big thing let out a WHOOF and ran downstream, bigger than ever, through the creek with a shower of water and round the corner, heading up into the bush on the other side.

Then Willy and Zag came tearing down after him and that got me moving again. I yelled at them and ran to head them off, and when they hesitated I grabbed them by the scruffs and held them back. Willy had a four-inch rip up his back leg, but it didn't seem to be bothering him too much. Uncle Hec came sliding down.

"Did you get a look at it?" he said.

"Did I! It was standing right there, looking at me."

He hadn't seen it at all. It had broken away before he could get there, but he believed me how big it was when we found its footprints in the sand where it had crossed the creek. The heel of Uncle Hec's No. 9 boot just fitted into the boar's hoofprint. It was a spiritual experience for me, that, the discovery that there were some scary things in this bush.

"No good to us, a thing that size," Uncle Hec said, examining Willy's ripped leg and giving him a slap on the rump. "We don't want any big old boars or twelve-point stags — leave those to the sportsmen. We need meat, and if one of these dogs gets put out of action it could ruin our whole act."

"What do we do if they get a big one bailed up?" I asked.

"Call the dogs off it and if they come, walk away and leave it there. We've got to try and get it through their heads that we don't want boars."

"Could we shoot a big boar like that with the .22?"

"Sure, if you know what you're doing. There's a hollow in the side of a pig's head between its eye and its ear. If you can hit 'em in there at the right angle with the .22 they'll go down all right. Don't you try it, though."

"Even big boars like the one I just saw?"

"The biggest, mate. I'll show you one of these days."

He did, too. Many times. *Crack* — and down they went, except once, but that was a disaster which happened much later.

“I don’t know if I ever want to see anything like that again,” I said.

“Garn,” he said, “in a couple of weeks you’ll be going in on pigs like that with your knife,” and he reached out to pretend to ruffle my hair, so I ducked and pretended to flatten him with a punch in the ribs and we grabbed our packs and carried on down the valley, keeping the dogs in behind until we were well past where that great big boar had gone up the side.

Half an hour further down the creek we were cutting across a bush flat and the dogs took off and found a big black and tan razorback sow. They were out on the river stones where they’d caught her and she was so skinny and putting up such a brave fight that we decided to let her go. We grabbed the dogs and held them off, waiting for the pig to take off into the bush, but she turned and charged us. I had to let Willy go to dodge her, but the dog grabbed her again so Zag had to be released to help keep her still. By this time she had Willy by the skin of his ribs and they were standing there shaking each other.

This time we got the pig down on the ground where Uncle Hec held it while I took the dogs about fifty yards away and grabbed their necks. Then he let go of the pig and shoved it round facing the bush. But it turned straight round and charged him, chasing him over to the bank. He almost made it to the top when he slid back down again, right into the pig. He kicked at its head but it grabbed his boot in its mouth and there he was, hopping around on one leg trying to keep his balance with this big skinny Urewera pig on the end of his other leg.

I released the dogs again but by the time they got to the pig Uncle Hec was on the ground. The dogs flew into the pig and pinned it as it stood astride Uncle Hec, squealing in his face. I was laughing so much I had trouble dragging him clear, but Uncle Hec wasn’t amused. He leapt up, grabbed the pig, tipped it over and stuck it before kicking and yelling at the dogs till they settled down again.

“What’s so funny?” he said, putting his knife back in its sheath.

"You should have seen it," I told him, "when it had you by the foot and you were hopping round..." I broke up laughing again.

"It wouldn't have looked so funny if it'd had *you* down on your fat bum," he said, examining the marks in the leather of his boot from the pig's teeth. "Anyway, let's get out of this valley before we run into any more of these pigs. They're crazy round here."

We hardly ever stayed more than two or three nights in any hut on the same visit, mainly because it usually only took that long to pick off the animals nearby and clean up most of what we found to eat in the hut. We nearly always got a pig or a bird or some watercress or something to eat between huts. For a while we ate well on grey ducks, which seemed to be everywhere, but then they got scarce and we had a spell on smoked eel from the river.

At the Onepu Hut we laid a big bushy manuka tree in a pool with a lump of stinking meat tied in the middle of it, and when we pulled it out and shook it over the stones nine freshwater crayfish fell out. Kura, the Maori calls them. They're just like little brown crayfish and steamed in salty water they're delicious, but you'd have to work at it to get enough to live on.

When it rains in the bush there's nothing to say it's not going to keep it up forever, and quite often we had to move on in the wet to find something to eat. Walking in the rain can be not unpleasant once you're properly wet and moving, in fact we did some of our best times between huts and camps in the rain. And we'd arrive at our destination each with a branch broken off a dead tree. By the time I'd broken up the wood for him and got out of my wet clothes Uncle Hec would have a fire going that would roast the rain away from us and our gear, cook our food, dry our rifle and make everything worthwhile. The dogs would sneak in as though we hadn't seen them and lie very still at the side of the fire out of the way, in case someone noticed them and sent them outside.

When the weather was fine we sometimes camped out in

the open and built up nice big fires. I'm one of those people who have an annoying attraction for smoke. Whenever I sit by a fire the smoke changes direction so it can blow on me and it's no use changing my position because the smoke always follows me around. I usually spend a lot of time sitting holding my breath with my eyes tight shut and my hand over my mug of tea, waiting for a gust of smoke and heat and ashes to blow past.

There was none of that with Uncle Hec's fires. They were positive, they were alive, they talked to you. He built up a stack of blazing logs that sucked the steam from round your socks and carried the flames and light jumping out through the trees, and the smoke had nowhere to go but upwards. When I used to try and build good fires they never came alive properly until Uncle Hec started mucking around with them.

"There's a knack in it," he'd say, and a few minutes later we'd have to shift everything further back from the heat.

Early afternoon one day we were still twenty minutes from the Pukareao Hut when we smelt wood smoke. Someone was around. We climbed onto the bush face opposite the hut and watched. They had no dogs as far as we could see, and we kept ours right beside us. There were two of them, a man and a woman, youngish. Trampers by the look of them and their gear. Their packs were sitting on the ground outside the hut and they were going in and out packing up their stuff. We only had to wait half an hour or so for them to take off in the direction from which we'd come.

I must say it felt a bit strange, sitting there watching other people and knowing we couldn't go up and talk to them without landing in trouble.

"What do we do if we suddenly come across people like that?"

"Play it by ear, I suppose. There's not much anyone can do to us in here anyway."

The trampers hadn't left much food behind them — a packet of instant oxtail soup, half a bottle of tomato sauce and a nearly-empty tin of condensed milk. There was a Leon Uris I hadn't read there though — *Trinity*. But we had no candle and I couldn't read at night.

The next morning I was a few minutes walk up the Pukareao stream looking for watercress when suddenly I saw this deer standing among some logs across the river. I ducked round behind some toe-toe and ran back to the hut, where Uncle Hec had just lit the fire. We grabbed the rifle and ran back up to the flat to get there before the deer smelt our smoke. The deer was walking across the stream towards the bush on our side. Uncle Hec leant the rifle across a log and next thing — *crack* — and the deer dropped into the creek right where it was. We went over and bled it. A yearling hind, shot right through the head. He was a good shot, my Uncle Hec.

We dragged the deer back to the hut and skinned it and hung it in a tree. The next day we started on the backsteaks, as many thick juicy tasty steaks as we could eat. They were delicious. We ate all the steaks and chops and made a big rich camp-oven stew. Uncle Hec poked me in the stomach and tried to put it across that I'd eaten a whole deer practically on my own in four days. I can't help it if I happen to like venison, but I'd had enough of it by the time we left.

From Pukareao we travelled on to Totaepukepuke hut, and then on to the Poplars in the Horomanga Valley. Uncle Hec had a few rules about the huts but sometimes I thought he went a bit far with them. We never skinned a hut right out of food, even if we only left a brew of tea there, and we had to leave a good heap of wood at every hut we used, and make everything nice and tidy "for the next man". That next man burnt a whole lot more of our firewood than we burnt of his, that's all I can say.

Mangapouri hut . . . Opaheru . . . Mangarawhia hut — pretty soon we had the best eating utensils you could find anywhere. It was just a matter of swapping something of yours for a better one whenever you found it. We used plastic mugs and plates because they were lighter and made less noise than tin ones.

The Bullring hut . . . Mangakahika hut . . . Central Waiau . . . Te Waiotukapiti. We found plenty of clothes in the huts — shirts, socks, coats, even pants. Nothing was in pairs or fitted us properly, but we could keep ourselves clothed, which was the main thing.

Boots were another thing. Our feet were hardly ever dry and I'd had my boots for nearly a year. We knew they were going to pack it in and they did — in a side-creek of the Waikare River. The sole of my right boot came right away from the upper. We flapped around and perched ourselves on a low ridge and watched the main track to the Waikare hut. We were hoping to find something at the hut to fix my boot with, wire or something, but towards evening a bunch of trampers came up the track. We heard one of the women laughing minutes before they came in sight. Two men and two women, obviously intending to stay the night in the Waikare hut.

That was the end of any idea of fixing my boot that night, and we couldn't get far with it as it was. We had to adapt, so we sidled around in the bush to where we could see the hut. Four pairs of boots were propped upside-down against the steps to drain — and the people were all inside, eating and talking and laughing. So I snuck round and exchanged my boots for the nearest-sized pair and crept away in my socks before someone came out and saw me.

We would have liked to wait around to see what happened when they discovered the boot-switch, but it was getting dark and we had to go for it to get to a camping place under an overhang we'd used once before. My new boots were so good to walk in that I felt a bit remorseful about taking them. I hope they made it out to the road with my old boots, whoever they were.

Parahaki hut... Whakataka hut... Manuoha. It was only when we were going round some of the huts for the second or third time that I started to learn the actual lay of the land. The whole of the Urewera has two main ranges, the Huiarau and the Ikawhenua, with the Whakatane River valley between them. If you could keep your position related to some point on one of those ranges you could usually tell which valley you were in. And if the water was running the right way you were probably in the right creek or river. It was very hit and miss and we spent a lot of time uncertain exactly where we were. Most of the trouble was not being able to see out through the bush; you get a lot of mist in the Urewera, too.

I got to studying the bits of maps we found in various huts and gradually built up an understanding of the way the ridges and rivers ran. Everything was right there on the maps. In the Upper Whirinaki hut one night I tried to point out something I'd found on a map to Uncle Hec, and I suddenly realised he didn't know what I was talking about. Uncle Hec couldn't even read a map.

"You can't even read a map," I accused him. "Can you!"

"Never needed to," he said.

"But that's why we have to guess where we *are* half the time," I said. "That's what maps are for, so you can tell exactly where you are. Don't you realise that?"

"I usually get there," he said.

He was impossible — too old-fashioned. I decided to take over some of our navigation and it wasn't long before I knew more about some of the areas than Uncle Hec. I also knew enough not to let him know it. He fancies himself in the bush, Uncle Hec, but there were two places where we'd walked for hours up gorgy creeks when a track had been benched into the face since he'd known it in the old days.

None of the smaller creeks had names on the maps so we usually had to refer to them by something that happened there. So we had an Earache Creek, Cast-antler Creek, Milkpowder-tin Creek, Always-raining Creek, Cowbones Creek — names like that. At Deep Creek, we had to follow the right bank for more than an hour to find a place to get across; at Cathedral Creek we camped among a stand of huge totara trees, rising straight out of the ground like big pillars.

How Log-jamb Creek got its name was a bit scary. We'd slept beside this creek, under a sheet of black polythene we'd found in one of the huts. It had been raining and drizzling on and off for a couple of days and the main river was up about a metre. We kept a fire going with lumps of shattered rata and just after dawn I went over to the creek to get a billy of water, and noticed that it had almost stopped flowing altogether. I thought this was a bit strange and told Uncle

Hec, "The creek's stopped flowing and the river's flooded."

"What?" He hurried over to see for himself, then rushed back to the camp and started pulling down the polythene.

"Get packed up and get the hell out of here," he said urgently.

"What's the hurry?" I said, stuffing things into my pack.

"A slip's come down in the night and blocked off the creek," he said. "The water builds up behind 'em and when they go they can be like a dirty great tidal wave."

We went straight up onto a small terrace on the ridge above and got a new fire going with burning sticks from the old one. Then we set up our shelter and sat there, about 300 feet above the creek.

"You've got to watch out for this sort of thing," Uncle Hec said. "I've seen one of those slip dams bury a hut under thirty metres of shingle when it — listen!"

And we could hear it coming with a rumbling grinding noise. A big slow wave of water and logs and branches, an enormous brown stew, surged around the corner of the creek from where we were, smashing flat and breaking off the bush at the sides and shaking and bruising the bark off the big trees. It was like a tidal wave, tearing past us like a giant train through the bush and fading off down the valley. Then there was only the rain hissing onto the leaves all around us.

We looked at each other but didn't say anything. There was only one thing to say and we both knew it. We'd beaten that destruction by under an hour.

Next morning on our way out we went down and looked at the flat where we'd camped. A two-metre wall of water and mud and broken timber had swept right through it, leaving some places ankle-deep in sloppy silt and others washed away completely. The whole creek had been altered forever in that one rush of water, and only Uncle Hec and I in the whole world knew what the name of Log-jamb Creek really meant.

Another place we named was Mossy Rocks — and that was a close shave, too. We were crossing this gorgy rocky place on a big rimu log about fifteen feet above the creek. The dogs were barking on something up around the corner and we were in a hurry to catch up and see what they had.

We weren't being careful enough. I was in front and I stood on a slippery part of the log. My foot shot out from under me and Uncle Hec grabbed my pack to try and steady me. We almost made it, but ever so slowly we both fell off the log and down through the air, crashing down onto some mossy rocks at the edge of the creek. Like when a stone explodes in the fire and a splinter snicks past your eye, your mind concentrates for a flash on how very far from any outside help you are if you get hurt.

We lay there for a moment, wondering how seriously hurt we were. We stood up slowly and looked at each other. No broken arms or legs, not even a bruise or scratch that we could see. Uncle Hec picked the rifle up out of the water. There was a dent bruised into the wood on the forestock. We shook the water out of it and had a couple of shots each at stones in a bank. It was okay.

"There was someone in our corner that time," said Uncle Hec, looking up at the log we'd just fallen off.

Our camps had to have names, too. There was Shag-rookery Camp, Wet-bread Cliffs, Stag-wallow Saddle, Lost-soap Pool, Duck-egg Flats, Kaka Ridge, Sparrowhawk Bend — in fact if there'd been anyone around to hear us talking they wouldn't have known where we were talking about.

One night we camped at the Kanohirua Hut on the Maungapohatu Track, and Uncle Hec went down to the Ruatahuna Settlement to try and contact a friend of his called Russ. He was away all night and as soon as he got back to the hut next day we had to go up to the Huiarau road to pick up a beautiful big load of food from the mysterious Russ's wife.

I was a bit hacked-off with Uncle Hec because he'd promised to ask if they had any spare books and he'd forgotten. He had some interesting news, though. We'd been in the newspapers. He had a newspaper cutting about us, so I made him stop on the track while I read it.

It said that Hector William Faulkner, aged fifty-three years, and his nephew, Richard Morehu Baker, a part-Maori aged thirteen, had disappeared from the Faulkners' Apopo farm over three months before. They were believed to be somewhere in the Urewera Country and fears were held for their safety. Although Hector Faulkner was known to be an experienced bushman, his relatives were concerned about his state of mind since the recent loss of his wife. The Forest Service and National Park Rangers had been alerted to keep a lookout for the pair, and anyone sighting them should inform the nearest ranger or police station immediately.

"They reckon it's been over the radio a few times too," said Uncle Hec. "They seem to be making a hell of a fuss about it."

"Do you think they'll come looking for us?" I said.

"Not seriously," he said. "There's too much bush for us to hide ourselves in. My guess is that they'll wait for us to crack up and go out and give ourselves up."

"That'll be the day."

"They probably think we won't be able to handle the winter. It gets a bit heavy in here some years."

"We can hold out through the winter, can't we?"

"Sure we can. They won't get us that way, but we'd better try and avoid being spotted by anyone in case they send a search party after us. They're doing some pretty weird things out there these days. I sure wouldn't have thought they'd have been all that interested in us."

Not long after that (five days), we were in the Tawhiwhi hut on the Whakatane River. Mid-morning it was, and suddenly there was a rifle shot just down the end of the flat. We didn't wait to tidy up for the next man, not that time. Luckily we were getting ready to leave for the Takurua at the time and our packs were sitting on the floor of the hut. We threw everything of ours we could see into the packs, untied the dogs, and took off quietly into the bush behind the hut. We must have been only just out of sight when we heard someone shout, "Hey Mike! You there mate?"

We climbed straight up the ridge behind the hut. Fortunately the night was fine and still, so we camped by a stag-wallow on a saddle high on the Te Wharau Ridge. That was where we discovered we'd left our tea billy behind at the Tawhiwhi Hut, and we had to boil water in our mugs against the embers of the fire to make a brew.

We arrived at the Otanetea hut the next day and saw our new brew-billy sitting on the table. It was a tin of golden peaches, a large one. It was sitting on a note that said, FOR JOAN AND REG, COMPLIMENTS OF RAY AND DAVID.

We ate the peaches and later on, when we'd had something to eat, we made holes in the peach tin with a nail worked out of the wall of the hut and put a wire handle in it. Just right for two mugs of tea.

If we'd known then some of the things that were going to happen to us while that peach tin was our brew-billy we mightn't have got quite so much fun out of swapping a third of a jar of expired yeast for it on the note on the table of the Otanetea hut.

Five

BROKEN-FOOT CAMP

On our next trip round the huts, about two weeks later, we'd left the right branch of the Manuoha Creek one day, heading for the Mangawhero Forks, and on a narrow track down a ridge we ran into two men and two women coming the other way. Even the dogs were taken by surprise. The only thing to do was stop and talk — we couldn't walk *through* them. It was the first other people I'd been this close to since Aunty Bella's funeral. My heart was thumping.

"Hello there," someone said.

"G'day," said Uncle Hec. "Where are you lot heading?"

"We're on our way out to the road from — hey! You're not the ones they're looking for, are you?"

"What do you mean looking for?" said Uncle Hec.

"Everyone's been asked to keep a lookout for a middle-aged man and a young Maori boy. They've been missing in the bush for over three months."

"No kidding," said Uncle Hec.

"Sure, haven't you heard about it?"

"Couldn't be us mate. We've only come in here for the weekend. Hunting."

One of the women caught me sneaking a look at the watch to see what day of the week it was. Thursday.

"Well if you do see anyone like that, tell them they're supposed to report to the nearest police station urgently."

"Okay, we'll do that," said Uncle Hec moving past them. "Have a nice walk."

"Thanks, the same to you."

And we were away from them along the track. We didn't stop or say anything until we'd reached the creek at the bottom of the ridge.

"Do you think they knew it was us?" I asked after we'd

dropped our packs and had the billy hanging in the fire.

"For sure," said Uncle Hec. "They'd have to be pretty dumb not to. They'll go straight out and tell the police they saw us."

"What would the police want us for?"

"It's *me* they want."

"Why?"

"Taking you off into the bush, I suppose."

"But there's no law against that, is there?"

"If there's not they'll probably make one," he said. "They're doing some pretty strange things out there these days."

"Why can't they just leave us alone," I said. "It's not fair."

"If you're looking for a fair deal, forget it," said Uncle Hec. "You'd only ever run into one of those by accident."

Knowing that those trampers would probably report seeing us, and where, we climbed onto the main ridge and dropped over into the Pukareao Stream and stayed the night in the Pukareao Hut. And the next day on our way to Ngahirimai we walked straight into two men with rifles in the Whakatane River. We walked right up to them and past them.

"G'day," said one of them.

"G'day," said Uncle Hec without stopping.

And when we were twenty or so yards past them one of them called out, "Hey!"

We stopped and looked back.

"You two are supposed to report to the nearest police station urgently."

"Yeah," said Uncle Hec. "We already got the message."

And we walked on away from them.

"We'd better get out of this area," said Uncle Hec. "It's crawling with other people around here."

So we climbed another long ridge, over the Te Mauia Range and down the other side to a big creek, where we caught a skinny pig and camped on a sandy river-beach. From there we crossed the Kairaka Range and picked up a stash of food we had hidden near the Te Pua hut. Another day's walking brought us to a jumble of short steep ridges and waterfally creeks. There was plenty of deer and pig sign around and we caught a good pig and camped where the creek we were following opened out into a fairly wide area of shingle and bush-flats. It was the hardest, longest walk we'd done for a long time.

"We might get left alone here for a bit," said Uncle Hec. "But we'll still have to keep out of sight of the choppers. I wouldn't be surprised if they've been told to keep a watch out for us."

"Where are we, anyway?" I said.

"Right in the guts of it," he said.

And it was easy to believe him. The bush here was steeper and more primitive-looking than over in the Whakatane Valley. The creeks were narrower and steeper and the pigs skinnier and nastier — they chased the dogs. Harder sort of country — even the same ferns seemed coarser and scratchier here.

As far as I could figure out from the torn scrap of map I had of the area, we were in a side-creek in the headwaters of the Ruakituri River. Right, as Uncle Hec said, in the guts of it. Strange territory, lost among more strange territory. When it rained the day after we got there even the downpour seemed wetter than usual, but we soon had a worse problem than just getting wet — when we were setting up our camp a certain Uncle pulled a big rock out of the bank to shield one side of the fireplace, and it fell onto his boot against another rock and broke a bone in his foot.

In an hour we knew he couldn't walk, and it was going to be a long time before he was going to get a boot on that foot again. We were stuck right there until his foot mended, and boy, he didn't like the idea of *that* very much.

When the rain stopped we built a really good camp in a grove of trees back from the stream. We cut poles with the slasher-head we'd found on a track over in the Whakatane, and tied them between the trees with vines to make punga walls and bunks. We used punga-fronds a foot thick over a sheet of black polythene for thatching, tied down with thin poles. And we built a big fireplace between Uncle Hec's big rock and the bank, a few feet from the doorway.

We'd bound up his broken foot with shirtsleeves and he could hobble around with a stick, tying knots and giving bad-tempered orders — but that was about all. I was going to have to do all the hunting till his foot mended, however long that was going to take. We had to have meat or our other food would be gone in a few days. I was going to be busy.

We were out of meat by the time I went for my first hunt and I *had* to get something. The dogs got interested in the wind from a narrow side-creek about twenty minutes upstream from our camp, and when I investigated I found a small mob of goats on a rocky slip down near the creek. There were six of them. I shot a young nanny goat through the neck and the others all ran into the bush. The dogs scrambled up through the jumbled rocks and bailed up a billygoat on top of a boulder as big as a Forestry hut. He was a white one with a long yellow beard and mane, and his horns curled out from his head in thick twists of bone. And he really stank. He fought the dogs off for about ten minutes — no way were they getting up on his rock if he had any say in it. He shunted them off one after the other as they tried to claw their way up the slope of the boulder to get at him. And he was still looking for more. A brave goat, that one.

I called the dogs off and we left him there in charge of his boulder. I then carried the goat I'd shot back to camp. If it was as easy as this to get meat around here... but it wasn't.

"Where'd you get this?" said Uncle Hec, flopping the dead goat from side to side.

"Second creek on the right up the left fork. Brave Goat Creek."

"Many there?"

"Five left out of the mob I saw, and another billygoat. There could be more there — I only got two minutes up the creek."

"Could come in handy."

He never asked me how it got to be called Brave Goat Creek — we just always called it Brave Goat Creek after that. Not bad meat, goat, but I always preferred mutton or pork or venison.

The next time I went out I got right up into the head of a creek before the dogs got onto a mean little boar that was only just worth eating. It gave Willy a rip up the shoulder and it took me three and a half hours to get it back to the camp.

Meantime Uncle Hec hobbled around with his stick, throwing every bit of firewood he could reach into a huge heap beside the camp. His foot looked pretty painful to me but he never said much about it. He hated having anything wrong with him, Uncle Hec.

Next time I left him soaking his foot in the edge of the creek and went downstream where I walked all day without even seeing any fresh sign. The game that had been so plentiful when we had arrived had moved away. I got back to camp an hour or so after dark, wet and miserable with rain and failure. The dogs hadn't had a run all day.

But Uncle Hec was looking smug about something and I didn't find out what it was until he raked a big rainbow trout, baked in clay, out of the embers of the fire. He'd hobbled over to the big pool at the forks, about 150 metres, and caught it with a cricket on a hook and reel of nylon we had with our gear. It must have been tricky getting it landed without breaking the nylon because you usually had to run up and down among the stones, following the trout till it tired and you could ease it into the shallows. It must have been quite a performance, the way Uncle Hec was fixed for running, but he never said anything about it. The trout was delicious, though, stuffed with watercress and wineberry. In fact I could have eaten the whole thing on my own if I'd had a chance.

The next day I climbed up onto the ridge at the head of Broken-foot Creek — nothing. It was getting dark and I was half an hour from the camp, empty-handed, and ready to give up when the dogs found something under a branchy log lying head-down the creek bank. There was an animal under there, probably a possum, but it might be a duck or something. I climbed up, pulled a shattered branch away, and Willy dived in. Something black shot out behind me and Zag grabbed it and shook it once before I got it off him. It was a big dark-brown kiwi with a broken neck.

I'd never seen a kiwi close up before. This one was about the same size as an ordinary rooster, with thick brown legs, long thin beak and ferrety little eyes. It had stumps of wings and hairyish speckled feathers, and it felt as if I was holding something prehistoric in my hands. There seemed to be plenty of meat on it so I carried it back to camp. By the time I got it there my hands were cramped with the weight of it.

"Never eaten one meself," said Uncle Hec, flopping the dead kiwi around in the firelight. "You game to give it a go?"

"It's the only meat we've got," I said.

We took the ferny-feathered skin off the dark red flesh and fried it in pieces in the camp-oven we'd carried all the way from Te Pua. Then we worked it up into a kind of casserole with some onion and other stuff we had, but no matter how long we cooked it, it was still like chewing musty fishy rubber.

"You can leave the next one of *them* where you find it," said Uncle Hec, throwing a piece back into the camp oven.

I had to agree with him, and so did the dogs, but it filled a gap till I got a big pig not far from the camp next day.

I managed to keep up with it for the next three weeks. One night it was a big eel I kicked up out of the shallows when I was almost back to the camp with nothing. Another time the dogs grabbed a paradise duck in some long grass. Then we'd catch a pig and have a few day's rest from hunting.

We got lucky too. One day I was having a rake with the dogs through a place I called White-sow Creek, where I'd picked up one or two feeds. Towards the head of the creek the dogs disappeared, so I carried on up, listening for them. Suddenly a red-brown smudge ran through scattered trees and stopped on a little slip, looking back at me. A deer, about forty metres away. I tried to get a bead on its neck but couldn't hold the rifle steady. Shooting at real deer can make you nervous.

The deer turned its head away to move again, so I took wild aim and fired. I knew I'd hit it somewhere by the way it bucked a bit as it jumped out of sight, so I ran round to where it had been standing and started following its marks around the game-trail looking for blood. Then Willy and Zag shot straight past me. There was a single bark in the creekbed 100 metres ahead, and when I got there the dogs were panting around at the foot of the bank beside my deer, dripping and wagging as though they'd done it all by themselves. I'd hit it through the chest — a lung-shot. It was a four-point stag. A big one.

After I'd gutted it I found I could just get it onto my back. I had about an hour to walk down White-sow Creek and then an hour and a half up to the camp with the back legs over my shoulders, the blood dripping down my leg-backs, the deer-smell, the dogs, and the rifle slung across — I was right into the spirit of being a hunter that day, bringing home the meat.

By the time I reached the main creek I'd had to cut the head off because it kept tripping me up. The bones were digging into my shoulders and back and the rifle was banging on my head or knee or elbow — I needed both hands to keep the deer balanced. I fell over a few times and had to have a number of rests, but I was determined to walk into camp with that deer on my back.

I was so tired by the time I saw Uncle Hec's big fire shining in the trees up at the next bend that I had to lean my load on a log and have a little cry about Aunty Bella. After I had staggered into camp Uncle Hec took over the deer and skinned it in the firelight, while I thankfully drank a full billy of tea. There was resting and feasting at Broken-foot for a good spell after that.

After a few days, and while we still had a bit of meat in the camp, I walked over to the Te Panaa Hut to look for food. I got back to Broken-foot next night with a big load of flour and quite a bit of other stuff—candles, two magazines, a sheet of plastic, some wire and a tin for a new billy, for watercress because of some boils we were getting on us.

It was a long walk, but it stopped Uncle Hec getting so worried every time I went somewhere on my own. He used to say it was because he didn't like not having the rifle around him in the bush.

I was learning a few things from living in the bush. One of them was that there's a big difference between hunting for fun and having to do it to eat. Hunting had become like work that had to be done. Sneaking through the bush, always looking for something to kill and eat. Having to do it. Needing the meat. There was something savage about it, something kind of primitive.

"Do you think it's good for anyone to kill things all the time, Uncle Hec?"

"What sort of things?"

"Animals. Pigs, deer, fish. Stuff like that."

"Long as y' don't start enjoying cutting throats there's nothin' t' worry about."

No fear of that with me. And there were always the nice things, like the birds. I always liked birds and I'd got to know most of them in the Urewera. The shining cuckoo, arriving each year from across the world to lead the dawn chorus in the Urewera — how about that? And the silly cheeky old weka, spearing around in the undergrowth. The soft grey bush robin, and the pretty moppy little fantail. Then there was the beautifully-dressed green and white bush pigeon, and the acrobatic kaka showing off in the high beeches. The fluffy morepork owl, ruru, hooting to his mates all night across the gully, and the dangerous diving sparrowhawk, hurtling through the treetops. The green little bellbird with the melodious voice, and the blue-black tui in the yellow kowhai tree. The wind-up walk of the pukeko; the fearless blue-mountain duck bobbing through the rapids, and the hovering harrier hawk, looking for a mouse or a frog or something dead. There was the bushman's friend, the miromiro I think he was, the shape and colour of a kid's drawing, and the jagged shag, sitting on a stick in the river with a bellyful of trout fingerlings, holding his wings out to dry so he can lift off. The white-faced heron, pale and delicate and shy, minding his own business out there along the edge of the river.

There were more birds than that, but you mightn't like them as much as I do. In fact I spent a lot of hours watching birds when I suppose I should have been hunting. One of my games was pretending to be a wildlife photographer, commissioned to get shots of birds in their natural habitat for a big nature magazine — *National Geographic*, perhaps. And if my chunk of wood had been a camera I'd have taken some interesting photos. It was more like practice really, in case I decided to take it up as a career, or something.

A funny thing happened about that. One day I was creeping after a kaka I'd seen from the camp, trying to get a shot of its orange underwings, using the rifle as a camera. Uncle Hec, dragging a big dead tawa branch, spotted me sneaking along.

"What are you up to?" he said.

"I was just trying to sneak up on that kaka."

"What for? You don't want to eat them. There's not enough on one to fill the holes in your teeth."

"I was trying to see if I could get a photograph of it, if I had a camera," I confessed.

He squatted down against a tree and started breaking up a stick of wood.

"Is that what you want to get into?" he asked.

"Wouldn't mind," I said. "What's wrong with that? I know a lot about birds. I watch them all the time. I bet I know more about them than you do."

"Photographing 'em might turn out to be a bit trickier than just looking at 'em," he said.

"I can learn photography," I told him. "I've read a bit about it. Enough to know the kind of camera and lenses you need. They might even have better gear out by now, but I know I can suss it out pretty quick."

"All you'd have left to do after that is suss out how to get close enough to the birds."

"I already know that," I said. I spend hours just watching..."

Uncle Hec flicked the end of his stick at me and it hit me in the chest. "I mean close," he said. "You don't understand the first thing about birds. You're going the wrong way about it for a start."

"I suppose you know all there is to know about them," I said, getting ready to dodge a flattening. I reckoned I could outrun him these days, especially with him having a lame foot.

"Birds are some of the hardest things to sneak up on you'll ever find," he went on. "Even for another bird. And here you are creeping along staring at them like a hungry cat." He shook his head at the sheer stupidity of it.

"What am I supposed to do then?"

"Well look at it this way. A bird'll sit on a sheep's back, it'll feed round a horse's feet — it'll even sit in a crocodile's mouth and pick his teeth — but the same bird won't come within a stag's roar of a human being. What do you reckon causes that?"

"Don't know," I said.

"It's because human beings are so unpredictable," he said. "One of the sheep isn't going to leap up and chuck a stone all of a sudden. They're indifferent to the birds. That's your clue.

"Birds are territorial, mostly, and the best way to get near 'em is to move into their territory and ignore them. You can keep an eye on 'em without staring at 'em. You don't want to stay too still, either. Things waiting in ambush do that. You just move quietly around minding your own business. Like a sheep. Then it's a matter of your own patience."

"Patience?"

"Yeah. You might have to wait an hour or more for the bird life in a place to settle down, once you disturb it, and not many people like to stick around that long. Especially young blokes." He looked at me.

"It's not like waiting to me," I told him.

He shrugged and stood up. "I won't stop you," he said. "Get into it if you want to. You're not going to be in here all your life."

He grabbed the end of his tawa branch and started limping down the creekbed with it towards the camp. I picked up some lighting-sticks and followed him.

"Where did you learn about birds, Uncle Hec?"

"Mostly from an old aboriginal lady I was bushed with once up in Arnhem Land."

"An old lady? What were you doing there?"

"Hunting."

"Hunting what?"

"Snakes, grubs, lizards, birds — anything we could get to eat. The Mornington Islanders had stolen our canoe and all our gear and a load of salted dugong meat. We were cut off by the wet season and all we had was a knife and a burning gum-branch."

"How long did you do that for?"

"About eight weeks. We crossed the Roper River on a log and made it out to the Gulf in the finish and got to a place called Borroloola on the MacArthur River. I got through to Darwin after that and waited out the wet."

"What happened to the old lady?"

"She went back to her tribe on the Limmin River, but I reckon I'd have been dingo meat if it hadn't been for her. I've been in the bush with a few people, but that old abo lady could run rings around anyone else I ever seen."

"How?"

"She just moved so good through the bush she never hassled an ant. She could tell you by the state of the insects what birds were likely to be around, and she could tell by the birds what animals were in their area. She could tell by the mud crabs just where to wait for a barramundi with a burnt sharpened stick. The birds used to carry on as though she wasn't there, and when I'd sneak up behind her they'd start squeaking and flying around as though someone had fired a couple of shots. When we were looking for tucker I had to stay so far behind her I could hardly keep her in sight — I was so clumsy compared with her. I'm not bad in the scrub myself, but the only use I was to her was carrying the fire-stick and helping her roll logs over to get at the grubs."

We walked on for a bit and then he said, "I'd have died on my own. There's no one can sneak like an abo."

"Must have been pretty tough going," I said.

We'd come out on the flat near the camp by this time and he stopped and looked round at me.

"It was no tougher than this."

Uncle Hec had said one of those things I couldn't forget. *"There's no one can sneak like an abo."* And every time it came onto my mind I couldn't help imagining this old black lady taking Uncle Hec out into the desert, years ago in another land, and giving him a message about birds to pass on years later to young black Ricky Baker in the Urewera bush. I felt kind of grateful to her from a long way off. Maybe she was an ancestor of mine or something, or maybe I needed something to fill the gaps of not having much to do with other people. Whatever it was that old lady, the Bird-lady, was with me in the bush whenever I thought about her after that. I even sneaked different, as though she was watching to see if I did it right. She taught me to *like* the vines and roots and bluffs and boulders that got in my way, and suddenly they'd be behind me and nice to have known you. You walk lighter on the land when you like the land you walk on, and you can see your way through a tangle of vines or a heap of rocks or a tricky river before you even reach them. Distance becomes a different thing, too. And time. It alters your pace, to do it right. You move slower but you get there sooner, and quieter, and more convinced than last time that in a mysterious kind of way it's all one big living thing. I had a whole new relationship with the birds to explore, too, and I could get into their scenes real easy once I got used to it. Uncle Hec was right. There's no one can sneak like an abo.

The night after I got back from Te Panaa Hut with the load of flour and stuff we had the first heavy frost of the winter. Keeping warm became very important, so we improved our little whare to make it more rain and wind-proof, made a goatskin door laced onto a framework of wineberry sticks, built up round our fireplace with flat rocks, doubled the depth of crown fern on our bunks and tied extra poles along the roof to hold down the polythene and thatching. It ended up real cosy, especially when the light and heat from the fire reflected right into the hut at night.

The dogs were snug too. Zag had a bunk under the roots of an upturned rimu, and Willy had a speargrass nest under the bank near the fireplace. They were doing fine on the biggest blackest possums Uncle Hec had seen for years.

"There's an unusually good colony of possums round here," he said half a dozen times.

One real cold morning it was just getting daylight and I was lighting the fire when I heard something that sent me ducking in to wake Uncle Hec up.

"Wake up," I said, giving him a shake.

"What's up?" he said, sitting up in his sleeping bag.

"The stags are roaring," I said. "Listen."

We went outside. A distant moan came wafting down from high on the range at the head of the valley, to be followed by a loud bellowing from up behind the camp. There was another roar from further away, and then silence, except for the birds.

"They're roaring all right," he said. "We'll have to be extra careful for the next few weeks. The Urewera will be crawling with trophy-hunters — they go everywhere. The choppers'll be busy too. You'd better take the slasher and see how many trees you can drop across that old helicopter pad you found the other day."

So we lit no fires in the daytime and listened and watched for signs of other people. It was an extra worry when I was away scrounging for food, and every time I got back to camp it was a relief to find out that Uncle Hec hadn't had a visit from anyone while I was away. We were very vulnerable just then, with Uncle Hec's foot, and I could tell he was worried about it by his bad temper. I heard two shots one day from way over on the next watershed, and I found gumboot marks crossing our creek two hours downstream from the camp, but nothing worth mentioning to Uncle Hec.

The stags roared around there for four weeks, morning and evening mostly. The big old one high up in the beech country would moan two or three times, then the noisy one on Pigeon Ridge would bellow like a calf, and when he'd had his say the one we called Hookgrass Harry would bellow and bark and grunt in several bursts. He was on a swampy bend in the heads of the little creek opposite the camp, about a quarter of a mile away. Those were the regulars but Uncle Hec said he'd identified twenty-six different stags he'd heard from the camp during the roar. I wondered where they all disappeared to when I was out hunting.

One afternoon at the height of the roar I tied up the dogs and climbed up to see how close to Hookgrass Harry I could sneak. For a start I just headed up in his general direction, and I'd climbed right past him when he let out a roar about fifty yards away. I went prickly with fright. Even the Bird-lady froze. No idea it was going to be *that* loud. I stood there with a bit more than half my attention on a tree I could get up quick, and then he roared again — a rattling rasping bellow that could only come out of something real dangerous, and big.

I knew not to be scared, but I still was. I sneaked slowly round to where the noise was coming from. The wind was gusty and blowing everywhere at once, so with a bit of luck it might scent me and run away. It roared again and I skipped a bit closer. The Bird-lady seemed to have stayed back by the leaning tree. Again it roared and I made about twenty yards towards it. I heard something crashing, like gorillas. I moved up behind another tree in a gust of wind and then I saw him.

He was an eight-pointer stag, walking up and down a ten-yard flat place, stopping every now and then to roar again, or rip his antlers through a tanekaha bush that was hanging in shreds of stripped bark and broken branches. It was the biggest deer I'd seen, and I could see why Uncle Hec had said, "Don't try it with the .22, you'll only tickle him."

He had a dark shaggy mane of hair round his neck and a big yellow ring round his rump. The rest of him was thick greyish hair apart from his belly, which was black like his legs. His antlers were brown from tanekaha bark and shining white at the tips. He roared again and gave four or five huge grunts.

I don't know how long I stood there looking at him, perhaps ten minutes, when I turned back from listening to another stag roar further round the face and found that Hookgrass Harry was looking straight at me. He'd seen my head move. It was a nasty moment, that. I've never been looked at so hard by anything in my life, except maybe Uncle Hec when he was getting ready to flatten me. But this was different — a wild animal that roared like a dragon and ripped things to bits with its antlers. I got ready to fire a shot to try and frighten it away, but the stag moved first. He gave a grunt and leapt away, down and across through the bush and he was gone.

I stood there wondering about it. What would a twelve-pointer be like to come across in the roar. Pretty impressive,

I imagined. But when I did see one later on the Pohukura Ridge my imaginings were nothing like it. He's a mighty animal, the red stag. You had to have respect for him.

Anyway, the wind had been getting more gusty for an hour or so, and as I made my way back down through the bush it started getting very strong. By the time I got to camp Uncle Hec was hopping around tying down the roof, and the trees were thrashing about in the sudden gusts as though they were throwing fits.

I thought it was going to be a bit of fun at first, but this wasn't any ordinary wind, it was Urewera wind. A roaring, shunting gale developed, broken up by the bush and ridges into aimless buffeting blasts that hit you from any old direction. I realised it was getting serious when the whole fire suddenly blew out of the fireplace with a swirl of ashes and embers and burning bits of wood, streaming sparks and smoke out across the flat, while we stood a few yards away and watched it with no more than a bit of disturbed air blowing around us at the time.

We staggered round with logs from the creek bed to lay on our roof, which was going to lift off and blow away at any moment, groping our way through the wind and stopping and hanging on in the gusts. Every now and then we'd be caught in a driven rain of spray whipped up off the surface of the creek. The whole bush-face opposite the camp was writhing.

When we'd done everything we could to hold the roof on and put rocks on everything that hadn't already blown away, we went inside and sat on our bunks, listening to the power and destruction of it. A big tree came crashing down in the bush across from the camp — one of the dead ratas. The rising roar of the storm tore at the bush until all we could do was to sit in our flimsy lifting whare and grin when we survived another big one.

The wind left our ragged-out valley just before dark that night, to be followed by a thick layer of blue cloud and heavy rain before we could even get the fire going. Urewera rain, it doesn't fall in drops like ordinary rain; it starts like a bucketful of marbles being tipped out on the roof and then it's a continuous stream of white lines, hissing and splashing into the bush, beating everything flat and keeping it there, bouncing spray off every surface.

By dark our creek was up a foot, and by morning — it was still raining — it was more than 2 metres above normal. We could hear the rocks and logs booming and rumbling down through the heaving brown torrent that had once been our little creek. The rain had its own cold little wind with it which swept the spattering rain through the gaps round the door of our whare, so the only dryish place was in our sleeping bags on our bunks. We just stayed in bed until the rain eased off into ordinary showers, a couple of hours after daylight. Then we started a tiny fire with a candle-stub, and built it up into a real big one with the aid of man-sized logs brought out of the bush by Uncle Hec on his one leg. Soon everything was steaming and drying out and looking much better with mugs of tea made with dirty water and fresh damper, and the last of the pork and a billy of watercress. What good stuff fire is!

We kept the fire going all that night because it was freezing. Next day we had a frost followed by an overcast sky. The creek was so flooded that you couldn't go anywhere except straight up behind the camp, and it was never any good up there. All we could do was keep the fire going and try to eat as little as possible. The next day was fine but freezing. The creek had gone nearly back to normal, leaving everything changed and swept clean with logs and driftwood piled up in different places and the creekbed itself on a new course across the shingle flats.

I made a quick trip over to the Tataweka hut to try for supplies, and I found that the chopper I'd heard just before I got there had dropped off a fantastic load of stuff — probably for a team of track-cutters. The first thing I did was punch holes in a tin of condensed milk and drink the lot. Then I loaded Uncle Hec's pack with milk, sugar, flour, butter, two loaves of fresh bread, a cabbage, two books and a stretch bandage out of the first-aid box. It was a big load and there was still plenty left. Those Forestry blokes certainly looked after themselves.

I stashed a few tins of peas and cheese and milk under a tawa down the flat from the hut and then had another poke through to see if there was anything I ought to add to my load. But the sound of a chopper sent me off down the track in a hurry. Just as well, too, because that load almost did for me, getting it back to Broken-foot.

Uncle Hec was pleased to see me and my big load of goodies. "You needn't have brought all that," he said, "But let's get one of those cans of tomato soup open."

The food from the hut kept us going through a lean time of hunting — we'd been in the area for too long to hope for any easy meat. I shot three more goats out of Brave Goat Creek, and a few more pigs by hunting further away all the time, but it was getting harder. We were nearly down to eating possum several times.

I got lost one day and nearly spent the night in the bush. I had no idea where I was, but just on dark I dropped down off a ridge and came out on the creek bed just where I'd lit a fire a few days earlier to have a brew. I reached camp an hour after dark, but I didn't say anything to Uncle Hec about getting bushed. I was supposed to be able to remember exactly where I was at all times.

Uncle Hec's foot was improving, especially after we changed the shirtsleeves for a proper bandage. He could take a bit of weight on it and get around more easily, but he still couldn't get his boot on. It made him real crotchety, that foot. I was reading *Don Quixote* again and he used to say it was turning my head. But he was only looking for something to grumble about. It's a good book, that.

The winter was half-over by the time he could walk on his foot again. We were down to fried eel and damper by this time and the dogs were definitely eating better than we were. We'd been at Broken-foot Camp for just under eight weeks and we would have to move on soon to stay eating. As a matter of fact I suspected I was losing weight from not enough to eat. My pants were getting loose.

We made it to the Te Pua hut the first day and had to do a starve for another few days because we'd overdone it on Uncle Hec's foot. When we got to the Tauwharana Hut we finally found some food — flour, rice, powdered milk, instant mashed potato, and half a tin of Golden Syrup. There was a notice on the wall. I read it out.

To Hector William Faulkner, of Apopo Valley Road, Gisborne County: You are required to present yourself and Richard Morehu Baker at the nearest police station immediately. If you have failed to comply with this order within fourteen days of June 30th, you will be deemed to be a fugitive from the law and a warrant will be issued for your immediate arrest.

N. Craddock,
Clerk of the Court,
Gisborne County.

Note: Any person or persons offering assistance to the above-named in any way renders himself/themselves liable to a fine not exceeding 1,000 dollars or a maximum of six months imprisonment.

Here it was again. Other people interfering with us. Uncle Hec tore the poster off the wall and used it to light the fire.

"They're getting serious," he said. "We'll have to be more careful from now on."

I liked the way Uncle Hec never thought of giving in. And judging by the number of notices we found they must have stuck one of them in just about every hut in the Urewera.

There was no going back now. We were fugitives from the law. Our freedom was threatened.

Six

A FRIEND

AS WE MADE our way through the bush we developed a new set of rules. We had to assume that every ranger, forestry worker, hunter, tramper and chopper pilot would know about us and be on the watch for us. The track-cutting gangs didn't worry us.

"The only thing that makes more noise than a track-cutter in the bush is a helicopter," said Uncle Hec.

We weren't so concerned about the possum trappers, either.

"Anyone who'd leave a camp full of skins and walk out to report us to the cops wouldn't be very bright," Uncle Hec pointed out. "Possum trappers don't dob people in as a rule, anyway. They've usually got more to worry about."

Whenever we travelled on a main track we made it a rule that one of us went fifty or sixty metres ahead. It cut down on any talking and it gave us a chance for the one behind to get out of sight if we ran into anyone. We agreed to brush our teeth and have a proper wash at least every two days, in case we slipped into getting dirty without noticing. Uncle Hec kept his beard down to bristles with a little pair of scissors we'd found in one of the huts. Before that we'd been giving each other haircuts by setting fire to each other's hair with a candle and brushing it out before it went too far, with not very good results.

We were getting better at knowing where to find supplies of food. Some of the huts were always being replenished by trampers and hunters who spent their last night in the bush there. And there were huts that never seemed to have anything in them at all. It always worked out that the more food, the more people, and the risk of being spotted by someone and we'd have to move away to some other part of the Urewera. But we were certainly eating better now we could move around.

When it rained we usually sneaked up and checked out

one of the huts, and if there was no one around we'd move in and make ourselves comfortable. It was fairly safe to stay in a hut while the rivers were flooded because no one could get through the tracks. The choppers hardly ever stopped at the huts — they cost too much to run for any flying time that wasn't hunting. They had to catch an animal an hour just to cover their costs and we'd heard that most of them were having a struggle to stay in business. The price of live deer was about half what it was the year before and lifting out venison didn't cover the cost of running the machine. We never had much to do with the chopper people, they lived in a different world from us.

On fine days we often camped on a bush terrace up a side creek somewhere and slept or read books until it was dark and safe to light a fire. At night it was a different matter. We had the whole Urewera to ourselves and could wander round in the open and build up huge fires if we felt like it. We even talked louder at night, to make up for the whispers of the daytime. We were becoming nocturnal.

Another thing we discovered was that the paradise duck, the putangitangi, had changed from being a noisy nuisance to a perfect alarm system. No one can sneak up on a paradise duck, apart perhaps from an abo, and we found that if we camped on their territory they'd fly up and down kicking up a mighty racket for about half an hour. Then they'd settle down again, but remain super alert. Whenever anyone else appeared from any direction the ducks would warn us in time for us to grab our gear and disappear into the bush before they could get within sight. We had only one genuine alarm from the putangitangi, and some false ones, but you could relax a few notches when you knew they were there watching out for you.

Towards the end of the winter the pigs, our main meat, became skinnier and more scarce until we couldn't find any anywhere. Even Uncle Hec had given up guessing where they might be. In the finish we had to go right out to the edge of the bush and compete with the weekend hunters to get a bit of decent pork. Then the rain made us go back to one of the huts.

We did have one memorable feed about that time. We were skimming through some of the best huts but there weren't many people in the bush at that time of year. The last thing we'd eaten was half a weka each and a packet of instant noodles we'd found in the Onepu hut — and that was hours before. We crossed the Kahikatea Range and dropped down a steep shingly tawa creek-head of the Otapukawa Stream. And suddenly we saw dozens of wood-pigeons eating the miro berries. We were going to eat.

We chose a good spot in a grove of miro trees and waited for the pigeons to come flapping in, whistling with weight, to land on the branches. Then we plonked them with the .22. They were so fat that some of them burst, an inch of bright yellow fat all over them, when they hit the ground. When we had eight of them we set up our camp by a trickle of water and smothered the birds in clay (feathers and guts and all) until they looked in the firelight like a row of loaves of bread. Then we rolled them into the embers of the fire and built it up around them. We waited for just over an hour before raking them out and breaking them open like Easter eggs. The feathers came away with the clay, as did most of the skin. They were falling apart and were very delicious and tasty. Uncle Hec ate two on his own while the Bird-lady and I ate one and a half each. The rest of them we wrapped in leaves and took with us when we moved on to Manuoha the next day.

Next we visited a few more huts before sheltering from the rain at Hautapu for two days. When the weather cleared we headed towards the northern end of the Urewera to meet the spring. And on the way there we had our worst argument ever.

We'd been walking for hours with heavy packs and we'd come down the wrong ridge off the Maungataniwha Range and found ourselves in a steep, waterfally, log-jammed, bush-lawyery, slippery little creek.

"I told you we should have gone further along the main range," I told Uncle Hec.

He looked back at me up some rocks he had just slid down beside a waterfall and said, "If you tell me that once more

I'll flatten you, you smart little bastard."

"You're wrong and you won't admit it," I said. "You snore, too!"

"I hit pretty hard as well," he said looking dangerous.

"You'd better not hit me," I told him.

He jumped forward grabbing at my leg and I got out of the way just in time. If he'd got hold of me then he'd have flattened me all right. I ran back up the creek a few yards for a head start, but he didn't come after me. We stood looking over this waterfall at each other for a while, and then he turned and walked off down the creek.

"Come on then," I think he said, and that was the last thing either of us said to each other for two days and nights, which was a bit hard-case considering what happened to us just after that. When we finally crawled out of the mouth of that creek and set off up the river towards Central Waiau Hut, we suddenly heard a strange noise, so we stopped.

The trees were shivering. The ground was shaking and trembling under our feet. The movement got heavier and suddenly we were in the middle of a great big earthquake. Dislodged rocks started crashing off a bluff above us, hurtling down through the bush and bounding out into the air, breaking up and landing all round us. All we could do was watch them coming and try to dodge the rocks of all sizes and shapes pelting like rain at us. On the other side something big crashed into the river but we were too busy to dare look round, even when rotten broken lumps of wood flew out past me onto the stones. Then we were up to our ankles in water. The riverbed had lifted and pushed the water out across the shingle flat, before draining away again.

Then the earthquake stopped. Just like that. There was no time even to get scared. One moment we were being belted with rocks pelting all round us and the river was going mad, the next everything was back to normal again, except the stones were wet, a big dead matai tree had fallen across the river and its shattered branches were lying scattered around, and there was broken rock everywhere. Otherwise it was hard to believe what we'd just seen happening. I looked at Uncle Hec to see what he was going to say about it, but he didn't say anything at all until two nights later when we were over in the Whakatane Valley.

It had rained half the night and most of the day and we'd dropped down to the river in another of Uncle Hec's bad places and found it flooded from bank to bank. We had to cross if we didn't want to spend the night in the rain. There was a big Forestry hut half an hour downstream on the other side and we had some rice and powdered milk stashed in a plastic bag near there.

We would normally have stopped and talked about it but this time Uncle Hec didn't even pause. He walked straight out into the current and let it carry him waist-deep across to the sweep of the bend on the far side. By this time I'd felt my way out into the current as well and suddenly the force grabbed my legs and I had to go with it, running in slow-motion under the brown water, bobbing downstream in the surge of it, easing my way across the stones towards the far side, already well downstream of Uncle Hec.

Suddenly I was in serious trouble. A broken-off branch started to sweep and roll along with me, carrying me right down the rapids under the water, rolling round and round and then out into a big swirl with my pack the only thing that floated me upright, and then down into another straight. Just when I thought I was going to fall through the next rapids my foot got a shove on a rock and I clawed and crawled and splashed my way out into shallow water where I lay coughing and gasping and realising how easy it'd be to get drowned.

Uncle Hec came hurrying over and dragged me onto my feet. I coughed up some water I'd swallowed.

"Next time you can do that on your own," I said between coughs.

"Next time we'll wait for the river to go down a bit, eh," he said.

And we were talking again.

Springtime came and then disappeared for a week before returning. We'd made it through the winter. All of a sudden there were deer and pigs in every creek and riverbed; the huts were stocked with new food, and a new clutch of helicopters slapped their way across the ridges every night and morning. The Urewera was coming alive again, and the dawn chorus of the birds became noisier every day. There were people everywhere, but with plenty to eat we had the leisure to be able to keep out of their way. It was a quiet life after the hassles of the winter, and in spite of having to be extra careful we soon had stocks of food stashed near several of the huts in case of emergencies. We also knew the location of the keys to four of the Forestry food cupboards which had just been stocked up for the summer season. We had plenty of food for the time being, but I wasn't going to forget the lessons of Broken-foot Camp for a while.

We'd been sleeping by a creek on a grassy bank one day until the sandflies drove us awake, when we sidled out and waited on the bluff opposite the Koranga Forks hut until the sun went down. There was no sign of life, so we came down from the bluff in the last of the twilight. It was dark by the time we rounded the track to the hut, certain that we had the place to ourselves for the night. But Uncle Hec suddenly stopped and held up his hand to be quiet.

"What's up?" I whispered.

"Someone's been here recently," he said. "Like today. I can smell the fire. Hasn't been out long enough."

We threw a piece of wood on the roof to see if anyone was sleeping in there. No response.

"I'll go in and have a look," said Uncle Hec.

He entered the hut and I saw a match flare up and the candle flame inside.

"Come here!" he called out.

I went into the hut and saw a man lying on one of the bunks. I thought he must have been dead at first, but his arm hanging over the side of the bunk twitched in the candlelight.

"What's wrong with him?" I said, peering.

"Don't know. Hold this candle."

Uncle Hec bent over the man and gave him a shake.

"Hey mate. Wake up."

He was a big young man, bleary and pale and unshaven.

He stank a bit. His eyes opened into wet slits and he looked towards us, trying to say something, but no sound came out.

"This bloke's crook," said Uncle Hec. "Get some wood and water in here and I'll get a fire going."

We found another candle and when I came back from the creek with a billy of water Uncle Hec poured some into a mug and tried to get the sick man to drink. But he started coughing and choking and I thought he was going to die right then. Then he lay back gasping and seemed to go to sleep again.

"Let's have a brew, anyway," said Uncle Hec.

"What's wrong with him?" I whispered.

"No idea, but he's not going to last much longer, by the look of him."

"What'll we do?"

"One of us'll have to go out and get a chopper in for him. There's a sheep station about an hour and a half up the Koranga from here. Good track all the way. Someone'll have to go out and get them to ring up for a chopper at daylight. Don't know if this rooster's going to last till then, but it's the best we can do."

"We'll both go," I suggested.

"No," he said. "One of us ought to stay here and make sure he doesn't choke or something."

"I'll go then," I said, not really liking the idea of being left alone in the hut with the dying man and half a candle.

"Okay," said Uncle Hec. "We'll get a feed into you and I'll show you where the track starts. You have to be sure to remember where it comes out of the bush at the other end. Could be tricky to find in the dark."

"I'll remember," I promised.

He cut a cross with my knife in the side of a milk-powder tin and poked a candle into it. It made a nifty torch which lit up the track in front of me brightly. I grabbed another third of a candle and some matches and I was ready.

"Yell out from above the house and wake them up. Get them to ring the police in Matawai and tell them there's a bloke dying in the Forks hut. Needs urgent medical attention..."

"All right," I said. "I've got it."

I powered up the track and came out on farmland almost before I was ready for it. I located the farmhouse by a light in one of the windows. Dogs started barking as I approached and I shouted "Hey! Anyone home?"

Another light came on before the door opened and a man came out into the light. I could see him but he couldn't see me and the Bird-lady in some fern up the hill.

"What's going on?" he called out, shielding his eyes and looking round.

"There's a man dying in the Forks hut," I called back. "Can you ring the police and get them to send a helicopter for him in the morning?"

"I suppose so. How long has he been sick? What's the matter with him?"

"We don't know. Just arrived there and found him. We don't know if he'll live till morning."

"Okay. I'll give 'em a ring. Would you like a cup of tea and something to eat?"

It was a thrilling idea but... "No thanks. I'll have to get back. You'll ring up then?"

"Sure. You can come in and ring them yourself if you like. We won't eat you."

"No thanks," I called back, and dropped over onto the road to go back to the track, because I could tell that no one was going to chase after me. All the same that Bird-lady had me ready to leap up the bank into the bush at the first sound of a motor starting up behind me.

It wasn't so good going back to the hut. I was worn out and down to my last stub of spare candle when I stumbled across the swingbridge and into the hut. Uncle Hec revived me with tea and scone-loaf and a tin of lambs' tongues.

The man was still alive. He'd been awake for a few minutes and had drunk some tea. Uncle Hec had been able to make out that he was a diabetic, but he hadn't been able to say any more than that.

I'd never read anything about diabetics, and Uncle Hec didn't know about them either.

"I think it's got something to do with sugar," he said.

"Anyway it looks like he might just hang on till morning. You're sure they're going to ring up?"

I nodded. "Far as I could tell."

"We'd better be ready for them then. They might just try to grab us along with our patient here."

We stashed our packs in the bush behind the hut before I slept. When Uncle Hec woke me with a feed before daylight, the sick man hadn't stirred, but he was still breathing. I stood outside with my mug of tea, listening. Then I caught a faint vibration in the air down the valley.

"Chopper!" I yelled.

"Right," said Uncle Hec. "Let's go."

He took a quick look at the man on the bunk and we grabbed our packs and climbed up onto the ridge in the bush, keeping the dogs close in behind. We'd just settled down when a Hughes 500 dived in and landed by the hut. Two men in overalls jumped out and ran ducking under the blades to the hut. Then they came back to fetch a stretcher from the chopper and brought the sick man out on it and loaded him into the machine. Soon they lifted off and climbed away down the valley.

"Hope he makes it," said Uncle Hec.

"What now?" I asked.

"Well, they know we're around here somewhere. If they're going to try and round us up this'd be a good time for them to try."

He thought for a while. "I reckon if we climbed back onto that bluff where we were yesterday we could keep an eye on the place and see what happens."

"Won't that be dangerous?"

"No more than anything else we do. They'd be expecting us to be an hour away from here by this time, but I wouldn't put it past them to try and catch us. Let's move."

We cut round to the Kahanui branch and left a few footprints leading upstream, before coming back down, walking in the water, and climbing up onto the bluff opposite the hut. No sooner had we tied the dogs up in some fern when the same chopper dropped back in and let four men off, three of them with rifles. Then the chopper took off again, up the Kahanui, and two of the men went up the Koranga and the others up the ridge behind the hut.

By the time they were out of sight Uncle Hec was curled up in his sleeping bag among some tree-roots. He hadn't slept all the previous night. I had some cheese and bread before climbing into my sleeping bag and falling asleep too.

The sound of the chopper returning woke us up. It was late afternoon and the last of the sun was just leaving our level. Down in the shadow we saw the four men get into the chopper before it lifted off. It flew right past where we were crouched in the fern and as soon as it had gone we gathered our gear together, untied the dogs and went back to the hut for a feed of rice risotto, beef noodles, buttered damper and condensed milk in our tea.

We both felt indignant about them searching for us like that, so we hung around the Forks hut till we'd eaten nearly all the food there. Then we took it easy up the Kahanui River to Tawa hut where there was someone installed so we watched from a low ridge downstream. A short dark man came out of the hut and started chopping wood. Uncle Hec knew him, he was an old trapping mate of his called Brian — Quiet Brian, because he never talked much. There was no one else about so we went down and said g'day and had a big feed of his meat and spuds.

Quiet Brian had been trapping around Tawa all winter and he had a good line of skins. He'd done well and was going to pay off his house in Gisborne this trip. He had plenty of supplies and no one else had been there for weeks, so we camped with him for a few days and gave him a hand tacking out skins and shifting a line of traps. He'd been warned by the rangers to keep a lookout for us.

The first night we were there Quiet Brian cooked up some juicy venison steaks in his cast-iron camp-oven — very nice. I ate a whole back-steak on my own, about fifteen pieces. Next day he was showing us his possum-skin set-up in a separate shed when Uncle Hec noticed the big bulge in the muslin cloth hanging dripping into a dirty yoghurt pottle.

"What's this?" he said.

"Possum fat," said Quiet Brian. "I put all the scrapings

off my skins through it. Strains it."

"What for?" I asked uneasily.

"I do all my cooking in it," he said.

I suddenly recognised the unfamiliar taste I'd noticed about the venison the night before. Quiet Brian's maggotty possum skins! I was just about sick, and I never ate anything out of his oven after that. Instead I found an old aluminium frying pan and cleaned it up to cook my stuff in. Quiet Brian was genuinely sorry for me, not being able to digest possum fat like that. Uncle Hec didn't like it, either. He went out in the rain one day and came back with a whole mutton. Plenty of proper dripping to cook in, but you could still tell that Quiet Brian actually preferred possum fat.

It would have been nice to stay on at Tawa for a while, it was so peaceful I started feeling ordinary again. But after eight days Uncle Hec became uneasy about the possibility of other people being around and we decided to move on. Quiet Brian and Uncle Hec swapped boots and arranged for Quiet Brian to leave a packhorse of supplies under a certain bank for us. He wouldn't let us pay him anything for them and seemed really sad when we parted. The dogs were sad too — they were so full of possum they could hardly walk.

I liked Quiet Brian, he was our friend — maybe our only friend in all that bush. I didn't realise why Uncle Hec was so keen to get away from him until we ran into a bunch of people less than an hour away from Tawa, heading in that direction. If they'd found us camped there Quiet Brian would have been liable to a maximum fine of 1,000 dollars or a term of imprisonment not exceeding six months.

There were four people in the party and they sprang us out on the open riverbed. They were trampers — two girls, a boy and an older man. Uncle Hec employed his usual evasive tactics and kept walking straight towards them without altering stride. I followed him and as we walked past them one of the girls said, "Ooooh — it's them! The ones the police are looking for!"

"Shhhh!" said the older man.

And we just kept walking until we were clear of them.

We'd now been seen twice in the same valley in two weeks,

so we struck out for the far side of the Urewera, and six days later we rested up in a wreck of a hut in the Mokomokonui. At night we could hear the trucks grinding over the Taupo-Napier Highway, but we were as safe here as anywhere else we could think of, except, perhaps, at Brokenfoot Camp.

There were some fat wild sheep in the Mokomokonui so we stayed there for ten days and took a big supply of roasted mutton with us when we moved on. It was good to know we didn't have to catch a pig or go hungry. We had so much meat we didn't know what to do with it.

Uncle Hec had talked about a hot pool beside a creek on an old deer block of his, and on a scrounging trip through the Hautapu I talked him into making a detour. It was a two-day walk and he wasn't sure if it was still there or not, but we eventually found it. You could smell the sulphur everywhere, but it took us a while to find the actual hot water, a red seepage steaming at the bottom of a bank a few feet from the creek.

It took us a good hour to clear enough stones out of the hole for us to bathe, and we found that it filled up with seepage from the creek almost as fast as we could dig it. We were wet and white-fingered by the time we'd hollowed the bath out and all we had for our trouble was a patch of smelly tepid water at one edge of a big hole full of pure cold bush creek. We'd had it for the day.

We found a site just downstream where there was plenty of firewood and risked a big warm-up. Next morning light rain and sleet was falling and it was very wet and gloomy. I wandered up to have a look at the big hole we'd dug the day before and the whole surface was steaming. It had hotted up during the night. I swirled my hand through it and started yelling out for Uncle Hec.

We could just stand the heat in the cooler water near the creek, but the electric flakes of sleet drove us deeper like nails into the hot water, right up to our ears. It took half an hour to ease our way over to the hot edge near the bank, before we staggered out steaming like ghosts in the rain until the cold started stinging through and we slipped back into the hot water again.

When we'd had too much of the experience we fumbled weakly around pulling our clothes on and building up a big fire to dry everything out. I had one more soak in the hot pool later that day when the rain stopped, but Uncle Hec said he was already soggy enough and gave it a miss. Three days later at Pohukura we still stank of sulphur, but it was worth it to have had that mighty bath.

From Pohukura we moved across into the Waiau Valley, and it was there, in the Te Waiotukapiti hut, that they finally caught us.

Seven

SERIOUS TROUBLE

IT HAD BEEN raining on and off all that day, so we stayed in the Te Waiotukapiti hut, burning a big pile of tawa branches we'd thrown down out of the bush. Uncle Hec was cutting up the last of the mutton to add to a stew and I was re-reading *The Thorn Birds*. The main sound was the rain spattering onto the roof through trees. It was cosy and peaceful.

One of the dogs barked once and suddenly three big young men were standing in the hut dripping water. Two of them had rifles with telescopic sights, and it wasn't cosy and peaceful any more. My main thought was how different from us they looked. I could smell some kind of scented soap off them. They dropped their packs on the floor and introduced themselves, Hugh, Joe and Ron, all National Park rangers, checking the tracks and huts in the area.

"Stinks in here," the one called Ron said, looking up and down us.

We didn't say anything. They got out mugs and filled them from our billy over our fire and had tea, sitting on the edges of the bunks. The one called Hugh seemed to be their leader.

"You two are supposed to be over in the Waioeka," he said.

"First I heard of it," said Uncle Hec.

"You were seen over there about a month ago."

"No kidding."

"Come on, old man. We know who you are. You're Faulkner, and this is Baker. We knew we'd pick you up sooner or later."

"That a fact?"

"You're caught, you might as well admit it."

"What are you going to do about it?"

"We'll have to take you out to the base, of course."

"Why?"

"Because you're wanted, that's why."

"Who wants us?"

"The police, that's who."

"You're not the police."

"No, we're Park Board rangers."

"Then *you* don't want us."

"Not us personally. We've got nothing against you. We know the guy you looked after at the Koranga Forks. We're all grateful to you for that."

"Leave us alone then."

I could tell they had no intention of leaving us alone. These heroes were going to bring us in and give us to the Social Welfare Department and the police, no matter what we said or did.

"You're just making it tougher on yourselves," the one called Hugh went on. "The longer you keep up this attitude you'll only make it worse."

"You're the worst thing that's happened to us for months," Uncle Hec told him.

"Well, you've had your bit of fun. You can come out with us in the morning and get it over with."

"We'll be coming out when we're ready."

"We don't want to tie you up, old man, but we will if we have to. If you try sneaking away we'll tie you and young baggy-britches here to a tree until we're ready to march you out to the road. The party's over, old man." And he grinned around at his mates.

The one called Joe took our .22 off a bunk, checked it, and put it with theirs behind the door.

"What do you shoot with this thing — sparrows?" They laughed.

I didn't like these men. They were casual about us, as though we were already locked up. It looked as though it was the end of the party all right. Even Uncle Hec could see how hopeless it was. He sat on the edge of a bunk and said nothing, while the rangers muttered among themselves, not really caring if we heard or not. The one called Ron wanted to tie us up, but the other two said to wait unless we made it necessary.

"They're harmless," one of them said. And still Uncle Hec didn't say anything.

Whenever either of us moved, one of them would shift between us and the door. If we had to go outside two of them came with us — we were prisoners. They took it in turns to sit by the door in front of the rifles, in case we tried making a run for it. When I climbed into my sleeping bag that night, topping and tailing with Uncle Hec on the same bunk, I couldn't sleep for hours. I was worried as I'd ever been, and wished that something really nasty would happen to those rangers, like a meteorite crashing through the roof of the hut and breaking all their legs.

I must have gone to sleep in the end, because the next thing I heard was Uncle Hec calling out my name. I sat up and so did the three rangers. The one in the chair by the door was the last to wake up. It was just getting light.

Uncle Hec called out again from outside. "Ricky!"

"What?" I yelled back, getting out of my sleeping bag.

"Get out here!"

I knew something critical was on as did the rangers. I went to the door and they crowded behind me, a big hand grabbing me above the elbow and holding me there. It had stopped raining and the whole valley was sodden and soaked in mist. Uncle Hec was standing by the woodblock with the .22 in one hand.

"Grab our packs and load 'em up, Ricky. We're snatching it from here, and if one of those blokes touches you, yell out and get under the end bunk quick."

"He's mad," muttered one of the rangers, and I had to agree it looked like it. Uncle Hec can look very hot round the eyes when he gets in that mood of his.

"You boys just keep out of our way. Anyone touches one of us, gets it."

The grip round my arm slid away.

"You've done it now," the one called Hugh said. "You realise. . ."

"I know what I'm doing, sonny. You just keep right out of the way and you won't get hurt. Ricky, move it!"

I ducked round them into the hut and started stuffing our

gear into the packs. No one tried to stop me; they were still standing at the door, talking to Uncle Hec, so I scooped a few cans of their food into our packs.

"You wouldn't shoot us," the one called Joe said.

"You just try me, young feller," said Uncle Hec. "You're easier to hit than a sparrow. I'd drop you before you could move."

I didn't like going too near him, but I lugged our packs in his direction.

"Get the dogs."

I untied them and we picked up our packs and moved away downstream, looking back to make sure they didn't come after us.

"What have you done with our rifles?" one of them shouted.

"Under the hut," called back Uncle Hec. "And if any of you try following us you'll deserve what you get."

"You'll never get away with this," the one called Hugh yelled after us, and then we were out of sight of them and free again.

Two crossings down the river we climbed up onto a bush spur, dropped our packs, tied up the dogs and sat against a tree for a while. I was still shaky. When we'd had a spell we sidled back past the hut up in the bush and found a place in some ferns where we could watch the main track out to the road.

"What happens now?" I said.

"It could get a bit tricky for a while. My bet is that they'll head straight out and raise the alarm."

"Would you have shot them?" I couldn't help asking.

"Hard to say. Shut up, they're due past here any time now."

About half an hour later the three rangers came up the track and passed by thirty feet below. They weren't trying to follow us, but you could tell by their faces and the way they were half-running that Uncle Hec and I were in trouble with other people again. Serious trouble this time.

When they had gone we went back to the hut and took all the food and books it could spare and carried them in a sack to where we'd left our packs and dogs. Then we climbed up through the dripping bush onto the Pukekohu Range and camped that night on a flat rock by the Manganuiohou River on the other side.

Next morning, right on daylight, it started. Choppers swept up and down the valley, slapping across the tree-tops, and others came and went dropping people off at various vantage points. It was as well for us that there weren't many places where they could land, but we had to be particularly careful of the choppers because we knew some of them had infra-red gear that could pick up an animal or a person, so we had to stay in deep bush, the tall timber.

We never used to put more than three or four bullets in the magazine of the rifle at once, but this day Uncle Hec put the full fifteen in and stuck a handful of extra ones in his pocket, so I knew we were in for a heavy day. I was scared.

We worked our way round to a ridge that would take us further away from most of the activity and after a couple of hours we were just coming up onto the crest of the ridge when we became suspicious. The birds were too quiet. We stopped to listen and we'd just looked at each other to see whether we should move on when we heard a radio crackle and hiss up on the ridge and someone call out, "I'm over here!" We knew there was more than one of them, so we sidled away through the bush and tried the only direction we had left.

It can make you nervous, hiding day and night. We had to stay super-quiet, and couldn't talk above a whisper for days and nights. Every now and again we walked for a few minutes up a side creek and then doubled back in the water, in case they were tracking us with dogs. Willy and Zag must have thought we were crazy that day, as they weren't even allowed to chase nice fat pigs that jumped up right in front of us.

We heard some shots and shouting out on our left on another ridge and eased away from there. The main search seemed to be concentrated over in the Waiau and Te Hoe valleys, and it looked as though they'd guessed we'd gone that way, but then they swung round in a wide circle and surrounded us. We were cut off from the main part of the Urewera.

This was serious. We stashed some of our load where we could find it again and set off on a mad game of hide and seek through 25,000 hectares of bush and streams and ridges and slips and waterfalls and cliffs.

For three days we dodged them back and forth across the watershed, using Uncle Hec's strategy of sticking around to keep an eye on what everyone else was up to. There was always the chance that we might try it once too often, and that we might be caught any moment, any hour. They had dogs this time too — we'd heard them bark a few times. The dogs must have known we were still around there somewhere, but they kept losing our trail, because we kept them a mile behind us, running up and down false trails.

"Them kinda dogs can't wind-find in the bush," whispered Uncle Hec. "They have to track you."

So we formed a pattern and used it every now and then, especially if we'd heard any barking close by. We'd look at each other, nod, and then split up and go in opposite directions, round into a side-creek and back to the main stream, walking in the water. The scent of our dogs only seemed to add to the confusion behind us. When we needed a rest we'd climb up into a steep creek-head somewhere and rest up, listening to make sure they didn't come too close.

There were certainly plenty of people and choppers and dogs. It took them only a few minutes to pick people up and drop them right over on the other side of the watershed, so they could get from behind us to in front of us before we could move 200 metres. They only needed to sight us once and surround us, but they were so clumsy and noisy in the bush that we could always tell where they were. Some of them actually shouted out to one another.

"They couldn't track an elephant through six feet of snow, those clowns," whispered Uncle Hec, looking down at the bushes thrashing around down in the gully, where someone seemed to be getting tangled up in the supplejack. But the people waiting on the ridges with radios were a bigger worry. Twice we smelt cigarette smoke and had to Bird-lady it in a wide circle around them.

They still should have caught us. One evening we were

looking for somewhere to camp on a bush flat along the bottom of a ridge, and we heard these two bushmen thumping and cracking and snapping in their big boots down the ridge. We stood in a clump of pepperwoods and watched them come tripping and fumbling down the ridge and onto the flat. They stopped about forty metres away in the trees and started talking loud about which way to go. One of them had a rifle and the other a radio on his belt. They were arguing. They were lost. Suddenly a vine I must have been half-standing on flicked up and hit Willy on the nose. He yelped.

"What was that?" said one of the bushmen.

"I didn't say anything," said the other one.

And they took off through the bush, no doubt to spend the night in the open because the hut they were looking for was nearly two hours in the other direction. But that's how alert they were.

We ate everything we had with us. It was cold, with no fires and no tea. We slept curled up in our bags in the roots of totara or rata trees — they're the warmest. It can make you very tired and hungry, living like that, and we were very relieved when the search spread out and away from us, deeper into the Urewera. Uncle Hec was right. They didn't think we'd be game to stick so close to where we'd been caught. They thought we must have got through to the main part of the Urewera.

On the fourth day we came up out of the tall timber and pushed and pulled each other and the dogs up onto the Kotare Ridge up a tricky gully. We didn't want to try the leading ridges because they were still too dangerous. We picked our way towards the southern end of the bush, away from most of the activity. It was real Bird-lady sneaking. Uncle Hec went in front and I kept him just in sight through the bush. The cover got a bit scattery in places and we had to dive for it whenever we heard a chopper come too close. They had a habit of coming suddenly up over a ridge or round a corner and they could be on you before you knew what was happening if you didn't watch out. I'd never been so nervous of a patch of open ground in my life.

We travelled along the Kotare for two and a half hours,

heading for a place Uncle Hec knew about from when he'd hunted goats there in 1966, but he was having trouble remembering exactly how to get there. After casting around for a while we found a place — all second-growth manuka and grassy clearings, with shelfed bluffs and rocky slips — where we could get over the side. We kept to the high ground and came out on a wide shelf where the bluff fell away to open sheep country. We could see anything coming for miles up there, and there were three directions of escape.

We made our camp under a big dry overhang of rock, almost a cave, and by dark that night we were invisible behind a wall of rocks and scrub.

"The only thing we can do now is wait," said Uncle Hec. "When they've burnt 'emselves out looking for us in there we'll get back over to the Ruakituri or somewhere."

We saw two lots of four-wheel-drive vehicles go up the valley next morning and come back out again in the evening. There was a lot of chopper activity, but none came near. It looked as though we had them tricked — it was a good place all right. We called it Cave Camp. We ate a lot of hares there, when it was safe to shoot, and there were two different mobs of goats further round the bluff. There was a gully full of pig-rooting half an hour up the Otoi side, and plenty of sheep down on the grass if we got desperate.

We didn't like to steal sheep off the farmers around the edges of the bush because it would have turned them against us, and we had enough enemies as it was, but the mutton was always there as a backstop. There was no need to swipe mutton at Cave Camp, as it turned out. The worst thing was being stuck up there not able to move around. We lay around all day, reading and sleeping, and as soon as the last chopper had gone past down the valley we could let the dogs off and come out into the open, where we could sit round the fire eating and talking till the early hours of the morning.

We could tell when they scaled down the hunt for us as though they'd told us. The choppers stopped blatting around all over the place and the only ones left went straight up the valley and came out again with deer slung underneath. They weren't looking for people. The vehicles and people stopped going up and down the valley, and anyway we knew without any of that. It felt different to walk round in the open in daylight.

We were now low on food, so Uncle Hec made a trip back to the hut where we'd got caught, Te Waiotukapiti, and got back next day with a packful of flour and tinned food, plus packets and sachets, a dozen eggs, a bottle of tomato sauce and extra salt. He even brought some books. He'd also shot a deer just along the Kotare Ridge and hung it in a tree, so we had plenty to eat.

Clearly they'd been using the Te Waiotukapiti hut as a base while they were looking for us, and they'd stocked it up well. Uncle Hec had stashed another load of food near the hut for next time. There was still untouched hunting around us, and we had plenty of time to sort out the camp. We put in a punga screen, disguised it with ferns, and built our fire so that the smoke went up the face of the bluff and you couldn't tell it from the mist, if there was any of that about, which was just about every morning. We built our bunks up with mingi-mingi vines till they were like my inner-sprung back at the farm. We collected our water from a spring in a clump of fern thirty metres round the base of the bluff, and there was more dead manuka around than even Uncle Hec could burn.

The only bad thing about Cave Camp was that it was so high up you always had to climb up to it with whatever you'd caught or shot. It was a long drag at the end of a hunt, but it was worth it once you were up there.

When it was time to go back to Te Waiotukapiti for more supplies we both went, taking the dogs and the books to exchange. We tied the dogs on the ridge above the hut and went down to find no one around. They'd stocked up the hut *again*.

There were candles, which we were short of, and tins of peas and cheese and meat and puddings, plus an unopened ten-kg bag of self-raising flour — but only one book this time. Uncle Hec showed me where he'd stashed the other stuff, in a hole under a big rata's roots, so we added more to it and left it there for next time. Then we each carried a good load home — and there was still plenty left. A good hut, that.

We returned to Cave Camp in the dark and had a big meal of stewed apricots with condensed milk and tins of chocolate pudding. Everything tastes good when you've been walking for nine hours across the Kotare. It's what Uncle Hec called a "gutbuster".

We soon got to know all the country where everything was for hours in every direction from Cave Camp, except the farmhouse you could see down in the valley from the end of the bluff. Someone was living down there but he or she never came up our way and we'd given up worrying about them. Then we went and got caught again.

This is how it happened. We'd been down at the river doing some washing and we were climbing up one of our main tracks back to Cave Camp when we came across a set of horse's hoofprints going straight up towards the camp. *Shod* hoofprints. I was getting ready to run for it, but Uncle Hec said to hold it, so I held it, and we sneaked up and had a look.

A horse with a saddle on was feeding outside the cave and a man with a woolly hat was leaning there. We watched him for a while. He was a big young man, a clean one, the sort that always meant trouble for us. Then Uncle Hec stood up.

"Come on," he said. "We'll go and see what he wants. We've got a gun and he hasn't."

I was shaky with apprehension as we walked over to meet the stranger. Every time something like this happened our lives tended to take a violent swerve in another direction. There was sadness, too. We'd got to like our Cave Camp; it was safe and comfortable and easy living, but because this man was standing there it could never be any of those things to us any more.

"G'day," said Uncle Hec.

"Hello there," said the man, smiling a bit.

"What brings you up here?" asked Uncle Hec, leaning the rifle against the rock.

"Seeing as we've been neighbours for the past few weeks I thought it was about time we got acquainted. My name's

Rob Barton — they call me Robby."

He shook hands with Uncle Hec and I moved out of the way and started pushing the embers of the fire together in case he tried to shake hands with me too.

"This your place here?" asked Uncle Hec.

"No, I'm caretaking the place for the stock and station agents. It's a bankrupt sheep station and I'm keeping it more or less running till they decide what they want to do with it."

"How long have you known we were here?"

"Since a few days after you got away from the Park Board boys," he said.

"Anyone else know we're here?"

He shook his head, "Only me. I'm on my own down there."

"How did you find us?"

"Don't worry, it was a sheer fluke. I was looking across the bluffs to see where the goats were, I use them for dog-tucker sometimes, and I spotted your mate here and his dogs digging a possum out of the flax up on the shelf there. They still had the big search on at the time, so I left you alone until it died down. You're safe enough now, though. You were supposed to have broken into a bach over on the Te Kaha coast a couple of days ago. I'm pretty sure no one suspects you're anywhere near here."

"*You* know we're here," pointed out Uncle Hec. "That's not no one."

"If I was going to turn you in I'd have done it before this," he said. "Look, how would you two like to come down to the homestead for a meal and a bath. I've just got some food in and you look as though you could do with a clean-up and a change of clothes."

"No thanks mate," said Uncle Hec. "We're okay the way we are. We'd appreciate it if you'd give us a day or two to get well away from here, that's all."

"Okay, suit yourself," the man called Robby said, "but I've got some information you ought to know."

"What?"

"I'll tell you in private."

"You can say anything you like in front of my mate," said Uncle Hec.

"— there's a price on your head."

Even the horse stopped eating and looked up.

"How much?" said Uncle Hec.

"Two thousand five hundred dollars for information leading to your apprehension. There's already been a few parties gone in looking for you, hoping to pick up the reward. They carry two-way radios to call up the choppers if they spot you. You've been classified as dangerous, not to be approached."

"What are they accusing me of?"

"Abducting a minor and presenting a firearm to facilitate escaping from lawful custody — they're the main ones. They're treating the firearm one pretty seriously. You lost quite a bit of public support over that."

"What do you mean, public support?"

"Well when you chaps first took to the bush a lot of people took your side. Didn't you know about that?"

"No. What else?"

"Well when you saved that ranger's life over at the Koranga Forks you became kind of heroes. The papers made a big thing of it."

"Was he a bloody *ranger*!"

Uncle Hec and I looked at each other, not really hearing what the man called Robby went on saying.

". . . in a diabetic coma. They only just saved him. A lot of people took your side after that, some pretty high-up types, too. They were all saying you should be left alone and they were wasting public money looking for you."

"I don't believe any of this, but go on."

"When you pulled the rifle on those Park Board rangers they declared you dangerous. They called in the Armed Offenders Squad, police with tracker dogs, the army Iroquois crowd. They even recruited members of the public. Some of their best bushmen and hunters were on the job for a while. The Forestry had men with radios in half the huts in the Urewera. None of them came up with any confirmed sightings, but you were supposed to have been seen all over the place. It's died right down just lately — a lot of people have been saying you're being hunted like animals and that sort of thing. You've still got a fair bit of public sympathy."

"It's a bit hard to believe some of that," said Uncle Hec. "But thanks anyway."

"I've kept all the newspaper cuttings I've come across lately," said the man called Robby, reaching over to pick up his horse's reins off the ground before climbing into the saddle. "I'll put an extra potato in the pot in case you feel like coming down to the house tonight. You ought to have a look over those newspaper cuttings before you take off from here. But if you don't want to you needn't worry about me telling anyone about you. I don't operate that way."

"Thanks . . . er . . . what did you say your name was mate?"

"Robby," I reminded him, speaking for the first time in front of the stranger.

"Well thanks, Robby," said Uncle Hec. "We'll think it over and come down after dark if we decide to."

"Okay, I'll expect you if you turn up. In any case, good luck."

He rode off over the edge and about twenty minutes later we saw him ride like an ant out across the riverbed and disappear towards the red roof of the homestead.

We had either to trust that little dot down there or move away somewhere else. "He seems to know a fair bit about us," said Uncle Hec. "Some of it might just be useful, if they're that anxious to get their hands on us."

"What if it's a trap?" I asked. "All that stuff about a reward on our heads and that. I don't believe it."

"It could easily be true," said Uncle Hec. "I know blokes like that — what's his name again?"

"Robby," I told him.

". . . like that Robby, and I don't reckon he'd put us crook. I'm inclined to think he's straight up."

"What if he's not?"

"That's the risky bit. What do you reckon?"

We talked it over for a while and decided to risk it. I don't know about Uncle Hec, but it was an apprehensive decision as far as I was concerned. If other people didn't leave us alone I was going to flatten one of them one of these days. Our Cave Camp was blown now.

Eight

ANOTHER NOTCH

BUT A LOT happened to us that night. We sneaked up on Robby's farmhouse in the evening, and as soon as we were out in the open grass country it felt as if the whole world had changed. It was so bare everywhere — hardly a tree in sight and nowhere to hide. I would have been quite happy if Uncle Hec had changed his mind and we'd turned back to Cave Camp.

"Naked, eh!" he whispered when we were getting over the fence behind the woolshed. That's just what it feels like when you go out into the open after hiding in the bush for a year and seven weeks — naked.

We tied our dogs in the woolshed yards and whistled out from near the house, and Robby came out and took us inside, into the brightest light at night I could remember. It took a while to get used to it. We sat around the kitchen table and enjoyed the warmth while Robby made us cups of tea. We could tell that no one else was around and started to relax. Robby took a small pile of stuff torn out of newspapers from a drawer in the kitchen and we started to read.

It was hard to believe those newspaper reports were about us — probably because we didn't know exactly what had been happening. It had been a big search all right, just as Robby had said. You could tell they'd expected to round us up in the first day or two, and you could also tell they hadn't been very happy about not succeeding. One search co-ordinator had said it was highly unlikely that Faulkner and Baker could survive in the bush without outside help. Then there were some letters and editorials saying how ridiculous it was for them to be spending all that money and effort in fruitless attempts to outwit a doddering old bush rat and a half-witted youth.

Another interesting thing was that some of the journalists

had declared that the Park Board rangers had had no right to detain Baker in the Te Waiotukapiti hut because there were no charges against him. One even suggested that Faulkner was within his rights to protect his nephew from being unlawfully detained. And no one could say whether the rifle had been loaded or not.

The whole collection of articles added up to a load of garbage, but it certainly gave us our first inkling of what had actually been going on and what people were saying.

We sat at the kitchen table and ate boiled beef and cabbage and bread and as much butter as we wanted. Uncle Hec and Robby talked across the other end of the table. It was the first time I'd been inside a proper house since Aunty Bella died and I didn't have much to say at first. After I'd done the dishes Robby said to help myself to a bath.

"You can use as much hot water as you like, there's tons of it. There's some clean clothes on the bed in that room there, if you feel like putting them on. They'll be a bit big for you, but they'll keep you warm."

So I went and filled the bath, and just when I was getting into it I saw my face in the mirror. I stopped and looked at myself because we hadn't seen a proper mirror since the farm. I was pulling a few faces at myself, like you do, and then I noticed something. I looked at my body, then climbed on to the edge of the bath to get a better look in the mirror. I looked over my shoulder and turned around. I looked back at my front to make certain. There are some things you actually know about but you don't like testing them in case it turns out not to be true. This was one of those things, and it was true!

I wrapped a towel round my waist and ran out into the kitchen. Uncle Hec and Robby looked round from where they were talking with a bottle of whisky between them.

"I'm thin!" I shouted at Uncle Hec.

They just sat there.

"I'm thin," I said again.

"Yeah, I know," said Uncle Hec.

"I'm thin," I said. "You're not allowed to call me fat any more."

"I don't," he said, drinking whisky out of a tea cup. "Haven't called you that for months."

"Ever again," I said.

Robby was grinning but I didn't care.

"Depends if you get fat again," said Uncle Hec. "You're not fat so you don't get called fat."

"Why didn't you tell me," I said. "I'm not fat any more. I'm thin!"

They were both laughing at me, but that didn't matter. Being thin can alter your whole outlook when you're used to being a fat person. I went back into the bathroom and put my thin self into the bath and had a big thin soak. I even washed my hair — a thin person's hair. I was thin all right. Thin face, thin stomach and legs and bum. Thin arms and hands. I was bony, and one of the main things I felt at the time was resentment about how long I must have been thin without realising it.

I climbed into Robby's jeans and big red woolly shirt. It was all a bit loose for a thin person like me, but the socks nearly fitted. When I came out into the kitchen Uncle Hec and Robby were deep into talk about what it was like round there in the "early days". I sat there listening to Uncle Hec talking more than I'd ever heard him, and exploring my ribs with my fingers through Robby's red woolly shirt.

I must have been yawning because Robby showed me where to sleep, in the room where the clothes were. There were two beds there, very clean-looking, with sheets and all that. I didn't like to get in the sheets so I left my clothes on and got under the top two blankets. Out in the kitchen Uncle Hec and our new friend laughed sillier and sillier with the whisky, and then I slept. Thin.

We were used to staying awake at night, but Uncle Hec wasn't used to whisky, and when he finally staggered his way to bed, shouting out to ask if I was asleep or not, he had to get up again immediately and be sick out of the window. I didn't mind, I was thin. Like Uncle Hec.

We stayed at the sheep station with Robby for nearly two weeks. The first day we helped him put 2000 ewes through the spray-dip. He'd been wanting to get that done and it was too much for one man on his own. Robby had four dogs, black and tan ones, and they weren't bad, Uncle Hec said, but Willy and Zag were easily as good as any he had.

"You blokes have got great control over those dogs of yours," said Robby, when we were having a brew of tea and a spell at the sheepyards. "Never seen anything like it."

"You have to have 'em like that when you live the way we do," said Uncle Hec.

"How about seeing what you can do with that bitch pup of mine, Hec. She's a well-bred thing and she ought to be working by now, but I can't do a thing with her."

"I'll have a look at her," said Uncle Hec. And a few days later he had the little black and tan bitch, Dream of all names, working to the whistle like a champion.

"That uncle of yours is the best man with dogs I've ever seen," said Robby one day when we were watching Uncle Hec away up the hill on a horse, bringing in 250 wethers with the help of Dream on her own.

"He's a good shot as well," I told him, feeling proud of him.

Uncle Hec and Robby shod all the station horses, eight of them, and I fixed up the fowl run and rounded up all the chooks. Robby thought we were great workers, but we were really having a good time doing ordinary things. It was like a holiday.

It rained one day and we sat round in the kitchen talking. Robby had spent a few years at Lincoln College and had managed several big sheep and cattle runs around the back country. He had a wife and two kids, girls, living with her parents in town so the kids could go to school. He used to go in and see them in his old Land Rover most weekends, and when he left us alone we were worried until he came back, alone, the following night.

He brought a load of stuff for us — boots, socks, pants, shirts and a new knife for me, as my old one was worn down to a spike. Two hundred rounds of .22 ammo, and quite a bit of other stuff. But the best of all was a transistor radio Robby said had been lying around his in-laws' place with nobody using it, and a whole box of batteries. Uncle Hec and I were a bit embarrassed by Robby's generosity. We'd agreed to let him buy us a pair of boots each till we could pay him, but the clothes and the radio and stuff were his idea. We knew he didn't have much money, and he was doing his best to help us.

Uncle Hec and I had already discussed the need for some money, to make life easier for us until I turned fifteen in nine months' time. And we owed Robby over 300 dollars already.

"I keep thinking about those possums over in the Ruakituri," said Uncle Hec. He didn't like calling it Broken-foot because it reminded him. "If they're like they were last winter you wouldn't have to get many to whack up a decent cheque."

So we made plans to trap possums at Broken-foot, up the other end of the Urewera, and pack the skins back to Robby for him to sell for us.

"I trap a few round here," he said. "Nobody'd notice if I take in a line of skins."

He was so genuine about trying to get us to stay longer at the station we had to make excuses to get away. If we were caught there we'd all be in trouble and we couldn't let Robby risk it. Twice we'd had to duck away and hide in the woolshed when cars came up the road. It was time to move.

"It's only about six weeks until the skins'll be ready," said Uncle Hec. "We'll need all that time to stock up the camp and get set up."

Robby loaded so much food and gear on us that we had to stash some of it when we got up to the Cave Camp. We stayed one night there to get our bush legs back and then headed off for Whakataka on the Huiarau Range, on our way up through the middle of the Urewera.

Life was different now. The main thing as far as I was concerned was me being thin — I even walked thin these days. But there were other important changes as well. There was a price on us now. We were wanted for a serious crime and a thing like that can alter every leaf and rock, if you let it get to you. Then there was the fact that we had new boots and clothes, socks in proper pairs without holes, and our own singlets. It gives a man respect, having a bit of decent gear.

But the thing that made the biggest difference was the radio. Whenever we camped one of the first things we did was unwrap the tranny (Uncle Hec still called it the wireless) and unwind the extra aerial Robby had given us which we'd hang in a tree and tune in to whatever we could get. Instant contact with the outside world — it was great to listen to music again. Uncle Hec hated missing the evening news and he used to get impatient when we were a bit late reaching a camping place. We half-ran down a long spur to a creek one night and just got tuned in in time to hear ourselves being mentioned on the news.

The Urewera Fugitives, Hector Faulkner, and his nephew, Richard Baker, were reportedly sighted by a tramping party in the vicinity of the Te Puna Hut, on the shores of Lake Waikaremoana yesterday. A team of police with tracker dogs was flown in to the area at first light, but no trace of the pair was found.

The officer in charge of the operation, Sergeant Bowling of the Gisborne C.I.D., told our reporter that he expected the pair to surrender themselves to the authorities by the time winter sets in properly in the mountains.

Faulkner and Baker now face their second winter in the bush. The pair have been at large now for fourteen months, and continue to frustrate all efforts to apprehend them. Anyone sighting them should not approach them, but inform the nearest police station.

That was us they were talking about.

"Fourteen months," I said to Uncle Hec. "That's a pretty long time."

"Seems longer than that to me," he said. "We've been lucky so far, but we're going to have to be more careful than ever from now on."

But in spite of us taking extra care a nasty thing happened to us one day. We were sitting in the Te Pourewa hut when we heard a chopper coming, low up the valley. We were always ready to move in a hurry, and we grabbed our stuff and were up in the bush when we heard it land at the hut. We climbed up a ridge and were about a third of the way to the top when we heard a dog bark behind us. Willy and Zag were a few yards out in front of us when we stopped and looked round. Rushing towards us was a big black Alsatian with a short lead hanging off it. It stopped to bark, then ran at us snarling. It was attacking us!

I went over one side of the ridge and Uncle Hec went over the other. I was slithering and sliding and rolling down the slope with my pack up over my head, and as I grabbed something and was getting myself the right way up, a whole tangle of dogs, Willy and Zag and the Alsatian, came rolling down the side, snarling and ripping and tearing at each other. They went sprawling down past me and ended up in a muddy wallow.

It was a fight to the death. Uncle Hec arrived and all we could do was stand and watch — there was no way we could stop them.

"Your own dog'd take a hunk out of you if you went in there," said Uncle Hec, breaking off a branch and snapping it shorter under his boot. I did the same.

The fight didn't last long. Soon Willy and Zag had the Alsatian beaten and it was yodelling and gurgling and half-drowning in the mud with no fight left in it. We dragged our dogs off, and the Alsatian got onto its feet staggering all over the place and limped away through the bush, dragging one front leg and yelping every now and then.

"He'll recover," said Uncle Hec. "But two of them might have been a different story."

"They're still tracking us down with dogs!" I said. "Dangerous ones!"

"Yeah. One of the choppers must have spotted us around here yesterday and put the police onto us. We'd better get the hell out of here. They mightn't be too far behind that dog, and they might have more of them. They could easily have heard that racket."

We slipped away up the ridge and hared it over into the Ruakituri where there was less chance of being disturbed, and where we worked out a plan in case we were attacked by police dogs again. Straight up a tree and if our dogs couldn't handle them we'd just have to shoot them.

"I sure hope we don't have to do that," I said.

"So do I," said Uncle Hec. "I can't think of a better way to antagonise the police than to knock off a couple of their dogs, but if they attack me I'll shoot 'em all right. Don't worry about that."

"Maybe they'll stop sending dogs after us when they see what happened to the one we sent them back."

"Start thinkin' that and you'll have one of them Alsatians swingin' off your arm before you know it."

They were using dogs on us, big savage ones. The very thought of it cranked our trouble-scale up another notch. Being tracked down by dogs is different than being hunted by choppers and other people. It makes you feel a sort of desperation whenever you think about it. Every creak of a branch in the wind becomes the bark you're half-expecting all the time. Whenever we were separated from each other we were even more worried.

We made it our policy to keep out of the huts as much as possible, checking them out for supplies and moving on to camp in a different place. "Like a couple of old boars chucked out of the mob," Uncle Hec remarked.

We packed a load of stuff into Broken-foot Camp. Our little whare was still there and everything was just as we'd stashed it. We stripped all the dried-up thatching off the roof, retied the poles with nylon cord and recovered it with a sheet of polythene we carried from Cave Camp. Then we put down another layer of ferns, laid poles to hold it all down and it was cosier than ever. It was like coming home.

It was still too early for the possum skins to be at their best, but they were coming right, Uncle Hec said. "Still a bit of mating-damage on this one. We might have to give 'em a week or two yet."

We spent our time packing supplies from everywhere within reach of Broken-foot. We had no intention of going hungry this time. We collected a line of traps that someone had sprung and left over in the Whakatane Valley. They were very rusty, but most of them still worked. We pulled the rusting staples out of the trees with a sharpening-steel and packed the traps back to Broken-foot, thirty-three of them. We collected every nail and staple we could lever out of the walls of the huts, and took all the string and rope and wire and sacking and plastic — everything we could find, and lumped it all over to Broken-foot.

We were busy round the camp for a few days, and by the time we were ready to start trapping we had everything ready for the winter. Our food was stored in two wooden boxes between the bunks with a candle in a tin on the top for reading in bed. The main stash of supplies remained under a rock across the bush flat, buried in plastic bags and tins. Sacks were useful. They provided the floor and the door, and made good mattresses when stuffed with ferns on our bunks. Our spare clothes were stored under Uncle Hec's bunk and our packs and dry firewood under mine. We even had a calendar from two years before hanging on the wall. It had a cow standing in a swamp on it.

The slasher-head we'd found the year before was one of the most useful things around. We'd put a short kanuka handle in it and sharpened it with a file Robbie had given us. We cut all our pungas and ferns and light stuff with it. The flat back edge was our hammer and the broad end of the blade was the best thing we had to dig with. One of the worst offences around Broken-foot was hitting a rock and blunting the slasher.

And of course we had the radio. We couldn't get reception at Broken-foot in the daytime — too many hills in the way I suppose — but at night we could nearly always get the National Programme. This suited Uncle Hec all right, but the music they played was always yukky. We didn't hear ourselves mentioned on the news again, even after the police dog episode, but we reckoned it was more likely to have been on the local station and we couldn't receive that where we were. No news was good news as far as we were concerned.

"How come everyone gets us wrong all the time, Uncle Hec?" I asked him one night when we were sitting down looking into the fire.

"What do you mean?"

"Well every single time we have anything to do with other people we get into more trouble."

"What about Robby, and Quiet Brian? They don't give us any trouble."

"Yes they do," I said.

"How do you make that out?"

"We can't stay near them or *they'll* get into trouble, and that means more trouble for us. But I mean those rangers, and the police, and the Social Welfare — why can't we get them to leave us alone?"

"They can't afford to leave us alone."

"But why?"

"Because if they let us get away with living in here they'd have to let anyone else who wants to, and most of 'em couldn't handle it. They'd get themselves straight into trouble and have to be rescued. Some of them'd get lost and die — the police can't afford to let it happen. They'd be mad if they did."

"You mean you *agree* with them?"

Uncle Hec loaded two more hunks of matai branch onto the fire.

"The police and me've got nothin' against one another," he said. "We just don't agree how to go about things, that's all."

"But the more we try to keep away from them, the harder they chase us," I said. "Not just the police, either. All of them. It's not fair. You're the only one I can trust out of everyone."

He looked at me and said, "You don't want to go trusting people, mate. You'll only disappoint yourself if you do that."

Then he mucked around with the fire a bit and said, "Now shut up, will you. I'm trying to listen to the wireless."

Hard to talk to sometimes, Uncle Hec. In fact we hardly ever talked these days, since we'd got the radio.

At last Uncle Hec pronounced that the skins weren't going to get much better than the ones we were catching around the camp for the dogs. They were very black and shiny, those furs, and I could see what he meant when he said they were unusually good ones.

We set our thirty-three traps up a ridge to the top and

down another one, with long spaces between each trap so they could be shifted if they didn't catch. We put them on runs and against trees and roots and on logs — wherever we found a good set and plenty of possum sign. We couldn't afford flour to bait our sets so we used little scraps of white paper to attract them, which Uncle Hec said was as good as anything where the possums hadn't been trapped before. Uncle Hec could set the traps with his hands but I had to put my foot on them to push the springs down.

I couldn't wait to get out round the line next morning to see what we'd caught. Fifteen possums, two blue bush rats and two sprung traps. We stunned the possums, bled them and hung them up near the trap. Eight of them had real good skins, so Uncle Hec was pleased.

Next day we got eight more good skins, skinned the ones from the day before and stretched the skins over pieces of driftwood and dead branch about as thick as your leg, if you've got thin legs, like me. We hung them under a skin-shelter on wires strung between two trees and soon we had fifty of them in there. They all had to be opened out and scraped and shaken loose and hung in bundles. Uncle Hec was fussy about how we prepared the skins, and we only took the very best of them.

In spite of several patches of dirty weather and having to shift the traps around all the time to keep them catching, we ended up after six weeks with 288 dried, scraped, pressed, and bundled skins.

"Could be one of the best lines of skins I've seen," admitted Uncle Hec.

We were low on food by this time because we'd been doing a lot of eating and not much hunting, so we stashed everything and humped our packs over to Maungapohatu on our way down to Cave Camp and Robby's sheep station.

Next day we climbed up onto the Huiarau Range. We knew it had been snowing up here and the snow was still lying around in big patches. In the distance it had looked as bright and clean as manuka flowers after rain, but close up it was slushy and wet with a crusty sound when you walked in it. Black pools of water lay in the hollows along the ridge, reflecting the tree tops and the sky. There was not a sound except the scrunching of our feet on the saturated ground. They were good conditions for pretending to be fur-trappers, making our way across the frozen wastes to the trading post at Hudson Bay.

We hadn't seen a single other person since we'd left Robby three months before.

Nine

SIX MONTHS

WE ARRIVED at Cave Camp in the afternoon and stayed the night there. We'd come a long way and waited a long time to get to Robby and we were looking forward to seeing him, but now that he was just a thousand feet down the ridge from us we weren't in any hurry. Our biggest worry wasn't whether he was still there, but whether he was still the same, still our friend. When you don't see any other people for a long time you start to wonder if what you remember about them is right. It makes you a bit nervous about seeing them again.

We heard someone banging something down at the station next day, and that night we sneaked down and gave our whistle for Robby which set his dogs barking. He was there, and judging by the way he greeted us you'd think he hadn't seen any other people either.

Robby said he'd been thinking about us for the past two days. "You skinny pair of bush-rats," he said, pouring us a cup of tea, not knowing that there's no such thing as skinny when you've been a fat person.

We had a clean-up and sat round the table reading the newspaper cuttings Robby had saved for us. Then we ate a huge feed, including everything green he had in the place. Uncle Hec and I had been seen in several places during the winter, including the Ruahine Ranges, 300 kilometres to the south. But the main news was that the firearms charge against Uncle Hec had been reduced to one of behaving in a threatening manner, owing to "discrepancies in the statements of Bremner, Houghton and Drew", the rangers who'd caught us at Te Waiotukapiti. Our old friend, Sergeant Bowling, was quoted as saying that the police were no longer actively searching for Faulkner and Baker. It was unlikely that they were still in the bush and were probably being sheltered by accomplices somewhere in the back country. Faulkner was still wanted for questioning in connection with a number of offences and a general watch was being kept for the pair. They should still be approached with caution.

"It looks like they've given up on you," said Robby.

"Wouldn't get too carried away with that idea," said Uncle Hec.

We talked until after midnight that night. Robby had some good news. He'd been as good as told that if he applied for the managership of the station he'd get the job.

"I know I can make the place pay," he said. "But what about you blokes?"

"What about us?" said Uncle Hec.

"When do you turn fifteen, Ricky?"

"Six and a half months," I told him. "And four days."

"Have you thought what you're going to do after that?"

"No," I said. "Not really."

"We'll take care of that when we come to it," Uncle Hec said. "Ricky'll be all right. They won't be able to do much to him."

"What about you?"

"Don't worry about me. I'll be able to keep out of their way for a while yet."

"What do you reckon'd happen if you went out and gave yourselves up?" said Robby.

"Forget it."

"No, seriously. What do you reckon you'd get?"

"Hard to say. A man'd be lookin' at six months in the slammer, I'd reckon. At the least. As well as a lot of other hassles."

"Ricky could stay here until you got out, but you mightn't necessarily *get* locked up."

"You want to bet?"

"I've seen a lawyer about your case. A friend of mine."

Uncle Hec and I both jumped up from the table.

"You what!" I said.

"You bastard!" said Uncle Hec.

"Settle down," said Robby. "He'd lose his licence to practise if he told anyone else about it."

"Does he know we're here?" demanded Uncle Hec.

"He doesn't know where you are, and he wouldn't turn you in if he did."

"What did the lawyer say?" I asked him.

"He's pretty sure he can get the abduction charge dropped on a technicality. You were never properly served with the warrant in the first place. He thinks that's why they had to withdraw the reward officially for your apprehension."

"What about the other charge?" I asked.

"It all depends whether the rifle was loaded or not. If it wasn't and Hec says he was only trying to bluff them, there's a good chance of him being able to get them to reduce the charge even further. You could get off with a suspended sentence, Hec."

"What if they don't suspend it?" I asked.

"Six months," said Robby. "Something like that."

"Was it loaded, Uncle Hec?"

"Mind your own bloody business," he said.

"Even if you *said* it wasn't loaded," said Robby.

But Uncle Hec said, "Nice of you to try mate, but I think I'll just hang on and see what turns up."

"Okay," said Robby, sighing. "It's your decision. But you ought to give it a bit of thought."

"Okay," said Uncle Hec. "We'll think about it."

Robby was due to go into town anyway, so the next day he took our skins in to sell and to get us some supplies we wanted. As it was the first money I'd ever actually earned myself I asked him to buy me a book about photography because I still wanted to give it a go. While Robby was gone I tried to talk to Uncle Hec about the idea of our giving ourselves up, but he was being difficult. I read a book while he cleared a drain at the side of the house. We had a meal cooking when Robby arrived back with all our stuff and more we hadn't asked for. He'd got $2764 for our skins.

"They'll take as many skins like that as I can get them" said Robby. "They're the best that's come in this season."

He'd brought my book, *Photography for Beginners*. I had almost memorised it by the time I went to sleep that night.

We couldn't stay with Robby. Some valuers were due to

start working there any day, so we made arrangements to come again in a few weeks. If the doors at the top of the woolshed ramp were open it would be safe to come down. We loaded our packs, untied the dogs and said goodbye to Robby and left for Cave Camp. The next day we left on a trip over to the western side of the Urewera.

Every time we travelled out along the Kotare Ridge our situation had changed, and it was different again this time. The reward for our apprehension had been officially withdrawn, and if the police weren't seriously looking for us, other people weren't likely to bother. We weren't news any more, and the worst they could do to us was stick Uncle Hec in the "slammer" for a few months and me in a Social Welfare home. The main change this time was that the seriousness had gone out of our situation, and that was important, but it was nothing to the changes waiting for us over in the Whakatane Valley.

We found we could use the tracks and huts like anyone else. In fact it seemed as though we had the whole area to ourselves. It was a week before we ran into anyone at all. But the less we avoided them the more they seemed to avoid us. We found two hunters in the Parahaki hut one night, and they were so nervous of us that they gave us some of their food and left in the rain for Central Waiau rather than spend the night in the same hut with us. Makes you feel as if there's something wrong with you, that sort of thing. And it got worse. Those people we did meet would get off the track and let us pass, glad to see us go. They didn't know if we were still supposed to be dangerous or not, I suppose, but it can certainly get to you, being approached with caution.

We arrived at Totara hut one day and when I grabbed the door handle to open it someone was holding it from the inside.

"Go away," a squeaky voice called out. "The hut's full. There's no room. You'll have to go away!"

Uncle Hec and I looked at each other and left the poor bloke there on his own and went on to Skipper's hut.

Just after that we passed a bunch of people on the Lake

Track and I heard an overweight lady say, "They're filthy!"

"We're thin though," I yelled back at her.

Fat people don't forget things like that.

We tried to swap a leg of pork for a loaf of bread with some people living in a bus at the edge of the Galatea side, but they were vegetarians. A chopper landed near us in a clearing one day and we went over for a chat with them, but when we were halfway there they took off again. I found myself half-hoping we'd meet up with people on every track, so we could find out how we stood with them.

Then we had a stroke of terrible luck. We were on a leading ridge, heading over to Te Raki to pick up a stash of food we had there, and the dogs found this boar on the top of the ridge and ran it right down to the creek and started bailing hard on it.

"Sounds like they're settled in down there," said Uncle Hec. "We'll have to go and give them a hand."

So we dropped our packs and slid and groped our way through the supplejack and steep roots, guided by the frantic barking. When we arrived they had the pig down in an almost-dry creek with three-metre sides like a ditch. The boar, a big one, was backed in against the bank. It was black and white and hairy, with half its face white and the other half black, which made it look more dangerous. Its hackles were sticking up and you could hear its tusks working on its grinders from where we were at the top of the bank. It made a high skreaking noise.

"Doesn't look too good to me," said Uncle Hec. The angle's wrong. Don't know if I can drop him from here."

Just then the boar charged the dogs and they had to go for their lives down the creekbed. The pig ran back to his spot and bailed up there, facing the dogs.

"We'll have to give it a go. He's going to get one of the dogs in a minute."

He leant the rifle across a small tree at the top of the bank, *crack* — and the pig went down on its front knees and the dogs moved in and started tearing at its head and neck. Then the boar stood up and flicked Zag into the air, rammed Willy against the bank and started ripping into him. I just had to stand and watch. Willy was a helpless yowling mess of blood, with Zag hopelessly tugging at one of the boar's back legs. Uncle Hec kept shooting — *crack — crack — crack* — and not making any difference either. Another *crack,* and he got it. The boar fell kicking in the mud it had churned up. Uncle Hec went straight over the bank and dragged the bucking carcase with Zag still tugging at it away from Willy, who was trying to get up on his front feet. Uncle Hec knifed the boar, and I was down there lifting Willy away from the foot of the bank. I remember every stone in that bank. He was covered with blood and it was hard to tell exactly where he'd been ripped, but there was a lot of flesh hanging down one side of his neck.

Uncle Hec reached past me and lifted Willy's head.

"He's had it, Ricky. You'd better get out of here. I might have to finish him off."

"But can't we . . ."

"*Take off, Ricky*!"

You don't argue with him when he talks like that. I stepped over the dead boar without looking at it again and went down the creek until I found a place to climb out and trudged back to the packs on the ridge. A bit later Uncle Hec arrived. He put his hand on my shoulder.

"Sorry about that, Ricky," he said, still breathing heavily. "I just couldn't get a decent shot at that pig. He killed Willy. He was dead before you were out of sight. His neck was broke. I pulled some rocks down on him. Good dog that. Turned out all right."

"I hate bloody pigs," I said, and I meant it. They'd killed my dog. My Willy.

"I know how you feel, mate. I've lost a few like that."

"How are we going to manage with only one dog?"

"We'll have to find out. We'd better hope we don't run into any more boars like that one. Zag's getting a bit slow for that kind of pig."

I wasn't very pleased with life after that, but three nights after Willy's death an important thing happened by accident. A talk with Uncle Hec.

We'd got mucked up on a ridge and ended up camped in

a deep gorge with the Te Hoe River roaring past a few yards away. There was a log-jamb there and we built up a big fire to make up for not having enough to eat. It was a drastic place — wild. We were sitting on a log drying our sleeping bags and I wanted to ask him something.

"Uncle Hec?" I said.

"Look Ricky," he said. "There's no need to call me uncle all the time. We both know I'm your uncle. I don't call you nephew all the time, do I?"

"It's all right, Uncle Hec," I told him. "I know you don't like me. But don't you worry, as soon as I'm fifteen I'll be off your hands and you'll never have to see me ever again if you don't want to." And I don't know how it happened but all of a sudden I was crying. Right there in front of him. Bawling my eyes out. Couldn't help it.

Then Uncle Hec went and reached out and grabbed me by the shoulder of the shirt and dragged me right up against him where he was sitting and held me there with his arm round me. Right up against him without either of us looking away from the fire.

"Come on old mate," he said. "I know you've had a rough trot, but you can handle it."

Well, him saying something like that, and giving me a bit of a squeeze as well, must have been too much for me. I blubbered my stupid head off. Told him a few things, too. Personal stuff about him and me and the way he treated me. Things he'd done and said. Unfair stuff. And I told him about my dog. My Willy. The only thing I ever had of my own and killed by that black and white boar in the Te Raki. Uncle Hec didn't say anything.

When all the crying was gone we sat there for a while, just looking at the fire and hearing the river roaring past out there in the dark. Then he said, "You want to hear my side of it?"

I wiped my face on my sleeve, looked up and nodded.

"When Bella died like that I didn't care much what the hell happened. I didn't want to see you stuck in a home, but there was nothin' I could do about it. I certainly couldn't be bothered arguing with you about it. You can be a stubborn little bastard when you want to be.

"So I made up my mind to take you into the bush and give you a hard time so you'd want to chuck it in. Then you'd be off my hands. That's why I made you walk so far that first day. There are two huts closer to the farm than Mangatoatoa."

"Is that why you don't like us going over that way," I said. "Scared I'll find out?"

"Shut up. I didn't think you'd be able to handle it, but I've been stuck with you ever since."

"Stuck with me? How?"

"I'd made up my mind to keep it up till you couldn't take it any more and would want to quit. But you still haven't quit. You're a stubborn coot all right."

"Do you mean if I said I'd wanted to quit you *would* have?"

"Yeah. Any time. I'd've had to."

"What were you going to do?"

"I don't know. Trot you out and turn you in at the nearest Social Welfare office, I suppose."

"Well you don't *have* to put up with me," I told him. "You can hand me over to them whenever you like."

He reached out and shook the end of a log that was sticking out of the fire and the whole thing collapsed inwards in a shower of sparks and flame. "You're not very smart sometimes, are you mate?" he said.

"What do you mean?"

"You seem to think a man'd be stupid enough to go through all this with someone he wants to get rid of. I'm proud a y', mate. Y' got more guts than I ever gave y' credit for."

"Well I don't know unless you tell me, do I. You never tell me anything. I can't even tell if you want me around or not."

"Forgetting something, aren't you Ricky."

"What?"

"We're related, mate. Same family, remember?"

When Uncle Hec said that to me nothing else he'd said or done mattered. It was the first time I'd ever had a relative who admitted it straight out, and who was proud of me as well. We liked each other a bit better after that, and Uncle

Hec treated me more equally. We got onto fewer wrong ridges.

As a matter of fact I tried out calling him Hec one day. It was his turn walking in front with the rifle and we were splashing along down an easy creek into the Whakatane, and I said, "How far is it out to the river, Hec?"

"An hour and a bit," he said over his shoulder.

When he got to the next crossing he stopped and looked round at me, and when he turned back and splashed into the crossing he was just starting to grin. I saw him.

Glad you didn't look round again after that, Uncle Hec. I was too pleased just then to have anyone looking at me.

We ran into a few more people on the tracks and round the huts and they all treated us as if we had Aids. But one day something really funny happened. We were bowling along the Te Wai-iti Track and ran into our good friend Hugh, the Park Board ranger and another bloke.

They stopped when they saw us coming and hurried back the way they'd come. Uncle Hec and I grinned at each other and trotted after them. We found where their marks left the track and we chased them through the bush making just enough noise to let them know they were being followed. They were too scared even to split up.

After a few hundred yards of this Zag showed us where they were both hiding up a tree. We stood there and looked at them. Hugh dropped his big rifle with the telescopic sights and it fell down the hill and slid out of sight among the leaves. His mate didn't have one.

"I stuck up for you guys!" Hugh called out.

We didn't say anything. We just went away and left them there. I like the way Uncle Hec does things sometimes. Kind of neat.

Ten

OKAY

WE WERE sitting by one of our big fires in the open at Hanamahihi, and there was something Uncle Hec had been avoiding.

"We have to make a decision about that stuff Robby was talking about," I said. "About us staying in the bush or giving ourselves up. We have to decide, Uncle Hec."

"We couldn't decide at Robby's place," he said.

"Why not?"

"We've got something else to decide about first, and it wasn't the right time."

"When's the right time?"

"Now'd be as good as any."

"What is it?"

He mucked around with the fire a bit and then sat back on the chunk of beech he was using for a seat. I could always tell when he had something special to say.

"You remember those kokako we came across on the Huiarau that day the choppers were chasing us. Those birds we found?"

I remembered it. We'd had to keep off the ridges and we'd just seen them drop someone off about half a mile ahead of us. Going back was too risky, so we dropped off the Huiarau Range in a tricky place and sidled round some bluffs. We came to a little clearing where a tree had fallen and Uncle Hec stopped and waved me to come up quietly.

"Look," he whispered. "See that bird?"

A big shiny bird with an orange tuft on its neck was hopping around in the branches of a dead beech tree, picking grubs out of the peeling bark. Another one, a bit smaller with a smaller, straighter beak and not so brilliant, flew in and hopped and skipped up the same branch.

"What . . . ?" I whispered.

"Shut up."

So we watched these big black birds jumping around in the tree until another one, blue-black in the sunlight, glided in and joined them. Then another one arrived. Four big birds, two pairs it looked like, hopping around in this dead tree making high and low whistling noises and some strange clucking sounds.

We really should have been moving on — there was an army chopper working just along from us.

"What are they?" I whispered.

"Kokako."

"Kokako?"

"Yeah, a kind of native parrot. They're pretty scarce. If you can prove there's kokako in a block you can stop 'em milling the timber."

I don't think they heard us whispering, but one of the birds gave a loud whistle and glided right past us, so close we could hear the air whistling through its feathers. Then the others, one two three, dropped out of the dead beech and glided past us and out of sight through the bush.

"Do you reckon you could find this place again?" asked Uncle Hec.

"Yeah, sure," I said. "We'd better move, hadn't we. We'll get caught, standing around here."

"This exact spot. That tree there," he insisted.

"Sure," I said. "You just come over the side of the Huiarau out of that pepperwood saddle and sidle down till you come to that grove of tawhara. You have to come round above that slip and stay at the same level till you come to these bluffs."

"Okay," he said, "but what if we had to find it from the other direction. Could you find it if we came in from that ridge over there?"

"I could once we've been that way. Let's go, eh."

"How sure are you?"

"Sure as I can be. Let's *go*."

So we went. Uncle Hec kept looking around for landmarks, but I think he must have been taking his bearings off the clouds because when we looked back from the next ridge he picked out the wrong bluffs.

Yes, I remembered the kokako. Better than Uncle Hec did probably.

"What about them?" I said.

"They weren't kokako."

"What were they then?"

He exploded the fire with a kick.

"I'm pretty sure they're huia," he said.

"Huia?"

"Yeah. They're supposed to have died out years ago. Those must be the only ones left alive."

"That makes it a pretty important discovery, doesn't it?"

"More than I can imagine, and I've been thinkin' about it."

"Why didn't you tell me before?"

"Had to make up me mind whether I was going t' tell you at all."

"Why?"

"We were attracting a fair bit of attention as it was that day, but it's nothing to the attention you'll get when they find out you've discovered an extinct bird. It'll be news all over the bloody world."

"What shall we do?"

"Might pay us to make sure before we go too much further. I'd like to get another look at those birds. D'you reckon you could find that place again?"

"Kokako Bluffs? — sure," I said. I wasn't exactly sure, but I wasn't letting on to Uncle Hec.

We got up onto the Huiarau next day and Uncle Hec led the expedition. I don't know if he could have found Kokako Bluffs again if it wasn't for me. He went the wrong way three times and would have ended up hundreds of feet too low on the face of the range. He was bad-tempered with embarrassment by the time we came to the bluffs, right near where I'd been telling him they were.

We were still a quarter of a mile or so from where we'd seen the birds the first time when we heard them again — low clear whistles, some very high ones, and then some clucking sounds. They were skipping around in the branches of a miro tree this time. Only one pair of them. The female was very bright and shiny, blue-black, the male smaller and duller. They had orange tufts at their throats.

We watched them for about an hour, following them when they flew off to another tree. They were very tame and easy to get close to — especially for us.

"That's huias all right," whispered Uncle Hec. "I'm bloody sure of it."

"Are you absolutely certain?"

"Certain as I can be. There's nothin' else I know of looks anything like 'em. Look at that white on the end of their tails. The Maoris used to use them feathers for decorations. There's nothin' else they could be."

I had a feeling he was right. "Let's get away from here and work out what we're going to do about it," I said. "We've got to get out of this place yet."

Getting out of that place was easier said than done. We'd been lucky the time before, and desperate. We couldn't go back up onto the ridge because we'd slid down shingle, and we tried two other routes but got into trouble both times. In the finish I had to drop Zag over a fifteen-foot ledge and Uncle Hec caught him and threw him across a split in the rock and we climbed down a tree onto the easier slope below the bluffs. We had to make the last bit to the Huiarau hut that night with a candle in a tin.

I want to say right here that I regard Uncle Hec as the discoverer of the huias. He saw them first and it was he who identified them. Besides, no one but Uncle Hec would have ever dropped over the side of the Huiarau Range in a place like that. You could say it was the fruits of his unique bushmanship, but he kept talking as though I was the one who'd made the discovery and he was just tagging along. I didn't wake up to him at first.

"I reckon I could get photographs of those huias," I said.

"You reckon?"

"I reckon."

"If you could do that — I don't know what they'd be worth, but it'd be thousands of dollars."

"Thousands of dollars?"

"Hundreds of thousands, probably. Enough to set you up with whatever you wanted. — You know what huiarau means?"

"No, what?"

"Huia-rau. Rau means a hundred, a hundred huias. There must have been plenty of them round there in the early days. There'll be one hell of a stink when they find out there's still some left."

"What do you think we should do about it?" I asked.

"I don't really want anything to do with it," he said.

"But Uncle Hec, it's an important discovery."

"Yeah, I know. But I couldn't handle all the publicity and stuff. I'm too old for that sort of caper. Why don't you get into it? You like birds, don't you?"

"What about Robby's idea of our giving ourselves up," I said. "We still haven't talked about that yet."

"Haven't we?"

"No. Someone keeps putting it off. We've got to decide about that sooner or later, Uncle Hec, but you just won't talk about it."

"How long is it now until you're fifteen?"

"Five months and one week," I told him. "And six days."

"You'd probably be all right then," he said. "It'll take them about that long to sort out what to do with you."

"What about you?" I said.

"I'll be okay. They won't catch me."

I'd been scared he was going to be like this.

"We mightn't even get locked up. Robby said it all depends if the rifle was loaded or not."

"That's what he reckons."

"Was it loaded Uncle Hec? We could always say it wasn't anyway, but *was* it?"

He shrugged, "You know that as well as I do."

"No I don't," I said. "Stop mucking around Uncle Hec. This is important. Was it loaded or not?"

He did something unnecessary to the fire and then he said, "Who was carrying the rifle when we first got to that hut?"

". . . Me."

"Who unloaded it?"

"I did."

"What did you do with the bullets?"

"They were in my pocket."

"Where was the rest of the ammunition?"

"In the plastic bag in the bottom of my pack — Uncle Hec! You didn't even have any bullets in the rifle! You're a great actor!"

"It would have been loaded if I could have," he grumbled. "And I'd've used it if I'd had to."

"That's not the point. We can prove it *wasn't* loaded. You mightn't have to go to jail at all. Robby's lawyer said so."

"Who's going to listen to us? No mate, if we stick our heads out there we're lookin' at gettin' locked up. You're kiddin' yourself if you think any different."

That's where you leave it for later with Uncle Hec. The conversation goes flat if you push him beyond this stage, if you know what I mean.

We camped in the Ohaua Hut the next night, but Uncle Hec's foot was giving him trouble. It was the night after that, camped in the Kakewahine streambed, that I brought the subject up again. There was nothing you could hear properly on the radio, the fire was one of our big ones and we were sitting back from it with our backs against a rimu log. It was a still dark night, not a star in sight. The moreporks seemed to think it was going to rain so we had our sheet of black polythene out ready. The loudest noise came from a lump of totara sparking and cracking in the fire. It was as good a time as any. He'd said something humorous that afternoon, which was a good sign.

"I quit, Uncle Hec," I said to him.

"What are you talking about?"

"I want to quit. I've had enough. I want to get out of the bush."

He looked at me with his face turned off.

"You're no quitter," he said. "What's brought this on?"

"I just don't want to stay in the bush any more. I want to chuck it in."

"What about the Social Welfare? I thought you were scared

of that crowd."

"I can handle it," I said. "It's only a few months, and I'm thin now."

"What the hell's that got to do with it?"

"Lots," I told him. "Come on, how about it, Uncle Hec?"

"They'll probably stick you in a home till you're fifteen."

"They might, but that's nothing. You might have to spend the same time in jail. It's the least time we'd have to be split up, this way. Please Uncle Hec. We've gone through all this together, we've got to stick together now."

"I'm not going out there and give myself up to them drongoes. You can forget it. I'll think about it again when you're fifteen."

"But that's when we can be free. After that we can sell photographs of the huias and go anywhere and do anything we like. You said so yourself. Please, Uncle Hec! If we don't do it this way it's going to be a *whole year*!"

"Nar."

"Forgetting something, aren't you Uncle Hec?" I said.

"What's that?"

"We're related mate. Same family, remember?"

He got up and poked around with the fire and stayed standing, lit from behind in the firelight he'd stirred up.

"Okay. If that's the way you want it. After this little lot a few months in the slammer'd be a picnic. I've never had such a gutful of the bush in me bloody life."

It was a little while before I could talk after he said that. Our most important decision had been brought out in the open at last. And it had been made, resolved. It was as if all the things that had happened to us made sense now. Our lives were going somewhere. Together.

There are some things you know about but you don't like to test them in case they turn out not to be true. The big question that had been hanging between Uncle Hec and me was what we were going to do when I turned fifteen. Each of us had been scared the other wouldn't want us to stay together. Now we both knew we did.

"You know what, Uncle Hec?" I said to him.

"What?"

"I'm not the only stubborn bastard around here."

He looks real nice when he smiles.

With all that out of the way all we had to do was to eat and make plans. The bush was different again. We were going to leave the Urewera. There was a limit to it. We decided that until I could get skilled and take some photographs of the huias we'd keep our discovery to ourselves. No one would believe us anyway, without proof. We reckoned that if we released one good colour photo of a pair of supposedly extinct huias through an agent — possibly Robby's lawyer friend — we mightn't ever have to go near them again, and they'd be protected from conservationists and bird-lovers and rangers and naturalists and all their other friends.

"If they couldn't find us in here, there's not much chance of them finding a handful of birds," said Uncle Hec.

Meantime the huias were up our sleeve, our trump card, our back-stop — perhaps even our future. It was a good feeling that made our other hassles seem less significant. But the main thing about it all was still me and Uncle Hec. After all, we were family, and that's the most important thing. We were sticking together.

We told Robby about our decision to give ourselves up when we next visited, but we didn't say anything about the huias. We mightn't ever be able to find them again, as far as we knew, and it was better to keep it under our hats for the time being. He was very anxious to help us in any way he could, but we didn't want him doing too much. It was our hassle — family business.

We had $1800 left with Robby from our possum skins. Uncle Hec asked him to look after Zag for us and we left the .22 with him too, in case it got confiscated. He gave us the name and address of his lawyer but we lost it somewhere and all I could remember when we got back into the bush was that his name was Charles.

"Whatever happens to us out there, we meet back here," I reminded Uncle Hec in front of Robby.

And they both agreed.

Robby had actually been saving supplies for us, most of

which we had to leave behind. This time when we travelled the Kotare Ridge into the Urewera things were different again. It was the end of something we'd lived, and the beginning of something new. Walking along behind Uncle Hec with no rifle, no dogs and no need to watch out for other people, I got into remembering it all.

I remembered back down three thousand kilometres of bush tracks to the little farm at Apopo. I remembered Aunty Bella and the big feeds and her ruffling my hair and calling me lamb — there was always a bit of sadness there. Then the hunting and getting my own dog, Willy. Then the funeral and Uncle Hec and I deciding to hide out in the bush till I was fifteen. The big grey boar looking at me in the creek at Kahikatea... scrounging around the huts for food. The smell of the sun on hot rock at Broken-foot, and Uncle Hec hobbling around with his foot, and me worrying about getting us enough to eat. Carrying the stag out of Blue-sow Creek... and the Bird-lady, gone back to her tribe on the Limmin River in Arnhem Land.

Finding the poster in the Tauwharana hut saying we were wanted by the police... the sick ranger in the Koranga Forks hut... Quiet Brian, friendliness and possum fat. Then the rangers in the Te Waiotukapiti hut, and Uncle Hec standing out there in the mist by the woodblock with no bullets in the rifle, telling them they wouldn't get hurt if they didn't interfere with us. I got so carried away when I remembered about that I couldn't help reaching forward and touching Uncle Hec on the back of the arm.

"What are you doin'? he said.

"Nothing, Uncle Hec."

"Keep back a bit, will y'. You'll trip a man up."

"Okay."

Then the big search for us... dodging the searchers and choppers and dogs through the bush. We'd been lucky a lot of times. Then Cave Camp, and Robby, and discovering I was thin in Robby's bathroom mirror. The police dog and the big fight with Willy and Zag at Te Pourewa... trapping the possums at Broken-foot... the radio hanging in a konini tree, telling us we'd been seen by trampers over beyond Lake

Waikaremoana . . . the big ugly black and white boar that killed my dog in the dry creek at Te Raki. My Willy.

All our old camps and the places we'd given names to. The constant scrounging and hunting and hoping for food. The times we were so hungry we could only think about finding an animal with our dogs, to kill it and take its meat and eat it. And underneath all that was the underlying feeling of us having discovered the huias and what it might mean in our lives. It was hard to fit it all into nineteen months in my mind, but that's how long Uncle Hec and I had lasted it out in the bush. Nineteen months.

We came in here with nothing, and now we were going out with a good chance of being able to have anything we could think of and go anywhere we liked, without being interfered with by other people. But there was more to it than that — I'd learnt something from the bush.

The Urewera country had taken things off me and given me things. It had sheltered me and frightened me. The bush still stands there growing and minding its own business. The ridges are just as high and broken as they ever were. The streams and rivers still tumble and rush and flood down the valleys. The rain and snow and sun and wind still please themselves what they do without being interested in me. But I see it differently now.

It'd taught me something other people never could. It'd taught me how to stick to rules that weren't my rules, just like everything else had to. In fact I was beginning to see how it all works. The rock gives in to the vegetable kingdom. The vegetable world takes from the mineral and gives up itself to the animal world. And then me, human beings, people — the last in the whole arrangement. But I could only take advantage of my place in it by sticking to the rules, and to step out of line could get me killed. It taught you respect, realising a thing like that. It might be the same with everything, for all I know, and just go on forever.

We hung around a few of our favourite places until there was really nothing left to talk about. We were more like two people going on holiday than a pair of bush rats wanted by the police, going out to give themselves up.

"You'll have to do most of the talking," said Uncle Hec. "I'd only end up flattenin' somebody. Do you reckon you can handle it?"

"Sure," I said. "I can handle it."

"You'd better, you skinny young coot, or I'll flatten you for a start."

"If you ruffle my hair like that again, Hec," I said, "I'll stick you across my knee and flatten your backside."

And we shoved each other around a bit in the sand in front of the fire.

He does look nice when he smiles.

The day after that there was nothing else to do. We slid down a bank onto the Waikaremoana Road and stuck our thumbs out when we heard the venison truck coming up behind us.

We've got a few hassles coming up, but we can handle them. We're okay now.

Eleven

EPITAPH

I'M ROBBY BARTON, Hec and Ricky's friend, and I feel impelled to add what I know to Ricky's story.

The first I saw of Hec and Ricky was some smoke up on the bluffs at the back of the station. Then I saw Ricky and his dogs one day. I guessed they were the ones the big search was on for when they stayed there for so long, and when the hue and cry had died down I rode up there, found their camp, and waited.

Their camp was a mouldy nest of ponga-fronds under an overhang of rock, albeit rather cunningly concealed, and their few pathetic possessions were hidden under some pulled fern. Their sleeping-bags were disgusting.

They appeared suddenly from among the rocks, from where they must have been watching me, and it was all I could do to keep the shock off my face. They were both dressed in rags tied around them with strips of torn cloth and flax. Where a button was missing they'd poked the cloth through the button-hole and inserted a piece of stick through it. One of the boy's trouser-legs had frayed off above the knee and the leg was covered with old bruises and scratches and he had a large scab on his knee that didn't look at all healthy.

Similarly, one of the old man's shirtsleeves was torn off at the shoulder; his arm was scratched and scarred and there was a filthy piece of rag tied around a deep graze on his wrist. Their boots were falling to pieces and by all rights should have crippled them.

The old man, Hec, was gaunt and stringy, with a straggly grey hacked-off beard and sunken piercing eyes. He had a pronounced limp, which I learned later was the result of an accident to his foot that had never healed properly.

The boy, Ricky, was a good-looking Maori chap. His hair stuck out in tufts from his head and his hands and face were streaked with inground dirt. There was something almost primitive-looking about him.

And they stank. Badly. Both of them.

The old man carried a battered old pea-rifle and they had two very thin dogs with them. They were both very nervous, especially the boy. They had a habit of glancing at one another every few seconds, for reassurance perhaps. One got the impression that the wrong word or action could put them into full flight at a moment's notice.

I talked to them for some minutes and assured them they were safe with me and invited them down to the homestead for a wash and a meal. I didn't know whether to expect them or not, but they arrived out of the dark that night like two wild animals, blinking in the light, looking around suspiciously and glancing quickly at each other at every sound. It was quite unnerving, to be honest.

I got some greens into them and they ate like animals. In fact I wasn't sure when they were going to stop eating. They even consumed the scraps I normally throw out to the fowls.

The boy, Ricky, discovered he was thin for the first time when he went to take a bath here. It was really quite touching. Evidently he was quite a plump lad when they'd gone into the bush, more than a year earlier.

Their story was a simple one. Hec's wife, Ricky's aunt, had died suddenly. They'd taken to the bush to wait until Ricky was fifteen, so that he wouldn't have to go back into a welfare home, and they'd been hounded ever since. It was my opinion that the lad would have been better off in any sort of home, but they'd made up their minds and no thought of giving up their original resolution seemed to have occurred to them. One had to be very careful what one said, especially in front of Hec, and especially at first. He relaxed considerably on acquaintance, and so did Ricky.

They stayed with me here for about a fortnight, during which time I got them cleaned up and dressed and fed. They would have appeared perfectly normal, except that every unusual sound, and quite a few usual ones as well, would cause them to freeze, glance quickly at one another and look around for the nearest thing to hide behind.

They were pathetically anxious to help round the station. They were good workers and knew their way around the stock. Their dogs were remarkably obedient. All they needed was more time to adjust to normal living. Unfortunately they could think of nothing but going back into the bush. They left here just as winter was setting in, to trap some opossums they knew of over in the Ruakituri somewhere.

I was quite concerned about Hec and Ricky by this time. I consulted Charles Roper, a lawyer and friend of mine, about their case. He made a few discreet enquiries for me in legal and police circles, and the consensus of opinion was that Hec would be fortunate to get off with less than six months' imprisonment, but if he was co-operative a suspended sentence wasn't entirely out of the question. I couldn't imagine Hec co-operating with his pursuers.

It was three months before I saw them again. I was cooking my meal one evening when they came sneaking in through the yards with two bundles of opossum skins in sacks wrapped with vines. The clothes I'd sent them off in were hanging on them in greasy rags and they stank of sweat and opossum fat and a kind of wood-smoke smell they always had about them. They were as wild-eyed and suspicious as ever, but seemed to relax a little sooner than they had the first time. They hadn't seen another soul since they'd left here, which they regarded as great good fortune.

I made them have a bath and got them into clothes that didn't smell and fed them. There *are* limits. I sold their furs for them, over 2000 dollars worth, and bought them some supplies they needed. They were both so hopeless with money that I opened an account with myself for them. They actually had more cash than I did at that time because that was before I was made manager here. My wife and the girls were still living in town at that stage and knew nothing about my strange visitors.

By this time the charges against Hec had been reduced to behaving in a threatening manner (due largely to a legal technicality), and abducting a minor. This charge was seen by many as legally flimsy. The reward for information leading to his arrest had been officially withdrawn and the police were obviously sick of the whole affair.

Hec and Ricky were actually less endangered than they themselves imagined. They were quite out of touch. I tried to point out that it was a good time for them to give themselves up, but they were determined to stick it out until Ricky was fifteen, which at this stage was in about six months. They were very stubborn, both of them.

They left here on some trip or other and three weeks later they arrived back, already filthy, and said that they'd decided to give themselves up to the police after all.

They were determined to be independent about the matter and wouldn't even let me contact Charles for them. They had to do it their own way. I gave them Charles's name and phone number, but I found it when I was airing their bedding after they'd gone again.

They'd lost one of their dogs and left their remaining one with me, a tough old header they called Zag. He was about twelve years old and they'd run the poor old fellow off his feet. He was exhausted; I couldn't put any condition on him and he died during that winter.

They also left their old Winchester .22 with me because they were afraid it might be confiscated. It's still here, that rifle. I run an oily rag over it sometimes when I'm cleaning my own gun. I wouldn't fire the thing, it's very worn and knocked about. I keep it as a reminder of those two, because I don't believe they'll ever be coming back to collect it.

When they went back into the bush I didn't hear any more of them until the story of their surrender to the police broke in the news. They were very anxious not to involve me and my name was never mentioned, even though I was with them through so much of the ensuing legalities and publicity that people couldn't help speculating on my role in it.

Ricky got his five months in a welfare home. Hec, after a much-publicised trial, got a nine-month suspended sentence, a $1000 fine, and was put on a good behaviour bond for two years. Honour was satisfied. Charles did a splendid job of defending him.

Hec gave me a hand on the station and came with me

into town each week to visit Ricky until his time was up. They both adjusted quite admirably, but I could have sworn those two were fretting for each other. They only seemed to be completely comfortable when they were together.

In spite of his natural reserve, Ricky got to be something of a favourite in the home and he didn't seem to be particularly unhappy there. He was growing into a remarkably handsome lad, with a most engaging shy smile, fine teeth and large brown eyes. He was to all outward appearances settling into civilised life quite well, although during one visit, I did accidentally overhear Hec admonishing him not to attempt escaping from there. It went something along the lines of:

"But Uncle Hec, I could get out of here any time I like now. They even let me go down to the shops!"

"You turn up out at Robby's one day before your time's up, and I'll bloody well flatten you!"

At which point I passed out of earshot.

The day we picked Ricky up from the home he and Hec did some shopping. They only had 600-odd dollars to their names, but they spent nearly all of it on photographic equipment. I was initially very pleased to see the boy developing an interest like that, but when I realised that they were planning another trip into the bush I became concerned. If anyone should have had enough of trips into the Urewera it was those two, but they seemed quite enthusiastic about it — just when I was beginning to believe they were returning to normal. I even had Hec looking quite respectable.

I couldn't talk them out of it. They had some implausible tale about wanting to photograph some of the places they'd seen in there. Ricky had been out of the home for less than a month, most of the time spent messing about with photography, when they packed their gear and left on "a short trip round a few of the huts".

That was two years ago now and I haven't seen them since. Nor has anybody else, so far as can be ascertained. When they'd been gone for three months I went into the Gisborne Police Station and reported them missing, somewhere in the Urewera. You may well imagine the response I got.

Many people are of the opinion, kept alive by occasional

reported sightings, that Faulkner and Baker are still dodging around the huts in the Ureweras. They still get blamed for much of the mischief done in there. I never believed it. And since I found Ricky's story, written in visitors' books taken from the huts and wrapped in a torn piece of black polythene among the stuff they left here, I've formed my own theory about what happened to them.

It's taken me nearly all winter to unravel Ricky's handwriting and get his story written down more or less how he meant it. One of his books has been wet and one whole passage is indecipherable. I could tell, though, from a few phrases I was able to follow, that Hec and Ricky planned to buy this station and present it to me in return for my having helped them. Another piece I was able to pick out was Ricky saying to Hec, "Maori skin isn't so brown on thin people as fat ones. True. I tell you!"

One or two other things he's left out of his story, such as the scene I remember in the kitchen here when Ricky discovered that Hec was illiterate. And later the touching little scene when Hec told Ricky he could have the .22 on his fifteenth birthday.

I must say here that everything I knew about in Ricky's story was quite true, and consistent with what they'd both told me. As for the huia, I don't know, but Ricky's description of them tallies in all respects with every reference I can find to them. If I had to guess, I'd say that those huia still exist, and that Hec and Ricky found them.

Owen Mallory, who was here last summer with his team, practising for one of his Himalayan expeditions, described any attempt to tackle those Huiarau bluffs without the proper equipment and experience in rock-climbing as "extremely foolhardy".

And that's what I think must have happened to them. Hec and Ricky must have dropped off one more ridge in a tricky place — too tricky. I do believe they're still out there in the Urewera bush, two ragged skeletons lying at the bottom of some bluffs, somewhere along the Huiarau Range. Kokako Bluffs.

And yet if I walked outside right now and saw that wisp

of smoke I always look for up on Cave Camp Bluffs — but no, it's been too long now.

That's all I have to tell, except that whenever I notice their old rifle there in the corner I think of Hec and Ricky, and I recall those last few words of Ricky's story:

"We've got a few hassles coming up, but we can handle them. We're okay now."

I'm not a particularly religious man, but if there's any justice in this life Ricky and his Uncle Hec *are* okay. Still sticking it out together and handling their own hassles in their own way. I hope so.

Books by Barry Crump

A Good Keen Man (1960)
Hang On a Minute Mate (1961)
One of Us (1962)
There and Back (1963)
Gulf (1964) — now titled *Crocodile Country*
Scrapwaggon (1965)
The Odd Spot of Bother (1967)
No Reference Intended (1968)
Warm Beer and Other Stories (1969)
A Good Keen Girl (1970)
Bastards I Have Met (1971)
Fred (1972)
Shorty (1980)
Puha Road (1982)
The Adventures of Sam Cash (1985)
Wild Pork and Watercress (1986)
Barry Crump's Bedtime Yarns (1988)
Bullock Creek (1989)
The Life and Times of a Good Keen Man (1992)
Gold and Greenstone (1993)
Arty and the Fox (1994)
Forty Yarns and a Song (1994)
Mrs Windyflax and the Pungapeople (1995)
Crumpy's Campfire Companion (1996)
As the Saying Goes (1996)
Song of a Drifter (1996)
Back Down the Track (1998) — photographs by Barry Crump
The Pungapeople of Ninety Mile Beach (1999)
Harry Hobnail and the Pungapeople (2002)
Mr Tanglewood and the Pungapeople (2005)

Books about Barry Crump

A Tribute to Crumpy: Barry Crump 1936–1996 (1996)
A Life in Loose Strides: The Story of Barry Crump (2000) — Colin Hogg